Advance Praise for *Ch...*

Visionary Fiction authors often have per....story roots that span centuries of metaphysical exploration. The legendary twentieth-century Nazi search for the Holy Grail draws author Vic Smith into ancient realms of mysticism. Smith's extensive on-location research and scholarship spans the Cathar and Templar époques of the twelfth century up to 1939, when the Nazi obsession with the Holy Grail is at its peak. The vehicle of fiction masks a unique visionary access that only Smith's dedication can bring to distant dramatic events.

Monty Joynes, author of *The Booker Series*

A well-constructed narrative woven around the two interlinking time periods...the reader will appreciate the author's depth and scope of historical knowledge that underlies the story. The subject matter and its key linkages—Grail, Cathars, Templars, reincarnation, Nazis obsession with the occult—are very topical.

Nigel Graddon, author of *Otto Rahn and Quest for the Holy Grail*

This historical novel is a brilliant marriage of two different, though similar, periods in European history. Presented from a refreshing new angle, it is the brainchild of an author who, through his personal passion for fact and truth, leaves no stone unturned in understanding a seemingly unsolvable and recurring mystery. Highly recommended!

Jeanne D'Août, author of *The Forbidden Relic (White Lie)*

An impressive dual-period novel. Prodigious in his research and with a keen eye for spiritual detail, Victor Smith has provided esotericists, Rahn enthusiasts, and Grail searchers with a worthy addition to their shelves devoted to the Cathar and Gnostic mysteries of old Occitania.

Glen Craney, author of *The Fire and the Light*

A fresh and masterful blending of historical and visionary fiction, which transitions between the mad and nightmarish Cathar period (between 1299-1325) and Nazi Germany (in the 1930's), two well-known, yet not so well-known, times in world history. Questions introduced by this thought-provoking novel include: Do the painful lessons of history repeat themselves to no end or do they inspire growth and transformation in mankind? And, Will the identity and whereabouts of Holy Grail ever be solved, or is it something that can only be possessed spiritually and is hidden in plain sight?

Margaret Duarte, author of *Between Will and Surrender*, founding member Visionary Fiction Alliance

"The kingdom is within you..." (the Gospel of Thomas). Victor Smith has woven a fascinating tapestry of historical fiction and nonfiction to create this engaging, esoteric tale. My favorite part in Channel of the Grail was the no-holds-barred romance between the German-Jewish grail historian, SS Obersturmführer Otto Wilhelm Rahn, and Raymond Perrier, which, from their 13th century Cathar counterparts to their World War II era selves, transcends time itself. If you are intrigued by Otto Rahn, the Cathars, the Crusades, the Knights Templar, and the quest for the Holy Grail, I highly recommend this book!

Melissa St. Hilaire, co-author of the *Saurimonde* series

ALSO BY VICTOR E. SMITH

The Anathemas, a Novel of Reincarnation and Restitution (Outskirts Press, 2010)

Channel of the Grail
A Novel of Cathars, Templars, and a Nazi Grail Hunter

By Victor E. Smith

Quantum Leap Publishing
Tucson, Arizona

Channel of the Grail
A Novel of Cathars, Templars, and a Nazi Grail Hunter
All Rights Reserved.
Copyright © 2016 Victor E. Smith

Cover Art: Jeff Danelek

Quantum Leap Publishing
Tucson Arizona

ISBN: 978-0-9974188-0-4

Library of Congress Control Number: 2016937563

PUBLISHED IN THE UNITED STATES OF AMERICA

DEDICATION

To my great-grandmother, Fanny Moser, who perished in a Nazi concentration camp.

To my grandmother, Catherine Gretz, who had the foresight to move her children to safety once the Nazis came to power in Germany.

And to my mother, Eva Smith, who left her homeland in her late teens to start anew and raise a family of ten children in America.

TO THE READER

While Channel of the Grail is a work of fiction, it is carefully based on the known facts about certain historical characters and the time periods in which they lived. While these people and places will be familiar to some readers, others might benefit from a brief overview of the major subject areas (Catharism, Knights Templar, Holy Grail, Otto Rahn) prior to reading the book. Summaries of all these topics can easily be found on the Internet including Wikipedia. Having such information beforehand will not act as a spoiler. A Cast of Major Characters and Timelines for both the Cathar Period and Otto Rahn's life are provided in the book's appendix area to aid the reader.

Although unconventional for fiction, this work uses endnotes. Without attempting to provide the extensive referencing required for non-fiction, these endnotes are used in two situations: 1) for uncommon persons, places, or terms that readers might not find in a reference tool like Wikipedia; and 2) to cite the published reference works for obscure historical facts or theories included in the story line. The latter might interest those who wish to research the foundations for the story beyond the novel's scope.

A more complete bibliography, supplementary information of various topics in the novel, and forums for discussion can be found on the author's website, vic@victoresmith.com. Feel free to peruse these pages and join in the conversations the novel is intended to evoke.

Victor E. Smith
3/11/16

Contents

Channel of the Grail

Bei einem Schneesturm in den Bergen kam im März d.J. der

SS. Obersturmführer

Otto Rahn

auf tragische Weise ums Leben

Wir betrauern in diesem toten Kameraden einen anstän-
digen SS. Mann und den Schöpfer ausgezeichneter, geschicht-
lich-wissenschaftlicher Werke.

Der Chef des Pers.-Stabes RF SS

Völkische Beobachter
18/5/1939

Wolff
SS Gruppenführer

"SS - Obersturmführer OTTO RAHN died tragically in
March of this year in a snow storm in the mountains.
We mourn the loss of our comrade, a decent SS-man and
creator of outstanding historical-scholarly works.
SS Chief of Staff, SS-GruppenFührer Wolff."

[*Völkische Beobachter* May 18, 1939]

PROLOGUE: KONSTANZ, GERMANY, June, 1938

"**I**t took two months, but General Wolff finally confirmed it. Otto Rahn is now officially dead," I said, pointing to the circled obituary in the newspaper spread out on the table between us. It was dated May 18, 1939, just over a week earlier.

Gabriele Winckler-Dechend dabbed at the tears streaming from her eyes. "I know," she said.

I allowed her grief its moment but then probed for the details I had risked crossing from Switzerland to the German border city of Konstanz to get. "Why now and like this?" I asked. "It makes it sound like an accident that befell one of their own. Otto was an experienced hiker and equal to any March snowstorm in the Alpine foothills. And he was certainly not in good graces with the SS at the time of his alleged death."

The 31-year-old new mother sniffled and put her finger to her lips. "Don't wake the baby," she cautioned.

I lowered my voice. "Did Wolff or your husband tell you anything more?"

She shook her head. "It's been two years since I worked for Himmler, and my husband has barely been home since we got married. The SS takes precedence over family, you know. It's no longer the way you might remember. I have no inside information. I know how very important he was to you, Raymond. He was important to me too. I'm sorry, but I can't help."

My gamble, as a Swiss national crossing the border to visit Otto Rahn's closest associate from his earlier and more innocent days with the fledgling archeological and cultural history wing of the SS, the Ahnenerbe, was not paying off. And there was no time to spare. The flow of reliable information, even among friends, between Germany and the rest of the world was slowing to a trickle. Rahn had warned that I might become a high-profile target after his death. Further, I had come to Konstanz without authorization from my own associates, who would judge my foray into Nazi territory as reckless, personally motivated, and counter to the group's purpose.

Employing a term of endearment I had heard her use for the Reichsführer-SS Heinrich Himmler, I said, "Hard to imagine that Uncle Heinrich would shut you out completely. He knew you were close to Otto."

She flinched but quickly covered the inadvertent gesture. "If something is amiss about Otto's death, as you insinuate, Himmler had nothing to do with it. He treated Otto like a son."

She was sincere in her assessment—but wrong. I grimaced to show incredulity. "Karl Wolff, his chief-of-staff, could order Rahn's death without his superior's consent?"

She leaned towards me and further lowered her voice. "No one's talking about anyone ordering Rahn's death except you, but Wolff despised Otto for his precious tendencies as a man and artist, a hatred Otto aggravated by flaunting his proclivities. I warned you the last time we met, 'Beware of the wolf who serves two masters.' Neither you nor Otto took me seriously enough. That's all I have to say about it."

She got up and brought the coffee pot from the kitchen. The summer storm, which had raged throughout the morning trip from Basel to Konstanz, lashed against the window panes. "More?" she asked, pouring before I could respond.

She then crossed to the sideboard and held up a book. *Kreuzzug gegen den Gral,* Otto Rahn's *Crusade Against the Grail.* She opened to a marked page. "My turn for a question. We three had conversations about the Cathar practice called the *endura*, which Otto morbidly reverenced."

I shuddered at the mention of the pre-death rite of that medieval heretical sect, also known as the Pure Ones, about which Otto had written in the book. Before a member received the sacrament administered to the dying called the *consolamentum*, he or she swore to forgo all food and drink from that point forward. This voluntary cessation of vital nourishment led Cathar critics to call the practice suicide.

"It's fair to presume," Gabriele continued, "that Otto recognized that his status in the SS was in such jeopardy that his only tolerable option was to take his own life. I've heard of several such cases. And knowing his devotion to the Cathar way, he would likely have entered the endura to prepare for death."

More in tune with Otto's character than I had presumed, Gabriele might as well have been present at the final meeting between Otto and me before his disappearance, a rendezvous I could not reveal to her as having taken place.

She went on, "But if this scenario is accurate, something puzzles me about it." She looked down at the book. "He writes here about the endura: 'If you have not lived in vain as a person, if you have only done good and perfected yourself, this is when, according to the Cathars, you can take the definitive step as a Perfect.'"

I knew what came next. She continued to read. "'Two always practiced the endura together. After sharing years of continuous effort and intensive spiritualization in the most sublime friendship, only together could the Brothers decide to co-participate in the next life, the true life of the intuitive beauties of the Hereafter, and the knowledge of the divine laws that move worlds.'"[1]

She closed the book and glared at me. "If this is true, why did he go to his death alone?"

Her voice oozed accusation. Even though we had never spoken to her about it directly, she knew Otto and I were lovers. If two always practiced the endura together, I should have been at his side at the end. Of all people, she had every right to know, but I could not yet reveal that the two of us had indeed undertaken the endura together on a March evening in Freiburg three months earlier even though only one of us was to die then while the other had to live on.

With tears in her eyes, she kissed the book and put it on the table. The infant in the adjacent bedroom was starting to cry.

Constrained to witness in silence the events precipitated and enacted by those around me, I stared down at the book written by Otto Rahn. Gabriele too had loved him. For him the nightmare was over. For her it was still to come. Since I could not leave her without some consolation. I shared my most precious memory of our departed friend.

"Otto and I first met during a film shoot on the outskirts of Berlin in 1928," I told her. "I was 19, and he was five years older. I felt like he was watching me throughout that day like an attentive older brother, but something much more. I couldn't stop looking at him either. As we were all leaving for the night, he sought me out and held my eyes until I felt naked under his gaze. That moment was sensual, magical, and ecstatic. I felt he was about to kiss me.

"Instead, he raised his right hand and let it rest on my head. His touch sent heat coursing through my body, and we both seemed to glow in the dark. It was unlike anything I had ever experienced: a combination of the baptism of John, the confirmation of Pentecost, and the mythical sacred marriage in a single gesture, stronger and more beautiful than a kiss." I touched my heart. "At that moment I knew that our destinies had been entwined before. We had found each other. Our destinies were entwined again."

Gabriele smiled for an instant, but then, as if to show that it was unseemly for a man to speak of another man in such terms, she turned away.

I reached for my raincoat. "Go and tend to your child, my friend," I said. "I'll let myself out."

CHAPTER 1: TOULOUSE, Spring, 1317

Frater Bernard Gui. So terrifying to the students of the Saint Sernin Abbey School was the reputation of the Grand Inquisitor of Toulouse that they only whispered his name and scrupulously circumvented the rear monastery wing where he held office. They knew that this zealous Dominican and his team of investigators could prove anyone, even a seemingly saintly priest or nun, to be a heretic, a Jew, or a sorcerer and thus deserving of death at the stake, imprisonment, or, at the very least, public humiliation. Gui's vaunted system of interrogation could parlay the report of one person making a single derogatory remark against the church into the conviction of a dozen of the originally accused's associates. During Gui's eleven years in office, hundreds had been convicted of various heresies and dozens turned over to the secular authorities for execution.

Thus, the order to appear in the Grand Inquisitor office at nine o'clock the following morning so perturbed Jaques de Sabart, a fourth-year student only weeks from graduation as class valedictorian, that he had to steer his shaking body to the nearest wall to stay on his feet. He leaned hard and slowed his breathing, something he had trained himself to do when he needed to regain his balance.

Roger, a friend and classmate, happened by and noticed Jaques's distress. This son of a distinguished local magistrate of Toulouse, a gangling popular fellow, laughed when Jaques explained his situation.

"You're no Cathar or witch, right?" he asked.

Jaques shook his head.

"There's nothing to be afraid of then. Frater Gui is a big dog but all bark if you're Catholic by his definition. My father had him over to dinner a few times. He hated me; I'm too frivolous for his tastes, but you two should get along. He's a man of the mind. Like you." The tall youth gripped Jaques's shoulders. "It's the end of the term, Jaques. I'm sure he wants to offer you a plum position. With your mind, I certainly would."

The unique friendship between a studious peasant from the rural south and a flighty aristocratic from the capital city sprang from an ugly incident that occurred in their first months at the school four years earlier. Unaware that protocol required those of lower breeding to never embarrass their social betters, Jaques too eagerly raised his hand to answer teachers' questions while the sons of noble or wealthy merchant families giggled among themselves or yawned with disinterest. He also failed to heed the glares darted his way when instructors praised his eagerness in contrast to their lassitude.

The youngest and smallest in the class, Jaques's voice had not yet changed while many of the other boys were already sporting whiskers and flexing hard muscles gained in jousting and knocking each other about. Taking Jaques's quickness in the classroom as blatant disrespect for their superior station, several bigger youths decided to put him in his proper place with their fists. They pounced on him one day after class.

During the beating, one tough, twice his weight, grabbed Jaques' cheeks and pulled them outward. He then kissed the younger boy on the mouth and forced his tongue between his lips.

"*Joli Jaques,*" the assailant sneered. "Pretty little teacher's pet."

The others joined in, making a mocking refrain out of what was to become a permanent nickname. "*Joli Jaques. Joli Jaques. Joli, joli, joli.*"

Then Roger stepped in. Too willowy to counter physically, he wielded the clout of status and popularity to shame and scatter the attackers. Understanding Jaques's utter humiliation, Roger encouraged the smaller boy to turn the table on such shaming. "*Joli* can mean *good, charming* and *agreeable* as easily as *pretty or precious*. You are a handsome young fellow. Don't let guys like that bully get to you," he advised.

"Who is he?" Jaques asked, curious because the one who had kissed him had a similar southern accent to his own.

"Arnaud Sicre-Baille. Thinks he's a big man because his father is a court accountant here in Toulouse. He doesn't mention that he grew up in Ax in the Ariège Valley and only moved here with his father after his mother was captured and executed as a heretical priestess."

Jaques had heard of such sad happenings. He could not help but feel some compassion for this brash fellow, by rights his countryman. "He is perhaps to be pitied then," he said, choosing his words carefully. Any sign of sympathy towards heretics could be reported as a crime.

"You're too kind," Roger replied. "Don't be fooled. His mother may have been a saint. The son's the opposite."

Some weeks after the aborted beating, Roger again took Jaques aside. He playfully slapped the smaller boy on the back. "So you learned your lesson," he said. "Not so fast with the hand up, right, Joli?"

He then went on seriously. "But you still know the answers. Since you're so good at this school thing, I'm not sure you can understand this, but some of us just can't get it, no matter how hard we try. Take me. I can study all day, repeating those Latin conjugations a thousand times. Then I go to sleep and wake up, and it's all gone. If I am to get through here, Jaques—and my father will disown me if I don't—you've got to let me in on your secret. Here you're still singing soprano but can reel off your lessons better than the professors who teach them. Will you help me?"

And so began a relationship that spanned their full four years at Saint Sernin. While tutoring Roger on a regular basis, it was he, Jaques realized in the later stages of the effort, who derived a benefit more valuable than all the book learning he imparted to his charge: insight into the human mind and its faculty of memory.

The following morning as Jaques made his way around the imposing cathedral and through the cloister to the Grand Inquisitor's office in the far wing of the quadrangle, Roger's optimistic appraisal of the situation had replaced the more dreaded possibilities. He had reviewed and validated his immediate occupational objective. His talents were considerable and valuable to several sectors of society: the church, the monastery, the secular courts, to name a few that had already made overtures.

The Dominicans, as proprietors of Saint Sernin, were first in line to attempt to recruit him. Several times, an earnest friar had taken him aside and exhorted him, sometimes with undue flattery, to devote his life to the Order of Preachers, touting how, in a mere hundred years of existence, the congregation had produced saints and scholars like its founder Dominic Guzman, Albert the Great, and Thomas Aquinas. It had established monasteries and schools throughout Europe and staffed the critical Office of the Inquisition, honing it into a lethal ecclesiastical weapon for fighting ubiquitous heterodoxy, which ranged in cause from primitive ignorance to sophistical heresy. But, little inclined towards the monastery or seminary, Jaques deflected the blandishments of the Dominicans.

Instead he saw an opportunity in the current radical reshuffling of the relationship between church and state that had given birth to a complex legal system that frequently saw the two powers on opposing sides. The so-called Albigensian Crusade, initiated by the Papacy against the heretical Cathars in the previous century, had only succeeded with French military backing. The Capetian kings generously contributed troops as the Crown anticipated extending its rule to the long-coveted County of Toulouse, then ruled by a noble family sympathetic to the heretics. During the war, injustices perpetrated by either ecclesiastical or secular authorities against the region's citizens, all virulently anti-French whether Cathar or not, were condoned by both Rome and Paris.

But at the end of hostilities, the defeated territories became royal provinces and its people French citizens. The papal courts of the Inquisition, left in place to eradicate the stubborn vestiges of Catharism and prevent any recurrence of the heresy, were thus required to satisfy French as well as their own legal requirements. Since Canon Law dictated that those convicted in ecclesiastical courts were to be handed over to the civil authorities for actual punishment, the Inquisition had to provide proof, if challenged, that current civil law, including rules of evidence about the use of torture to obtain confessions, had been followed.

The need to accurately record legal proceedings spurred the revival of the once esteemed profession of scribe or court-recorder, but the position's requirements were stringent. Expected to transcribe a trial often conducted in several tongues—Latin was the official language but lay participants spoke French or the Occitan and other dialects—a qualified scribe had to be multi-lingual. Further, since it was impossible to write down every word as spoken, the candidate must have mastered a system of shorthand backed by a flawless memory that could later complete the full wording and supply any gestures and inflections that might affect the literal meaning.

Certain strict character traits were also prerequisite. A scribe had to sit unperturbed for hours in an arena where emotions, including the screams of the tortured, created havoc. He was to speak only to request clarification of a phrase or when asked to read back a participant's earlier statement. On taking his place at the writing desk to the side of the dais where the presiding judges sat, the scribe had to expel all personal opinions or feelings and make himself a polished mirror reflecting the events unfolding around him. As an agent of the court, he was sworn to secrecy about matters witnessed. Any violation, even inadvertent, made him subject to dismissal and punishment. While political and religious orthodoxy were assumed, zealotry in any direction could disqualify. The scribe was expected to be polite with all, even the accused, and familiar with none, even his employers. A scribe, it was jested, was the only saintly presence allowed in the inquisitorial courtroom.

While far from saintly, Jaques knew he had the technical and language skills to excel in the position. To meet the personal requirements, he had learned sufficient tact, diplomacy, and humility from his mentor, Père Fontaine, his church pastor while growing up in Tarascon. His political and religious positions were under development; he felt he knew too little about either to form an opinion. And he could only surmise that he could keep an oath of secrecy, never having been put to that test before. He was, however, tight-lipped enough to not mention his aspiration to anyone other than to Roger; he despised the petty rivalry that typified those who vied for the few available positions in the field.

The rough-hewn door to the Grand Inquisitor's office was closed when Jaques arrived a few minutes before the hour. He watched the few monks pacing, meditating, or reading their breviaries in the courtyard until the cathedral bells began chiming nine o'clock. On cue, the door behind him squeaked open. He turned.

Exiting through it was Arnaud Sicre, dressed in Sunday finery in contrast to Jaques's simple student's uniform. But Saint Sernin's loudest and proudest peacock now looked dreadfully pale, his broad shoulders hunched as he shuffled out of Frater Gui's office.

He almost ran into Jaques before he noticed him. He returned to character momentarily. "He'll eat you alive, Joli, and spit you out in little pieces," he muttered as he scurried off.

Only then did Jaques remember that his former tormentor too aspired to become a scribe. Once he had encountered a group of students to whom his fellow countryman was boasting about his qualifications. Arnaud, who never spoke to Jaques directly, raised his voice when he saw Jaques approaching. With hyperbole too obvious, he praised the Dominican effort to eradicate the despicable Cathars and quoted from Gui's works to make his claim to a position at the scribe's table in the Inquisitor's court. His way, Jaques interpreted at the time, of warning a strong potential rival away from the prize he already considered his.

"Jaques de Sabart, you are next," a flat voice, higher than expected, called out. Jaques took a deep breath and entered the room where it had not gone well for Arnaud.

Adjusting his eyes to the low light made murkier by the drab walls and dark furniture, he stepped towards the straight-backed chair indicated by the monk, who did not look up from his desk heaped with papers and books splayed helter-skelter.

"Good morning, Frater." Jaques dared to greet the hollow-cheeked monk, although silence until he had been spoken to may have been more prudent.

"Your good reputation as a student precedes you," Gui finally said, "and, unlike most good reputations, it seems merited."

Jaques relaxed for a breath although the monk still had not looked up.

"You refused to join the Dominican Order." Gui's head swiveled suddenly and caught Jaques's eyes with a look. "Why?"

"I did not hear the call, Frater," Jaques said evenly. He expected the question although not so abruptly.

"Several brothers invited you on different occasions. The call through them was not good enough evidently. You need to hear it from God directly. But you're young with plenty of time to change your mind." Thinking Gui looked a trifle amused, Jaques remained silent.

The monk looked at a paper in the middle of his desk. "Proficient in Latin, Greek, French and several local dialects, I understand."

"Yes."

"With an excellent ear for what is said and the ability to record it accurately."

Jaques nodded.

Again the turn and direct eye contact. Jaques braced himself. Every nuance in the way Gui was conducting the interview, even the pauses and their duration, seemed choreographed. "Your teachers call you a prodigy. Were you aware of that?"

"Yes."

The monk looked to the side. "Unusual talent like yours can be more the work of the devil—magic, witchcraft—than a gift of God. True?"

"Some people think so," Jaques replied, suppressing a tremor that warbled in his words. "My experience is too limited to judge."

"But you know you have extraordinary intelligence and memory. Where does that come from?"

Jaques paused for a moment, hazarding that the monk would appreciate depth over speed. "During my early schooling with Père Fontaine in Tarascon, I was the only student," he finally explained. "I had no one else to compare myself with. Most of the village children didn't read or write. Not that they couldn't, but they didn't learn. I never thought my memory was any different from theirs. I thought everyone remembered everything they heard and saw once they heard and saw it. When people said they forgot, I assumed it was intentional—put out the candle and you can't see the page. Or a form of sluggishness—don't relight the candle."

"We can assume that yours are gifts from God then," the monk pronounced with a finality that somehow disappointed the youth even though he was relieved to not have to further explain what ultimately he did not understand.

"Père Fontaine from Tarascon, you say. What is the parish there again?" the monk asked.

"Notre Dame de Sabart." Tears sprang to Jacques's eyes. "But Père passed away last year." He wiped his cheek. "Pardon. By the time I found out he was fatally ill, it was too late to go to his bedside. I never had the chance to say goodbye. He was the only father I ever knew."

The monk waited until Jaques stopped sniffling. "He arranged for your admission to Saint Sernin even though you were only twelve," he then said. "Did he think you had a religious vocation?"

Jaques shook his head. "Even though I was his altar boy before I was tall enough to move the massive missal at Gospel time, he never pushed me. Quite the opposite. When I found out that Mother and he were thinking of sending me here, I was concerned that I would have to become a priest or monk even if I didn't want to. Père was clear: 'No one *must* enter the church or become a priest,' he told me. 'And let no one convince you otherwise. God calls us to our right vocation from within, not from without.' He then smiled and patted me on the head. 'You understand, Jaques. You are one of us.' His advice has served me well."

There was a slight tightening around Gui's eyes as he leaned towards Jaques. "You are aware, of course, of your region's reputation as one of the last refuges of the Cathar heretics. The cowards hide in caves up on the cliffs along the Ariège while the more brazen ones live right in the village, contaminating unsuspecting Catholics with their vile doctrines." He leaned even closer. "Did you not come into contact with Cathars while growing up there?"

Jaques recoiled. He clasped his hands to hide their sudden quivering. Gui drew back a bit. "Your priest must have warned you that they infested Tarascon like vermin."

"He told me about the Crusade against them in the last century and of their defeat at Montsegur in 1244. He explained that the Inquisition was then established to permanently eradicate the heresy."

"Was he sympathetic to their cause, perhaps saying the church's treatment of them was too harsh?"

Sensing that the interview was veering in a dangerous direction, Jaques checked his umbrage at the unwarranted insinuation. "Père Fontaine was an Occitanian. He regretted our loss of independence to the French. But he and all of his parishioners were good Christians, and he was a saintly man."

Gui sat up straight. "They called themselves good *Christians*, not good *Catholics*?"

Jaques shrugged. "Is there a difference?" he asked.

The monk seemed momentarily piqued, but then appeared to calm down. "Pardon me, young man. I've been an inquisitor too long. I only took this position in obedience to our Holy Father, who is now gratefully—and this is in confidence between us until its public announcement—about to relieve me of much of the weight of this office."

Jaques gulped.

Gui responded to his reaction. "You wonder why I called you here then."

The monk rose and began to pace the length of the room, his spare body moving catlike beneath his white cassock topped front and back with a black scapular, the habit of the Dominicans. "The Office of the Inquisition in Toulouse is to be drastically reduced. The civil government has demanded that its primary operation now be in the hands of the regular clergy rather than with our order. Jacques Fournier, even though he is a Cistercian, has been appointed bishop of Pamiers, and he will now direct the Inquisition in this region. The Dominicans that remain involved will report to him. So, to the point of me inviting you here. It is for a position in his court, not mine, that I am looking to hire a scribe."

A sadness fell across the older man's face; a glisten showed in his eyes. Jaques felt a sudden sympathy for him in his isolation, which his loss of position as Grand Inquisitor would only worsen. He blurted out, "And what will you do now, Frater?"

The monk stopped short. "Kind of you to ask. Our Holy Father, John XXII, has called me to the papal court in Avignon. Unlike his predecessor who tolerated the disobedience of the Franciscan group from Béziers and Narbonne that calls itself the Spirituals, he recently ordered the rebellious monks to Avignon to stand trial. Upon arrival, their spokesman, Bernard Délicieux, notorious for his rabble-rousing against us Dominicans and our management of the Inquisition, was arrested."

Gui stared at the floor. "His Holiness, educated in civil and canon law by the Dominicans, has entrusted me along with Bishop Bernard de Castanet of Albi to draw up charges against Delicieux and his fellow monks. Rather than continue the fight against the church's enemies from without, I must now battle the foe within."

Even the Saint Sernin students had wondered why Bernard Gui, despite his service to several popes as a diplomatic envoy, church historian, and inquisitor, had never been named a cardinal or even a bishop while many lesser churchmen had been elevated. Some attributed the oversight to Gui's reputation for harshness, some to his genuine humility, and others to a personal timidity underlying his intractable exterior. The interview, so far, brought Jaques no closer to understanding what motivated this austere man.

Again, daring to be brazen, he asked, "But what would you really rather do?"

The hint of a smile flickered at the corners of the monk's pale lips. "So long have I been cast as the scourge of the Inquisition—I know my reputation, deserved or not—that I would prefer to return to my home monastery in Limoges, my birthplace, to be alone with my books and my writing." He sighed. "But this will happen only if and when God and Holy Mother Church so wills it."

He sat back down and leaned forward with a look that felt like he was trying to inscribe an indelible message into Jaques's brain. "You too have been given a specific mission, young man, and, in a way unknown to either of us, it is an extension of my own. As Bishop Fournier will soon discover, the inquisitor's role requires constant vigilance. We became complacent for several decades after our victory at Montsegur, allowing the Cathar heresy to reassert itself with the Authier[2] brothers. Many more souls have been lost in the process of defeating it a second time. Relax against internal enemies, and revisionists like Delicieux and his Spirituals will spring up like poisonous weeds to seduce the many sheep already so prone to wandering."

The monk finally dropped his eyes. "But I did not call you here to discuss ecclesiastical policy. In your future position, you are best far apart from the conflicting opinions and prejudices involved with that."

He took a large volume from the shelf behind him and held it up. It was a book entitled *Flores Chronicorum*, or "Anthology of the Chronicles," with his own name in Latin, *Bernardus Guidonis*, inscribed in gold letters. "The final accurate report is the only product a scribe should take pride in. This is history, an account of what actually occurred, that I, through my scribes, was blessed to be able to compile. This will outlast all of us and is potentially eternal. Not the physical book or even the words; it is in Latin, which few understand any more. But the ideas and images stored here will travel across time and space, leaping through the minds of one generation to the minds of the next, a ripple in the stream that composes the great Mind common to us all. Without this record, the events written about here might as well not have happened. Only this remains to testify to the reality of the past." With a reverent touch he returned the book to the shelf.

"I'm not a diviner, Jaques, but I believe that we are each endowed with an individual destiny. That out of the Ariège, the heretics' last haven, should come one like yourself so gifted in the skills needed by the inquisitional courts is not an accident. That your Languedocian hand should pen the final act of the work that I brought forward with all due diligence, even if its completion is to be achieved by another, is a direct act of Providence.

"Go to Pamiers and serve the Cistercian Bishop Fournier's court well. Do not succumb to the laxity and sophistry you will encounter there. Adhere to the discipline of body, mind, and soul that you have learned here among the Dominicans. See all and record all without adulterating what you observe with anyone's opinion—including your own." Frater Gui touched Jaques on the shoulder. "It's a humble position, lad, but a vital one. We will attentively read what you write, and your work too will belong to the centuries."

Chapter 2: Berlin, 1935

Otto Rahn stood waiting in the drizzle on the platform as my train from Geneva pulled into the Berlin station. There was no mistaking the black fedora cocked over his right eye, the open trench coat inflating his spare figure, and the trademark cigarette blurring his face in smoke. Barely three days had elapsed since I had received his unexpected invitation to visit with him in the capital. I spotted him again immediately on disembarking, but he was scanning in the opposite direction and only saw me when I stood in front of him. He flicked his butt, and we embraced, but without the usual pummeling or flirtatious suggestions that we stand back to get a better look at all of each other. Several days' worth of dark stubble replaced his usually clean-shaved look. It lent him an appealing machismo.

"The beard would go better with a beret," I quipped.

"Too French, *mon ami*," he retorted. "Not the vogue in Hitler's Berlin."

Since I had last visited the German capital, the National Socialist banner—red with a white circle enclosing the stark black *hakenkreuze* or swastika—had replaced the black, red, and gold bars of the Weimar Republic, and the Nazi colors now flew from every possible place where a flag could be hung.

He grabbed my bag and hailed a cab. During the ride he seemed to be talking to the driver rather than to me, rambling on loudly about the nasty weather and pointing out familiar sites as if this was my first visit to the city.

In our earlier time here, the depression of the late '20s, we had to make do with shabby quarters when relatives or friends could not take us in, so I was relieved when the cab stopped in front of a handsome townhouse on fashionable Tiergartenstrasse, the eponymous urban forest park just beyond it.

Still, when leading me down a flight of steps from street level, Otto was apologetic. "This basement apartment is temporary," he explained. "Next time, it'll be an upper floor or maybe in a better neighborhood like Brandenburg."

Otto had always disdained city life, revering instead rural landscapes similar to his native Odenwald, the lush forest region in Hesse that served as the setting for the *Nibelungenlied*[3], the homeland of dragon-slayer Siegfried and his avenging wife Kriemheld, a vast mythic region that had seduced him to take up writing as a career. His taste had evidently changed in the two years since we had been together in Geneva.

Once inside the flat, the door locked behind us, he popped open a bottle of the previous year's Rhine wine without removing his hat and coat. "It's not French or even vintage Riesling," he said as we tapped glasses. "Did you know, Raymond, that it is now patriotic in Germany to drink wine?" He flashed his first genuine smile since my arrival.

"I thought it was always beer for you Krauts."

"Not this year. While '34's hot and dry growing season was disastrous for the rest of our agriculture, it was perfect for the Rhineland vineyards. Too perfect. Over-production meant waste unless Germans could be induced to drink more wine. The National Socialist propaganda bureau went to work. And at least this year it's everyone's patriotic duty to help empty the Rhenish wine cellars. And you know Germans and duty."

He finished his drink and refilled his glass, topping off mine even though I had barely sipped from it. I didn't recall him drinking so avidly before. The few times he had indulged he had gotten ill and did not touch alcohol for long stretches afterwards.

"But I didn't beg you to come to Berlin to get rid of more of this lousy German wine." he said while ceremoniously laying a book on the coffee table in front of me. "Here's the real reason for my invitation."

I picked up the volume with both hands: *Kreuzzug gegen den Gral [Crusade Against the Grail] by Otto Rahn, Urban Verlag Publisher*. I felt a surge of pride and elation.

"You did it, Otto. It's published. Congratulations."

"Open the cover."

I did. Inside he had written:

To my dearest friend, Raymond.
Your love gave me the courage and will to seek the Grail.
Love forever.
Otto Rahn.

The memory of his years of study, research, travel, and personal deprivation on this project brought tears to my eyes. I leapt up, intending to give him a long celebratory hug. He accepted my embrace but too briefly it seemed for this momentous occasion.

"You probably don't even need to read it. You've listened while I struggled with just about every word in it," he said, stepping backwards.

I forced aside the bite of implied rejection. "I'm so happy for you, Otto. You deserve your new-found fame and affluence. I'm glad it's selling well. The winds of fortune have indeed changed in the blink of an eye."

He looked away. "The sales are not quite there yet but will be soon I have been assured by all the right people."

"Then it must have earned a handsome advance."

"A pittance." He sniffed. "And left up to the publisher, it wouldn't have sold enough copies to repay even that."

I glanced around his well-furnished apartment. "How then—?"

He put his finger to his lips, walked to the window, and closed the drapes. He then sat across from me, his brow furrowed. "It's why I wanted you to come as soon as possible." He glanced at his watch. "I want you to meet a new acquaintance of mine. In just over an hour, we're scheduled to have dinner with her. Her name is Gabriele Dechend. I owe much of this to her."

My throat clamped. Uncontrollable feelings, jealousy mainly, ripped through my body. I forced them and the assumptions behind them to the back of my mind.

"Who is she?"

Either missing or choosing to ignore my discomfort, he went on evenly. "Until two weeks ago, I didn't know her at all. Still very little I know about her for sure. I was minding my own business in Freiburg, actually trying to peddle my books for food and cigarettes, when a telegram arrived at my rooming house telling me to come to 8 Albrechtstrasse in Berlin to meet some folks interested in my recently published book. I was to contact Fraulein Dechend[4] upon arrival. I wheedled train fare from friends and showed up at the given destination. I almost wet my pants when I found myself in front of Gestapo headquarters. By all rights, I should have run far and fast. But the compliment paid to my writing in the telegram along with curiosity and poverty made me brave. I went in and asked for Fraulein Dechend. A pretty brunette about my age came right over and ushered me into a private parlor."

"Did she say how they found you?"

"A published book is a public record. She contacted Urban Verlag in Freiburg and talked to Otto Vogelsgang, my publisher. He knew my whereabouts."

"So she's a government agent?"

He squinted. "Not sure. Certainly not typical. Officially, she's a nanny."

"For somebody's child?"

He chuckled. "For an eccentric old man without all his wits about him. Have you heard of SS-Colonel Karl Maria Weisthor?" I had not.

Rahn lit a fresh cigarette. "Most haven't. Formerly named Wiligut, on joining the SS he adopted the alias Weisthor, for *Wise Thor,* a hint to the extent of his self-esteem. Austrian, late 60's, claims to be of Aryan royal blood and titles himself 'the secret king'—of what I don't know. An oddball for a hard-nosed paramilitary force like the SS." He glanced at his watch. "Perhaps Gabriele will explain more during dinner."

He drained and refilled his wine glass, not offering to top mine this time. "Let me finish on the Albrechtstrasse meeting," he said. "Her reason for wanting to meet with me proved logical enough. A scholar in her own right, she came across my book, read it, was impressed, and recommended it to Weisthor. He read it, was also impressed, and brought it to Reichsführer-SS Heinrich Himmler's attention. She didn't say if he read it, but he was also impressed. He told Gabriele to find and bring me to Berlin."

My stomach knotted. Otto had brought the name of the notorious Reichsführer-SS into the conversation as if the man was the next-door neighbor. "Why is Himmler interested in a book about medieval history and the mythical Holy Grail?" I asked.

"Why wouldn't he be?" Otto gibed, and then caught himself. "Still ready with the tough questions, Raymond. Things moved too quickly to think through such things, I admit. Evidently, they expected I'd respond to the telegram. They were ready for me. That first evening Gabriele settled me here, made sure the pantry was full and the wine rack stocked, left me more spending money than I'd seen in a year, and told me to speak up if I needed anything else. When I inquired what to expect going forward, she asked about my current writing projects. 'Keep going with those for now,' she said.

"Next on my schedule is this dinner tonight, an impromptu affair at the Nobel Restaurant, a favorite with SS officials. 'Your first chance to be seen,' she chortled on telling me of the event as if relishing the opportunity to show me off as her personal trophy."

"Does she know you invited me along?"

He nodded. "No problem. She liked that you were Swiss with connections in government and industry. With the Olympics here next year, the Party takes every opportunity to demonstrate German worthiness to again perform on the world stage."

Discomforting as it was to be cast as a goodwill ambassador in a Nazi melodrama, I wanted more to determine if a plot was underway to co-opt Otto's talent for the Party's vulgar purposes. I was brimming with objections that might have brought him to question his seeming good fortune. But to avoid the probable errors incurred by rushing to judgment, I decided to let things play out further.

During the ride to the restaurant through the Berlin streets, evidence of construction and refurbishment in preparation for the Olympic Games everywhere, Otto seemed preoccupied.

"I told Paul Ladame that I would be seeing you, and he sends his regards," I said, keeping the conversation neutral

Otto brightened. "Best spelunker in Europe," he exclaimed. In the early '30s, while combing the hazardous caves above the French Ariège Valley for evidence to support his theory that the medieval Cathar heretics took refuge there to escape the Catholic Inquisition, Otto had hired Ladame as his guide. "Too bad he was such a cynic. What's he doing these days?"

"He finished his degree at the University of Geneva. Political Science, although, true to form, he says he doubts that there is really any science to politics. It's all skullduggery. He admires the techniques of your Minister of Propaganda Joseph Goebbels although he loathes the way he uses them. I think he imagines himself as turning Goebbels' tactics against the enemies of western democracy."

Otto laughed. "A career well suited to Paul, although I think he'll wish he stuck to caving if he butts heads with Goebbels and company."

When we arrived, the Nobel was over-crowded and over-decorated. Otto pointed to a smartly dressed young woman conversing with two SS men in black uniforms and swastika armbands. "Gabriele Dechend," he said.

The woman excused herself and pushed towards us, turning heads with her exuberant energy as well as good looks as she passed through.

"You must be Raymond," she gushed before Rahn could introduce me. "My great pleasure to meet you. Come." She took our hands and pulled us toward the back. "I've reserved a table for four and asked them to watch for Weisthor. They'll show him over." Rahn held her chair as she sat. "But let's make the best of the few minutes we'll have to ourselves before he gets here. He's notorious for monopolizing conversations."

She cast Rahn a knowing wink and patted his arm as we took our seats. "I've known Otto for just over week," she said to me, "but we feel like we've known each other forever. Of course, his wonderful book let me into his marvelous head before we met."

Rahn blushed. "Don't try to promote me to Raymond. He knows me too well to buy the celebrity version."

She clucked. "Modest, too." She touched his arm again. "Glory in your destiny, my friend."

She turned to me. "Do you believe, Raymond, that all this good fortune—Otto writing his book, me finding it, reading it, and passing it up the line, with us now about to celebrate his achievement—happened by accident?"

Sensing that the unfolding of events was more courtesy of the Nazi machine than either Providence or happenstance, I was tongue-tied.

Otto came to my rescue. "I've already told Raymond that you are the fairy godmother who whisked me out of abject poverty in the remote provinces to unaccustomed luxury here in the capital. It seems like a miracle"—he glanced off for a second— "and yet it was somehow expected." He again paused and looked upward, squinting as if trying to make out something at a distance. It was a stance I had seen several times before, the seer awaiting a vision. The face of Otto Rahn I had not only come to love but to revere.

Gabriele too saw the transformation, and only after his silence became conspicuous did she prod him. "How is that?"

He lowered his head and shook it. "I'm not sure. The book's message about the Cathars and the Grail are bigger than me. It is as if I was born only to give it birth." He frowned. "I am suddenly concerned that any children I conceive from now on will be still-born or freaks."

Gabriele threw her arm around him as I reached for his hand. "Such silly talk," she said. "It is only the first of a fruitful career. Now that you have patrons in high places, *Crusade* will soon have many proud companion volumes."

I slid my hand away from his, and, despite wanting to show support for the more authentic Otto who had just spoken, I opted for a lower key. "I know firsthand how hard Otto worked on *Crusade* and so appreciate your role in promoting him. He deserves it." I said to Gabriele.

She nodded. "He came prepared and already productive. In the new Reich the best people are given the opportunity to do their best work. Should it not be so everywhere?"

Otto again stepped in to answer for me. "Raymond, as a Swiss citizen who mostly speaks French, might not yet see eye-to-eye with the new Germany. We still have to prove ourselves worthy of the rest of the world's admiration, it seems to me."

Bottles of champagne, Rhenish still, appeared on the table, and Otto again made it his task to keep the glasses full.

Gabriele remained engaged. "Precisely why the Reichsführer-SS invests in the talents of artists, teachers, and writers like Otto," she said to me. "It was he, not a Frenchman, who dug for, found, and wrote about the secrets of Languedoc, even though they were right there on French soil for hundreds of years."

Rahn topped her glass. "We can't minimize the French role,"

he reminded her. "Without a number of them—Maurice Magre, Deodat Roché, Antonin Gadal, Countess Pujol-Murat, to name a few—there would have been no book."

Gabriele picked up his hand and kissed his fingers. "Still more French than German, Monsieur Rahn. Better keep that under your fedora though."

She turned back to me. "I'm no Francophobe, but the Reich has the right to reassert itself after the treacherous 1918 Armistice pushed on us by France and the western Allies. Can you blame us?"

I side-stepped her question if awkwardly. "I understand your main job is to mind Colonel Weisthor while handling clients like Otto on the side."

She twitched her nose. "You make me sound like a babysitter. I may be young and a woman, but I'm as qualified in German history and linguistics as the self-proclaimed wizard I have to take care of. Once, while I was wiping drool from his whiskers, I caught him copying from my article in *Nordic World* on the meaning of a rune that had evaded him. I only address him as vati and let him call me his daughter because Uncle Heinrich asked me to."

Otto saw my questioning look. "Himmler," he said.

"The Reichsführer is your uncle?"

She giggled. "Not literally. My way of showing appreciation for a terribly misunderstood man."

The maître d' was approaching the table with an elderly man in an ill-fitting SS uniform in tow. "Here's Colonel Weisthor. Ignore his grandiosity. In his mind he never leaves center stage," Gabriele said.

My immediate impression of SS-Colonel Karl Maria Weisthor in a sentence: if he was the best the Nazis could muster, the world had nothing to fear. A cartoon character: short and stooped with bulbous belly and a face all gelatinous jowls. He wielded a cane, an elegant antique, that he readily turned into a crutch to steady himself.

"Good in getting here on your own," Gabriele said, pulling out his chair.

Otto rose to shake his hand. "Good evening, Colonel."

Weisthor stared at him. "*Ach, yah*," he finally said. "Rahn, the fellow who wants to prove that the Cathars and Templars had ancient Aryan roots. A theory."

Otto introduced me. "My longtime friend, Raymond Perrier from Geneva, here to help celebrate my good fortune, courtesy of the two of you and the Reichsführer."

"Gabriele, my drink," Weisthor barked.

"Coming, Vati."

The old man hesitated only long enough to lick his lips over the ample cleavage of the waitress leaning over to pour beer into his stein. Before she could finish, he snatched up the glass and slurped the brew, spewing foam on his mustache. "*Das ist gut*," he grunted, slamming the empty down for refilling.

"How did you and the Colonel became acquainted?" Otto asked Gabriele after an awkward silence occasioned by Weisthor's unabashed display of intemperance.

"Back in Austria, boy," Weisthor said. "Her mother and I were close before any of you were born."

"Yes, their families knew each other in Salzburg," Gabriele interjected. "Mother was fascinated by the books and articles he had written about his ancestry. Later she became concerned over reports of his persecution in Austria and the severe personal and family problems that was creating for him. She invited him to our house at Lake Constance where he and I met."

"And where did the Reichsführer come in?" Rahn asked Weisthor.

"Destiny," he said between gulps. "On the way to her mother's place, there was a National Socialist conference in Detmold. I met Himmler there and we fell in thick as thieves. Himmler admired my ancient craft, not like those Austrian fools who thought I was insane. He realized that I had the blood and the magic to legitimize the Party."

Gabriele continued. "Himmler invited him to Munich and provided him with an office and some assistants to work on several projects. Even then the Reichsführer-SS wanted to create a unit that would conduct scholarly and field research into German ancestral roots that would construct the science behind National Socialist theories of Aryan superiority. With the colonel in charge, Himmler established the Department for Pre- and Early History in the Main Office for Race and Settlement, RuSHA."

"And you were asked to go along as—"

"His personal assistant," she cut Otto off. "Himmler, always solicitous for his staff, wanted Vati, older than most personnel, to be adequately cared for. For me it was a hard decision as I had my own career to consider. But when they decided to move the office from Munich to Berlin, where everything important was happening, I agreed to take the position."

While Gabriele was talking, Weisthor seemed only interested in imbibing, but evidently he had also been listening. "To hear you tell it, Gabriele," he protested, "you'd think I'm a dimwit, a relic to be shelved and shielded from further deterioration.

"I am an historian, *Ja*, but a soldier first. Forty years in the service. The son of a soldier, I joined the Imperial Cadet School in Vienna at 14. By 17, I was serving in a Serbian infantry regiment. Promoted to lieutenant in the Austrian imperial army in 1888. During the war, I served on the southern and eastern fronts with many decorations, a colonel by 1917.

"But a real soldier does more than fight. I raised a family and researched and wrote a history of the Germanic people, the real history going back millennia, not the lazy one in vogue that starts with Bismarck.

"I published my first book, an epic poem about King Seyfried of Rabenstein in 1903. Then the *Neun Gebote Gots* [Nine Commandments of Gôt] in 1908. That established me as the heir to ancient Irminism,[5] the once and future true Aryan religion."

Gabriele turned towards me and rolled her eyes. I had to suppress a smile.

Weisthor, catching Gabriele's gesture, stood up and raised his voice. "Go ahead. Belittle me. No less than Theodor Czepl[6] of the Ordo Novi Templi described me ten years ago as 'a man martial in aspect, who revealed himself as bearer of a secret line of German kingship.'"

Gabriele eased him back into his seat. "No one's challenging your credentials, Vati," she soothed.

"I don't care about popular support," he carried on. "The people march to anyone's tune. Give them the right flags, songs and ceremonies, and they'll weep without knowing why. But we leaders will know what moves them, and move them we will."

The colonel might have continued on all evening had an abrupt silence not fallen on the room. Then chairs scraped back. The uniformed men rose as one, and, facing a private dining room door that has just opened, extended their arms in salute.

"Heil Hitler," they shouted in unison. A synchronized click of boot heels followed. Otto and Gabriele also got up, but not Weisthor. I half-stood and craned my head to get a look.

Three officers came through the door, led by a rather squat man with his cap under his arm. Dark-featured, mustached, and hairline receding— I had seen that face often enough in the papers to recognize the Reichsführer-SS, Heinrich Himmler. That he greeted the attention his appearance aroused with an expression of mixed pleasure and bashfulness was, however, unexpected.

"They usually go out through a private exit," Gabriele whispered.

Following Himmler were two officers wearing their peaked uniform caps. Both blond and clean-shaven with Aryan blue eyes that continuously scanned the assembly, they flanked their squat superior like bodyguards.

I turned to Gabriele. "On your left is Reinhard Heydrich, head of the *Sicherheitsdienst*, the Party Intelligence Service," she explained. "On the right, Karl Wolff, the Reichsführer-SS's Chief of Staff. Now put on your best behavior. They are headed this way at my invitation."

Himmler motioned for everyone to be seated. Again chairs slid in concert, and conversations resumed as the officers crossed to our table.

For a queasy moment, it felt as if I was witnessing the opening scene in an epic play, its cast of main character advancing from the shadows and into the limelight for their preliminary bow on the broad stage of history.

"Ah, the family's out for the evening," Himmler exclaimed on reaching our table. "So thoughtful of you young people to include our eminent elder here." He nodded to Weisthor, who only muttered something unintelligible.

"And I'm glad you're showing our newest star that a life of dedication to country and party is not without perks," he said to Gabriele.

He then gestured towards the officer who had remained a few steps back from the table. "Obergruppenführer Reinhard Heydrich, Germany's top spy. You don't want to know him, although, I assure you, he knows you." Heydrich barely nodded. Himmler shrugged him off. "The Führer calls him the man with the iron heart for good reason." I was relieved that Heydrich stayed back. His stare was discomfiting enough from a distance.

Himmler then pointed Otto out to the other officer. "Wolffchen"— only the Reichsführer-SS dared to use a nickname for a fellow officer in public— "Otto Rahn, our author of *Crusade Against the Grail*. We expect great things from him." He winked at Rahn. "Someday he will be celebrated as the man who recovered the Grail itself and brought it home to Germany, where it belongs."

"My pleasure, Herr Rahn." With the aristocratic air more suited to the earlier imperial era, Wolff shook Otto's hand. "The Reichsführer-SS regards your work highly. As chief of his personal staff, I accept his initial assessment. Live up to your potential and perhaps you will be invited to wear the uniform of the Order." He then took a sharp step backwards. Otto seemed tongue-tied.

Himmler then noticed me. His eyes lost their twinkle as they studied me through his thick rounded glasses. "And you are?"

"Raymond Perrier, Otto's personal friend from Geneva, here to help him celebrate his book's success," Gabriele said in my stead.

"Well then," Himmler said, "a friend of Rahn's is a friend of mine. Welcome to the family, Raymond." The twinkle was back as he extended his hand.

"You gentlemen have meetings to attend to," he then said to his fellow officers. "If they'll allow me, I'd like to talk with this little group for a bit, so don't let me hold you up." Heydrich and Wolff saluted and departed.

Gabriele pulled a chair over from another table. Himmler kissed her on the cheek as he took a seat.

"As much as I loathe doing business outside the office," he said, "I have to take this opportunity with all of us here—you too, Raymond—to clarify your position, Otto.

"Consider yourself on special assignment. Most of your projects, like Colonel Weisthor's, are beyond the normal perimeter of the SS, at least currently. As you might have guessed, some of the subjects you write about seem irrelevant, nonsense even, to hard-nosed military men like the two gentlemen who just left us.

"Your work will largely be self-directed. With *Crusade*, you have already shown that you can produce quality work under more trying circumstances than you will ever have to endure with us. Most of your time can be spent writing what you chose.

"You will undertake a few tasks for me directly. These will be stipulated between us, and on them you will have direct access to me. They will, of course, remain confidential.

"But, since no one works well in prolonged isolation, you will also be part of a team." He nodded towards Weisthor who was finally paying some attention. "The colonel as head of RuSHA, now not connected to the regular SS, will be your official superior. His unit is conducting several low-profile archeological digs inside of Germany. Such activities may eventually expand beyond our borders. Your expertise will be useful. Agreed, Colonel?"

Weisthor nodded. "I'll take any extra hand who can work a

shovel—with the precision required of an archeologist."

Otto grinned and held up his hands. "Calluses," he said.

Himmler tapped Gabriele's wrist. "But the de facto coordinator of the group is Fraulein Dechend, as you might have already observed. She serves as my liaison for group projects."

"And, remember, Uncle Heinrich, I can work a shovel and write articles as well as any man," she said with a telling pout.

Himmler winked at Otto. "Take her out in the field with you sometimes, Rahn. And since you two live practically next door, there should be plenty of time to put your heads together."

Otto smiled and nodded. Suspecting that Himmler considered himself a matchmaker, I cringed inside.

"So," the Reichsführer said as he rose to leave, "our operation is underway." He looked at me. "And should you find yourself without enough to occupy your time in that idyllic little country of yours, Raymond, we can find something worthwhile for you to do here also."

After dinner, Otto and I accompanied Gabriele, with the inebriated Weisthor in tow, to their taxi.

On the way she said to me, "So, the fearsome Reichsführer-SS isn't quite the ogre your papers depict." I nodded half-heartedly.

She turned to Rahn. "You should know, Otto, that he followed your career with interest well before the summons to Berlin. He knows *Parzival* and has his own interpretation of von Eschenbach. He believes in reincarnation and believes he was Henry the Fowler, the founder of the German nation in medieval times and its first king. He sees himself as the modern day King Arthur holding court at the Round Table with his twelve noble knights."

"Camelot," Weisthor muttered. "Wewelsburg."

"Vati, bad." She slapped at the old man's hands as we reached the cab. "That's confidential."

Having seen them off, Otto suggested that we walk the mile back to his flat for exercise. We had gone several blocks side-by-side in an unsettled silence before he said, "You were quiet through most of that."

"A lot to absorb. Germany is now a foreign country to me. So organized compared to the chaos when we were boys just out of school here."

"So true." He whipped his head towards me, a skip in his step. "I was just thinking about our first time. You looked like a golden angel. I couldn't take my eyes off you. Do you remember?"

I smiled. "How could I forget? At the end of that day you placed your hand on my head. It was better than a kiss."

"I'm not so sure of that," he said. We both laughed.

That stirred up a palpable tension between us, a pulling together, a pushing apart, that pulsed in the darkness to the rhythm of the screeching crickets. "Do you still think we were right to embrace the celibacy recommended by the Georgekreis[7] so literally?" I finally asked.

"Not right, but prudent," he said. "Remember the ruckus when we dared to display a bit of affection for each other in public. German intolerance towards homosexuals is much higher than in Switzerland. But, cheer up. That could change. In '33, Goebbels even offered our Stephan George the presidency of the Academy for the Arts."

I knew that story. "But Stephan declined, knowing the Nazis regarded homosexuality as a perversion to either be cured or sublimated." Even though George and his followers renounced gay sex voluntarily, the poet refused to allow the government to hold him up as a model for all homosexuals. Instead, he headed to Switzerland where he died within the year. Many of his followers also migrated from Germany, fearing that the Nazis at any time might resume the strict enforcement of the notorious Paragraph 175[8] enacted during the Second Reich, which punished homosexuality with imprisonment. They drew caution from the gradually increasing prosecution of the Jews.

Otto laughed nervously. "I can't believe the country that gave birth to so many artists and humanitarians, many of them homosexual, will ever revert to the savagery of the hoodlums who once held sway in the Party."

We both turned pensive for the rest of the walk. I felt he was naïve for expecting the Nazis to remain moderate; but again I kept that opinion to myself.

When we reached his apartment building, he leaned against the iron railing surrounding the stairs going down and said, "We better hope I'm right about tolerance here improving. I'm a homosexual, as you know, and with my luck I'll get caught *in flagrante* someday. But I'm in no rush to find out what their discovery of my true sexual preference might entail. And so, my dear Raymond, I must insist, all natural urges to the contrary, that we keep to our separate beds tonight."

Chapter 3: Pamiers, Late 1317

"**I** am Jaques de Sabart reporting for duty to Bishop Fournier's office," the young man told the sentinel at the main entrance to the episcopal palace. The guard looked him over, sniffed at his student outfit, still tousled after being stuffed into his backpack for the two days it took to journey from Toulouse to Pamiers, and ordered, "Inside and down the first hall, boy. Wash up at the fountain and they'll give you a proper clerk's robe. They'll set you an appointment if you're due one."

He had been warned that relocating from the bustling capital to the plodding artisan community forty miles down the Ariège might be unnerving, and the transition from a student's routine to an adult career could prove daunting. To calm himself, Jaques focused on the novel surroundings, taking in details until his breathing and heartbeat slowed down.

The rest of his reception proved pleasant enough. After cleaning up and donning the gray thigh-length tunic and black hooded mantle proper to a secular apprentice, he had only a short wait in the vaulted ante-chamber, adorned with paintings of saints and knights, before his name was called: "De Sabart, the bishop will see you now."

While the office and person of Frater Gui had struck Jaques as stark, the quarters and stature of Bishop Fournier impressed him as opulent. Every wall and cornice of his spacious suite glowed with colorful art work or gilded filigree. The portly prelate, swathed in episcopal robes, loomed large behind his mahogany desk, a purple mountain garnished with a bejeweled pectoral cross of silver. The bishop had to be twice his width, Jaques gauged, and twice his height with a miter on. Without getting up, the prelate extended his glittering ring.

Jaques kissed it. "Good morning, your Excellency," he said, immediately self-conscious of his southern accent.

"Jaques de Sabart," the bishop murmured, giving him the once-over. "With that name, you have to be my countryman. I am from Saverdun, also on the Ariège but well after it has made its way through Tarascon. Sit, please."

Jaques perched on the edge of the plush chair although the bishop's informal air suggested that he ease back.

"You come highly recommended by Frater Gui and your teachers at Saint Sernin. Of course, they took issue with your refusal of the Dominican habit. Wise. The Dominicans are a young order in an old church and prone to over-zealousness. They tend to take every God-given pleasure as superfluous, if not sinful. But you do feel called to be court scribe and, most importantly, have the talent. Far excelling over the other students at the abbey, I understand." Fournier peered at him expectantly.

"Since I can only know myself with the talents I've been given, I can't make the comparisons teachers can. I was surprised, even upset, to see that others found it hard to learn what came so easily for me. I accept my gifts as given, not belittling others for lacking them or seeing myself as more important because I have them. I do the best with what I've got and strive always to enhance them," Jacques said.

"Well put." The bishop applauded. He then leaned forward. "Now who, pray tell, at the abbey rehearsed you to make that answer, knowing it would ring perfectly in my ears?"

Jaques felt a flash of irritation. Despite the outer display of nonchalance, the bishop was testing him. He took a deep breath.

"The words are mine, composed in the moment just before I spoke them," he said, "although I have to credit many people—teachers, fellow students, even passersby—for the education that informed me of the principles behind them."

Fournier rubbed his face as if to hide a smirk. "Thank God the Dominicans didn't get you first."

He eased back but suddenly lurched forward again, piercing Jaques with his eyes. "So, the crafty Gui could not make you one of them. Instead, he sent you here to spy for him."

When Jaques only looked perplexed, the bishop continued, "No again, eh? My apology. One can't be too careful with those radicals. Ambition will try any trick to protect its fiefdom. Had they developed even a bit of patience, compassion, or plain diplomacy, I wouldn't have to be here cleaning up after them."

Jaques attempted no reply. The bishop returned to the report on his desk. "I see that Gui worried that your extraordinary memory might have come from the fellow with the cloven hooves. They see demons everywhere. Once they bled the Cathar heresy to a trickle, the Dominicans had to find new nests of villains to exterminate, so they went after the Waldensians and the Béguins, and then on to Jews, sorcerers, and magicians. If Bernard Gui had his way, every woman since Eve would deserve the stake. Sure, they're all culpable of some chicanery or seduction—it's their nature. But ridding us of them all would doom the human race."

Jaques continued in his silence. He was aware of the rivalry among the religious orders but wondered why Fournier, and Gui earlier, did not keep their mutual distrust under their skullcaps at least in front of a lay person. The bishop seemed to pick up on his distaste and apologized. "I get overly incensed at such stupidity, especially in those who ought to know better."

But he could not resist carrying on. "Why I suspected Gui's motives in recommending you to me. The Dominicans believe that the rest of the church—we Cistercians among them—are lax on heretics, if not heretical ourselves. They forget that the Cistercians, under

Arnaud Amalric, abbot of Citeaux, led the original crusade against the Cathars.

"The Inquisition was founded only to eradicate the remnants of heresy after the war ended with the fall of Montsegur in 1244, some seventy-five years ago. Towards the end of the last century that goal was virtually accomplished. But the Inquisition, staffed by the Dominicans, fabricated heresy where there was none to perpetuate itself. Their inquiries and trials, directed against remote descendants of the Cathars, turned sophistic and meddlesome. Local secular governments, now realigned with royal rule, objected to the excesses of the inquisitorial courts in Carcassonne, Albi, and Toulouse. Other religious orders began to resent Dominican usurpation of legal and ecclesiastical authority. In 1303, the Franciscan friar and incurable rabble-rouser, Bernard Delicieux, induced a royal official to help him lead a mob in storming the Inquisition's notorious prison in Carcassonne and freeing its population. Paris endorsed the mutiny and pressed the church to subdue Dominican overzealousness.

"Then an unexpected Cathar resurgence, planned and perpetrated by Pierre and Jacques Authier of Ax-les-Thermes, vindicated the Inquisition and its Dominican leaders, Geoffrey d'Ablis[9] and Bernard Gui. Even so, by 1309, all but one of the known new Perfects, or Cathar clergy, including the Authier brothers, had been tried and executed, and the refurbished bureaucracy of the Inquisition was again short of victims.

"Unlike the original heretics, often wealthy landowners who enjoyed the patronage of the Counts of Foix, Toulouse, and Carcassonne, the cult's pathetic remnant is now composed of impoverished groups hiding in caves or nomads already fled south to Spain beyond our jurisdiction. Their current leader, Guilhem Belibaste, is a former shepherd from the Narbonne, long wanted by the bishop there for murdering a fellow worker, hardly a worthy quarry for the Holy Catholic Church. We will certainly hunt him and his followers and bring them to heel, but without the fanfare that stirs up animosity in the rest of the populace, a subtlety the Dominicans could not master. The church has enough enemies without breeding more with unnecessary severity."

The bells in the tower of the Cathedral of Saint Antonin de Pamiers, across the courtyard from the palace, rang the hour. Bishop Fournier seemed suddenly abashed. "Not like me to get so carried away," he said, "especially in a first interview." He then grinned. "You are a good listener to allow me go on at such length. But, remember, politics, civil or religious, internal or external, must be immaterial to a scribe."

Jaques nodded. "Frater Gui did advise me, 'See all and record all without adulterating what you observe with anyone's opinion—including your own.'"

"Give credit where it is due," Fournier said. "Such advice will serve you well as a novice. To start, you'll sit with elderly Brother Simon, whose place you will eventually take, at various types of hearings, mostly administrative. Because such tactics worked with my predecessor, these peasants assume that stubbornness will get them out of paying their taxes and tithes. Also some morals cases, matters passed to the ecclesiastical courts by civil magistrates too timid to decide them on their own authority.

"But, no mistake, your initial role will not be entirely passive. Brother Simon is a Dominican, who served under d'Ablis during his recent tenure as Grand Inquisitor of Carcassonne. A slip of the pen, which can always be attributed to Simon's age, might divert a tithe awarded to the diocese to the Dominican convent in Romegos. Or the tax levied against a Dominican benefactor can be reduced by dropping a zero. A suspect's name provided by a witness can be misspelled, thus voiding incriminating testimony. Put your fabled memory to work. Transcribe the proceedings mentally. Afterwards, I will give you Simon's transcript to review and revise, not officially as that is prohibited, but for my information as the final arbiter of the case."

He smiled and waved Jaques from the room. "This is just the beginning, Jaques de Sabart. Soon you will be scribing trials on your own. Now out with you. Have a look around the city. Find a good meal, some good wine, and maybe a good wench. I will see you in court."

As directed, Jaques monitored Brother Simon's transcripts, observing several alterations, few of which, however, seemed to concern Fournier when each evening he presented his findings to the bishop. More often than not the prelate showed more interest in the personal tendencies of his charge. If Jaques's eyelids drooped with fatigue after such long days, the bishop would offer encouragement. "This procedure makes you go through each court session not once, but twice," he would say, "and I know it's trying. But while the devil is in the details, so is the truth. 'Not one jot or one tittle shall pass from the law, till all be fulfilled.'"[10]

With each passing session, Jaques sensed that Fournier was more intrigued with the mechanics of his memory than in his notes on the day's court proceedings. The bishop would sit back and ask, as if impressed, about his techniques for remembering and how he discovered them. At first Jaques was embarrassed by the older man's questions and tried to slip past them by saying something about the issues in the transcript under consideration. Fournier allowed for such reluctance but eventually circled back to the inquiry.

Given such genteel prodding, Jaques started to share his still forming ideas about the talent he had taken for granted before Saint Sernin. He told the bishop about his private schooling under Père Fontaine in Tarascon and the way he assumed everyone learned and remembered as he did until he tutored the capitoul's son at the abbey.

"Roger made me realize," he explained, "that some people have a scrambler in their head that mixes up information after they store it there. For Roger to remember anything, we had to figure a way around that disruptive machine."

"Which you did?"

Jaques flashed a grin. "We found a trick, mental sleight-of-hand, that worked like magic. His problem was not with getting information into his head; that is as automatic as I assumed earlier. But if facts are stored willy-nilly, they are slow or impossible to retrieve when needed. We figured out that it was a lot easier to find one thing among many if the information is filed in some order from the start."

The bishop stroked his beard. "Storing memories methodically. Give me an example."

Jaques leaned forward, eager to share the discovery that enabled Roger to complete his schooling, although it had not made his protégé a genius. "We made up tags, easy to remember, out of words or short phrases. These then represented longer passages or groups of related ideas," he explained. "Think of it as one word standing for a chapter in a book. Recall that word and the mind serves up the full chapter. Remember the chapter tags in order and you can recall the entire book."

Fournier bobbed his head slowly. Jaques felt the satisfaction he often experienced when Père Fontaine approved his mastery of a lesson, a sensation that rarely happened during his strict schooling at the abbey.

"You have then read Marcus Tullius Cicero's discussion of the art of memory in *De Oratore*," the bishop said. Jaques nodded. He cherished this work on the art of public speaking by Rome's greatest orator.

"Cicero was not the first or last to attempt to master the process of memory, so natural a function that most people don't think about it until they lose it," Fournier continued. "His prescriptions are very specific. Mnemonics, as we still call them. Do you recall his devices?"

"He proposes several. One is the use of *loci* or places. As a first step, one imprints a series of places in a certain order on the memory, as simple as walking through a building and noting its various features: rooms, hallways, niches, and furnishings.

"Then strong images representing the sections of the speech are associated with these features. Finally, the actual words to be spoken are attached to the images. To deliver the speech, the orator has only to walk mentally through the building, visit the places in the preset order, retrieve the associated image from the place, and then recite the words associated with the image. The speech is accurately delivered."

The bishop laughed, his fleshy jowls wobbling. "Easy for you. I'd be hard pressed to even repeat what you just said. So you used Cicero's model in tutoring your friend?"

"Actually we were using our simpler system for a couple of years before I read *De Oratore*. I was pleased, though, to find similarities there with what we had worked out on our own. The more often the same idea appears in different places the more reliable we can take it to be."

Fournier again stroked his beard. "Remarkable. And these tags, this Ciceronian filing system, is the key to your extraordinary memory?"

Jaques shook his head. "That was a system I worked out for Roger. It's still slow and clumsy even if less elaborate than Cicero's. But if I had to go through all that in your courtroom, I'd always be hours behind. How I do it myself is infinitely simpler."

"And that is?"

Jaques hesitated. The few times he had pondered that question he found no words for the phenomenon. "I can't describe it—not yet. I focus on the activity I want to remember. Then something in the background activates and records automatically for as long as I keep my attention on the proceeding. To reverse the process and recall exactly what was said, there is something—like the tags I taught Roger to use, but—"

He paused and turned aside, trying to pierce the darkness that shrouded his mind whenever he got this far. Suddenly the blackness shifted. He heard a click.

"A key," he gasped, aware that Fournier was watching him intently. "An object that opens the door. Turn the key and it all comes back, as if it's happening again, only faster. And I can start and stop the action, go back and forward in time, skip past what is unimportant, and look more carefully at the important scenes. I sometimes glean further details that I missed during the actual event."

"Can you see or feel this key? Can you describe it?"

Jaques strained, but the darkness had congealed into a wall like solid coal. He tried to feel around but felt paralyzed. "I can't see anything," he moaned. "I can't go any further. I'm stuck."

When he opened his eyes, the bishop had rounded the desk and was standing next to him. "Enough for tonight, young man." Fournier said, holding out a hand to help him up. "You're exhausted. Tomorrow is Saturday. Take it off and relax. We will return to this some other time."

Jaques forced himself upright and staggered into the shadowy courtyard. Just beyond the exit from the palace, he stumbled into a ragtag body lying across the path. Struggling to keep his balance, he excused himself.

"The bishop's boy," the vagrant spat out.

Jaques tried to make out the features of a face covered with filth and patched over one eye. He recognized a particular street denizen, a marketplace heckler whose prattle insulted the clergy, the nobility, and every sacred institution to the great amusement of the passersby. Rather than have him apprehended, the area vendors protected him as an attraction that increased business traffic.

Jaques fumbled to find a coin.

"I ain't no bum," the fellow growled. "And I wouldn't take the filthy money of a kid who works for that fat cow, Jacques Fournier."

"His Excellency Bishop Jacques Fournier to us," Jaques corrected.

"And I'm His Highness, the reincarnated Baldwin the Leper King, so kiss my royal ass," the vagabond shouted in Occitanian to the frightened boy as he hurried away to his room.

Jaques huddled inside his hooded overcoat for protection against the brisk wind that blew up from the Ariège, at the same time grateful that it was not so cold that he had to stay inside on his day off. The chance encounter with the public nuisance had dispelled the previous evening's symptoms caused by his latest attempt to penetrate the mystery behind his memory. He recognized the name and title the man used as that of Baldwin IV of the House of Anjou, who reigned as king of the liberated Jerusalem between 1174 and 1185. Having contracted leprosy as a child and not expected to live long, Baldwin was nevertheless crowned king at age 13. Despite his handicap and the constant court intrigue to determine his successor, the boy went on to reign for eleven years, even garnering acclaim as a warrior by fighting with the force of Knights Templar that defeated the fearsome Saladin in the critical battle of Montgisard.

Jaques's night's sleep, however, had been disrupted by a lengthy dream set in a monotonous mathematics class back in the abbey school. While it never congealed into anything meaningful as a whole, two brief scenes lingered after he awoke. The first was of Arnaud Sicre just staring at him from the other side of the room. And the second, what startled him from sleep, was of a burly knight in a white surcoat emblazoned with a red cross bashing down the door with his sword and scattering the screaming students.

Then that morning, as he dressed to go out, he was surprised to recall an actual boyhood memory of a troop of mounted Templars pulling up to the church in Tarascon. Their leader dismounted and walked with Père Fontaine towards the cemetery where the two talked for some time. The next year, 1307, he remembered, the Templar Order, once the most disciplined military organization in Christendom and the most powerful financial establishment in Europe, was disgraced and disbanded virtually overnight.

There had to be a connection between current happenings and the dream material, Jaques thought as he wandered through the stalls manned by vendors crouched around their fires. He meandered through the square, and, finding little merchandise of interest, he simply took in the small talk, noticing that most of it was in his native Occitanian rather than the French more prevalent in Toulouse.

He was about to round a stall in a remote corner of the square when a conversation behind the tent's canvas wall caught his attention.

"No sense the church still running a court for hunting heretics here," a man was saying. "Haven't been any Cathars, nobody who even knew a Cathar, in Pamiers for years. Just another excuse to squeeze more taxes from us farmers, and all of us as Catholic as the pope."

"I wouldn't be so sure that the heretical rats have all been rounded up and drowned," a voice dreadfully familiar to Jaques replied.

It was Arnaud Sicre from the abbey school. Jaques thought to move away unseen, but curiosity about his nemesis, who had appeared unbidden first in the previous night's dream and now in person, made him linger.

"Some of us lost our rightful property, no fault of our own, because of some damned heretics in the family. And the Cathar hunt isn't over until we get back what's ours," Arnaud said.

"Speaking for yourself?" the first man asked.

"Damned right. I had the misfortune to be born in Ax at the height of the Authier revival there. Our property was in my mother's name, and she converted to the heretics, became a *perfecta*, a priestess—yeah, they have them—got caught and burnt at the stake. The church took everything she owned. My brother turned heretic too, so he has no rights. My father stayed Catholic, so my mother forced him out of the family house. He moved to Toulouse, and I went to live with him when I was only seven, so we can't be accused of consorting with heretics. But still the church is keeping what rightfully belongs to me and my father."

The first man laughed. "You actually think they'll give it back?"

"Not for nothing they won't. But if I were to serve up some Cathar leftovers, one of them a Perfect, I can name it as my price."

Jaques took a step back, intending to move away quietly. But a third man, huddled in rags beside the fire, who had said nothing thus far, noticed his movement. "What, ho, the bishop's boy!" he bellowed as if he had known Jaques was there all along.

Arnaud charged around the corner before Jaques could duck away. "Well, if it isn't Joli Jaques! More like the bishop's girl, and all ears, his spy, to boot," he sneered.

"Good morning, Arnaud," Jaques said, side-stepping the larger fellow. "What brings you to Pamiers?"

"The prospect of bloodying your pretty face with my fists," Arnaud retorted.

The vagrant, Baldwin the Leper King of the previous evening, sidled his rag-draped frame towards the pair. "You heard the man," he said to Jaques. "Heretics for sale, a Perfect among 'em. Damn cold winter's comin' and we'll need some blazin' bonfires. About time. No decent French cooking since they roasted Jacques de Molay over four years ago. You remember that one, don't you?" Baldwin asked the third man who had ducked into a far corner of the tent. He waved the question off.

"Damn shame you missed it," Baldwin continued. "Low fire, slow turning to brown on all sides. A pig on a spit." He tapped Jaques's chest with his fist. "But you know who got the last word, eh, bishop's boy?"

"My name is Jaques de Sabart."

Baldwin began to laugh. His cackle grew to a roar. "The bishop, the bishop's boy and de Molay. Jacques all around then. Well, the Pope and the King, together they cooked old Jaques de Molay. But the old soldier got the last laugh. He was just about done, his body perfectly roasted, when, from out of the fire, he called on the living God and prayed that his two arch-enemies would be as dead as he was about to become within a year and a day hence. And, I'll be damned, but it happened. Come April, Clement V died after a long and ugly illness. And in November, the king, who thought he was quite the hunter, got killed during the chase. And old de Molay didn't even need that extra day he prayed for."

"A myth concocted by de Molay's followers to make him a martyr," Arnaud snorted, "and you, old snot, should be hung for repeating it."

Embarrassed by the company and conversation, Jaques excused himself and hurried towards the cathedral across the square.

Before he was out of earshot, he heard the first man say to Arnaud, "You knew that kid?"

"From the abbey school in Toulouse. That kiss-ass stole my job."

"What ho," Baldwin said. "You wanted to be the bishop's boy? Why the hell would you want to do that?" He started to guffaw. "Ah, as bishop's boy you could rat out some Good Christians and their Perfect, make a name for yourself, and force them to give your mama's house back. Very clever, but Jaques beat you to the job."

"Shut up, you old bugger," Arnaud hissed. "As it is, he's likely to spill this all to Fournier. He'll try to have me charged. To not report knowledge about heretics is still a high crime, even if I am as anti-heretic as any Dominican."

Jaques crept into the quiet of the cathedral through the side door, letting it close behind him as if it could shut out the disturbances that had infiltrated his placid routine. He slipped into a pew in the nave, wishing that somehow Père Fontaine would emerge from the shadows and put his arm around him.

Instead there were the echoes of unwanted voices: Baldwin with his heretics for sale and de Molay's potent curse of pope and king; Arnaud Sicre's threats, boasts and suspicions; even the dire suggestion of Bernard Gui: *Unusual talent like yours can be more the work of the devil—magic, witchcraft—than a gift of God.*

Even though he had passed scrutiny by a Dominican and a Cistercian, how could he be so sure? He had passed out last night trying to explain his gift to the bishop. What if the devil dwelt in that darkness? The thought disturbed him so much that he gave up trying to pray and started down the aisle.

The key. He stumbled on a protruding flagstone. Barely breaking the fall, he chided his lapse in attention. Straightening, he saw that he was in front of a side altar over which stood a statue of the Virgin Mary, her arms upraised—she held no child—and her eyes lifted skyward rather than looking towards him. The White Lady. He regarded the image in the flickering candle light without devotion.

The church where he had served as an altar boy in Tarascon, Notre

Dame de Sabart, had two statues of the Madonna. The first, clothed in white and light skinned like the prettiest girls in the village, was placed prominently in a niche to the right of the main altar. She too had her eyes and arms raised towards the heavens and was without her child. The other statue, the historical Notre Dame de Sabart after whom the church was named, was housed in a shadowed alcove to the rear of the church. This image was made of dark wood, the faces of the seated woman and the child on her lap black and primitive as if carved long ago by a prehistoric artist. As a young boy, he had been confused by the completely different representations and asked Père Fontaine if there were actually two Madonnas.

Père then told him the story of Notre Dame de Sabart, which for hundreds of years was the church's only effigy of the Virgin Mary.

Legend had it, the priest explained, that in 778 Charlemagne, the Frankish king, followed the Saracens with whom he was at war to the Ariège region. On the evening of September 8, he came to the mouth of a valley where he intended to engage his foe in battle. Suddenly his horse refused to move forward. Charlemagne dug in his spurs, but the beast stayed put; it would not enter the valley. After a third try, a luminous vision of the Virgin appeared. Charlemagne was so awestruck that he decided to delay the fight. Then the Virgin disappeared. At dawn the emperor assembled his army at the spot of the apparition. They dug and discovered a wooden statue upon which was written "Notre Dame de Sabart," Our Lady of Victory. The soldiers, realizing that the horse's stubbornness had prevented Charlemagne from falling into a Saracen trap, erected a stone altar on that spot.

The emperor, however, had the statue carried to the abbey of St. Volusien in nearby Foix. But on two attempts to enshrine it there, the statue vanished, only to reappear on the stone altar on the spot of its original discovery. Understanding that the Madonna only wanted to be venerated in this sacred place, Charlemagne ordered a chapel built around the original altar to house her.

"And now you know, little Jaques de Sabart, how the virgin, this church, this valley, and you yourself were named. All are Victory, Sabart," Père Fontaine said in conclusion.

Jaques was happy to have his special story but still curious. "But why is she black and the others are white?" he asked.

The priest shook his head. "No one seems to know, but there are several very special statues of the Black Madonna throughout Europe, all older than those of the White Lady."

Jaques persisted, "But how can the same person be both black and white?"

Père tousled his hair gently. "It is the right question, Jaques, but not one that can be answered with words, no matter how wise or beautiful they may be. That answer and many others are already within you even if you don't see or understand them yet. Keep asking and the answers will come."

Now standing in front of the Blessed Virgin's altar in Pamiers, Jaques shook himself to break loose from the memory of the boy and the priest in Tarascon. He was still asking and would continue to do so. His one regret was that Père Fontaine would not be around when the answers came.

Chapter 4: Berlin, August 1936

"**A**s wary as I am of their ultimate intentions, I applaud the German flare for pageantry," Paul Ladame remarked as we watched the spectators pour from the massive *Olympiastadion* at the conclusion of the day's session of the 1936 Olympic Games. "Five years ago, this defeated country was dragging its hind quarters in the dirt, in the midst of a depression with five million people unemployed. But now this. Substitute the fasces for the ubiquitous swastika, and it could be Rome in the Empire's heyday."

"With all credit applied to the Nazis and their leader, Adolph Hitler," I said.

"Masterful propaganda. They co-opted the one event on the planet that celebrates human ability without regard to race, color, or creed and turned it into a showcase for National Socialism. A two-week demonstration that shows Germany is once again a leading economic and military power despite the shackles put on her at Versailles; that she has shaken the Great Depression and put her people back to work faster than other western countries; and that most Germans are happier with their standard of living than practically all others in a very disgruntled world." Paul shook his head. "If I could disregard the price that will have to be paid for this, I too could embrace their agenda."

"There even seems to have been some relaxation in official policy against the Jews," I noted. "Signs barring Jews from public places, which were posted everywhere when I was here a year ago, have disappeared; and I haven't seen any anti-Semitic rants in their newspapers. They even tout that two Jews, Rudi Ball, an ice-hockey player, and Helene Mayer, a world-class fencing champion, are stars on their Olympic team."

"Omitting that both reside outside of Germany and are here only for the games," Paul said. "Details. Blind the public with the sun of power and glory, and all kinds of outrages can occur unnoticed on the periphery. Propaganda changes perception and thus changes people. With all the technological advances now—film, radio, television, photography—at which the Germans are geniuses, the opportunity to spread a message, not to be confused with truth, to millions simultaneously gives unprecedented power to those who control the transmissions."

"And they expect that we foreigners will depart these games, if not bedecked with swastika paraphernalia, as good-will ambassadors for the Nazi cause," I said.

Other than an occasional postcard from one of the archeological sites on which he worked, I had heard little from Otto since my visit to Berlin in mid-1935. Just this June my letter to him was answered by a secretary, who stated that he was on a confidential research mission to Iceland for a month. But then came his unexpected invitation to join him for the Games. Anticipating the occasion as a reunion of the three of us who became friends on the movie sets in Berlin in 1928, I invited Paul Ladame to accompany me from Geneva. The trip north was uneventful except for an uncomfortable delay at the border while German officials pulled Ladame aside for a brief but inconsequential questioning.

Now we waited in the designated place for Rahn to join us. "I'm curious how Otto has handled the propaganda, especially since he works for Himmler, whose Schutzstaffel is the cream of Nazi zealots," Paul said.

I felt compelled to defend my friend. "He answers to Himmler but not as part of the SS. He's still writing his books and only does research related to his field. He can hold his own."

Paul turned and grimaced. "I hope you're right."

"He called you the best spelunker in Europe but one of the worst skeptics when it came to his work."

"Don't let personal friendship blind you to Otto's weaknesses. He's in dangerous company where certain flaws could prove disastrous. This is not the gang of amateur Parisian occultists, the *Polaires*, who backed his venture in the Languedoc. I'd have bet the house against him finding any buried treasure but went along to make sure he didn't break his neck. I did have to rescue him from a crowd of irate Tarasconians who caught him chalking up an inscription in their sacred caves. He wasn't cheating, he said, just trying to bring out some features so he could photograph them. They still chased him out of town as a charlatan and German spy. I admit I wasn't much of a believer in his theories, and much of the time he did little to convince me otherwise."

"Do you then think it was more than luck that Himmler was impressed by his book and brought him here to Berlin?" I asked, finally voicing the question that had nagged me since I last saw Otto.

Paul sighed. "The Nazis, and Himmler with them, have a very long range plan for Europe. They do nothing that doesn't forward that plan. Rahn is not an exception."

My intended objection to Paul's facile inclusion of Otto with the Nazi ilk was cut off by the laughing shout of a woman. "Raymond, Raymond, over here."

It was Gabriele Dechend with an SS officer holding her arm. She pulled away from the man and embraced me. "I thought we'd never find you in this crowd," she burbled. "And this must be Professor Ladame." She hugged Paul as well. "Otto"—she nodded to the officer— "has told me so much about you and the old days."

Paul and I froze. The filled-out face above a black uniform emblazoned with Nazi insignias and below the peaked cap adorned with the ominous *Totenkopf*, the "dead man's head" of the SS, was indeed that of Otto Rahn.

"Doesn't he look splendid in uniform?" Gabriele chortled, patting his arm with affection. Then she noticed our stupefaction. "You didn't recognize him either," she said. "No surprise. I saw him in it for the first time this morning and thought it couldn't be Otto without the fedora and trench coat. But I've gotten used to it. So manly."

Rahn cleared his throat, removed his cap, and stuck it under his arm. He then fumbled through his pockets and produced a pack of cigarettes. "Gentlemen," he offered, although he knew we didn't smoke.

While Otto lit up, I gave Paul a look to check whatever imprudent comment he was about to make. Too late.

"Why the hell are you wearing that outfit?" he asked Otto.

Dead silence until Gabriele, again giggling, explained. "After so many significant contributions, Otto was chosen to represent the *Ahnenerbe* staff, still civilian, in the Führer's honor guard. For that, SS membership, an officer's rank, and occasionally wearing the uniform are required."

Otto came towards us, took us both by the arm and turned us away from the crowd. "My dear friends," he whispered, "It is merely a practical matter. A man's got to eat."

Gabriele circled around and faced us, her camera cocked. "Smile," she said and clicked.

"Let me take one of the three of you," Paul said.

Gabriele came between us and we linked arms. Paul snapped the photo. Then, as we both realized we had not yet greeted each other properly, Otto and I put our outer arms around each other forming a circle of three. We leaned forward and our heads briefly touched at the center of the circle. There was a distinct snap.

Gabriele drew back. "Did you feel that?" she gasped.

"A sign that we three have been together like this, but in a very different time and place," Otto declared.

I had felt such electricity before. It happened when Otto placed his hand on my head the first time we met. But now Gabriele was also included. "You probably already know this," she said to me, "but Otto sees and hears things that nobody else does."

Paul shattered the intensity of the moment. "Come on. We're in public. Open displays of affection, particularly *ménage a trois*, are verboten."

We joined the line at the restaurant entrance. Most of the men, tall, blonde and blue-eyed, were in SS uniforms with doting dates, also tall, blonde and blue-eyed, dangling from their crooked right arms. Gabriele again linked with Otto and tossed him the required flirtatious glance, even though neither of them—short, dark-haired and brown-eyed—fit the true Aryan profile.

Unlike the other men who largely ignored their partners, Otto rewarded Gabriele's attention with smiles, which got her to cuddle closer. Their interaction brought on a pang of jealousy. Was the display, like the uniform, meant for everyone except me? Or was it precisely Otto's way of showing me that his affections too, like everything else, had switched radically?

At the restaurant Gabriele asked for a table to seat four. "No Papa Weisthor tonight then?" I asked to distract myself.

"Too drunk too soon. I'm bad but I made sure of that."

"So you're still his nurse?"

"Not for long, I hope. I've asked to be relieved. I'll stay only as long as Uncle Heinrich insists."

"Uncle Heinrich?" Ladame asked.

"Himmler." I gave him a look that said I would explain later.

"Reichsführer-SS Heinrich Himmler," Rahn interjected. "Only Gabby gets to call him *uncle*." Then, chin up and shoulders squared, he paraded Gabriele through the room, exchanging robust *Heil Hitler's* with his fellow officers.

"Something of a good old boys' club," I said as we were seated.

Rahn nodded. "One of the few places in Berlin that won't be intolerably overcrowded this evening."

"Reserved exclusively for SS men and guests throughout the games," Gabriele said.

"Any chance we'll run into some big Nazi fish here?" Ladame asked.

"Not the Führer, if that's who you mean. He left the games before the medal ceremony again this afternoon," Gabriele said. "His way, it's rumored, of keeping his word to the Olympic committee. They objected when he only shook hands with the Germans who medaled on opening day and insisted he honor victors of all nations equally. So now Hitler greets no one, although I'm sure he will duly honor the German winners in private."

As drinks were poured and dinner ordered, Otto picked out an acquaintance, a civilian at a table in the corner. He waved, and the man, wearing a press badge, came over to our table.

"My friend and patron, Adolph Frisé, allowed in with some privileged journalists as they cover the games for the German press," Otto said. There were introductions all around.

"A well-known publisher here," Otto continued, "he normally works only with established writers. Some years ago he made an exception for me and promoted my book in radio broadcasts when I was still unknown. Later, when he happened upon me in Freiburg, a virtual pauper, he gave me money out of his own pocket."

"Otto's guardian angel," Ladame quipped as he greeted Frisé. I sensed some camaraderie between them, as if they already knew each other, but neither acknowledged any prior acquaintance.

As the meal proceeded and the liquor flowed, Otto, contrary to his admitted bashfulness in public, took to dominating the conversation. He became the teacher addressing his students, which, as he got louder, came to include some folks at the surrounding tables. He ate little but smoked and drank continuously. With Gabriele goading him to elaborate on his adventures, he held forth on his privileged life as a researcher and writer, crediting the Reichsführer and the SS as the source of his good fortune. No salesman could have advertised a product better. He recalled how bad things had been until recently and how good they were now with smart uniforms, good food, plentiful wine, and more cigarettes than even he could smoke. And all this, he added with a wide grin, while getting paid to write. He glowed as he painted an even more spectacular future. His thousand-page masterpiece, the novel *Sebastian*, was almost finished, as was his non-fiction work about the murderous inquisitor Conrad of Marburg, Pope Innocent III's blunt instrument for crushing heretics in Germany while his holy Crusade was destroying the Cathars in neighboring France.

"Thus demonstrating that the suppression of heresy was not exclusively a French pastime," I interjected.

"You were talking about Conrad when we were exploring the caves years ago, Otto," Ladame said. "That story needs to be in print. When can we expect it?"

Rahn glanced off. "I'm kept busy otherwise. When I'm not digging through ruins in the Odenwald or around the stones of Externsteine[11] to prove out Colonel Weisthor's ancestral theories, I am in Iceland[12] searching for evidence of our Aryan roots in cave carvings. The Reichsführer-SS also wants a sequel to *Crusade Against the Grail* by next year and a third in that series the year after that." He turned back to the table with a deep sigh. "And always there is Montsegur, the passion to return to France, to the Languedoc, to finish the business I started there."

While Otto was holding court, four junior officers and their dates at an adjacent table were acting up at his expense. Taking bits of his speech and quipping over them, their boisterous competing conversation became laced with cursing and obscenities. Several times Otto glanced their way with irritation.

"French whore," one fellow shouted at Otto's latest statement. Rahn glared at the speaker, whose hand had found its way beneath the bodice of the woman next to him.

"Pig," Otto shouted at the offender. "I thought we got rid of the thugs when Ernst Röhm and the SA[13] were shut down two years ago. Evidently not. Exchanging a brown uniform for a black one won't turn a barbarian into a gentleman."

The junior officer jerked his hand from the woman's blouse and half rose. "You talking about me, punk?" he challenged.

"Heinz, sit," one of his companions whispered. "He's an officer."

"Officer, my ass," Heinz sneered, straightening up. "From a civilian unit. A bookworm who wouldn't shoot if a Jew if it was raping his mother."

"Sit, Heinz," Rahn roared with an intensity I did not know he had. "When you wear the SS uniform, you are to act as a model of the evolved species that has left his depraved humanity behind."

Slowly, derisively, Heinz began to clap. "And you, sir," he sneered, "are a flaming faggot."

The crowd, attracted to the altercation, groaned. Chairs scraped back, and shouts supporting either side rang out. Hands went to holstered pistols. The bloody suppression of Röhm's SA and its absorption into Himmler's SS was a *fait accompli*, but resentment still festered in those forced to switch allegiance from the hard-drinking soldier to the more temperate administrator. Otto's derogation of Röhm had opened old wounds. An unseemly row was only averted when two enormous bouncers grabbed the drunken Heinz and dragged him off.

After that, attempts to resume normal conversation among ourselves sputtered and failed. Ladame, silent throughout the incident, shuffled his feet as if anxious to leave. Jokes about the confrontation fell flat.

"Shouldn't you be checking on Colonel Weisthor soon? I can get you a car," Otto suggested to Gabriele.

She nodded. "I'll leave you with your friends."

Paul stood up. "I'd better get back to my hotel. I have an early morning appointment but am free in the afternoon if you want to meet," he said to Otto and me.

And so it was arranged that I would spend the night with Otto at his Tiergartenstrasse apartment with Ladame joining us there the next day.

Despite the previous evening's turmoil and the amount of wine he had imbibed in its course, Otto was remarkably chipper the next morning. Before I was fully awake, he was padding about the kitchen and setting the table on a covered patio behind the apartment. Steaming coffee and a substantial breakfast awaited me when I emerged from the washroom.

As we sat to eat, Otto was cheerfully proper, not mentioning the prior night's events other than to wonder over how much time we had to ourselves before Paul arrived.

He was in the mood to reminisce, assembling the years of our acquaintance, eight now in total, into blocks that demonstrated that our past produced our present and thus might be used to predict our future.

After skating past the dizzying weeks of our early courtship on the movie sets, back street bars, and park benches of Berlin as the "short time it took for us to realize that we were born to be together," he cherry-picked our remaining nomadic student years to highlight our most intense times together: in Michelstadt at his parents' house, in Geneva with my folks, and in the squalid Berlin flat for the brief period we were on our own. "A thoroughly desperate time," he concluded. "Fortunately, we were still simple enough to see adventure in living from hand to mouth. We had our parents and friends when we needed them, each other all the time, and endless dreams for the future."

"*Parzival*," I said. "You were studying *Parzival* then and became convinced, like Schliemann,[14] that it was your destiny to prove that von Eschenbach's Grail story, far from being mythical, was actually an encoded history of the heretical Cathar movement and its belief system."

He sighed, but with a smile. "That obsession propelled me to the next stage, one where we were separated except for quick visits whenever I passed through Geneva. My travels took me to Paris and the Polaires[15] group, which had already done preliminary research on the Cathars and their lost heritage, and to maestro Maurice Magre,[16] who introduced me to his Occitan friends, my dear Comtesse Miryanne de Pujol-Murat,[17] Arthur Caussou,[18] and Ladame too, although he would deny any involvement with the Polaires."

Knowing Otto, I sensed that his reprise was more than casual conversation. "And that stage concluded with the successful publication of *Crusade Against the Grail*," I said, to push him towards his intended conclusion. "Since then, you've been in another phase that hasn't afforded us much proximity, and the SS uniform you now wear bodes no better for the future."

Otto broke into an incongruous grin. "The uniform was for yesterday. It's now in the closet to stay, and my official status need not alter our relationship. In fact, I have a specific proposal to make that could greatly improve it."

I was wary but curious.

"As I hope you understand, Raymond, I'm always looking for opportunities for us to be together. A few weeks ago, the Reichsführer-SS called me into his office and made a personal and confidential request."

"Which, of course, you can't really tell me about," I said when he paused for effect.

"*Au contraire, mon ami.* It is something you can do with me."

"I—do something personal and confidential for Himmler? I am a Swiss."

"We are both European. As we have discussed, nation-states have to become a thing of the past. Hear me out before you decide. It recently became a requirement that every SS member, current and future, complete a detailed and accurate *Ahnenpass* or genealogical profile, which traces his family tree back to the year 1750. Only those who can prove that both paternal and maternal ancestors are without Jewish or colored blood will be allowed to remain in or join the SS. For anyone else in Germany, this would be a routine administrative matter, but we're talking about the Reichsführer-SS here. Himmler needs to meet the gold standard he has set for the rest. Trusting my research ability, he asked me to resolve several open links in his chart. As long as I am discreet, how I do it is up to me. Funds are, of course, no problem."

While the implications of the procedure revolted me, I was curious not only as to how Otto rationalized his involvement with the practice but also why the powerful Himmler would entrust so sensitive a task to a pair of rookies, one not even a German citizen. At the same time, I sensed an opportunity. I had happened onto a portal through which the outside world could glimpse the inner workings of the confounding Nazi racial apparatus.

"I am flattered but flabbergasted," I said. "But so many questions. Why did Himmler choose you? Why would you accept? And what in hell could it have to do with me?"

Otto smiled. "Like most political figures, Himmler has both a public and private personality. He can be the fearsome Reichsführer-SS to the nation and the world but Uncle Heinrich to Gabriele and his close friends. That he included me in the latter category is reassuring. Perhaps the deep, if unorthodox, ideas in my book, along with endorsements from Gabriele and Weisthor, prompted it." He paused and looked off. "But there is something more that's still to emerge. Let's call it a sense of destiny for now.

"There are other good reasons to accept the task. I remember the way it was in Freiburg and earlier. Everything I have now I owe to his patronage, and he is the Reichsführer-SS. How could I say no?

"Also another matter I've never mentioned to you before because it was irrelevant—until now. I was raised Protestant, as you know, and know nothing of Judaism. But my blood, it turns out, is not as pure as the new regulations require. Since I am an SS officer, General Wolff from Personnel ordered that I too submit my ahnenpass immediately. Some preliminary work shows that my mother's maiden name, Hamburger, is frequently found in central European Jews. Further, her mother's mother was Lea Cucer, likely from Cocer, certainly Jewish."[19]

"Not that it should matter, but that makes you Jewish, since the heritage passes through the mother's side," I said.

He grimaced. "So I might need a big favor when my turn comes, and who better to have on my side than the Reichsführer-SS?"

With that he got up and started to pace, stopping occasionally to finger the flowers blooming in the planters lining the patio. "And to your third question: what does it have to do with you? I would never have brought you into this, Raymond, had not an inexplicable sequence of events impressed the idea upon me. Our times together have become scarcer in recent years, especially with the political situation. After meeting you in the Nobel restaurant last year and observing our friendship, Himmler originated the suggestion that you work with me on the ahnenpass. Since some of his ancestors came from areas beyond German borders, particularly Savoy, it made sense, he said, that you, living in Geneva, take on that portion of the research."

"Does Himmler suspect that there is, or was, something more than platonic between us?" I asked.

"*Was*—nice." He frowned. "From observation I'm guessing that there's a divergence in opinion between the public and private Himmler on homosexuality."

"So, for insurance, you are playing it both ways," I said, unable to check my pique at the amorous performance he had staged with Gabriele the previous evening.

"Himmler aside, most SS men would cut everything out from between the legs of a suspected gay man. I have to play the he-man to the hilt."

"And Gabriele doesn't mind being your cover?"

"Alone, we are quite comfortable, like brother and sister. It's never been an issue."

"*Hell hath no fury like a woman scorned.* Be careful, Otto."

"I will," he said without genuine concern.

"So you're going along with this whole genealogy project just so we can get together outside Germany where we don't have to stick to the Stephan George celibacy routine."

He grinned. "Not too often because I don't want to drive myself crazy, but that did cross my mind. Evidently Himmler too has ulterior motives for suggesting we work together."

Again, alarm. "He said something more about that?"

"He always does his homework. He knows your uncle, Brett Perrier, Geneva's Honorary-Chancellor of the Republic, has political clout.[20] He's also aware of the family's beverage distribution business and its current virtual monopoly in the German market. An arrangement, he mentioned, that might be in jeopardy in the current anti-capitalist environment here. 'However,' he added as if musing, 'there is the possibility of a mutually profitable arrangement between the Perrier operation and the SS, which has an eye on the lucrative beverage market for its continued funding.'"

"Generous. Steal the loaf and let Perrier keep the crumbs. But does he realize that I have no voice or interest in the company?"

"You hold shares, and, as a family member, you can influence the Board," Otto said.

A brisk knock echoed through the living room from the front door. Otto glanced at his watch. "Too soon for Paul. Wonder who that is." He answered and sounded irritated at the unexpected interruption, but then they started to whisper. After several minutes, the caller left, and Otto, stuffing an envelope into his breast pocket, returned to the patio.

"Kalkstein, my secretary from the office. Never a moment of peace with this outfit." He stood thinking and then asked, "When did Ladame say he'd be here?"

"Not specific. Sometime this afternoon. Do we need to change plans?"

He shook his head. "Just something I have to speak to him about."

Predictably punctual, Paul Ladame arrived at one o'clock. A coolness between the two was palpable as Otto ushered him into the living room. The atmosphere felt charged like the air prior to an electric storm as we sat down, Rahn and I on the couch, Ladame in an easy chair across the coffee table from us.

After a few uncomfortable moments when no one even looked

at the others, Paul began to shake his head.

"Spit it out, Professor," Rahn said. "Say what you're thinking."

"All right then." Paul leaned forward. "I have to admit that I don't know you any more, Otto. Whatever happened to that knight with whom I searched the caves of the Sabarthès for the Holy Grail? To the passionate troubadour poet who sang of the gentle *amor* that would triumph over tyrannical *Roma*? To the mystic with whom I soared to the top of Montsegur? To the dreamer who envisioned *Pan Europa*—not German or French or English or Swiss—a continent united in prosperous peace instead of perpetual war? Where is he, Otto? And who is this uniformed upstart so inflated with self-importance that he doesn't see his minders snickering at his naiveté?"

As Paul spoke, I watched Otto from the side: no reaction, not even a blink. When Ladame finished, Otto reached for a cigarette, lit it, then puffed and exhaled three times before he spoke, looking more towards me than Paul.

"I know how all this appears," he said, "to someone from the outside. And you may have a valid point, Paul, but I am German; these are my people. We have suffered defeat, depression, and despair. And, Heaven knows, what the Nazis are now offering may prove worse. The pageantry and patriotism, so evident with the Games, does not impress me as much as I let on it does. And I know that many of my countrymen are being fooled, their minds twisted into an insidious hatred already expressed in vile demonstrations with worse still to come. But does one abandon the ship just because some rats have climbed aboard?"

Although his conclusion was uncertain, his words gave me some relief. This was the man I knew and loved speaking, not SS officer Otto Rahn.

"You think you can change the Nazis by becoming one of them?" Paul challenged.

"Who knows? I'm not a prophet, although there is an attempt to make me one. *Crusade* is now required reading for SS officers in training, and Himmler plans to present a leather-bound copy of my book to Hitler as a birthday present next year."

Ladame threw up his hands. "And the Führer will read it and be so inspired that he will make a complete about-face. He will reinstate the humane authors previously banned— Remarque, Mann, Kästner, Gläser, Hemingway, even Helen Keller, whose *faux pas* was to champion the disabled—and burn instead the hate-filled works of Lanz, von Liebenfelz, Sebbentdorff, Eicke, Rosenberg, and even his own *Mein Kampf.*"

"You mock me now, Paul," Otto replied, an unflattering whine to his voice, "just as you belittled the wonders in the caves along the Ariège. Where Antonin Gadal, Arthur Cassou, and I beheld the Altar and the Cathedral of the Cathars in those caverns, you saw only stalactites and stalagmites. While we perceived visions of the Cathar commander Raymond de Pereille, their bishop Guilhabert de Castres, and the fabled white lady Esclarmonde de Foix in the moonlight on the heights of Montsegur, you saw only a rock pile, the weathered remnants of a French fortress built on top of the sacred shrine of the Pure Ones."

"So, I don't have your flare for mysticism and poetry," Paul shot back, "but without me you would have drowned in those caves or been crippled falling from those cliffs. And yet"—he pointed to a copy of *Crusade* on the coffee table— "in the 'Afterword' you acknowledge Gadal, the Countess, and even your secondary school teacher, Baron von Gall—everyone's contributions, but mine."

"So, that's it, Paul?" Otto asked, lighting another cigarette. "Your disrespect is not for my SS uniform but because of my simple oversight: I didn't give you the credit you deserved."

Ladame flushed. "Not so fast," he barked, "in making me the petty one."

"Gentlemen." I had to intervene. "Let's not turn this into a personal tit-for-tat. Otto admits the mistake; it can be fixed in the next edition. And, Otto, I know Paul is truly a friend."

I looked at Ladame first; he was sitting back ready to accept the ceasefire. And then at Rahn. He remained tense, staying on his feet and pulling Kalkstein's envelope from his pocket. Dramatically unfolding the paper it contained, he said to Paul, "Why did you go into the Soviet embassy on Unter den Linden just past nine this morning?"

Paul jerked upright. "What does that have to do with anything?"

"So you confirm that you were there?"

"I confirm or deny nothing. It's my business."

Put off by Otto's accusatory tone, I was tempted to side with Paul. But again choosing to witness rather than intervene, I let it play out.

"In Germany can one foreign national not visit the embassy of another country? Are you inferring some subterfuge, perhaps that I'm a Soviet spy?" Paul asked.

"I'm inferring nothing. I am paying you the courtesy of relaying what my intelligence sources passed to me. I can't control what others will infer from this," Otto said.

"Your intelligence sources? So you are spying on me?"

Otto nodded. I gasped in disbelief. Paul's fists tightened. Otto stepped towards Paul, who took a step backwards.

"Yes, Paul," Otto explained, "I have orders to watch you. Aside from your professional specialty, I was given no reason for their interest in you. Nor do I know how they connected us together—it wasn't from my book, since, as was just discussed, it doesn't mention you by name. But evidently they want you enough that, even though you are a foreign national, they will arrest you. That's as much as I can say."

"So you, my supposed friend, are their hound dog," Paul said.

I got up and positioned myself between them. Paul glared at me. "Hear Otto out," I pleaded with Ladame. "He's putting himself on the line by telling you what's going on."

Otto continued. "Since they value the Swiss government's neutrality, they won't do anything until the Games are over. But right afterwards, they will move. Get out of Germany now, Paul, and don't come back. That's my best advice."

Paul sat down and held his head in hands for several minutes. Otto smoked and I watched.

"I will go now," Ladame finally said. "Raymond, will you walk with me while I find a cab?"

As we were going out the door, Otto reached out his hand to the professor. At first it looked like Paul was going to refuse it, but then he grasped it, embraced Otto, and murmured, "Thanks."

"Let's hope they do think I'm a Soviet spy. It will lead them nowhere, which is precisely where we want them to go," Ladame remarked while we waited for a taxi to pass.

This further confused me, but, recalling that Ladame had drawn scrutiny from officials when we entered Germany, I asked, "Is there more than your professorship to make them suspicious?"

Paul patted me on the shoulder. "In the political world today, and perhaps always, there is one certainty: nothing is what it seems to be."

Otto's pending proposition that I work with him on Himmler's ahnenpass came to mind. Even though I was likely violating a trust, I summarized the situation for Ladame. "I'll have to give him an answer one way or the other before I leave," I concluded. "What do you suggest?"

Only after he was seated in the cab did Paul reply. "I can't decide for you. It is an opportunity and a risk, and your friendship with Otto is not negligible. My vote: if you can't commit to their proposal yet, keep the option open. Then come and talk to me when you get back to Geneva."

We had already exchanged parting greetings when he added, "Remember Adolph Frisé from the restaurant last night? Between us only, he is safe. Before you leave, make it a point to tell Otto that he can trust Frisé if he gets into trouble."

Chapter 5: Pamiers, Spring 1318

Six months into the position in Bishop Fournier's court, Jaques felt sufficiently acclimated to his role, now expanded to principal scribe with Brother Simon's retirement at the prior year's end, that it seemed possible to add some personal activities to his official duties. With spring coming, he looked forward to hiking the trails along the Ariège, soon to be cresting with snowmelt from the high Pyrenees. He pictured the foaming waters rushing white through greening meadows alive again with birds calling for mates and flowers bursting with color. The evenings would still be bright when he left the dank court chambers after a tedious day spent with pen poised and ears attuned to nuanced words and intense emotions.

During the winter, once the nightly meetings with the bishop to review Brother Simon's transcriptions were no longer required, he spent his meager free time pursuing his mental interests in the ample library Fournier made available to him. Through some rare volumes of their work he discovered, he developed a taste for the troubadour poets. These itinerant composers and singers had graced the region's salons in the previous century, enthralling the noble women with melodious Occitanian verse. Always, as was required by the Courtly Love tradition of the beguiling Queen Eleanor of Aquitaine, their rapturous pining for their chosen lady love fell short of carnal conquest. Also intriguing among the tomes were treatises about the Old Testament period of Solomon that resulted in the construction of the First Temple of Jerusalem. Jaques passed many a dark winter evening mentally wandering through that fabled edifice, awed by both its vastness and minutiae, which he could see in his mind's eye in more detail than could be found in any book.

Nevertheless, his body ached for the vigorous exercise provided by scaling cliffs, clambering through caves, and swimming in icy waters. Together with Père Fontaine's mental disciplines, outdoor activity was so much a part of his growing years that he did not consciously see the connection between the health of the body and the vigor of the mind until he was deprived of physical exertion.

On one such promising spring day, after the court recessed early when a witness failed to appear, Jaques had just decided to take a vigorous hike in the afternoon sunshine when a page summoned him to Fournier's office.

Contrary to custom, the bishop was not at his desk when Jaques arrived. His cape removed, he sat instead in a plush settee before a low table set with a bottle of wine and two crystal glasses.

"Have a seat, young man." He waved Jaques to the upholstered high-back chair across from him. He tapped the flask. "A gift from the monks of Fontfroide. They miss their former abbot. We'll share a glass."

As he poured, the bishop invited the youth to sit back. "Court is not in session," he said, "so we can let our hair down a bit." He chuckled as he ran his hand over his tonsure. "A simile more suited to the ladies, but you get the idea."

He crossed his legs beneath his cassock and sipped his wine. "I won't pretend that this meeting, casual though it seems, is not important, even though it is not about our usual business. I have only the highest praise for your regular performance. Your transcriptions are flawless, and the side notes on facial expressions and body movements add action, color, and even humor to proceedings that would bore anyone not enamored with legal quibbling to death."

Jaques slid back a bit and took a sip of the excellent wine but stayed alert lest Fournier's easy manner catch him unaware. The bishop's nonchalance had baited many an indictee into confessing what torture failed to extract.

The prelate leaned forward. "But, I sometimes wonder, Jaques, do you enjoy the work?"

The question was unexpected and double-edged. Jaques wanted to keep his job without seeming over-enthused. "The very nature of the work rules out extremities," he said.

"Hmm, as expected." The bishop sipped from his glass and motioned for Jaques to do the same. "Opportunity is a staircase that goes up several floors," he said. "Some never go beyond the first floor. The more ambitious go to the next floor and so on. You have easily mastered the art and craft of the scribe, but will that be enough for you?"

Jaques grimaced. "I'm not inclined to be either a cleric or lawyer. Aren't those the only upper floors available here?"

The bishop rubbed his chubby fingers over his pectoral cross. "Ostensibly, yes," he said, "but there are less obvious and more exciting opportunities for those willing to take a risk."

Jaques waited, allowing his face to show that he did not follow.

Fournier sat up and stroked his ample jowls several times, his eyes no longer as merry. For a moment Jaques's habitual wariness toward the powerful churchman turned to revulsion against a harsh autocrat who sentenced men to death or life in prison without sympathy.

The bishop said, "Your confidentiality pledge as a scribe has grave penalties, but it is a handshake compared to the sanctity of the vow of silence required before I proceed. Nothing will protect you against a breach of this contract you make solely with me. I assume you understand."

Jaques nodded vigorously to show that he grasped the gravity of such an agreement should he choose to enter into it.

But Fournier pushed on as if his nod was a gesture of full assent. "You are bright, but still you must follow me carefully. This path is winding and leads to unexpected places." He finished his glass and poured another. "In our few months together, we have both been learning on the job. When I first interviewed you, I was perhaps too judgmental of the zealotry of Gui, d'Ablis and the Dominican form of inquisition. Not that I now applaud or intend to imitate it, but I've come to understand their impatience.

"As you have witnessed in the trials so far, the church's enemies are extremely clever. The ignorant peasants will give what little worthwhile information they have for the promise of a meal, but the more resourceful among the heretics have studied our laws and learned to use the loopholes in them to their advantage. Ironically, it is our own laws that now prevent us from exterminating these vermin. The court prosecuting a heretic is hobbled by limitations in both canon law and the civil laws of the local jurisdiction. For instance, canon law forbids spilling blood to extract a confession, limiting the forms of coercion we can use to get to the truth. Nor can the church directly administer capital punishment; we must depend on the local authorities to carry out our mandated executions."

"The one pronounced guilty dies by order of the church no matter who performs the execution," Jaques said, "so why not revise ecclesiastical law to allow the church to carry out its sentences?"

"That's taking the bull by the horns," the bishop quipped. "The obvious solution, of course, but only if the lawmaker is absolute. Today the once-supreme power of the papacy is challenged from within; John XXII rules from Avignon because rebellious prelates occupy his rightful seat in Rome. It is also threatened from without; the King of France and the Holy Roman Emperor now scoff at the once compelling threat of excommunication. Until we have someone on the papal throne like Innocent III, we have to work around the laws as they are written."

The bishop leaned forward, his hands clenched in front of him. "Let's take an even deeper look. Pope Innocent possessed seemingly absolute power. He negated unsuitable laws, excommunicated balky emperors and kings, and enforced his will by any means necessary. Do you know, Jaques, how the first battle of Innocent's Crusade against the Cathar heretics turned out?"

The youth hesitated. Aware of the history but uncertain how Fournier intended him to interpret the event, he stayed close to the reported facts. "Hardly a battle," he replied. "The sacking and burning of the city of Béziers on July 22, 1209. In 1208 Pope Innocent III declared a crusade to eliminate Catharism in the Languedoc. In early July 1209, the crusader army, 10,000 strong, consisting of knights mostly from northern France with their retinues—professional soldiers, mercenaries, and pilgrims— marched south from Lyon. Béziers, a stronghold with mixed Cathar-Catholic population, was the first major town the crusaders encountered. Viscount Raymond Roger Trencavel fortified and provisioned Béziers to withstand a long siege, but he then pulled back to bivouac with his main army in Carcassonne.

"Under the command of the papal legate, the Cistercian Abbot of Citeaux Arnaud Amalric, the crusader army reached the outskirts of Béziers on July 21, 1209. To avert bloodshed, the Catholic bishop of the city tried to negotiate. It was agreed that the town would be spared if its heretics were handed over. The bishop drew up a list of 222 likely leaders of the Cathar community. But the townsfolk, meeting at the cathedral, voted against surrendering so many of their own citizens. The bishop then left town with just a few of the Catholics, the rest opting to stay to defend their city.

"On July 22, the crusaders were busy preparing for the siege proper. An armed group from the town charged through the city gate overlooking the Orb River and began harassing a mercenary unit of the crusader army. The attackers, however, found themselves outnumbered, so they retreated along the same route by which they came, leaving the gate open behind them. The mercenaries took advantage and, without orders, stormed the walls and entered the city through that gate.

"The outcome is best summarized in Abbot Amalric's own report to Innocent III, in which he wrote: 'While discussions were still going on with the barons about the release of those in the city who were deemed to be Catholics, the servants and other persons of low rank and unarmed attacked the city without waiting for orders from their leaders. To our amazement, crying "to arms, to arms!" within the space of two or three hours they crossed the ditches and the walls and Béziers was taken. Our men spared no one, irrespective of rank, sex, or age, and put to the sword almost 20,000 people. After this great slaughter the whole city was despoiled and burnt.'"[21]

"Bravo!" The bishop applauded the recitation.

"One thing more," Jaques said. "The Cistercian historian Caesarius of Heisterbach attributed a curious quote to the Crusader commander. When it was brought to his attention that there were Catholics still mingled with the heretics in the fallen city, Abbot Amalric declared: *'Caedite eos. Novit enim Dominus qui sunt eius.'*"

Fournier smiled, quite incongruously Jaques thought. "'Kill them all and let God sort them out.' A cruel-sounding phrase as reported twenty years after the fact. But does it not embody the tenor of that battle and all the successful ones that followed right up to the fall of Montsegur 35 years later?"

"Excellency, I am a scribe, not a strategist or historian. How I might interpret such things matters little."

"Hah, there is safety in neutrality." Fournier finished his wine, poured himself more and topped off Jaques's barely diminished glass. "But here we are looking up to the next level where, without losing the scribe's objectivity, one begins to develop the art of interpretation. There is meaning in the sequence of events.

"It should not surprise you that I, a Cistercian, once agreed with Amalric's position and Innocent III's endorsement of it. Had absolute force been brought to bear consistently by their successors, I conjectured that the war would have been won sooner and no heretics would have remained afterwards to rekindle an Authier revival or recontaminate towns like Montaillou,[22] as we are discovering to have happened in our current trials.

"But neither the Crusade itself nor the subsequent inquisition served to accomplish the church's purpose, the eradication of the

Cathar heresy. In fact, we have to ask: with all their ingenuity, what did our predecessors overlook that made their solution so short of final?"

The bishop sat back and peered at Jaques, who shifted in the overly comfortable chair. Fournier could not expect him to answer such a question.

"If I could answer that riddle with certainty, I could well be the pope the church now so sorely needs," Fournier finally said as if thinking out loud. "The Cathar Crusade, starting with Béziers, was rife with terror, blood, destruction, and death. The Inquisition, after the war and until now, does not lack for torture, imprisonment, and stinking pyres of burning flesh. And yet—" He swished the wine in his glass, his brow furrowed.

He then continued. "The Catholic Church professes to have been seeded by the blood of martyrs. Yes, martyrs, but martyrdom alone is not enough. A martyr merely surrenders his present life for a cause he conceives to be worth more than that life. But dying for a cause is not sufficient to propagate a legacy. A martyr whose reputation does not continue among the living is just another corpse."

The bishop crossed himself. "Without the epilogue of his resurrection, without the tangible transfer of his wisdom and power to the next generation at Pentecost, without the record of the Gospel's witnesses, Jesus Christ after his death on Calvary would have been as anonymous as the tens of thousands of others the Romans crucified."

Jaques could only nod and wonder what all this might have to do with his personal future. Fournier was taking a winding if intriguing path.

"The blood. The seed," Fournier mused. "Without a vital cause as his seed to be passed on, the martyr is no more than a suicidal maniac, crackpot, or accidental victim, maybe mourned briefly but then buried. The executed leader of a mob rioting for better food is forgotten once people again have full bellies. Follow, Jaques?"

"Somewhat," the scribe said. "The martyr must first be a hero. His death remains meaningful because he has both lived and died for a cause worthy enough for others to embrace and carry forward, even if that means martyrdom for them in turn, as happened with the Apostles."

"But if the cause is weak or local or selfish?" the bishop quizzed.

"The movement quickly collapses."

The bishop got up and began to pace the width of the room, his hands behind his back. "That's what Innocent and Amalric gambled on at the start of the Crusade. So certain of quick victory were they that volunteers only had to sign on for forty days to gain the promised plenary indulgence and all the booty they could carry. And Catharism should have collapsed, if not after Béziers, then after the fall of Carcassonne and the death in prison of their champion Raymond Roger Trencavel. Certainly it should have happened after the fall of Montsegur with the execution of the two hundred remaining Perfects and all who would not abjure the heretical faith.

"But some uncanny power, this time in the guise of stupidity on our side, came to their rescue prior to the consummation of the surrender. Once the decisive battle on March 1 forced the Cathar commanders, Raymond de Perella and Pierre-Roger de Mirepoix, to negotiate terms for surrender, against all logic the conquerors permitted the heretics a fifteen-day grace period before actually entering and taking over the fortress. This bizarre display of mercy, probably obtained through the intercession of the double-dealing Count Raymond VII of Toulouse, gave the Cathars time to spirit away a considerable cache of material wealth to a safe location and manage, contrary to the terms of surrender, the escape of four heretics, at least one of them a Perfect. The breakout was so well executed that knowledge of it only came to light years later when some of the survivors, Commander de Perella among them, confessed to the Inquisition."

Jaques's interest perked up at the prospect of intrigue and hidden riches. "Is the treasure still out there somewhere?"

"Don't get carried away by the glitter of gold, young man," the bishop chided. "Any wealth they possessed has long been used up in providing for those hiding from the law. Of greater concern should be the escaped Perfect."

"Would he not be dead by now?"

"Yes, but by their rules one Perfect can consecrate another Perfect to succeed him. Like rabbits they can reproduce into the future. The two hundred who willingly threw themselves into the fires of the Camp de Cremat did so knowing damned well that at least one of their kind had escaped with the ultimate treasure of their faith— the seed. The flames that consumed them had barely turned cold before the meadows of the Languedoc were again sprouting heretical Good Christians, as they prefer to call themselves to mock the established church."

Even while he was struggling to grasp the bishop's complex narrative, Jaques was startled by his use of the term *Good Christians*. In the interview at Saint Sernin, Bernard Gui seemed irked that the people of Père Fontaine's parish in Tarascon called themselves Good Christians rather than Catholics. And Baldwin too had used the phrase when referring to the Cathars.

Yes, Baldwin—with Arnaud in the Mercado the previous fall. The scene came rushing back with the force of the Ariège swollen by snow melt.

The vagabond fingering his former classmate's source of resentment: *Ah, as bishop's boy you could rat out some Good Christians and their Perfect, make a name for yourself, and force them to give your mama's house back. Very clever, but Jaques beat you to the job.*

And Arnaud's awareness, as Jaques was reminded daily in court, that any connection to a heretic was grounds for prosecution. *As it is, he's likely to spill this all to Fournier. He'll try to have me charged. To not report knowledge about heretics is still a high crime, even if I am as anti-heretic as any Dominican.*

Would serve him right. Jaques caught the judgmental thought and rejected it. Arnaud was a bully but had done him no harm that warranted the cruel punishments meted out to heretics.

A further thought set his heart thumping faster. If Arnaud's boast, likely a bluff, made his schoolmate culpable, did not the same law oblige him to report what he had overheard in the marketplace? Would Fournier, who was known to sentence a wife to prison for failing to disclose her husband's accidental contact with a heretic, not fault him as well? The notion seemed laughable: stretch the law that far and they might as well arrest everyone.

Jaques looked up. Fournier was watching him closely. "You drifted for a moment, my boy," he said. "Does something about this disturb you?"

He dared not lie completely. "The term *Good Christians*," he said. "Odd that it is used for heretics."

"In their arrogance they apply it to themselves." The prelate shifted his bulk around in the chair. "Have you heard it used elsewhere?"

Cautious on reflex, Jaques skipped over the reference to Père Fontaine's parishioners and mentioned the conversation in the square instead. "It was in ridicule, but I overheard it used among three fellows gossiping in the marketplace last fall."

The bishop pounced. "Their names?"

Jaques steeled himself. "I only know one for sure. A former St. Sernin schoolmate. I was surprised to see him here in Pamiers. He lives in Toulouse where he works in his father's notary business."

"Arnaud Sicre-Baille," the bishop said, sitting back with a leer. "The Sicres and Bailles again. Those names have also surfaced in the Montaillou investigation. Arnaud's mother was a *Perfecta* from Ax executed some years back, but his father claims to be a devout Catholic. I'd wondered what happened to the boy." He wiggled his fingers as if he were playing on a keyboard. "You know him well then?"

"We spent four years in school together but never became friends. He too aspired to become a court scribe. He resented that I got the position instead."

"Nor would I have accepted him. He and his father have made themselves pests trying to get the Perfecta's property back. He was probably here to press his claim with my office, which will do him no good since the Bishop of Ax holds the property."

"That came up in the conversation. One of the men said that he was chasing the impossible, but Arnaud was having none of it. He—" Jaques checked himself.

"He what?"

"Oh, some wild plan to force the church to reconsider. He tends to brag."

"What did he say he planned to do?"

Jaques thought for a moment. He would have to tell the truth carefully enough to avoid incriminating himself. "Are there Perfects still alive and at large?" he asked.

The bishop held up his index finger. "Only one."

"Is it known who he is and where he's hiding?"

"Who? No doubt. Their current leader, Guilhem Belibaste."

Jaques was surprised. "You spoke of him earlier. I thought he was a shepherd and known murderer. This man is a Perfect?"

Fournier smiled. "Evidently, even among the so-called 'Pure Ones,' it is only the strong who survive. After shepherding and murdering, he escaped the law and abandoned his family, only to fall under the influence of Pierre Authier, who converted him to Catharism. He was later ordained a Perfect, his bloody past not an obstacle. In 1309 on information from a disillusioned believer, he was arrested along with several other Perfects. They were imprisoned pending trial in Carcassonne, but he and another, Philippe d'Alayrac, the man who ordained him, escaped. They crossed into Catalonia beyond our jurisdiction. Philippe unwisely returned on a mission, was recaptured, and burned with all the remaining Perfects of the Authier revival. Only Belibaste, ironically the least perfect among them, remains at large. Exactly where is still a mystery."

But if I were to serve up some Cathar leftovers, one of them a Perfect, I can name my price. Arnaud Sicre's boast in the square thundered through Jaques's head so forcefully that his neck quivered visibly.

The bishop caught the reaction. "Does Belibaste have something to do with Arnaud Sicre and his plan to get his mother's property back?" he probed.

"I don't know if he was only boasting, but I overheard Arnaud say that if he were to hand over some Cathars, one of them a Perfect, he could name his price. I assume he had the property in mind, and if Belibaste is the only Perfect left, Arnaud could only have meant him."

His brow furrowed, the bishop drummed slowly on the desk with his thick fingers. He finally broke from his brooding with a self-satisfied smile. "Ah, Jaques," he exclaimed, "it is with the unexpected event, whether sublime or bizarre, that a higher intelligence grabs our attention. A shame that after the initial amazement such portents are so easily discounted as anomalies or accidents."

Jaques frowned to show that he was not quite following.

Fournier sat up. "When seemingly unrelated pieces fall together and fit perfectly," he explained, "it is not luck or chance, but a sign pointing the way forward. I called you here, my scribe, this afternoon on a hunch that it was time to discuss your future role with us. You just happened to go to school with Arnaud Sicre, the disgruntled son of a Cathar Perfecta, who wants his property back from the church. You just happened to have been in the marketplace last fall when this same Arnaud, who wasn't supposed to be in Pamiers at all, bragged about bargaining a Cathar Perfect for his mother's property. I, as the inquisitor, know that only one Perfect remains at large. If Belibaste is brought in before he breeds another of his kind, it will be the end of the Cathar Perfect line. And if he is captured alive and delivered to me, I will have one last chance to retrieve that mysterious seed we talked about earlier."

The bishop closed his eyes, brought his hands together and sighed. "I see the way forward," he said. "The sentence against our Holy Mother the Church, which I feared might be irreversible, might still be lifted. You have not only observed the dawn of an historic event, Jaques de Sabart, but you are an integral part of it."

Jaques blinked several times—a rare moment when he felt completely confused. "What, ah, would you have me do?" he stammered.

The bishop beamed. "In the beginning, nothing more than you do in court: keep your ears open and record everything—in your mind, of course. Anything you notice that might lead to our objective: Guilhem Belibaste captured unawares and standing alive in my presence. Use your tongue sparingly, but ask if it will lead to further information. That's all—for now."

Jaques's body quivered. "Are you asking me to become a spy?" he blurted out.

"No, just my extension into places a prelate cannot go unnoticed. We are already on the path. You will find out what we need to know further. Remain awake to what comes up. Then observe and record."

It was Jaques's turn to ponder. Several times in his life he had just happened upon the exact bit of information he needed after he had previously failed to obtain it through the usual channels. Fournier's concatenation of recent events into a purposeful sequence rang true, and he showed no inclination to punish either Arnaud or himself for the crime of consorting with heretics. Instead, the bishop was inviting them to participate in the critical task of ending the Cathar heresy forever.

Despite a deep but vague reluctance to commit to something that felt somewhat sullied, Jaques agreed. "What's to lose? I have to go about doing what I am doing anyway. And I observe and remember regardless. It's a minor adjustment to keep one additional item in mind and report anything relevant."

"Very well then." Fournier rose and smoothed his cassock. "Drink up and be off while there's still daylight outside."

As Jaques opened the door to leave, the bishop cleared his throat. "Remember that you are under contract to me alone in this and fully aware of my terms," he said.

Jaques nodded and left. Fournier had assumed his agreement. Now there was no going back. Their pact was without force in a court of law, but the bishop, Jaques now understood, was the law.

For the first weeks after this meeting, Jaques was on full alert for Arnaud's reappearance in the square, in the pubs, or on the streets, but there was no sighting. He did not actually relish the prospect of bumping into his pugnacious former schoolmate; and, despite reviewing a dozen possible approaches, he saw no feasible way to turn a seeming chance encounter into a discussion about Belibaste without arousing Arnaud's suspicion. Nevertheless, time and the intrusion of other interests gradually reduced his attention on the matter, and he again found he could walk the streets without Arnaud Sicre in the front of his mind.

Thus, on a lovely evening in early May, light-hearted but hungry, he passed from the episcopal palace into the public square. Just beyond the gate, he spotted Baldwin mounted on a fruit crate delivering one of his usual tirades against the injustices of everything.

"The time is nigh when judgment will fall on those who judge," Baldwin was proclaiming to a small knot of amused shoppers. "Heretics destined for hell are leaping into the fire like martyrs singing their Pater Nosters. Templar sodomists and idol worshippers who kiss a cat's ass greet death praying like saints while the bishops who condemned them look on cursing like brigands. Stark naked Spirituals chained to the walls in their prisons cell make love with Lady Poverty while their Franciscan brothers diddle their giggling mistresses between slithering silk sheets."

"You're cutting close, old goat. Much more and they'll be comin' for you," one man shouted.

"Ah, let him go on," someone else yelled. "He'll bait 'em till they burn him. That'll make one big stink."

Jaques stopped just beyond the circle of listeners, his mind abruptly brought back to his assignment. He had last seen Arnaud with Baldwin. The vagabond might know something of his whereabouts.

"You, yo there, bishop's boy!" Of all the rotten luck, Baldwin was pointing in his direction. "You think this old bag of bones is a crazy fool, don't you, pretty fella?"

Baldwin lurched off his perch and headed toward him. The crowd separated to let him through. Jaques had to think quickly. Baldwin had enough wits to string together his monologues; he might remember something about Arnaud.

"You're no fool," he said when Baldwin was close enough that only he could hear. "You speak quite eloquently." He winked at the man. "Although what you say makes me worry about your safety."

"Is that why you're following me around, boy? You want to drag me into your bishop's court, eh?"

Jaques laughed, hoping to disarm him. "On the contrary, I haven't seen you for quite a while and was concerned about what became of you."

Baldwin muttered something under his breath and looked around. The crowd was dispersing.

"I was also wondering if you've seen my old schoolmate, Arnaud Sicre, around," Jaques added.

Baldwin grunted and wiped the dribble from his nose on a filthy sleeve. "All these people out here listening to me and I'm supposed to remember your chum?" he asked.

"You remembered enough to call me *bishop's boy*," Jaques countered. "A cold morning last fall. Arnaud was the one bragging about knowing where some Cathars were and how he could bring them in to get his property back from the church."

"Joli Jaques, joli Jaques," Baldwin chanted.

"That's the guy. I didn't like it, but he insisted on calling me *Joli Jacques*."

"So you want to arrest him."

"I'm just the bishop's boy, remember. A scribe. They have police and detectives to round up suspects."

"And spies all over," Baldwin added. "I could be a spy for the court and even you, bishop's boy, wouldn't know it."

Jaques only smiled. "So, have you seen Arnaud recently? Is he still here in Pamiers?"

"Baldwin the Leper King may be an ugly wretch," the man said, straightening up taller than Jaques thought possible, "but he's a man of honor who puts no one unnecessarily at risk. Should I see this Sicre, I'll tell him you asked about him. What happens after that is up to him."

Chapter 6: Dachau, Dornach, December, 1936

Munich's Marienplatz was festooned for the approaching winter holidays, I noticed as I disembarked from the train. A threesome—Otto in civilian clothes, Gabriele swaddled against the cold and on his arm, and Obersturmbannführer Willy Ullmann of the SS Personnel Department—greeted and ushered me to a waiting car. With the affable Ullmann at the wheel and Otto and Gabriele pointing out the city's landmarks, many related to the tumultuous early years of the Nazi party here, we drove northwest about sixteen kilometers into the flat frozen countryside, then through the quaint hamlet after which our destination was named, to *Konzentrationslager Dachau's* main entrance.

Ahead of schedule evidently, we were held up at the closed gate, which proclaimed in wrought iron, *"Arbeit macht frei"* ("Work makes you free"). Barked instructions from a loud speaker screeching with feedback leaked over the high walls topped with barbed wire. To drown it out and keep us occupied, Ullmann summarized the camp's history from its founding in 1933, only 51 days after Hitler became chancellor of Germany.

"The Dachau KZ is located on the grounds of an abandoned munitions factory, which is still standing but scheduled for demolition," Ullmann said as if reading from a script. "Himmler, then Munich's Chief of Police, described the facility as the first concentration camp for political prisoners established by the National Socialist government. Developed by Kommandant Theodor Eicke, now KZ Inspector General, it serves as the prototype in layout and organization for the expanding KZ system.

"We use the word *concentration* in naming these relocation facilities because they serve to consolidate populations that are considered likely to cause or be the objects of disturbance if left mixed with the general public. Dachau now accommodates about 5,000 with its current population, mainly German nationals detained for political reasons. Too many to be kept in the state prisons without overburdening, but too unstable to be released since they might continue to agitate against the duly elected government.

"Idleness is, of course, bad for morale, so detainees are kept busy working in the operation of the camp, on construction projects, and in handicraft industries on the grounds. Plans are in place to build factories adjacent to our camps, thus making the available labor more productive to the state and its related industries. This is where your company's interests come in, if I understand correctly, sir?" Ullmann nodded towards me.

In contrast to the sparkling winters in Switzerland, the scenery here on the flatlands of southern Germany was drab and bone-chilling. It only intensified the sense of foreboding that had settled over me after I agreed upon discussion with Ladame to accept Himmler's invitation relayed by Rahn to tour the Dachau facility. Research into the Reichsführer-SS's distant Savoyen ancestors was a palatable asking price for continued contact with my friend, but negotiating with the Nazis on behalf of a firm in which I had little power or interest was hard to digest.

Paul Ladame had hinted to broader ramifications: Hitler had already voiced the intention to form the Greater Reich, which would include the German-speaking portion of Switzerland as well as Austria and the Czechoslovakian province of Sudetenland. A clandestine counter-Nazi group, to which Paul was connected, had alerted the Perrier beverage firm that Himmler was looking for a business partner. The company's executives concluded that such an offer, regardless of war, peace, or neutrality between the two countries, was preferable to losing all their German business. They agreed to have me, already conveniently positioned through my friendship with Rahn, explore the overture further.

"But Perrier's profitability can hardly be your group's primary concern," I objected to Paul. "I sense here that some unnamed entity is inserting me, and Otto by association, to spy into the Nazi concentration camp network. A role, by the way, that the Swiss government could misconstrue as collaboration with the enemy."

"No one is at war yet," Paul replied. "But I think you can see the value of subterfuge here. The Nazis will only give valid information to convincing collaborators. By working with Rahn on his ahnenpass, you already have access to Himmler. Now you are being handed a ticket into one of their most notorious concentration camps. It's an intelligence agent's dream."

"Your intelligence agent is their spy. They shoot spies, as they intended to shoot you, Paul, had Otto not warned you to leave Germany. You could at least let me know who I am working for before I commit myself."

Ladame gathered himself and began. "It's called the Emerald Club, EC for short, which reeks of the idle rich, which we are not. Only insiders need to know that it is named after the famed Emerald Tablets of Hermes Tresmegistos, the divine Egyptian-Greek author of the *Hermetic Corpus,* from which comes the well-known aphorism, 'As above so below.'"

"A familiar ploy. An esoteric secret society masquerading as a good old boys' fraternity," I said.

"Some of our members may lean towards the occult, true," Ladame replied. "But, in every functional intelligence operation, each individual knows his part and little beyond it. My piece is, let's say, information logistics. I tailor the information or disinformation that reaches government officials and the public to match the EC's primary message.

"As far as I know, the Emerald Club was originally a watchdog group for the Pan-European Movement,[23] founded by Richard Nikolaus von Coudenhove-Kalergi in 1923 to promote the cause of European unification. Along with League of Nations, PEM was a strong political force for peace on this war-torn continent. When the organization was banned in Germany in 1933, thus diminishing its reach, the EC became indirectly connected with yet another effort towards peaceful European unification: the Third Way of Rudolph Steiner and his Anthroposophy movement."

"Which also was officially banned in Germany last year," I noted. As a Swiss, I was familiar with the life and work of Dr. Steiner, who well before his death in 1925 had moved his headquarters from Munich to Dornach, just south of Basel.

"So Steiner is your link to the hermetic tradition," I added.

Paul shrugged. "Not my bailiwick. Like I did with Otto and his Cathar theories when we were working the caves along the Ariège, I stick to the grunt work and leave the occult stuff to those more ethereally inclined. As it is, I get into enough trouble. As you said, I almost got arrested in Germany during the Olympics."

If Paul knew more about the operation of the Emerald Club, I saw no way to pull it out of him. He did, however, offer to arrange for me to meet with the EC's leader in Dornach on my way back from my mission to Dachau.

"And this man's name?" I asked.

Paul smiled. "He has no name. He goes by a number: 333."

Before I could respond to Ullmann's reference to the Perrier firm's interest in the Dachau installation, an SS officer from the guardhouse approached our car. He gave our papers a second glance and waved us past the outer iron gate and through the steel doors behind it. Beyond the high perimeter fence and partially obscured by a double row of poplar trees was a large open area tamped flat like a well-used parade ground. To its west was a sprawling building in disrepair with a brick smokestack poking skyward—the old factory, I presumed. I barely caught a glimpse of the long low huts with galvanized roofs to the south, a few men in striped outfits hanging about them, before Ullmann turned right and away from the barracks. He sped by several sturdier concrete buildings—where newcomers are admitted and processed, he explained—into a separate secure compound that contained the command center and staff living quarters. Although evidence of construction was everywhere, no actual work was going on at the time.

"You'll have to envision the potential, Raymond," Otto said as we got out of the car. "A work in progress, with a modern SS training facility now being added."

I kept my eyes down, listening to our feet crunch on the frozen gravel. Did Otto not see that this place's "potential" included slave labor as its work force?

Gabriele seemed to sense my disturbance. "I visited here earlier," she said, "and saw the possibility for abuse. As only a woman can, I voiced that concern to the Reichsführer-SS. He assured me that all precautions were being taken. Once inmates are re-educated and no longer risks to the state, they are released. For the majority it is only a short stay. Himmler has no tolerance for unwarranted cruelty. He personally dismissed the camp's first commandant, Hilmar Wäckerle, his own schoolmate and a founding National Socialist, and ordered that criminal charges be filed against him after a couple detainees died from punishments he ordered."

"The site will have multiple uses," Ullmann said. "Deputy Führer Rudolph Hess plans to experiment with crops in the fields beyond this compound. He is intrigued with the principles of Rudolf Steiner's biodynamic agriculture and imagines Dachau as something of a Garden of Eden."

Startled by the random insertion of Steiner's name into the conversation so soon after it had come up in the conversation with Ladame, I was alert for a trap. I side-stepped it. "If Himmler and Hess are Dachau's guarantors," I said, trying to sound impressed, "I think Perrier should give the proposition serious consideration."

I glanced towards Rahn as I spoke. His face was impassive.

"Are Jews detained here as well?" I then asked, hoping to catch them off balance.

"Not unless they are also political dissidents," Ullmann answered smoothly, "which some are. Since they are no longer German citizens by law, the Reich currently encourages Jews to emigrate to Palestine or wherever will have them."

"A Swiss firm," I stated, "will not tolerate the use of forced labor, especially if based on racial discrimination."

"Raymond, we are Germans, not savages," Otto protested with a passion that confounded me.

The remainder of the tour was unimpressive, the incomplete facilities as uninspired as the weather, and the four of us on edge in roles that limited the truth we dared to share with each other. There was relief all around when we arrived back at the Marienplatz, but there was one more twist to the plot before the other two left Otto and me to spend the evening together.

Before he drove off with Gabriele, Ullmann pulled me aside. "Otto is a good soul, Mr. Perrier," he whispered. "I read his book during SS training. But he's a poet, and that makes him a misfit with this corps. Know that you can call on me if he gets into trouble. I'll do what I can to help."

Once we were alone, the ugliness of day in the concentration camp behind us, I felt compelled to address Otto's disturbing implication that Dachau's potential might prove positive. Strained as I already was by my conflicting roles— Otto's closest friend and sometimes lover, his research assistant in the matter of Himmler's genealogy, and Ladame's reluctant spy posing as corporate matchmaker—I chose not to disguise my chagrin.

"As a rational human being, who believes in government based on the consent of the governed rather than the will of a ruling clique, how can I not think negatively of Dachau?" I asked.

"What?" Otto snapped, reaching for a cigarette. "You heard Gabriele. Himmler himself has it under control."

I tossed my head. "The word of your pretty girlfriend—."

"Don't go there, faggot," he barked, but then added a mitigating smirk.

"Who's to say she's reliable? Why did you have to invite her along today?"

"I didn't. I never told her I was coming here. She found out and invited herself."

"Convenient. Does it ever cross your mind that they may have her tailing you like you were ordered to tail Ladame?"

"They'd go that far?"

"I don't know, but you better think it possible. In the game you've gotten mixed up in, a healthy suspicion is advisable. And suppose you and she are right: Himmler is the commodious Aryan King Arthur out to make the world a happy place for everyone, including gypsies, Jews, and homosexuals. And you SS men are his noble knights industriously seeking the Holy Grail. There's still the inconvenient matter of one Adolf Hitler, der Führer, his boss, with the will and power, should Himmler merely pass gas in a way that displeases him, to cut him down instantly. Summon the specter of the Night of the Long Knives and Ernst Röhm if you need verification."

For an uncomfortably long time, Otto just stared at me. Then, like a morning glory closing under the warming sun, he curled his head into his hands and hunched over.

"What does everyone want from me?" he sniffled. "What do they—Himmler, Weisthor, Wolff, even Gabriele—expect of me? Ladame wanted to know what became of the Grail knight, the poet, the mystic, the dreamer I once was. He said he didn't know me anymore." There was an audible sob. "Well, I don't know me anymore either. I'm no politician or spy or soldier or ladies' man, but I'm expected to be them all. I'm sick of digging around for evidence of runes that prove crazy Weisthor's royal lineage; tired of searching archives and graveyards for ancestors with impossibly pure bloodlines; exhausted with plodding across the frozen wastes of Iceland looking for rocks that will confirm Hörbiger's bizarre Cosmic Ice Theory; suffocated with having to write books on demand that tout the superiority of everything German when I damned well know that Germans can be as depraved as anyone else, sometimes more so."

He wrung his hands. "I was led to the Languedoc years ago and given a glimpse of something supremely important there. Why me, I don't know. I wrote a book about it. I only do all of this"—he finally looked up— "so that I can get back there, to the Sabarthès, to Tarascon, to Montsegur. I must see it again and finish what was begun there. I have been to the top of the mountain, Raymond. I have known its ecstasy. Why, why then, I ask, all the clamor demanding that I come down from those heights and live apart from it? If you of all people cannot understand what I mean, Raymond, I might as well give up right now."

My inclination was to reach for him, wrap him in my arms, and kiss him until he was consoled. But something besides prudence or prudery restrained me. I reached out and lightly touched his shoulder.

"Otto," I commanded with unaccustomed intensity, "Do what you must do to get back to the Languedoc."

Although I could not have explained my sense of urgency to Otto or even to myself, I then resolved to do all in my power to expedite his return to his beloved southern France. Thus, on my way back from Munich to Geneva, although there was no apparent connection, I stopped in Dornach where Paul Ladame had arranged for me to meet with the mysterious 333.

Upon arriving at this tidy Swiss town about ten miles south of the German border, I asked the cab driver to take me to the Goetheanum, headquarters for Rudolf Steiner's Anthroposophy organization. He nodded straightaway, the location evidently a major attraction in town. A light flurry was dusting the rolling foothills as we climbed towards a building that looked like an enormous crouched creature with stain-glassed windows glinting on its flanks. Even with my limited architectural knowledge, I perceived that the edifice was intentionally unique. Designed by Rudolf Steiner to replace the movement's original headquarters destroyed by fire allegedly set by his enemies in 1922, this behemoth, wholly formed of cast concrete, was considered a masterpiece of 20th-century expressionist architecture. With its organically inspired rounded and curved forms instead of the conventional straight lines and right angles, it proclaimed a bold independence from traditional styling. Like a sphinx, it lay poised on its hilltop perch, awake, and watchful but at the same time comfortably at rest.

With only a limited knowledge of Steiner's enterprise and Ladame's sparse description of the person I was to meet, I approached the reception desk inside the Goetheanum's cavernous lobby.

"May I help you?" a pleasant middle-aged woman asked.

I hesitated, realizing I didn't have a proper name or title for the man I was looking for. "Ah, yes, please. My name is Raymond Perrier, a friend of Professor Paul Ladame of the University of Geneva. I was told to ask for 333. I hope you can help me."

"One moment, Mr. Perrier." She passed through a doorway into the main building, returning a few moments later to conduct me inside.

"Raymond, a pleasure," a professorial German-speaking gentleman, probably in his thirties and in business suit and glasses, greeted me. "Fortunate timing all around. I'm just closing things out here before leaving town"—luggage was piled off to the side—"and, after talking with Paul, I wanted us to meet, especially given your recent mission."

The receptionist returned with coffee, and 333 motioned for me to sit across the desk from him, at the same time glancing at his watch and apologizing for having to plunge right into things.

"You probably have a hundred questions: Who am I? Who do I work for? What's my interest in Otto Rahn? Why should you trust me? Why the ridiculous code name? I get some ribbing about 333 being half the number of the notorious beast of Revelations, 666, a code already adopted by the self-proclaimed evilest man in the world, Aleister Crowley. That should mean that I'm only half as vile as that wily British magician." He shrugged. "Just a number for easy identification. I suppose the '3' connects to the Third Way, Steiner's still untried formula for peace and cooperation in Europe."

"Paul Ladame mentioned that," I said, "along with the Emerald Club and von Coudenhove's Pan-European Movement. May I ask if all these organizations are part of the same effort to unite Europe?"

333 removed his glasses and looked downward. "It may take time before you understand what I am about to say next, but it is important. Unfortunately, at this point in history, human beings are not sufficiently developed to bear the responsibility for the self-governance required by true democracy. Along with many great leaders, Jesus preached that the kingdom of God existed within the individual, and yet within a century of its founding his church had become an authoritarian autocracy that condemned the natural urge of an individual to follow his own conscience and cognizance. And that trend continues to the present day. Karl Marx's community of the working class has devolved into Joseph Stalin's totalitarian Communism. Simply put: a united Europe today could only be a megalithic dictatorship."

333 put his glasses back on and again checked his watch. "So the answer to your question is 'no.' We—call our conglomerate the Emerald Club if you like—do not seek to unify Europe. Ours is a more limited objective, which excludes a Europe unified under any single authority, although it does not preclude a democratic European union in the future."

He smiled. "I can see that I may have overfed you with generalities. Given my time constraints, I'll trust that Professor Ladame will fill you in later on the philosophy, politics, and practice of all this. We now have to cover the more immediate matters."

I sighed to release a bit of exasperation. "It's all hazy," I said. "Going to Dachau was bizarre enough, but then coming here I feel like I have entered some further weird dimension where buildings look like huge mushrooms and people have numbers rather than names. I simply wanted some help for a good friend who is entangled with a dangerous cult in Germany, only to stumble into what seems like a coven in my own country. No offense. You seem normal enough, sir, and what you say makes sense, but what does it have to do with me and Otto Rahn?"

Despite being pressed for time, 333 addressed my objection. "We live in a desperate and demanding period, Raymond. You are part of it by virtue of being alive, and you wouldn't be here if you didn't take responsibility at some deeper level. Like Steiner's followers and Paul Ladame, I too am *persona non grata* in Germany, one with multiple counts against me according to the Nazi codes: a Jew, anthroposophist, occultist, and now perhaps what they would call a foreign agent. For the present, I have to ask you to allow me to remain something of a mystery, a number. It's for your safety and for the security of the mission. In return, I respect your right to tell me only as much as you think I ought to know. As we proceed, you will always have a channel to me, even when you don't know my physical location."

As nervous as the cloak-and-dagger routine made me, the man's matter-of-factness otherwise invited me to trust that he knew what he was doing. "Fair enough, sir," I said, "especially as I'm seeking your advice in a personal matter connected only peripherally to your work."

333 smiled again, too wisely for my comfort. "All things are connected although some more critically than others. My role requires that I remain informed, and I've long been abreast of events involving Rahn and yourself. Even before you two met in Berlin in 1928, there was a conjunction, although not direct contact, between Otto and me. During his graduate school years in Freiburg and Heidelberg, when his interest in *Parzival* and the Grail peaked, I was

teaching at Rudolph Steiner's Waldorf School next door in Stuttgart. There I produced my own book on *Parzival*."[24]

"Are you too then a Grail expert?"

"Expert, questionable. Aficionado, absolutely. As with Otto, Wolfram von Eschenbach's *Parzival* fascinates me. Even after I published my work on it, I remained alert for new material on the subject. I read Rahn's *Crusade Against the Grail* in 1933, was intrigued by his thesis quite different from my own, and wanted to meet him. Unfortunately, I had to leave Germany that same year."

"A shame you didn't beat Himmler in getting his attention."

"Things happen in the sequence they do for a reason," he remarked before summarizing his knowledge of Otto's checkered career as researcher, traveler, and writer, some details likely garnered from Ladame but others from sources unknown to me. He knew of Rahn's potentially incriminating Jewish ancestry; how Gabriele, Weisthor, and Himmler drew him into their circle; his current status as an SS officer with the Ahnenerbe; and how we were jointly working on Himmler's *ahnenpass*. And he made mention of our personal relationship without judgment against it although applauding our prudence in adhering to the Georgekreis code when on German soil.

Seeing that the man had done his homework, I was encouraged enough to express my concern for Otto's personal well-being. "It's evident that you are aware of Otto's strengths and weaknesses. He is a talented visionary who communicates his utopian dream with conviction. On the other hand, he thinks that everyone, the Nazis and Himmler included, share his idealism and honesty. I fear he will become victim to his own naiveté. While he can see the original telegram that drew him to SS headquarters as an act of providence, I can't shake the impression that it was an intentional act of manipulation by the Nazis from which no good will come to him."

"I understand your concern, and it may not help to point out that his call to Berlin might have been providential and seductive at the same time. That's now in the past, and the outcome lies indeterminate in the future. We can only work with what we have in the present with the intended goal serving as a beacon showing the way forward. Putting aside world affairs for now, let's focus on what's immediate. Given his current position, what do you suppose Otto Rahn would most want to have happen?"

I had to smile, recalling our recent conversation in Munich. "He'd want to return to the Languedoc and finish what he started there."

333 rose to mark the conclusion of the conversation. "That's actually two items," he said, extending his hand. "The first, the trip, will be arranged. The second depends on what happens when he gets there."

Chapter 7: Pamiers, Summer 1318

His knees clenched to hide the evidence of his arousal, Jaques sat just outside the circle of men gaping at the swirling and swaying gypsy who moved to the jangling tambourine she played in self-accompaniment. As soon as he would summon the resolve to be on his way, she'd catch his eye and flash a sensuous smile that riveted him further. Just another minute, he'd tell himself.

Suddenly, a pair of hands grabbed his shoulders from behind. "Well if it isn't Joli Jaques getting off gawking up a darkie's skirt." It was Arnaud Sicre. "And here I thought pretty boys only hankered after other pretty boys."

Jaques twisted out of Arnaud's grip. Those close by turned to watch. "So you're one who goes both ways," Arnaud added.

Jaques forced a smile. "Hello again," he said. "It so happens that I want to talk to you."

"I know." Arnaud started away from the crowd, motioning Jaques to follow. All other eyes went back to the gypsy.

"Baldwin told you?"

"Baldwin's an idiot. No, I heard from his friend." Baldwin had evidently spread the word.

When they reached a secluded corner, Arnaud lunged and shoved the smaller youth against the wall. "Let's get this damned straight from the start," he said, his foul breath hot on Jaques's face. "If you even think of snitching me out to your bloody bishop or anyone else, your body will be dead in a ditch before you can open its goddamned mouth. Understand?" He slammed Jaques hard against the boards before he let go. "Now what do you want?"

Jaques rubbed the back of his head. "You made your point." He spoke slowly, needing time to recover the script he had rehearsed for this occasion. He had pored over every available trial record that mentioned the Sicres or Bailles. He had put himself in Arnaud's unfortunate position as a child: pinched between his mother, a Cathar woman of means, and his father, a fortuneless Catholic expelled from the family home by a heretical wife. Embittered by his disenfranchisement, the elder Arnaud Sicre gained notoriety by heading the Inquisition's 1307 expedition against the Cathar community in Montaillou, which resulted in the capture and execution of several Perfects and the imprisonment of many of the townsfolk.[25] Forced to live with his journeyman father from age five, Arnaud coveted the Baille wealth from afar, only to see it confiscated by the church upon his mother's execution.

"Rather than remain an artisan all your life, Arnaud," Jaques said as boldly as he could make his voice sound, "you can still be a gentleman as befits the scion of the Bailles of Ax."

"If this is a trap, remember that ditch," Arnaud snorted. But Jaques noticed the telltale quiver of avarice in his shaking schoolmate's hands.

"On my word, no harm will come to you."

"Your word?" Arnaud spat. "Your word is shit, Joli."

"The solemn word of Bishop Fournier then."

"Better, if I can believe it. And what do I have to do for his Excellency to earn what is already mine?"

The direct approach should yield the truest response Jaques had surmised. "Find the Perfect Guilhem Belibaste and bring him in alive to Fournier's court."

"I remind you of that ditch again, Joli. What makes you or the bishop think I even know the man?"

"Put two and two together. In this square some months back,

you stated that you could hand over a group of Cathars, a Perfect among them. The bishop says that Belibaste is the last of the Cathar Perfects. He has to be your man."

Arnaud looked off. "Without a notarized statement of immunity from prosecution by all ecclesiastical or secular courts for any activities I undertake in pursuing this matter and an ample cash advance for travel and living expenses over the several months this will require, I assert that the statements you claim I made are lies." He too had rehearsed his part.

Satisfied that this was as far as he could take the matter on his own, Jaques said, "I will report your terms to the bishop. Meet me tomorrow at sunset at the Inn of the Doves. I'll give you his answer."

"Even a Sicre is not foolish enough to assume I would give such a promise in writing," said the portly Fournier with a derisive chuckle when Jaques relayed Arnaud's condition for immunity. "Such a document coming from me, if discovered, would set a precedent that could null the Inquisition's right to claim guilt by reason of simple association, intentional or not, with heretics. Of course, he has the dispensation, but he has to accept it on my word with you as sole witness."

"And if he refuses?" Jaques asked, regretting that he had so quickly guaranteed that no harm would come to Arnaud.

"He won't unless—" Fournier leaned forward, his brows drawn together. "Unless he's working for them and the document of immunity is what they're really after."

Jaques frowned. "A trick to get what will be valuable in future defenses?"

"Don't underestimate the enemy," Fournier said. "Arnaud Sicre was suckled by a mother who became a Perfecta. Any woman obstinate enough to gain ordination, even in a heretical faith, has to be a sorceress, a witch, or worse. As she stood dying in the flames, who knows what powerful curse she uttered against the church and the Inquisition."

Jaques shivered, recalling Baldwin's description of the dying Templar Grand Master Jacques de Molay's accurate prediction of death within the year of a pope and a king. "Arnaud's mother had magical powers?" he asked.

The bishop nodded. "And what better agent of vengeance than her son disguised as a heretic hunter."

"So Arnaud could be working for them while saying he's working for us?"

Fournier held up his forefinger. "Worse. He may actually think he is working for us when, in fact, he is working for them."

Jaques slapped his forehead. "Is he a puppet with no control over whomever is pulling his strings?"

"Heresy, young man, is an unforgiveable sin. We scatter the ashes of the heretic burnt at the stake to prevent further infection. Even those who recant must be imprisoned or marked with a yellow cross to warn others away from them. Disavowal does not erase their earlier defection; they are permanently diseased and thus contagious. As to their offspring, the book of Exodus is merciless: 'I, the Lord your God, am a jealous God, punishing children for the iniquity of parents, to the third and the fourth generation of those who reject me.'"[26]

For an instant Jaques's mind went back to the teachings of the gentle Père Fontaine, who often repeated the words of Jesus reported in the Gospel of John: *God is love*. Such contradictions in the same Bible.

Fournier did not seem to notice his moment of distraction. "But even the cleverest devil can be made to serve the church's purpose as long as we remain at least a step ahead of him in cleverness," the bishop continued. "Arnaud was infected in his mother's womb and will always remain so. No matter whom the puppet thinks is pulling its strings, it moves with the string that is pulled. We don't need Arnaud's loyalty, only control of his strings.

"As the son of a perfecta, Arnaud is uniquely qualified to locate, infiltrate, and identify the members of the community of Catalonia, the one fragment of the sect outside my control and thus capable of regenerating the heresy as the Authiers did despite the Cathar defeat at Montsegur. He is the hook that we have to keep on the end of our line. This is where you come in, Jaques. Like the fisherman, you will cast him out and reel him in."

Jaques was too abashed to reply coherently. Infantile as it sounded, he could only complain. "Arnaud Sicre would like nothing better than to bash my head in and bury me in a ditch, and he is a lot bigger than I am. I'd be crazy to think I could control him."

"Match his bluster with your brain," the bishop advised. "Just as he is suited for his role, so are you for yours. He's clumsy and will leave clues. Pick them up. With your capacity to assemble seemingly disassociated facts, piece things together well before they become evident to him. Stay that crucial step ahead. Remember that through me you have the power and funding of the church behind you, and your position becomes invulnerable."

The bishop's positive assessment did not wholly appease Jaques: was there something intrinsically wrong or dangerous about the proposition, or was he merely a coward?

Again Fournier picked up on his hesitation. "Of course, Sicre's stubborn, and he might refuse outright to take my word through you," he said, voicing what Jaques feared might be the first obstacle he would face.

"And what do I do then?"

Fournier reached into his desk drawer. "Arnaud may be very stubborn, but he is even greedier." He pulled out a small purse and tossed it on the desk, the coins within clanking as it fell. He pushed it towards Jaques. "If it looks like he is going to walk away, pull this purse out and throw it down in front of him so he hears that sound. He won't leave a table that has money on it."

"What's to keep him from taking the money and running, never to be seen again?"

"Good work, thinking ahead of him," the bishop applauded. "The purse contains only enough for a preliminary stage. He'll notice. Let him know there's a lot more where this came from. It's his if he returns with a feasible plan to haul in Belibaste."

Jaques felt light-hearted, almost giddy, as he walked to his meeting with Arnaud that evening. Shoulders back, breath flowing easily, and senses tuned to his surroundings, an aura of the importance of his task buoyed his steps. Feeling duly armed to counter Arnaud's inevitable outrage over Fournier's decision to withhold written immunity further bolstered his confidence.

His nemesis was waiting in the shadows behind the doorpost when he arrived at the Inn of the Doves. "We'll do our business out here," Arnaud said, taking a seat at an exterior table away from the windows. "The paper first."

"No paper," Jaques said. "You have Bishop Jacques Fournier's word. No harm will come to you from either the ecclesiastical or civil courts over any actions you take to complete this mission."

Arnaud's eyes narrowed. He glowered at Jaques for several taut moments. Then his fist crashed down on the table. "No Perfect then," he said, thrusting up from the bench.

Jaques pulled the money bag from his pocket and dropped it on the table between them. The coins clanked. Arnaud froze at the sound.

"To get things started," Jaques said, "we know Belibaste and his clan crossed the Pyrenees into Catalonia. It will take you time and money to track them and devise a plan. Belibaste must be lured back into the bishop's jurisdiction where he can be taken alive."

Arnaud grabbed the sack, opened it, and counted the coins. "I should just cut your throat and run off with the money," he snarled, pocketing the purse.

"It barely covers the preliminary stage. The *fait accompli* will take a lot more. You're clever, but this is a tricky business. Many ways it could go wrong. The bishop would like to review the final plan beforehand. Take your time, a year if you need it, to survey the situation and then report in. From there we'll decide our way forward."

Arnaud's face tensed. "I will report back to the bishop, not to his boy," he said.

Jaques shrugged. "That can be decided when you get back," he said, a bit too heedlessly he realized too late. Arnaud was up, around the table, and grabbing the front of his shirt before he could raise his hands in defense.

"Just remember, Joli, anything goes wrong and you pay. It'll be my cock up your ass and down your throat before you land dead in that ditch." He let go and stepped back, his face still contorted. "And that's not all. I'm sure you remember Père Fontaine, your parish priest in Tarascon."

Jacques nodded. "What does he have to do with this?"

"What if I told you that your beloved mentor was not the Catholic priest he posed to be but, in fact, a Cathar Perfect? Everything he taught you, including those memory tricks, was heresy and sorcery."

"I'd call you a liar," Jaques shouted back, instantly angrier than ever before. Arnaud had struck him in the groin.

"Then make damned sure that I don't have to reveal what I know. Imagine good Père Fontaine's body dug up and burned for the heretic he was. And his parishioners, your mother included, charged and imprisoned for being the heretics they are. Your own supposed gifts, which you flaunt so brazenly, branded as the devices of the devil."

He grabbed Jaques's collar and shook him a final time. "If you think I am exaggerating, Joli, just follow Fournier's current case in Montaillou. Fontaine isn't the only heretic to wear priest's clothing." He pushed off, jiggling the coins in his pocket. "I'll see you next summer. Have lots more of this ready," he said as he melted into the dark.

Unable to grasp how his advantage had evaporated so quickly and completely, Jaques stood panting in the shadows. He had played his part well, and against all odds Arnaud was off on the mission as intended. And yet he felt violated and already left for dead in the ditch. "It's a lie," he murmured, "the foulest of lies that only

Arnaud Sicre's wretched mind could concoct."

He finally summoned the will to drag himself down the alley towards his quarters, his eyes barely open. He stumbled over something.

"What, ho, boy. Watch where you're going." The vagabond Baldwin was propped against a wall with his legs sprawled into the roadway. Jaques had tripped over them.

"What the hell," Jacques yelped. "Not you again. Why don't you keep your damn legs to yourself?"

"Bad night, eh?" Baldwin said in a voice less strident than usual.

Jaques was in no mood for conversation. "Just let me go on," he said, wiping his eyes.

"Sit a minute," Baldwin said, patting the ground beside him. "You're in trouble. I can still listen. I may be an ogre now, but it wasn't always this way."

Compelled by the compassion where there should have been none, Jaques sat, still sniffling. "That damned Arnaud Sicre," he said.

"I saw you two talking by the Doves. A meaner man than me, and that's something," Baldwin said.

"I try to treat him decently, but he insists on kicking me in the teeth."

Baldwin began rocking, his hands clasped in front of his chest. "Rotten stuff happens. You can't depend on anyone, on anything, in this world. Play along or they'll lock you up. It's all a show. Don't fall for it, theirs or your own. You know what I mean, boy?"

There was little sense in the codger's words, but they did soothe Jaques a bit. "Somewhat. I should be ashamed of myself. Here I have everything anyone my age could want, and I'm upset because someone showed me disrespect. And there you are, half blind, in rags, the laughing stock of Pamiers, no place to spend the night, and you're consoling me."

"It's rumored you have an extraordinary gift." Baldwin said. "It's valuable, but, I warn you, also dangerous. Envious people will try to steal it from you even while singing your praises. Best to keep it within yourself. Don't offer it to the swine. Care for it as the one treasure that endures, the pearl of great price."

Amazed at the man's sudden sobriety, Jaques said, "You talk like one who knows. Before you said, 'It wasn't always this way.' Something happened to you. Did someone steal your treasure?"

Baldwin struggled to his feet. "Dumb question," he growled as he spat and started to slink away, his moment of sanity dissipating so quickly that Jaques wondered if he imagined it. "Get on with you. Be the good little bishop's boy. Let life pass you by and you'll get in no trouble."

Chapter 8: Geneva, Spring 1937

In the isolation imposed by the long winter nights at the start of 1937, my frenetic reassessments of the previous year's events curdled them from curiosity to conspiracy. I had already surrendered my romance with Otto to the demands of a continent groping for normalcy in the throes of the Great Depression. To honor social imperatives before individual preferences was legitimate, but allowing historical events, no matter how momentous, to overwhelm everything personal seemed patently unfair. That they would impact aspects of our intimate lives was sufferable, but to be thrust without consent into the vortex generating these events by those manufacturing them was mortifying. Himmler assuming the prerogative to co-opt Otto's life and work to forward the Nazi cause, no matter the incentives he offered, was high-handed. No less egregious was the Emerald Club's use of our relationship and my family connections to spy on Nazi internal affairs. And 333's claim that I had an innate responsibility to support his cause merely by virtue of being alive in this time and place was unduly presumptive.

As I pondered how we had been seduced into being so deeply involved, I became convinced that the timing of those who had embroiled us was too neat for the sequence to have occurred naturally. Had not 333, a stranger without a name, claimed without concern for our privacy that he had been monitoring Otto's activities from his schooldays? The mere possibility of such covert oversight, even if a ruse, had me suspecting manipulation at every turn.

Adding to my anxiety during those cold, dark weeks was Otto's silence following the Dachau visit. In Munich he mentioned that he had to commit the winter to the second book Himmler had demanded. That this kept him from making those promised visits to Geneva with which he induced me to work on Himmler's genealogy was understandable, but that all contact otherwise was limited to a couple of postcards seemed dismissive.

By the time the days got longer and warmer, I was habituated to projecting conspiracies and cataclysms even when no evidence of abnormality existed. Desperate to reclaim my balance, I remembered 333 saying that Ladame would fill me in on the philosophy, politics, and practice of the Emerald Club.

Paul greeted me affably when in late March we met in his modest office located just off the main campus of the University of Geneva. But, like 333 in Dornach, he seemed preoccupied, thus making me wary of consuming his time. After summarizing my winter musings, which I admitted I had largely done in a vacuum, and relaying what little I had heard from Otto, I asked for any news relative to the events initiated the previous year at Dachau and Dornach.

"It's been ominously quiet on the other side of the border for several months now," he replied, "since Hitler squeaked by with the Rhineland remilitarization last spring, an adventure his own generals considered premature that turned in his favor due to the timidity of the British and French. Since then, the Fuehrer has stepped back to confirm his allies and build up his forces. He now has treaties with Italy and Japan in place, his air force is practicing bombing runs in support of Franco in Spain, and Reich armament factories are working overtime. Meanwhile, he broadcasts Germany's peaceful intentions at every opportunity, a definite signal that he is preparing for war."

He shrugged diffidently. "My humble opinion. The Western allies are dreaming. They want to believe that the Nazis will behave if they are tossed an occasional cookie. Last year, the Rhineland

and with it the end of the Versailles Treaty. Austria is baking in the oven, and pieces of Czechoslovakia, Poland and Lithuania are in the mixing bowl. The French and British bakers can only hope the Nazi appetite will be satisfied before the cookie jar is empty."

"And what of the increased repression of political dissidents, Jews, and other minorities inside Germany?"

"At some time in its history, every country in Europe has had the blood of undesirables on its hands. Their own sins prohibit them from throwing stones."

"And Switzerland?"

Paul laughed. "We Swiss have an impervious cover: neutrality. We assume we did our part by providing the real estate and buildings for the League of Nations in this city. There the rest of the world can sit and decide if it will be peace or war. Whatever course they choose, we will finance—and profit from."

"But you believe the Nazis have already chosen war. Does the rest of the Emerald Club think the same?"

The professor sat back and squinted his left eye. "You didn't come to talk to me of things you can read about in the newspapers. You want to know who 333 is, what the EC does, and what all of this has to do with Rahn and yourself. When I last talked to him, 333 was surprised it was taking you so long to ask."

"So you will explain. No secrets?"

Again, he laughed. "There are never *no* secrets, Raymond. The intelligence business takes nothing for granted. For all you know, I could be working for the Nazis even though I'm signed with the EC." He pointed with his forefinger. "Worse. I could be a puppet, thinking I am working with the Emerald Club when actually Goebbels is pulling my strings."

A shock, as if I had touched a live wire, surged through me. The left side of my brain felt like it was slipping sideways. I jerked to the right to rebalance.

Ladame saw the reaction. "I'm not serious," he said.

"I didn't think so. But those words—*puppet, strings.*" I slapped the side of my head. "I've heard them before. Maybe recently, maybe long ago. I can't place it."

"Maybe in a dream," Ladame said. "If so, a rare case when a dream is worth something." His concern passed quickly. "So, what would you like to know?"

I took a deep breath. "From our conversation before Dachau and the one with 333 afterwards plus data from additional research, I've put together a reasonable outline of the various vectors intent on unifying Europe in the post-war period. Running parallel to the international efforts of the League of Nations, which advocates for capitalist democracy, and the Communist Party with its push for rule by the proletariat, there are several specifically Euro-centric movements.

"The three that affect us now all started just after the war, the first two with important events in the year 1923. First is the Pan European Movement, a more tolerant but still aristocratic offshoot of the defeated Austro-Hungarian Empire, previously the Holy Roman Empire, which had already dominated Europe for centuries. Its founding document, Count von Coudenhove-Kalergi's manifesto *Paneuropa*, which presented the concept of a unified Europe but still controlled by the Hapsburgs, was published in 1923.

"Second are the National Socialists, middle-class and militant, who based their legitimacy to rule the continent on Aryan or Nordic racial superiority, which they claim was undermined by inferior Latin and Semitic oppressors from the south. The Munich Beer Hall Putsch, Hitler's initial attempt to seize political power, occurred in 1923.

"Finally, there is Rudolph Steiner's Third Way, which ignored the boundaries of class and race with a system that harkened back to the motto of the French Revolution: *Liberty, Equality, Fraternity*. Three separate but interdependent social spheres, each with a different mode of regulation. *Liberty* in cultural life, which included education, science, art, and religion. *Equality* in a democratic political life. And non-coerced solidarity or *Fraternity* in economic life."

I paused and pulled on my ear lobe. "Steiner died in Dornach in 1925, but I don't know what he was doing in 1923."

Ladame eagerly filled in. "Hitler and Steiner were not strangers to each other. Both their movements incubated in Munich. They went toe to toe in 1921. Hitler, barely confirmed as the Nazi leader, attacked Steiner, long established as a public figure, in an article in the Party newspaper, labeling him a Jew and calling for a war against him and his followers. Steiner, in turn, publicly declared that it would be disaster if the National Socialists came to power.

"Steiner was physically attacked during a lecture he was giving in Munich in 1922. Stink bombs exploded and the lights went out as several people rushed the stage where he was speaking. He managed to escape through a back door.

"Then on New Year's Eve at the start of 1923, his headquarters, the first Goetheanum in Dornach, was destroyed by fire. No proof but there are grounds to suspect the Nazis of arson. After that, Steiner concluded that he was not safe in Germany. He sold his Berlin residence and severely limited his speaking engagements in the country.

"Neither did the attacks from the German press stop after his death. In 1930 Gregor Schwartz-Bostunitsch, a one-time follower turned Nazi, published a book claiming that Steiner was an agent of the Jewish world conspiracy."

"No surprise then," I added, "that last year his Anthroposophical Society was formally dissolved, its properties confiscated, and its books banned in the Reich. The grounds, given in Reinhard Heydrich's proclamation, were that Anthroposophy was internationally oriented and maintained close contacts to foreign freemasons, Jews, and pacifists; also that the methods of teaching practiced in its Waldorf schools were individualistic and human-oriented and thus incompatible with the principles of national socialistic education. Might Himmler too have developed a vendetta against Steiner's followers?" I then asked, aiming to return the discussion to Otto's predicament.

"He was born and lived in Munich and, coincidentally, joined the party there in 1923. Surely he keeps an eye on Steiner's followers."

I was alarmed. "Isn't it dangerous then for 333 and the EC to operate from Dornach?"

Ladame threw out his hands. "I had the same question. 333 just smiled and pointed out the second Goetheanum's solid concrete construction. 'Rudolf Steiner learned from the New Year's Eve fire,' he said. 'Fire won't destroy his work twice.'"

That explanation may have satisfied Paul, but I feared for Otto's security. "Blind faith is out of character for you," I said. "Look what happened to you in Germany during the Olympics. They were tailing you going in and all the time you were there. If not for Otto, they'd have gotten you."

He leaned forward. "Between us boys, we wanted them to see me going into the Soviet Embassy. A ruse to keep them looking in the wrong places. An elementary tactic, but effective." He clapped his hands. "But irrelevant here. You want to know what all this has to do with Otto and you. Rahn and the Nazis, the Emerald Club, the Pan Europeans, Steiner, 333, Hitler, Himmler, me for that matter—what's the common denominator?"

He had posed the key question, rhetorically I assumed. I waited expectantly.

"Think of the title of Rahn's book," he prodded when I did not answer.

"*The Crusade Against the Grail.*"

"The Grail." He nodded his head.

"Yes, *The Crusade Against the Grail.*"

"The Grail, Raymond, is the common denominator," he said, almost yelling.

I was caught dumbfounded. Not that I did not understand, but it was too much too fast. *The Grail.* That word. It turned on a thousand brilliant lights simultaneously, turning me giddy in the glare.

"I can't believe that came out of your mouth, Paul," I said. "You, the skeptic who thought Otto a mystic scatterbrain because he was searching for the Grail in the Lombrives."

"My opinion of him hasn't completely changed, and neither have I. But I'm in the business of information, and words and symbols are its most common carriers. Just across the border, a mustached little corporal twisted an ancient sacred symbol, the swastika, Sanskrit for *luck* or *auspiciousness*, and used it to reduce an advanced civilization into a berserk mob hailing him as a god."

"You'd equate the Grail and the swastika?"

"Both are simple symbols, but powerful. They are talismans, objects that unconsciously exert a profound influence on human feelings or actions. Talismans are self-accumulators. The longer they are around, the more attention or energy they attract to themselves, and thus the more potency they gain. Before it was chronicled in the Arthurian legends, the Grail already had a long history, going back even earlier than its best-known role as the cup of Jesus' Last Supper and Crucifixion. Some think it was one of the sacred objects in the lost Hebrew Ark of the Covenant. In *Crusade* Otto, following von Eschenbach, identifies the Grail as the precious stone that fell to earth from Lucifer's crown during his great rebellion against God at the beginning of time.

"Various other symbolic items—chalices, bowls, platters, and spears—in diverse places throughout history have been designated Grails or *graals*. Even the word's spelling and pronunciation are uncertain. How then can we ask: what exactly is this Grail, holy or otherwise?"

"Teacher, teacher." I raised my hand. "'There was a Thing that was called the Grail, the crown of all earthly wishes, fair fullness that ne'er shall fail.' I too remember my *Parzival*."

"Bravo. 'Fair fullness that ne'er shall fail.' The vessel of inexhaustible abundance that dispenses lavishly to each whatever they wish. The one treasure that endures. The pearl of great price."

There came that sudden shock again and the sensation of my brain slipping sideways. *The one treasure that endures. The pearl of great price.* And the flash of a human face—bruised and ugly—a tortured creature staring out of hell. But vanished too quickly to identify.

This time, though, Ladame appeared not to notice my distress. When I was gathered enough to again follow the discussion, he was already drawing his conclusion.

"With the Grail as the symbolic common denominator through-out much of the Western world for the highest good, Otto should have expected that the Nazis too would get interested when he wrote a book stating that he had discovered something very impor-tant, Grail-related, in the Pyrenees. Himmler, with his will to power and occult proclivity, got mighty curious and recruited him."

Surprised to pick up the flow of the conversation so quickly, I said, "And once the EC figured that Rahn might reveal what he found to Himmler and the Nazis, it too had to know what his dis-covery was, and so you recruited me."

Paul smiled and winked. "You catch on quickly," he said.

A month later, I was relieved to get a parcel from Otto addressed from a town in his native Hesse. From its shape it had to be a book. I surmised it was a copy of his next work, the one that Him-mler had pressed him to write. Given his prior enthusiasm about producing both the grand novel he called Sebastian and a candid history of the brutal German Inquisitor, Conrad of Marburg, I ex-pected it to be one or the other. On opening the package, I was mys-tified and a bit disappointed to find the moderate-sized book he had authored entitled *Luzifers Hofgesind*, or *Lucifer's Court*, with the subtitle, *Eine Reise zu den guten Geistern Europa (A Journey in Search of the Good Spirits of Europe)*.

The first sentence of its prologue, "The Journey Begins," expelled the mystery about the book's content: "*Lucifer's Court* is based on travel diaries begun in Germany, continued in the south, and com-pleted in Iceland." The table of contents, consisting of place names largely in France, Italy, Germany, and Iceland, confirmed that the book was a travelogue compiled from his notes taken from 1930, when he first visited Paris prior to exploring in Languedoc, to just last year, when he participated in the Ahnenerbe expedition to Iceland.

Nevertheless, the book's short introduction made clear that his affections were rooted in his native Odenwald while his attention remained fixed on the history he would rather have written. He concluded the prologue thus:

> A few hours separate my hometown from Marburg-am-Lahn. A son of this town, the "fright of Germany," also preached for Rome. The magister and inquisitor Konrad von Marburg crisscrossed his homeland on the back of a donkey, collecting Rosenwunder for the beatification of his enlightened confessor, Countess Elizabeth of Thuringia—and collecting heretics for execution. He had them burned in a place in his hometown which is still called Ketzerbach or "heretic ditch." My ancestors were pagans and my forebears were heretics.[27]

I was in the midst of figuring out how he might insert the Lucifer of the title into so mundane a format when I spotted a folded slip of paper between the book's pages.

With nervous fingers I opened the note. Undated, it read:

> My dear Raymond,
>
> Enclosed please find a copy of *Luzifers Hofgesind*, the fruit of my assignment, titled and revised to official specifications by my editor and publisher, Albert von Haller of Schwarzhaupter Verlag, Leipzig.
>
> The accomplishment here is not in the content, as it was with *Crusade Against the Grail,* or in my subsequent promotion to SS-Untersturmführer, but in the completion of my first major project on time that earns me the freedom to pursue the more worthy works closer to my heart.
>
> Which takes me to the point of this letter: my return to Languedoc for additional research has been approved. The time allocated is brief, a couple of weeks at most, and the agenda confi-

dential. You can mention it to the professor; he may have some pot-holing pointers to contribute even though I cannot enlist his services this time.

Based on your contribution to his ahnenpass as well as the favorable report you made to your Swiss associates about our manufacturing model near Munich, our client approved my request to include you in the expedition.

Several others will join us, Ullmann among them, although Gabriele has been designated, not so willingly, to remain behind as our liaison in Berlin.

We will gather at the Hotel de Ville, Pamiers, the evening of the last Friday in May, and proceed from there. Time is short, so reply quickly. A simple oui will do.

Your devoted friend,
Otto

Chapter 9: Carcassonne, October 1319

In the late summer of 1319, Pope John XXII selected Bishop Fournier to preside over the trial of the Franciscan agitator Brother Bernard Delicieux. Set to take place in the regional capital of Carcassonne along the Aude River, a day's journey east of Pamiers, the court was commissioned to examine the long bill of charges drawn up by Bernard Gui and his team of Dominican lawyers. Chief among the infractions: treason against the French king, murdering Pope Benedict XI, obstructing the Inquisition, and undermining the authority of the Franciscan Order by promoting and practicing the prohibited Spiritual interpretation of its rule.

With the required temporary relocation of the ecclesiastical court, this mandate came at an inconvenient time for the bishop, who was then tightening the noose around the village of Montaillou and its particularly stubborn coven of Cathars. But Jaques, figuring to be left in Pamiers to await the return of Arnaud Sicre, now gone about a year, welcomed the recess from his scribal duties. Since dispatching his former classmate to gather information on the Cathar colony headed by Guilhem Belibaste, he had largely kept to himself during any free time. Meticulous in meeting his professional obligations, he turned down most social invitations, even the bishop's, pleading engagements otherwise, most of them spurious. Not that he was idling away time. If it was Fournier inquiring, he attributed his intense reading and research to his role as Arnaud's minder.

Actually he was gathering information to refute Arnaud's untoward assertion that Père Fontaine, his mother, and many other Tarasconians were heretics in Catholic disguise.

Arnaud Sicre had correctly foreseen the renewed investigation of Montaillou. Even though that tiny community in the Pyrenean foothills was raided and supposedly cleansed of heretics in May 1308, Catharism had again taken root there in the decade since. Fournier had reopened the case against it, arrested several townspeople, and issued warrants for others who had fled, some supposedly to Belibaste's community in Catalonia. But Arnaud's prediction that a heretic disguised as a priest would turn up in Montaillou had not materialized. From a respectable family that included his brother who served as the town's mayor, Montaillou's only Catholic priest, Pierre Clergue, had actively participated in the Inquisition's 1308 raid, fingering for prosecution those parishioners he suspected of heretical tendencies. He was known to be equally cooperative during the current sweep.

Only once, a couple of months after Arnaud had left, did Jaques's preoccupied state attract the bishop's attention. Fournier called him in for a talk.

"You've turned serious and withdrawn lately, young man," the bishop began. "It won't do to have you wear out so early. Did something occur with your last meeting with Arnaud Sicre that disturbed you, something it might help to tell me about?"

Despite steeling himself against potential reactions should this sensitive area be broached, Jaques's hands quivered and his head shook at the question. Fournier missed nothing, so no point denying that a nerve had been struck.

To circumvent discussion of the unspeakable in his confrontation with Arnaud, Jaques looked duly perturbed and went with a half-truth. "I don't want to prove that bully correct and sound like a sissy," he said, "but he did threaten to kill me if anything went wrong with the deal."

Fournier leaned forward, seeming compassionate but saying nothing.

"Probably just an idle threat. Arnaud thrives on intimidation," Jaques added quickly.

"A threat is a threat, especially in this business," Fournier said. "Very prudent to watch your back. But he's now in Catalonia—or better be—and can't strike directly. Does he have accomplices who might act in his stead?"

Jaques started to shake his head.

"Look hard. Such people may not be obvious," Fournier advised.

"There's his father and a brother. Too recognizable though." He was about to give up when Baldwin came to mind. The vagabond had been in the marketplace the morning Arnaud bragged that he could bring in a Perfect. Then he popped up again, impromptu enough, to broker the meetings between the two former schoolmates, which resulted in the arrangement to apprehend Belibaste. Then again in the square for the distraught Jaques to trip over after he closed the deal at the Inn of the Doves.

"Ah," the bishop injected. "You came up with someone."

Jaques rued that his thought process was so transparent. Then, recalling Baldwin's moment of compassion during their last encounter, he waved off the poor fool as a threat. "Only circumstantial evidence," he said.

Fournier sat waiting, again saying nothing. Jaques felt obliged to elaborate. "I was thinking of the obnoxious old bum who hangs around the Mercado. I happened to trip over his legs in the dark after closing the deal with Arnaud. He saw I was upset and, out of character, he consoled me. And I felt better. A dog, for sure, but all bark and no bite."

The bishop began tapping his manicured nails on the polished desktop, a slow, deliberate rhythm. "I know the fellow. Crazy but probably harmless. Fancies himself a court jester who will make us all honest with his foul mouth. Interesting that you experienced a softer side; one of the Lord's odd instruments, perchance."

Fournier slowed his drumming fingers and peered at Jaques, smiling slightly. "I should call you to task for allowing Arnaud to get under your skin and then letting on about it to a stranger. No harm done in this case, so we'll count it as part of the learning process. But be aware that such activities—loss of composure and indiscretion—could prove fatal."

Jaques wanted to protest the bishop's harsh assessment but accepted the reproach with a humble nod.

"Has this Baldwin shown any interest in you since that night?" the bishop asked.

Jaques had to think. Even though the man had been in the Mercado regularly before his meeting with Arnaud, there was no sign of him afterwards. "I haven't seen him since I tripped over him," he said.

"Off for greener pastures," Fournier said. "But keep an eye out. Possibly just an unfortunate who appeared at the right time to help you, but then—" The unfinished sentence left Jaques suspended in speculation. Was that precisely what the bishop intended? he later would wonder.

Since Baldwin did not reappear in the Mercado and nothing yet developed with Arnaud Sicre, Jaques had no further need to meet with Fournier until Pope John put the bishop in charge of the critical trial in Carcassonne.

"I assume you've followed Brother Bernard Delicieux's case well enough to recognize that it is out of our ordinary line of investigation," the bishop said at the start of the meeting in which Jaques expected to be told that he would be left behind while the court convened in Carcassonne.

"Frater Gui mentioned that he would be working on it when he left Toulouse for Avignon," Jaques said.

"So you know that the Delicieux trial is different from the normal routine. In the Pamiers court, it is heresy, and the verdict follows the facts. They did or said so-and-so, which is deemed heretical, and so are guilty. In Carcassonne, however, it will be politics, with the verdict based on the dominant opinion, no matter the facts." Fournier grimaced. "Bad luck for Bernard and his Spirituals. You can't quote me, but there is little suspense about their fate."

Jaques gasped. "You mean he's guilty regardless?"

The bishop nodded. "If the initial evidence against him isn't sufficient for conviction, we continue until it becomes so. It may take some time. Delicieux will be clever and long-winded in his own defense. Years ago with Pope Clement V, he won the argument for his Spirituals and their extreme interpretation of the rule of Saint Francis of Assisi that retained a rigorous poverty distasteful to a wealthy church. But Pope John has aligned with the Conventuals, Bernard's opponents within the Franciscan order, and their Dominican allies. He has ruled the Spirituals rebels if not heretics."

"It doesn't seem fair to switch so much around every time there is a new pope," Jaques said.

The bishop smiled. "Politics, remember, not principles. The winner makes the rules. I am a Cistercian, an order older and more mature than both these bickering congregations. Perhaps why the pope threw me into the middle of this. Nevertheless, he made clear what the final verdict must be. Only the appearance of due process is up to me."

"How will you manage that?"

Fournier shook his head. "If we can cast Delicieux as a heretic, not merely a trouble-maker, the case is made." He began to scribble notes. "King Philip the Fair and his councilor Guillaume de Nogaret used such a strategy to take down the supposedly invincible Templars."

"But—"

"You're going to say that it's not fair again. Time to learn, my boy, that life is not always fair. This is why I've decided to take you to Carcassonne after all. Pay attention. God forbid you ever have to deal in church politics, but an inside knowledge of the way they operate will benefit you."

Jacques tried to hide his disappointment. "What if Arnaud Sicre returns while we're gone and doesn't find me here?"

"Hah, you should know your man better than that. He knows where the money is. He'll find us."

As Fournier had predicted, the trial took time. Four weeks into the proceedings, the beginning of October already, and the tedious process of presenting evidence dragged on with little prospect of a verdict anytime soon.

In the trial's first phase, Bernard Delicieux, despite having been in prison for two years already, had been spirited, irreverent, and at no loss for words. A skilled lawyer, the monk overworked the prosecution witnesses until most were tricked into contradicting themselves. His exposition was so deliberate and his demand for fact so exacting that the court was forced to deliberate for hours over details that should have been tabled in minutes.

Two weeks into the hearings, the Archbishop of Toulouse, co-president with Fournier, had tried to curtail the defendant's alternating bellicose diatribes and measured cross-examinations. But Fournier, fastidious about enforcing the few laws that protected the rights of the accused, overruled the archbishop's objections. As if betting that the monk would eventually slip and incriminate himself, Fournier allowed the defendant all the time he wanted.

It took several more weeks, but eventually Fournier's permissive strategy started to yield results. Bernard's fire slowed and then sputtered. With each new session, he looked more haggard. Rumor had it that his food and sleep were reduced in direct proportion to the recalcitrance he displayed in the courtroom, even though Fournier prohibited the use of outright torture. Jaques saw no signs of physical abuse nor did the monk complain of any.

Unlike in Pamiers, Jaques was not required—in fact, it was prohibited—to keep a written record. Apprised in advance of the bishop's strategy and the preordained verdict, little other than practiced discipline kept his attention on the often tedious proceedings. That is, until the name Ramon Llull was introduced into evidence during an early October session.

The question of extraordinary memory—whether a dark art or a divine gift—arose. A Brother Jerome, who had been at the Franciscan monastery of Narbonne with Delicieux, testified that Brother Bernard was an avid follower of the controversial Ramon Llull. This Majorcan writer, scientist, and mystic had died four years earlier at age 82 after having been wounded in a melee in North Africa, where he had gone on an ill-advised solo mission to convert some Muslims to his unorthodox brand of Christianity.

Brother Jerome testified that Delicieux taught a philosophy class that included Llull's occult theories derived from the forbidden study of alchemy. Bernard, he claimed, demonstrated memory techniques from Llull's banned text *Ars Magna*, methods the Majorcan had learned from Arab astrologers who used a mechanical memory device called a *zairja*. Both teachers disguised their source of the dark arts by stating that they were derived from a form of Christianity more authentic than that taught by the Roman church, a claim similar to those made by the heretical Cathars and the disbanded Knights Templar. If Jerome's testimony prevailed, Delicieux should also be charged with heresy.

Although now staggering when he walked and quivering when he talked, Bernard Delicieux realized that the fatal trap had been set, and Fournier was eager to spring it. He rallied to rebut Jerome with details about Ramon Llull that aimed to prove the man a devout mystic who deserved nothing less than sainthood. From memory Bernard quoted a description of Llull's conversion[28] from a dissolute life as a troubadour to Christian missionary: "One night he was sitting beside his bed, about to compose and write in his vulgar tongue a song to a lady whom he loved with a foolish love; and as he began to write this song, he looked to his right and saw our Lord Jesus Christ on the cross, as if suspended in midair."

From the first mention of Llull, Jaques observed, Bishop Fournier shifted from boredom to deep interest. He encouraged Bernard to expound further on Llull's virtuous life as a humble Franciscan lay monk and probed for more details on Llull's esoteric teachings, especially regarding enhanced memory.

Equally fascinated, Jaques began taking notes on the testimony, even while also keeping track of what he perceived as going on in the bishop's mind. Fournier was digging into Brother Delicieux's brain, hoping to extract the seed of Llull's genius from it just as he once attempted to tease the key to his remarkable memory from Jaques's own head. The prelate understood it to be a delicate operation: he had to extract the coveted treasure without alerting his victim or anyone in the courtroom that the theft was occurring. Brother Bernard possessed something of great value and the bishop wanted it above all else. *The only treasure that endures, the pearl of great price.* On a scrap of paper, which he slipped into his pocket, Jaques made a note of that important phrase, Baldwin's words to him the night he tripped over the vagabond's legs in the Mercado.

As if he too were reading the bishop's mind, Delicieux began to parry Fournier's questions with a form of baiting. He would whet his opponent's appetite by offering a cryptic morsel, only to pull the spoon back before the bishop could take a taste. Rather than explain the mechanics of artificial memory in Llull's *Ars Magna*, he questioned Jerome's application of the word *banned* to the book, pointing out that it had not been officially censured by papal bull or episcopal council.

For another hour the monk and bishop circled each other, their given roles in the courtroom sometimes reversed. The convoluted dance featured the judge trying to steal from the defendant, while Delicieux, aware of Fournier's intent, used convoluted legal questions to deflect his opponent's probes.

It was Fournier who finally yielded the round. "Llull's book is not on trial here," he pronounced. "The man's been dead for years. The witness is dismissed. Return the defendant to his cell with this court's permission to turn his night into whatever hell it takes to make him more cooperative tomorrow."

Granted a reprieve by Brother Bernard's bullheadedness, Jaques took the afternoon to explore the fabled city in which the trial had placed him. Carcassonne had been inhabited for over a millennium. Romans, Visigoths, and Septimanians had controlled the region from the fortified citadel on the hill above the Aude River for centuries before it became the capital of the House of Trencavel. In 1209, the first year of the war that ended only with the fall of Montsegur in 1244, the Cathar Count Raymond-Roger Trencavel failed to withstand the city's siege by the Crusader forces led by Simon de Montfort, and Carcassonne became the second major city, after Béziers, to fall to the invaders.

"The most exotic place in Languedoc," an envious associate had exclaimed when Jaques told him about his reassignment. "But disguise that Occitanian accent there. The town now belongs to the Dominicans, and just your way of speaking can be grounds to brand you a heretic," he warned.

Carcassonne was essentially a city within a city. Its commercial and residential districts sprawled outwards towards the surrounding farmland and river like the white of an egg. Its yolk was the fortified castle on the hill, which contained the edifices of the region's administration.

As Jaques made his way across the citadel's ecclesiastical quadrant with which he was familiar—the bishop's palace and other church offices arranged around a square over which towered the gothic Basilica of Saint-Nazaire—he turned to study the less prominent Tower of the Inquisition, inside which he had spent most of the past month. This external vantage point of the most ominous structure in southern France, headquarters to the Inquisition for a hundred years, led Jaques to think about the martyred heroes that Bishop Fournier once cited as the adversaries he most feared. What anguish the sight of that tower, symbol in stone of merciless dogma, must have struck in the heart of those dragged there for judgment. How did they endure the incessant questioning in its courtrooms, the harsh deprivations of its dungeons, and the pain inflicted by the machines in its torture chamber? What sort of person could endure the worst that the powerful could impose on them and still maintain their sanity and dignity as they walked through yonder doors and into this courtyard to meet death by rope, sword, or fire? What enabled such superhuman fortitude? This, Jaques finally understood, was the target of Bishop Fournier's fascination and the bane of his nightmares. These martyred heroes possessed the pearl of great price.

The first such perished in the tower before it became home to the Inquisition. Seeing that defeat was inevitable, Count Raymond Roger, induced by a promise of clemency, crossed alone into the Crusader camp to negotiate the honorable surrender of his starving city. In doing so, he walked into a trap, was taken, and imprisoned in the tower's dungeon after the city had fallen. There he was poisoned, making way for the hated de Montfort's appointment as the region's sovereign in his place. His courage juxtaposed against Simon's treachery transformed Raymond-Roger, previously a mediocre leader, into a martyred hero in the eyes of his countrymen, Cathar and otherwise. His name still evoked a proud patriotism in Languedocians and fueled a simmering resistance to French and Catholic rule.

Jaques shook his head at the irony of history. The gore that once slicked Roman amphitheaters as the early Christians were tossed to the lions now covered the courtyard of Carcassonne. Here those same Christians, now known as Roman Catholics, were not only executing Cathar heretics, who called themselves *true Christians*, but also Franciscan Spirituals, whose only crime was the practice of the strict poverty of their founder, Francis of Assisi, who embraced this discipline in imitation of Christ himself.

Was Brother Delicieux, already a hero for leading a rebellion against the Inquisition in this city a dozen years earlier, to be the next? In the battle of wills Jaques had just witnessed in the courtroom, the combatants had both left wounded, Delicieux by attrition,

Fournier by frustration. If Bernard continued in his current course, he would merit martyrdom, but he would make no quiet exit. *A martyr whose reputation does not continue among the living is just another corpse.* The wily Franciscan certainly understood what the bishop had once observed. Delicieux would embrace death as it was dealt him but with a fanfare that would be long remembered. Jaques shuddered as he turned away from the tower. The monk had baited the bishop into creating another martyred hero.

To distract himself, Jaques headed away from the clerical enclave towards the town's commercial center that fronted the former Count's palace. Rounding a corner, he was absorbed into a milling crowd. It was as if the entire population of the outer ring had squeezed itself into its center. He became dizzy at the unexpected jostling from people and animals squeezed into the narrow passageways between jutting sellers' stalls. He fought for breath and footing, losing his sense of direction. Vendors touted their wares in bawling staccato, and overeager customers cursed at those who refused to make way. A knight's horse brushed so close that Jaques felt the man's boot cut across his back. Sweating now, he too pushed to escape the chaos.

"The time is nigh when judgment will fall on those who judge," a rasping voice proclaimed to the throng around him. "Heretics headed for hell are leaping into the fire like martyrs, singing their Pater Nosters."

Jaques stopped on hearing the all too familiar voice.

"Templar sodomists and idol worshippers, who kiss the ass on a cat, meet death praying like saints while the bishops who condemned them stand by, cursing like commoners."

The Leper King, Jaques realized, was here in Carcassonne. He tried to push through the crowd surrounding the speaker. "Baldwin," he called out.

"Quit your bloody shoving," a burly fellow shouted at the determined youth. Something blunt struck him on the side of his head. He staggered and fell. The world went black.

He came to lying alone on the paving stones near the entrance to the Cathedral of Saint Nazaire. He pulled himself up. He had been trying to reach Baldwin in the marketplace, he remembered. Somehow he had been taken from there to here. He looked around. No Baldwin in sight. He shook his head to clear it. Had he imagined all that? He felt a sore spot above his ear. The lump left blood on his fingers. It had not been a dream.

To escape the heat that made his head throb worse, he went into the cathedral. After dipping his hand in the entrance font and crossing himself, he merged with the vast, cool quietness. Like the caves in the hillsides above the Ariège, he thought. He tiptoed so as not to ruffle the soothing silence. Staying to the right of the nave and moving toward the high altar, he scanned the alcoves and plaques along the wall. Here too, as in Notre Dame de Sabart and the cathedral of Pamiers, there would be an altar to the Madonna, perhaps a Black Madonna, in front of whom he could kneel and pray.

A red shaft from the stained glass on the opposite side splashed a garish light onto a plaque commemorating the sermon given on that spot by the founder of the Order of Preachers, on Easter Sunday 1213. Students from Saint Sernin were well versed in St. Dominic de Guzman's biography: a man of such holiness that Pope Gregory IX declared him a saint in 1234, the year of his death. Canonization usually took decades if not centuries.

Jaques tried to summon the emotions appropriate to standing in the footsteps of such sanctity; but a vague residue left over from the trials he witnessed in Pamiers and now here in Carcassonne diluted the due devotion. The Inquisition, Frater Gui once proudly claimed in a sermon, was Dominic's creation. While necessary for the regulation of the human element in the church, Jaques deemed the legalistic institution with its collateral brutality as somehow inconsistent with sainthood.

Without giving the plaque the customary kiss, Jaques moved up the aisle, more ill-at-ease now than when he had entered the building. He could maintain neutrality while recording events as they unfolded in court, but lately he found his balance disturbed if he pondered over his scripts afterwards. As despicable as the beliefs and persons of the Cathars, Waldensians, and Spirituals were supposed to be, he would sometimes feel more aligned with those judged than with those who condemned them. He wondered if Père Fontaine, the only person he could imagine revealing such deep misgivings to, had experienced a similar sympathy. His mind began to race. But, of course, if Père Fontaine was a Cathar Perfect rather than a Catholic priest—. He bit his lip to stop such thinking.

Toward the rear of the church, a door hinge creaked. Jaques turned and, holding his breath, waited for footsteps. No further sound. He shrugged it off as his own skittishness.

He came to a sarcophagus with a life-sized image carved into its marble lid: a soldier in armor, eyes closed in death, and hands clasped in prayer. An inscription identified this as the tomb of Simon de Montfort. Jaques was again startled. Here lay the most heroic or the most savage—depending upon one's political loyalty—leader of the French Crusader army during the Cathar wars. A man of extreme orthodoxy and an ardent Dominican ally, after taking Carcassonne de Montfort ravaged the Languedoc in a series of bloody battles that culminated in Muret in 1213. There, King Peter of Aragon, the south's strongest ally, was killed, and the Cathar resistance was crippled. Nevertheless, even after being titled lord of all the conquered territories with Raymond VII, the lawful Count, exiled to Aragon, Simon continued his merciless raids and punitive executions throughout the region.

In September 1216, word reached him that Raymond VII was fighting his way back to Toulouse where he remained popular. De Montfort abandoned his current siege of Beaucaire and preemptively ransacked parts of the capital city to punish its citizens for their suspected loyalty to their former lord. Still, Raymond retook Toulouse in October 1217, and Simon, now at the disadvantage, surrounded it in siege. In the ninth month of the standoff, on June 25, 1218, Simon was killed while fending off a sally by Raymond's troops. His head was smashed by a stone from a mangonel, operated, it was recorded, by the heroic "ladies and girls and women" of Toulouse.

Jaques placed a hand on the marble slab covering de Montfort's bones. Hardly a touch of admiration. As a southerner, one of the conquered ones, the gesture was more to ascertain that de Montfort remained as dead as he was reported to be.

Jaques then continued the quest for some consolation, but the altars, columns, and flickering candles of this basilica emblazoned with French fleur-de-lis instead of the cross of Toulouse made the church seem alien, sinister. Even the image of the Virgin, when he found her altar, was cast to resemble Blanche of Castile, Louis IX's mother, who as regent for the boy king, had finally subdued Raymond of Toulouse and permanently affixed the southern counties to Capetian France.

Suddenly conscious that his birthplace and language made him a foreigner here, one more suited to receive the punishments meted out to the heretics in the outer courtyard than to garner the spiritual consolation due the faithful in this house of God, Jaques stumbled into a pew and sat hunched with his head in his hands.

Only when the footsteps slapped right beside him did he hear them. Before he could look up, a hand roughly grabbed his shoulder.

"Joli Jaques," Arnaud Sicre hissed, "I'm back. With a Perfect in my sights for delivery to your bishop. Now for the money."

Chapter 10: Pamiers, Tarascon, June 1937

I passed the time on the long train trip from Geneva to Pamiers by rereading Rahn's *Lucifer's Court*. Shortly after receiving the book, I had passed the copy to Paul Ladame, who dismissed it as a dutiful travelogue containing little that we did not already know about our itinerant friend's adventures.

"I'd hoped he would provide further clues to what he discovered in the Languedoc," Paul said on returning the book to me.

A disappointment for me also. "He's explicit about places," I said, "but the time sequence is collapsed, perhaps intentionally obscured. He merges events that span from 1930, when he went to Paris to meet Magre and the Polaires, to 1936, when he made the research trip to Iceland for the Ahnenerbe, into what seems like a single journey that spanned just months."

"And nothing about his Nazi connections, his being in the SS and interacting with the likes of Himmler, Wolff and Weisthor."

I nodded. "As if none of that happened. He quotes Kurt Eggers, his fellow writer and SS member, extensively without naming him other than in the bibliography."

"Several random anti-Semitic remarks. In one place, he says he hopes to see Europe 'cleansed of all Jewish mythology.' Expected in a Nazi book but odd for Rahn with his admitted Jewish ancestry," Paul said.

"Perhaps one of von Haller's revisions."

"Would be interesting to see the original manuscript and compare."

I agreed and asked Paul's opinion about the invitation to join Otto and the Germans in France in a few weeks.

"Intentionally vague and understandably so," Paul said after reading Rahn's letter. "Not information you'd want in the wrong hands."

"But could the invitation be a trap?"

Paul grinned. "You're learning. Let's look at the possibilities. What's the best case scenario?" he asked.

I smirked. "I go. We lose the Nazis, recover the Grail, bring it here to Switzerland, and we all becomes famous. Won't happen."

Paul bobbed his head. "No, it won't. And for us, that wouldn't be optimal. The Emerald Club would lose its snoops inside Himmler's tent."

"You wouldn't need us. You'd have the Grail." I wanted to relish the positive dream before discussing the grimmer alternatives.

"What if you say *nein* and don't go?" Paul asked

"And let the Germans traipse through France without any idea what they are up to? They could find the Grail, take it back to Germany, and put it on Himmler's trophy shelf in Wewelsburg. They could come up empty, and Himmler would have Otto's head."

"So," Paul concluded, "your answer to his invitation has to be *Ja*."

As the train rolled south along the banks of the Ariège River, from the bucolic countryside and into the populated outskirts of the city of my destination, I glanced through the two pages of "Back Home," Rahn's closing chapter of *Lucifer's Court*. A single sentence, unconnected with what went before or came after and trailing off with an ellipsis, caught my eye: "I am carrying a Dietrich with me..." it read.

I smiled and closed the book. A Dietrich, a key. Genuine Otto, ending a rather bland travelogue with a poetic burst, a line of verse pregnant with mystery that begged for a sequel.

Before I could think through Otto's intent for concluding with this tantalizing hook, the train whistle shrieked to announce our arrival in Pamiers, and the passengers clogged the aisle with their luggage. A glance out the window at the shabby station was evidence enough that this town, known throughout history as the ugly stepsister of Toulouse to its north and of Foix to the south, still deserved a poor reputation. In *Lucifer's Court*, Rahn spoke of a friend who considered the climate of town to be unhealthy and "advised me not to stay in Pamiers because I would die of boredom."

The station was adjacent to the town's central marketplace. There I studied a tattered map posted on a kiosk. In his book, Rahn had noted the abundance of foreigners in the city. "Among the throngs of people that crowded the town's tiny streets, I saw many Senegalese and Arabs in uniform. I decided not to stay too long."

Using the map, I located myself as being on Rue de Jacques Fournier. That name, *Jacques Fournier,* was familiar from Otto's work although he did not appear in *Lucifer's Court*. He was Pamiers' most famous citizen, I soon discovered, its bishop between 1317 and 1327 and a renowned Inquisitor, who became Pope Benedict XII in 1334, succeeding John XXII.

Crossing the Mercado, as the marketplace was called since medieval times, towards the cathedral and bishop's palace at its west end, I became aware of the oppressive heat. Suddenly dizzy, I lowered my head, only to walk straight into the barrel chest of an enormous black man. With his turban he towered at least a foot above me. The print of my sweaty hand blotched his crisp white shirt. I mumbled an apology. He merely veered off. One of Otto's Senegalese, I thought.

Seeking relief from the heat, I entered the shadow of the deteriorating *Cathédrale Saint-Antonin de Pamiers*. A side door stood open. The dark cool interior was tempting, but Mass was in progress. I crossed instead to a cluster of trees around the double-gate that fronted the episcopal gardens and residence. A short rest revived me. I tugged at the heavy doors. They were locked. I glanced back towards the courtyard. Across the way I again spotted the huge Senegalese. He seemed to have been watching me, only to quickly shift his eyes elsewhere when I faced him. I moved along the wall enclosing the garden, periodically checking to see if he was follow-ing me, but he went in the opposite direction and disappeared. A case of overactive imagination or not, Ladame would have approved of my cautiousness.

Despite my eagerness to join Otto and share his continued ex-ploration of his beloved Languedoc, I did not look forward to shar-ing our experiences with a squad of Nazis. That I was effectually to serve as the EC's spy on the mission further perturbed me. "It only seems like you are going in solo," Ladame tried to assure me when I voiced this concern. "The coalition will provide cover as re-quired." He even gave me a sign with which these so-called under-cover agents would identify themselves: a triple flash of the three middle fingers of the right hand, a play no doubt on the number of the mysterious 333. Otherwise the professor had been frustratingly vague in delineating my role with the expedition.

Sufficiently fatigued by the journey and heat as well as unnerved by a subliminal sense of familiarity in a place I had never visited before, I gave up the sight-seeing and headed towards the Hotel de Ville to await the arrival of the Germans.

That evening they trooped in together, all with heavy backpacks and trying their best to pass for French hikers on holiday. Even Otto had traded his combed-back, clean-shaven look for mussed hair and three-day stubble. It made him look older than 32 and ruggedly handsome. We greeted with a warm handshake, forgoing the nor-mal hug in deference to present company. He then introduced me to the contingent's other three members.

"Ullmann you already know," he said of the blond blue-eyed officer who had been our driver in Dachau. The SS man seemed downright friendly without his uniform. "Willy is here by invitation from Uncle Henry." Code names were evidently de rigueur.

Next was another tall specimen but without Ullmann's Aryan coloration, which made him more passably French. His command of the language, it turned out, was also superior to that of the other two. "Our expedition leader, Ernst Steimel," Otto said. "We'll call him Ernie. He will monitor all trip details, including dress, schedule, and assignments. He reports to Karl." Steimel's handshake was perfunctory.

I immediately found it odd that Ullmann was Himmler's man, while Steimel took orders from Karl Wolff, Himmler's adjutant. I thought that one mole would have sufficed for both. Rahn's taking the lead in making the introductions showed that he had at least some status in the group. Nevertheless, my questions were mounting. I needed to talk to Rahn alone.

"And finally, because every group has to include its mad scientist, we have Rudolf Erfurt—Rudy for short, although he hates nicknames—from the DP," Otto said, introducing the third member. Much shorter than the others, his features swarthy, Rudy would only have looked at home in a laboratory. DP, I learned later, stood for *Deutsche Physik*, a nationalist movement in the German scientific community formed in the early 1930s to counter the Jewish physics of the already expelled Albert Einstein and his associates.

"Too much cloak and dagger stuff," Rudy muttered in German as he extended a hand moist with perspiration. "I don't know why they picked me. I hate hiking and climbing. I just hope we get out of this alive."

"Despite his retiring manner, Rudy is one of the brightest experimental scientists in the DP," Ullmann explained. And why does the expedition need an experimental scientist? I was tempted to ask. That too would have to wait until I was with Rahn alone.

"To round out the contingent, I believe mention should be made of the group's official liaison and my personal collaborator"—Ullmann and Steimel smirked at Otto's choice of term— "who is anchoring us at home: Gabriele Dechend, to be referred to as Gabby, of course. She wanted to come in person; but her aging protégé— simply *W* if we need to mention him— insisted that if she came, he too had a right to come. And with all due reverence for our elders, we know that W couldn't make this hike. Gabby will be standing by for our reports, decoding them, and distributing them to all who need to know."

That Otto mentioned Gabriele's role for my information was evident, but precisely why I could not decipher. His hinting at an intimate relationship with her implied to the other men that he was heterosexual. But was he also trying to tell me something about us by referring to her thus in public? Another question to clarify privately.

Knowing me to be an early riser, Otto tapped on my door at dawn the next morning. A silent nod indicated that he wanted to go for a walk before the others awoke.

I led the way down Rue de la République and turned right on the Rue des Jacobins, retracing the previous day's route back to the Mercado. Not until we made another right on Rue de Collége did we say anything.

"Coffee?" he asked, pointing to a bistro that had all empty tables in front. Walking stiffly as if still wearing his SS uniform, Otto brought coffee and croissants out to where I waited. I kept expecting a smile to break out on his face, some warmth to return to his manner.

"I hate this filthy town with a passion," he groused instead. "The most miserable place in Languedoc and they choose it." He glanced around, shuddered, lit a cigarette, and finally sat.

His was not a tune I wanted to harmonize with, but I nodded. "I sensed a weightiness I couldn't shake from the moment I got here yesterday. Maybe influenced by your book. What little you said about Pamiers wasn't good."

I reached across the table and squeezed his wrist. "But you're here now, Otto. In France, in Languedoc, only miles from the places you've yearned to return to for so many years. And we are here together. Maybe—"

"And I should be jumping for joy?" he snarled to my dismay. "Even after we leave this god-forsaken village later today, we head south to Tarascon. Five years ago they falsely accused me and threw me out of that town. Someone's got to remember. If Gabriele hadn't talked me into their plan, I would have refused to go there."

He smiled weakly. "She sends greetings and says she holds you responsible for my safe return. It came down to you or her in the end. She wanted to come and so argued against including you, even though she knew you were Himmler's choice. Wolff, she said, broke the deadlock by voting for you, preferring to keep her back as a surety."

"A hostage so you don't try to escape?"

Otto shrugged. "Where would I go? In any case, she was serious about committing my safety to you. She's aware of the threat from my old enemies down here and hinted that members of our party might harm me under certain circumstances. But she also knows that we might be tempted to concoct some scheme between us. 'Raymond does not actually sympathize with the Nazi cause,' she said. 'He's no German. Don't let him talk you into anything foolish.' My every step will be watched. It behooves me to return having what the Reichsführer wants in hand."

So many questions raced through my mind at once: Who was in charge of the expedition? Who was in control from Germany: Himmler or Wolff? Why the DP scientist? Where did Gabriele's loyalty lie? What was his current relationship with her? How did that affect us? And what the hell did he mean when he wrote that he was carrying the Dietrich with him? At the same time, I recalled Paul's advice given once it was decided that I would go to France.

"And what do I do when I get there?" I had asked.

"Observe carefully, but think quickly," he had answered.

Given Otto's current bitter mood, I chose to stand back rather than pepper him with my many questions. Paul and I both had assumed the expedition would head directly to the Cathar fortress of Montsegur where, in *Lucifer's Court*, Rahn says the treasure still lies.

"Whose idea was it to detour to Tarascon, and what do they hope to find there?" I asked gently.

"Himmler created the itinerary," he murmured. "He wants the stone."

In *Crusade* Otto wrote of a precious stone that fell to earth from the crown of the rebellious Lucifer when he was expelled with his legions from Heaven. Like Wolfram von Eschenbach in *Parzival*, Otto had equated this stone with the Grail.

"He thinks you will find Lucifer's stone in the Sabarthès?" I asked, my voice suddenly trembling. Paul and I had discussed the expectations of Rahn's superiors in Berlin and the dangerous burden that put on him. Was the Reichsführer-SS demanding he produce the highly improbable if not impossible?

Otto shook his head, a bitter smirk on his lips. "I doubt that anyone other than Himmler believes in the Grail. But they tested the small sample I brought back from my last visit, and they want a larger piece of it."

I shook my head, not understanding.

"I'm not clear about what they are after either," he said. "There are things they don't tell me about." He sighed, but then a bit of light came to his eyes. "But I have a hunch. In *Lucifer's Court*, which they blessed and so is part of the public record—no chance I'll get into trouble referring to it—I mention a particular devil's stone or *teufelstein*, this one tossed to earth by a demon intent on destroying the cathedral in Halberstadt. But his aim was off, and the boulder landed in the churchyard where it still remains. When I visited there and touched it, I felt a strong energetic emanation, a sustained electric shock. In the book, I modified this experience to a 'mild irradiance.' In fact, there was nothing mild about it."[29]

"I remember that passage," I said. "And it is that energy they're after. Is that why there's an engineer in the group?"

Otto's face clouded over; his eyes moistened. "We're here together in my beloved Languedoc for only a short time. There are things I cannot say. To do so could be fatal to both of us. Perhaps the time will come again when we can share like we used to. For now, I have to trust that you will see for yourself what I can't tell you in words."

A tear rolled down his cheek; he swatted it away. I reached out to touch his hand; he pulled away. We took deep breaths, finished our coffee, and headed toward the church and palace at the far end of the Mercado.

"This town is not without its history," I eventually said. "Yesterday I did some poking around and found that Bishop Jacques Fournier, who eventually became pope, is its hero. I could swear you mentioned him in your writing, but he's not in *Lucifer's Court*. I checked."

"*Crusade*," Otto snapped. "Last chapter, 'The Apotheosis of the Grail.' Come on, Raymond. You should know that. You remember everything."

His reproach felt like a rap with a rod across the knuckles. "I didn't bring my copy of that book with me," I said in mild protest.

"You what?" he fairly screamed.

Stunned by his reaction, I turned toward him. In seconds, his face had become purpled and weather-beaten. His eyes bulged, the pupils dilated.

"You did not bring the book?" His head gyrated as if he was straining to keep it attached to his neck. He punched himself in the face with his fists. "Without the book there is no salvation. Fournier wins and our cause is lost forever." He leaned toward me, his head still shaking. "Never let go of the book, Jacques."

I stepped back. He'd gone mad. He'd forgotten my name. He was talking to someone else. I reached gently for his shoulder. "Otto, it's me, Raymond."

His head twitched one last time. The crazed look evaporated. He sighed twice and glanced toward the cathedral and episcopal palace.

"Sorry," he muttered, "for a moment I went to some other time. But it was this same place, in this very courtyard that still stinks of Fournier's fires so many centuries later."

He had called me *Jacques*. The bishop of Pamiers was *Jacques* Fournier. Had he mistaken me for the notorious Grand Inquisitor? I wanted to ask but did not dare risk sending him back again. I took his arm and turned him in the direction of the hotel. "Enough sight-seeing for now, Otto."

Again I thought I glimpsed the Senegalese off to the side watching us, but he vanished before I could be sure. I held Otto's arm tighter. We both could be going mad.

"We better get back," I said. "The others will be getting up by now."

Before dawn on Sunday morning, our party, equipped with the warm clothing and gear required for a day in the mountain caves, piled into the open Citroen touring car procured before we left Pamiers. Ullmann was at the wheel with Otto next to him as navigator. Steimel and I sat in the back with Erfurt, our scientist, sandwiched between us. From the village of Ussat, where we had spent the night as the sole guests in its dilapidated hotel, we headed south to the Cave of Lombrives, Otto and Paul's destination some six years earlier. After crossing a rickety wooden bridge, we followed the Ariège on its west side, the sounds of the river roaring through the rocks and the auto's motor drowning out any attempt at conversation.

I noticed as we went that Otto was finally unwinding. Wrapped in such splendid surroundings lighted by the sunrise—the white water frothing through the ever deepening cleft, and the distant snow-capped Pyrenees appearing sporadically—he seemed to breathe more easily.

When we arrived in the area the previous day, he had sat tense and hunched as we passed through the town of Tarascon. He flinched when we passed the sign for the Hotel Marrionier, an establishment he had leased in 1932 when he was feeling confident about his fortunes, only to fall behind on his payments after a few months. His rivals and enemies floated rumors of other wrongdoings. Legal action followed, and he was virtually expelled from the county. He had waved the driver through Tarascon with its better accommodations and had him stop in the drab hamlet of Ussat instead.

But now, seemingly revived by a night's sleep and the scenic drive, Rahn directed Ullmann through the turns in a corkscrew dirt road that wound up from the river to the cave area. When we reached its dead-end, Ullmann stayed with the Citroen while the rest of us strained to keep pace with Otto, who led us up a steep footpath that rose for about half a mile to the mouth of Lombrives.

As we organized to enter the gaping maw of the cave, Rahn remained in charge. I bit my lip to restrain the wisecracks his officiousness evoked. Since we were alone on the mountainside, he reverted to German as he barked orders to put on extra clothing, retie boots, secure flashlights and tools to our belts, and stay paired up no matter what. Steimel, who outranked Otto, would co-lead with him. I was teamed with Erfurt, who, now free to use his own language, insisted that he hand-carry his Geiger counter, a sophisticated and delicate instrument customized to measure more than radiation, so he said.

"It will be at least a mile in over slick rocks and tight passages before you need it. You'll want your hands gloved and free. Stow it in your pack," Rahn ordered. Erfurt looked to Steimel, who nodded. The scientist reluctantly complied.

Rahn moved quickly after entering the cave, and Steimel kept up with him. Between Erfurt's clumsiness and the shadows shifting crazily in the glare of our lamps, I realized we might get separated from the forward team. I started to take mental notes of landmarks along the route so I could find the way back on my own if necessary.

"Time out," Rudy called after about twenty minutes. "I have to take a reading. If I'm to be fried by radioactivity, I want to know it's coming."

"Not yet," Rahn called back. But the scientist had already removed the instrument from his pack and turned it on. He played a flashlight over the dials, his ear cocked as if he expected the black box to talk to him. He then walked around and waved his wand towards the numerous cracks and cross caverns in the area.

Rahn too was watching him. "Anything?" he asked.

Rudy shook his head and returned the counter to his pack.

Otto came and stood next to me. He flashed his searchlight upward. "Look there," he said, momentarily dropping his guise as group leader. The beam revealed that we were in an enormous chamber, its ceiling lost in a darkness that could well have been the heavenly heights at night. Icicles of glistening stone, stalactites and stalagmites, graced the massive cavity that flowing and dripping water had hollowed out of solid rock over eons.

"The Cathedral," Otto whispered. "Inhabited since prehistoric times. Originally the underground palace of Pyrene, unrequited lover of Hercules, after whom the Pyrenees were named. The mysterious symbols and engravings on these walls go back to Stone Age times. After the fall of Montsegur, it became the secret cathedral of the Cathars. Their bishop, Amiel Aicard, who escaped from the besieged fortress the night before the chateau's surrender, brought some part of the sacred Cathar treasure here." He lowered his light to scan the walls. "In one of these side chambers are the bodies of 510 Cathars, immured alive here in 1328 on orders from Inquisitor Jacques Fournier."

I gulped. That name, and again associated with crime and cruelty.

Standing a few steps away, Steimel cleared his throat.

"We're close but not quite yet," Rahn said, all business again, "Carry on."

We pushed deeper into the dark through passages so tight and ledges so narrow that I would have gladly turned back if told to. Oddly, my partner Rudy, despite a wider girth and heavier pack, seemed to gain energy as we went.

Rahn, who also showed increasing stamina, pulled up after a further thirty minutes. We had reached a cul-de-sac. "Take a reading here," he said to the scientist.

"It only looks like the end of the line," he quipped. He shone his light on a crevice about four feet high on the wall. "The only way forward is through there."

"You're joking, Rahn." Steimel voiced my same reaction. "All this way to have to stop here."

"Getting through is not impossible. Getting back might be." Rahn glanced at Erfurt, who was still setting up his machine. "When I was last here," he broke into a story I recognized from *Crusade*, "I was fortunately accompanied by Habdu, my manservant, an enormous African almost seven feet tall." The Senegalese in the Mercado flashed into my mind. "He made a stirrup with his hands. I stepped into it and then boosted myself through that crevice."

"No seven-footers here," Steimel said, "and what's the problem with getting back?"

Rahn laughed. The sound echoed through the invisible honeycomb of chambers. "A fluke not likely to happen twice. There's a small platform on the other side. And beyond it a wide channel through which we were walking when suddenly there was the thunder of rushing water. Since we were in the river bed, it was instantly upon us.

"We rushed back to the platform, but it too became submerged under several feet of water. There was nowhere else to go, and the water was rapidly rising. In a short time, it was up to my shoulders. I could swim, but there was no safe place to swim to. I was about to panic when my manservant lifted me onto his shoulders. Must have been several hours that he stood with me that way. The water came up to his chin before it started to recede. He then boosted me back through the crevice. It took more luck and grit, but frozen wet and little left to light the way, we made it out before dark."

A rapid pinging from Erfurt's contraption caught everyone's attention. "Where did the wall of water come from?" I asked Rahn, as we hurried towards the scientist.

"Flash flood," he said. "While we were in the cave, there was a heavy downpour outside. Water soaks sponge-like into the porous mountain limestone until it reaches saturation point. Then it discharged the surplus into riverbeds that lace the interior caverns."

"What is it?" Steimel asked Erfurt about the waxing and waning sound.

Rudy, finally on center stage, put his finger to his lips and walked around waving his wand. Wherever the pings increased in frequency, he closed in until they slowed again. "More than one hot spot," he muttered as if it should not be that way. "A major field beyond the wall, for sure." He looked at Otto. "Did the sample we tested come from over there?"

Rahn nodded. "I had picked it up from the stream bed just before the water broke loose," he said.

"Did you have a detector with you?"

"Just my hands. It felt warm from a distance and much warmer to the touch."

"One of those," Erfurt muttered.

"Avoid burns. Don't pick anything up," Steimel quipped. I got goose bumps.

"Makes some sense, but—" Erfurt continued to scan.

"Watch where you're going," Rahn warned. "There are crevasses around here with the molten rivers of hell at the bottom. So deep we won't hear you splash on landing." No one laughed.

"There seems to be a more localized but stronger impulse coming from something on this side as well," Erfurt said.

"Let's hope," Steimel added, "especially if it means we don't have to climb through that keyhole."

The scientist stopped at a point lined up with the wall but several feet out from it. The counter started to screech. He kicked at the rock and dirt beneath his feet.

Rahn pushed Rudy aside. "Wait. Let me use my hands," he said

Erfurt stepped back. Otto got on his knees and spread his hands just above the ground as if warming them above a fire. He waved them over a broad area and then settled on one spot. There he began to dig with a trowel. We crowded around. Erfurt kept trying to poke his probe into the growing hole, but Rahn pushed it aside. "Give me a minute," he said, breathing hard.

"Ah," he finally grunted. "Got it." With both hands, he lifted out a stone weighing perhaps thirty pounds, egg-shaped with a fairly smooth surface but otherwise nondescript.

Erfurt poked his probe at it. The instrument screeched as if it were a person stabbed with a knife. He pulled it well back; the sound slowed to a more regular pulse. "That's it," he pronounced, not without awe, "radioactive as a horny bitch."

Steimel reached through and touched the rock, which Otto was clutching like he never intended to let go. "Looks and feels like an ordinary stone, but it's making quite an impression on Rudy's scope. Good enough for me. Seems odd it's the only one on this side though."

"They probably found it over there and pushed it through the slot, but lost it in the descent," Otto conjectured. "Whoever discovered it had no Geiger counter." Or sensitive touch like Rahn's, I thought.

I too then stretched my hand toward the stone, curious if I could feel from a distance what the Geiger counter was registering, what Rahn called irradiance in the rock at Hesterbach. I thought I sensed a vibration, but it could have been my body echoing the throbbing Geiger counter.

"Can you turn that off for a moment?" I asked Rudy. He obliged. The vibration, subtle, smooth, but not dramatic, remained consistent. I then placed my hands directly on the stone. The impression was little different than what I had experienced from a few inches away. Disappointed, I began to let go. As I did so, the outer edges of my palms brushed Otto's hands positioned at the ends of the stone. A bolt of lightning seared through my body. I choked off a scream.

Otto caught the reaction. A look told me that he understood what I had felt, but I better endure the pain in silence. The others must not know that something so dramatic had happened. Biting my lip, I moved back. As my distance from the stone increased, the effect of the shock subsided. I found a rock shelf and sat there until I recovered.

Steimel was talking to Erfurt. "Will that be enough for the DP's purpose?" he asked.

"Larger and with a stronger vibration than anything we previously had," Erfurt said, "but, if we are talking about radioactive source material, it's not enough to make anything with." He looked up at the crevice. "We need to send a mining crew in there."

Steimel grunted. "That would be tricky. This is French soil; and if it's what you think it is, the last thing we want to do is let the French know it's here."

Erfurt began packing his instrument. "It's more than enough to do the necessary testing. Getting France to play nice with Germany is a task above my rank," he said.

"Enough for your people too?" Steimel asked Rahn.

Rahn shivered as if he had just been woken up. "My people?"

"The Reichsführer SS. Will he accept that rock as mission accomplished?"

"It proves the claims in my books are true," Rahn said. He then hesitated. "But enough? It depends on what we come up with in Montsegur. This, remember, is the lesser half of the mission."

Chapter 11: Carcassonne, Late 1319

I n their brief meeting after he surprised Jaques in the Basilica of Saint-Nazaire, Arnaud Sicre had boasted of locating the Perfect Belibaste and his tribe of exiled Catalonian Cathars but again insisted that he would only divulge the details to Bishop Fournier. Jaques agreed to relay the message, but he did not go directly to the episcopal palace after the encounter as Arnaud demanded. Mere contact with his former schoolmate made him queasy, muddling even his normally reliable memory. Once apart from his nemesis, he tried to center himself by breathing deeply, but the air cramped in his lungs like a fetid gas. Something about Arnaud was not human. To deal with him required something equally inhuman. To have a chance with him, Jaques had to split himself, allowing one half to battle mercilessly with an unyielding adversary while the other half looked on, ready to yank the fighter should he seem in danger of losing his head or the bout.

It required an hour of pacing through cloistered hallways before Jaques was composed enough to speak to the bishop.

"Out of the question that I talk to him directly," Fournier restated when Jaques informed him of Arnaud's ultimatum. "As a high church official and the presiding judge, I can't be seen as involved with this until Belibaste is standing in my court as a defendant." He toyed with his pectoral cross. "But protocol aside, there is something infinitely more important than appearance here."

He told the youth to close the door. "What I have to say next is for your ears only," he continued when Jaques retook his seat. "I risk telling you such things so you understand the critical nature of our undertaking."

Jaques moved to the edge of his seat. The bishop had never been so intense and confiding before.

"We've already discussed how the church has been at war with the Cathar heretics for the past hundred years and how the theological wrangling between them went on for the hundred years prior to the Crusades—a period when even our saintliest, like the great Bernard of Clairvaux, could not change their erroneous thinking.

"But you should also know that the Cathar movement is only the most recent chapter in a conflict that goes back to the time of the Apostles. In one place, Jesus says, 'Thou art Peter and upon this rock I will build my church.' But in another he proclaims, 'Neither shall they say, 'See here!' or 'See there!' for, behold, the kingdom of God is within you.'

"The Roman church was founded upon Peter and his rock. But some early Christians, citing that Jesus taught that the kingdom of God was within the individual, placed personal revelation ahead of the authority of the established church. They called themselves Gnostics because they held that *gnosis*, personal inner knowledge and experience, took precedence over all authority. To maintain its position and public order, the Roman church declared Gnosticism a heresy, banned its adherents, and prohibited its practices. But that belief system was never completely eradicated; of this the Cathars are proof as they are essentially Gnostics."

Fournier sat back. "What I have to tell you next you will never hear preached from any pulpit. It involves a paradox, a seeming contradiction that evades simple believers including much of the clergy. Nor are you to speak of it after you leave this room."

With piercing eyes, Fournier fixed Jaques's attention. "Gnosticism cannot be eradicated because it contains some vital truth that has been lost to the Roman church. Truth cannot be permanently suppressed. Root it up in one place and, like weeds, it springs up in another, time and again throughout history. Do you understand?"

Jaques hesitated. Was the Inquisitor Fournier testing him? "What is this truth that the Gnostics have that the church doesn't?" he ventured to ask.

The bishop got up and paced the width of the room. "I am a bishop of the church, an ordained successor to the Apostles," he finally said, "and a supposed man of God, but I cannot answer your question. Against the Savior's prescription, I stand in the pulpit or in the courtroom, telling the faithful to 'See here' and 'See there.' Disregard the impulses of your own sinful hearts and do as we say. I judge and condemn the Cathar *bonhommes*, the Waldensian poor men, and the Franciscan spirituals, who set aside those church teachings that contradict what they know through personal experience, people so certain of their inner truth that they seem to pity me when I sentence them to life in prison or death at the stake."

Fournier suddenly halted, his face pale, and leaned over Jaques. "Do you know, boy, how galling it is for a bishop of the church to be taunted this way by rebels and heretics?" He shook his index finger in Jaques's face. "They have a secret. With your intelligence and memory, you must have some clue as to what it is. That key you mentioned once that opens the door. 'Turn the key and it all comes back, as if it's happening again, only faster,' you said."

Jaques gasped and gripped the arms of the chair. The last time they had talked of such things he had been immured in a black wall of stone.

A howling wind came up from behind him. He was tossed about on a huge gray sheet that billowed like the ocean waves driven by a storm. Struggling for balance, he pitched about crazily, only to land abruptly pen and scroll in hand amidst a sun-drenched crowd focused on an intense young man standing on a knoll several yards away. Pointing to the vast marble complex in the distance, the man exclaimed, "I will destroy this temple made with human hands and in three days will build another, not made with hands."

An angry buzz ran through the crowd. One of their leaders challenged the speaker, "It took forty-six years to build this temple, and you think you can raise it up in three days?" The people rose up and, grabbing sticks and stones, rushed towards the knoll, screaming, "Blasphemer." The writer and his scroll were crushed to the ground as the mob rumbled past him.

When Jaques opened his eyes, the bishop was again sitting across from him. He continued as if nothing untoward had occurred. "You might wonder what this has to do with Arnaud Sicre, Guilhem Belibaste, and your dealings with them. Listen carefully. If Belibaste is the last of the Perfects, individuals who claim that gnosis and its associated powers have been passed forward from antiquity into their hands, then he offers a rare if not final opportunity for the church to take back that knowledge and power, which was lost not long after Jesus walked the earth."

Perhaps lost well before Jesus completed his work, Jaques surmised, thinking of the melee in the vision he had just experienced.

"Belibaste, I understand," Fournier continued, "is the most imperfect of Perfects, a murderer, a fornicator, a poor speaker, greedy, lazy, and self-centered. Whatever spiritual powers he might have received through ordination have to be fading, ready to fall from the vine, ripe for picking."

"So, you don't want to capture him just to kill him?" Jaques asked.

"Not before he hands over the key to me."

"And you think Belibaste is so weak that he will surrender what all previous Perfects chose to die rather than give?"

The bishop grimaced. "We can hope. His feckless character could be broken in a number of ways. He has a mistress and had a child with her despite his vow of celibacy; obviously not a strict observer there. A Perfect takes a vow to never to tell a lie. Normally a huge advantage when interrogating one of them. They will verify the identities and hiding places of their fellow Perfects rather than speak an untruth. But will Belibaste keep that vow under examination?" He shrugged. "He's the last of the litter. Our final chance."

From his drawer Fournier withdrew another purse of coins, twice the size of the previous one, and pushed it across the desk to Jaques. "My coffers are open to be used at your discretion. I won't even monitor what you spend or how. Just have Arnaud arrange to bring in our man alive."

Jaques picked up the sack, the coins clinking. He grimaced to think of the many things that could go wrong. "So we're going to trust him?"

"Trust and Sicre can't fit in the same sentence," the bishop snorted. "If his story so far holds up, he's proved to be a clever spy. But the Cathars too have an effective spy network. He could be unmasked or even turned. Put your own considerable cleverness to use, Jaques. Before he goes back, get him to talk. Assume he will tell only what is necessary to insure his fee. Dig out as much of his plan as you can. Talk to him as a friend, then switch and turn bully if necessary. Blackmail in reserve is helpful. You have no vow not to lie. Get enough that, should he blunder or betray us, we can pick up where he left off."

"It would be easier if he didn't hate me," Jaques said.

"Do your best. Your role is important, but it is not in your hands alone. If it is the divine will that the lost key be restored to the church at this time, it will be done no matter what you, Arnaud, Belibaste, or I do. If it is not the right time, it will not happen."

Jaques nodded, mildly relieved. He pocketed the sack and turned to depart.

"One last thing. Perhaps inconsequential, but anything further on that rowdy from the Mercado?" the bishop asked.

Jaques turned back, surprised. "Baldwin?" The time he imagined he saw the Leper King in the marketplace here in Carcassonne could hardly count. He shook his head.

"Keep an eye out for him," Fournier reminded.

With his lack of enthusiasm for his task dragging heavier than the bag of coins in his pockets, Jaques again joined Arnaud in the predetermined alley. With a forced bravado to match Sicre's belligerence, he announced the bishop's decision. "His Excellency still cannot meet with you. I am authorized to handle all aspects of the deal, including dispensing funds. Work with me or not at all." He shifted his stance. The coins clinked in his pocket.

Arnaud's face darkened. He clenched his hands. "You think you're hot dung, Joli. Let's see how long it takes for my fists to cool you down for good."

Jaques ignored the threat. "What can you tell us about Belibaste and his Cathar community to prove that you've found him and have a reasonable chance to bring him in?"

Arnaud folded his arms. "What's it worth to you?"

Jaques handed him two gold coins.

"Three more," Arnaud said.

Jaques gave him two.

"As expected," Arnaud began to Jaques relief, "they've migrated across the Pyrenees into Catalonia well south of Fournier's jurisdiction."

"What town?"

Arnaud jangled the coins in his hand. "These pay for confirmation that there is treasure. Its exact location will cost a whole lot more and will only come a whole lot later. What's to keep you from taking my information, double-crossing me, and trying to find Belibaste on your own?" He showed his teeth. "But you know that won't work, don't you?"

"How so?"

"These people have practiced hiding from the Inquisition for a hundred years. They live in a closed circle. To get inside takes credentials. I'm family. You're not, even if you hail from Tarascon."

Arnaud's tongue was loosening; Jaques was encouraged. "No need to worry. I don't have your knack or stomach for spying. So, tell me about Belibaste. I assume you met him."

"Met him? A very forgettable experience but we slept together in the same bed a few times. And it's not what you're thinking, Joli. They're nomads, disgustingly poor. There was only one bed in the house."

"How'd you find him?"

"Luck, which you have too much of, and dogged persistence, of which you have none. After months of trekking back and forth across those god-forsaken plains in sweltering heat, I was almost out of the precious little money you provided. I suspected a particular town, and, being broke, I took some work with a cobbler whose shop fronted the main street. I could watch the local comings and goings through the window.

"A few days into the job, I heard a woman outside soliciting business for her corn mill. One of the fellows in the shop, who had recognized my accent as Occitanian, mentioned that this woman was from the same region as me. I stepped out and asked her where she was from. When she said, 'Saverdun,' I pointed out that her accent was from Prades and Montaillou. 'Who are you?' she asked suspiciously. When I explained that I was the son of Sybille Baille from Ax, she relaxed and suggested we get acquainted. Turned out that she was Guillemette Maury, sister to Piere Maury, who remembered me as a child before I was sent to live with my father in Toulouse.

"Guillemette and Piere took to me as one of them. That I could claim, based on a vague childhood memory, to have met the great Authier Perfects bolstered that perception. But Belibaste proved more skeptical. One day he visited the cobbler's shop with Guillemette. I recognized him from your description: a burly, bearded man with a guttural voice and rustic manners. He didn't introduce himself, but Guillemette kept prodding me, 'Do, do, sir, in the name of God.' This meant, I found out later, that I as a believer was supposed to perform the ritual *melioramentum* on meeting a Perfect. I couldn't do it because I didn't know how to. Belibaste left quite abruptly."

"Not a good start," Jaques said, noticing, though, that details of the story were credible. "You later wound up in his bed, so how did you get around that opening gaffe?"

Sicre grinned. "With Piere Maury's help, and his gullibility. A likeable fellow, he accepted my Cathar credentials as easily as he absorbed Belibaste's tedious preaching. After realizing that I had offended their leader, I explained to Piere that, although I remained true to my mother's faith at heart, I'd been taken away by my father at an early age and forced to live as a Catholic. He willingly instructed me in the ritual to be used to greet a Perfect."

"So the next time you met Belibaste you performed the *melioramentum* and won his approval?"

Arnaud stiffened. "Not so fast, Joli. That's a crime according to the Inquisition, you know, and your bishop refused to dispense me in writing."

Jaques chuckled. "You'll accept Fournier's gold but not his word. All right then, we'll skip the details. You worked your way in with him and that's what matters."

Arnaud nodded. "Everyone has a weakness. A Perfect is no better than the rest of us." He held up the coins in his hand.

"And what of the rumor that Belibaste keeps a woman?"

"Another weakness and the worst kept secret in Catalonia. He's supposed to be so damned holy, not even eating in the same room with a woman. That old hypocrite enjoys it both ways. His adoring flock reverences his chastity while allowing his liaison with Raymonde Marty-Piquier as a necessary cover against outsiders who might suspect him to be a Perfect. Even though Raymonde's sister walked in while the two of them were rutting like goats and nine months later their daughter Guillemette was born, his sheep can't believe their relationship is sexual."

Absorbing names, dates, and places as fast as Arnaud brought them up, Jaques compared what he was hearing against what he had learned about the Catalonian colony from the Inquisition files. The fellow was reporting credibly if not completely.

"Not all members of the group are equally infatuated with their leader or his teachings." Arnaud went on. "For instance, Jean Maury, Piere's brother, a usually quiet and sickly type, is prone to expressing contempt for Belibaste, calling him 'the Cathar Pope' to protest his hypocrisy."

"Does Piere correct his brother's irreverence?"

Arnaud shrugged. "Not that I saw. Piere is easy going, tolerant of everyone and everything. He coddles Belibaste but allows Jean to treat Belibaste as he chooses. Jean and Belibaste both take advantage of him; Piere is not stupid so he knows it. But he allows it. He's so generous that he should have nothing left. Yet he's actually the smartest of the bunch, certainly the most prosperous with the largest flocks and the most profitable business deals. Belibaste may be their spiritual leader, but Piere is their provider. The community could not survive a week without him. Nor would I have been accepted there without Piere's approval."

Curious as he was about the human aspects of these outcasts, time constraints forced Jaques to push on. "And how did you explain your discovery of their supposedly secret colony without arousing suspicion?"

"Despite my Catholic upbringing, given my mother's burning for heresy and the confiscation of her property, it stands to reason that I would desert the church responsible for such crimes and seek to realign with the remaining relatives of its victims. It was logical to look in the area where the Cathars are known to have migrated."

"So you told them that you were searching for specific lost family members?" Jaques asked.

"As the bishop's extensive records certainly show, I have two additional heretical relatives on my mother's side. First, and most important to move our plan forward, is my aunt Alazais, a wealthy woman with a teenage daughter, who a few years back slipped into hiding somewhere in the Pallars region."

"The Pallars is just south of the border. Did you go there and find your aunt and her daughter?" Jaques asked.

"You're throwing baited hooks into the stream again, Joli," Arnaud warned. "All you need to know about the Pallars is that, while still in Aragon, it borders the bishop's jurisdiction and is thus critical to the mission. When I left their settlement about a month ago to report back, I told them I was headed north to look for Auntie Alazais and her daughter in the Pallars. Conveniently located for our purposes across the pass from Pamiers, I told them I would at the same time sneak back into Languedoc to gather badly needed news and provisions before I returned. Not only do I have an alibi should I be recognized here, but I was given the names and addresses of heretics still in this area so that I might deliver messages from their Catalan relatives to them. Do you follow so far?"

Jaques nodded. "You've come away with a lot of intelligence about their operations on both sides of the Pyrenees."

Arnaud poked Jaques in the chest. "Indeed, but you and your bishop only get what you pay for after you've paid for it. Next, I must prove to the Catalonians that Aunt Alazais is actually hiding out in the Pallars; that she remains dedicated to the Cathar cause; that, although crippled by gout, she would dearly love to relocate to the community in the south; and that in the meantime she wants a good Cathar spouse for her marriageable daughter. To get them to believe all this, I must immediately provide evidence that Aunt Alazais is wealthy enough to make a bequest sufficient to ensure the survival and prosperity of Belibaste's community for years to come."

"And how will you do that?"

Arnaud stepped up and slapped Jaques in the pocket. The coins clinked. "That's where you come in. I do hope you brought enough. A gold piece offered at the proper time can induce a man to believe the most preposterous things, even those against his best instincts and interests. So, let's see what you brought."

Jaques held up a finger. "What about your other Cathar relative? You said there were two."

Arnaud shrugged. "My brother Bernard, also an ordained Perfect. Takes after my mother in everything. He provides me with further cover. Quite reasonable that I'd be looking for him too. According to sources, he was last seen over a year ago heading for Majorca and from there had likely gone on to Italy. Looking for him gives me another convenient excuse to scout around."

Jaques shook his head. "Your brother is a Perfect and still alive? Fournier is under the impression that Belibaste is the last Perfect."

Arnaud sneered. "No need to disabuse him. My brother too was a traitor to the family. I will find him and, after that, Belibaste will be the only Perfect left."

"But—"

"No more questions, Joli," Arnaud barked. "Let's see the money. It better be enough."

Jaques pulled the bag from his pocket. As he did so, a slip of paper came out with it and fell to the ground. Arnaud scooped it up and read it aloud: *The only treasure that endures, the pearl of great price.* The note Jaques had made for himself during the previous session of the Delicieux trial.

"I'd hoped for something important," Arnaud snorted, tossing the note back. "For now I'll take the treasure in that bag. Let's have it."

Jaques pulled back. "Hold on. You don't necessarily get all of it now."

"I'll decide that," Arnaud said, grabbing the sack and counting its contents. Finally, he looked up and smiled. "Enough to allow me to indulge Belibaste's more expensive tastes. The better to impress him with Auntie's potential largesse."

He pocketed the money and turned to leave but not without a final warning. "Remember this, Bishop's boy. I didn't tell you as much as I did because I trust you. I just want the bishop to see that I have a specific plan. It may take another year to set things up, but the trap will be ready when I next return."

He started to walk away but then turned back one last time. "By the way, Joli, I made some discreet inquiries among the Cathar faithful. For a priest of the Roman Church, they regarded your Père Fontaine quite highly."

Chapter 12: Tarascon, June 1937

T he evening after the trek through the Lombrives cave, with the three Germans fatigued enough to retire early and Otto so enthralled with his precious stone that his cigarettes went ignored, I stepped out of the hotel to get some air before retiring. *Sabart*—the source word, *victory*, for Sabarthès—kept repeating in my head as I followed a dirt path down to the east bank of the Ariège. There I sat on a rock and breathed in the soothing sound of the rapids and the calming sight of the sluices glinting in the moonlight. My chest relaxed enough to admit a huge gulp of the pine-scented evening air. I feel at home, I thought for no particular reason.

A nighthawk squawked, and I was about to mimic it when a huge paw was suddenly slapped over my mouth. Stunned by the unexpected assault, I failed to react before a powerful limb grabbed me around the middle. In that moment of panic, I thought I was being attacked by some enormous Sabarthian monster.

"You must be quiet. I am friend," my captor hissed. At least it was human. "Look down at my right hand, the one around your waist," he said, his accent distinctly foreign. I did. Without relaxing his arm, he flashed his three middle fingers three times.

The hand over my mouth loosened. "You understand?" he asked.

"333," I sputtered. He released his hold. Even in the dark I immediately recognized the Senegalese who had been spying on me in Pamiers.

"My name is Habdu."

"Ah, Rahn's manservant and his St. Christopher," I quipped, even though my heart was racing faster than the river rapids.

"We must not speak here. Follow me."

Gliding like a jungle cat, he led me through the woods, a mile or so, from Ussat back to Tarascon. He stopped behind a small house with dim lights coming through its rear windows. Approaching through a yard cluttered with shrubs and statuary, he knocked on the back door. A balding middle-aged man with thick round glasses, every bit the eccentric professor even in his robe, opened it.

"I have your man, Monsieur Gadal," Habdu said, "although I gave him a fright."

As surprised as I was by my abduction, I was shocked to discover that the staid Antonin Gadal was the man behind it. Otto and Paul had both mentioned Gadal as the custodian of all things Cathar in the Sabarthès. He grew up next door to the famed Tarasconian historian, Adolphe Garrigou, who in turn appointed Gadal heir to his extensive knowledge about the region's Cathar roots. Such expertise earned Gadal, a schoolteacher by profession, a place on the local tourist board. He had unlimited access to the area's caves and historical sites, which the intrepid docent then promoted to visitors as Cathar chapels and hiding places.

Although some friction was reported in their relationship, Gadal generously shared his theories and the physical evidence backing them with Rahn during the latter's stay in Tarascon in the early '30's. Otto in turn acknowledged this mentorship in *Crusade Against the Grail*: "It is an enormous satisfaction for me to be able to thank Monsieur Gadal here, and pay homage for his disinterested help,"[30] he had written.

"I truly apologize for the rough way you were brought here," Gadal said as he ushered me into a room that looked more like an unkempt combination of library and museum than a living area. "Ladame told you there would be a background presence. But Habdu grabbing you in the dark? We trusted you had a strong heart. It had to be done without the others, especially Rahn, knowing."

He poured glasses of wine and we sat. "Unusual times require unusual means," he said, raising his drink. "We enjoy the niceties as we can." They toasted and sipped.

"So what did the Germans bring back from up there today?" he then asked.

For a moment I hesitated. Ladame had warned about spies spying on spies. Habdu had given the required sign but Gadal had not. Impertinent as it felt to challenge the man, I demurred. "I don't understand," I said.

He looked puzzled, and then smiled. "Ah, hocus-pocus," he said, flashing the required set of triple-3s. "But your vigilance is to be commended."

I then summarized the day's events, pinpointing the location of the find and detailing the results evidenced on Erfurt's Geiger counter. Showing no surprise over the location or scientific nature of the stone, Gadal was intrigued by its varied effect on the members of the party. Erfurt's was unknown as his hands did not come into direct contact with the stone. Steimel felt nothing on touching it, although he was impressed enough to grant that the find met the mission's requirements. Otto was able to locate the stone by sensing it with his hands, and it induced a drug-like rapture in him afterwards. And I initially experienced a mild vibration followed by a powerful shock when Rahn's hands, my own, and the stone were in simultaneous contact.

"It should be enough to convince Himmler that Rahn is on to something significant," Gadal said when I had finished my report, "but not dangerous in its own right. Fortunately, the main lode is on French soil although the Germans might attempt to change that should they decide they need more of the same from the place where the stone came from."

That there was some mysterious science behind it all started to dawn. I tried to understand. "Given the differing reactions the stone produced, I think that the magnitude of effect is proportional to something associated with the person touching it. Something emotional, a subjective factor. But it also registered on Erfurt's machine, so it has to be objective also. When not being touched, it is neutral; its internal power can only be sensed as blips on the machine. But put it in contact with the appropriate human dynamo, and it's a whole different story."

"You're quite warm," Gadal said. "And we have to make sure that the Germans stay interested only in what they can read on their Geiger counters."

This puzzled me, but before I could frame my question about it, Gadal pushed on. "Where does your party intend to go from here and when?"

"Montsegur," I said. "In the morning, I believe. Tuesday the latest."

"And has Rahn spoken to you or the others about what he hopes to find there?"

I shook my head. "Not yet, but he has always been hell-bent to get back to that mountain."

"But now the stone has put him in some sort of altered state?"

"Intoxicated, at least."

"A dangerous development."

Another cryptic statement given without explanation, as seemed too frequently the mode of communication with these EC people. Again I worried that Otto's well-being was not a high enough priority for them.

Gadal noticed my discomfort; nevertheless, his response seemed severe. "It may appear that you have been tossed into the middle of this solely because of your relationship with Otto Rahn. But"—he wagged his index finger for emphasis— "there are no accidents. Typical of a Swiss, you might want to believe that you are immune to the forces of history that affect the rest of the world. No one is blessed—or can afford to be deluded—to that degree. Even the most neutral observer affects what he observes."

The docent's speech reminded me of 333's at Dornach when he insisted that I was a part of their movement just by virtue of being alive. Feeling that Gadal too was operating with information he was not willing or able to share with me, I turned petulant inside. I had come to France willing to contribute despite personal danger, and here I was being selectively shunted aside. I shifted in my seat.

Gadal seemed to read my mind. "A lot of this maneuvering may seem unnecessary to you," he said. "Languedoc has been a land of intrigue ever since the Crusader armies marched across it, intent on destroying its enlightened form of government, vibrant culture, and lofty aspirations. Its spirit did not die despite the best efforts of generals and inquisitors to kill it, but it did go underground, at first, literally, into the caves you visited today. And then organizationally into secret associations where admission is only by invitation and initiation. The surface story, which must be allowed to run its course, is unintelligible to those unaware of the deeper forces behind it."

Rather than consoled, I felt more confounded by this further abstraction. "Why do I feel that everyone else knows what's going on here, but I remain an outsider?" I demanded. "When Otto came here years ago, you welcomed him, took him through the caves, and taught him so much about the Cathars that he wrote a book—two books—about them. But I feel like I am in the middle of someone else's dream without a guide."

Gadal smiled, but I sensed his disappointment with my level of understanding. "Europe was very different when Otto came here in 1930," he explained. "In addition to the political instability after the Great War and the Treaty of Versailles, the world was in the middle of the Great Depression. In Germany Hitler's National Socialists were just one of several groups of thugs chasing power.

"Then the world knew little about the Languedoc and the Cathars, and cared less. But a few of us here—and there have always been a few of us—felt it was time for our history, our ways, and our secrets to be revealed. They would provide a powerful alternative for a world in chaos and rapidly getting worse. We sensed a powerful yearning for substantial change. The major established religions had proved themselves outdated. Radical spiritual thought and practice, some of it quite primitive, were being revived. Blavatsky, Gurdjieff, and Crowley. Some leaned towards a left-hand path more dangerous for the majority of people than the bland orthodoxy it aspired to replace. Mankind needed a balanced middle way. The current guardians of the Cathar tradition—Deodat Roche, myself, and our few dedicated supporters like the Countess Pujol-Murat—deemed it time for the Cathar tradition to rise again after 700 years underground.

"When the author and theosophist, Maurice Magre, published his novel about the Cathars in 1931, *The Blood of Toulouse*, we supported his effort to broadcast the story we had held in trust for so long. When his group, the Polaires, a Parisian society investigating esoteric phenomena, wanted to explore the physical remnants of Catharism here, we assisted them. That they were allied with certain German occult organizations like Thule Gesellschaft and entertained eccentric German theories like Hans Horbiger's World Ice Theory did not disqualify them. Who were we to call others' hypotheses bizarre? Otto Rahn came here with a Polaires credential, the appropriate education, talent for research and writing, and fervor for the Cathar cause. His linking Wolfram von Eschenbach's *Parzival* to Cathar history was the work of an intuitive genius, like that of Schliemann. That he was a foreigner meant that the message would be carried beyond France and to the world. He no more knew then that the Nazis would triumph than we did. Without political interest or aspirations and with limited personal resources, he accepted any support, German or otherwise, to get his research done, published, and promoted.

"Otto's difficulties began when his knowledge of the Cathars added up to more than it should have been, given what he studied and what we taught him. He began to say and write things, to discover objects and inscriptions, to manifest sensitivity to emanations from places and items like the stones of Lombrives that indicated he had the endowments of an initiate without ever having been initiated. In other words, Otto Rahn was more Cathar than we who have spent our entire lives studying Catharism."

"He may have been a Cathar in a previous life, and being here restored his memory of it," I said.

The docent nodded. "We considered that and tried to confirm it, but he can't be placed in our records. Something is still amiss," he said wistfully. "Perhaps his initiation was incomplete or interrupted since he falls short of the maturity that the full course of training and practice would have afforded. No doubt, a prodigy aware of his own talents but lacking a vital component that balances him."

I nodded. Gadal had pinpointed a peculiar agitation I sometimes sensed in my friend. "Which may explain," I said, "why disaster often overshadows his brilliance; why they expelled him from Tarascon then and the Nazis have him trapped now."

Irritation at my own predicament resurfaced. "But this sheds no light on my role here and what I can do to help him escape from a situation bound for disaster," I protested.

"Are you not overlooking the obvious?" Gadal said.

"I don't see how."

"Observe, Raymond. Where were you today? What did you see? Where are you now? What are you hearing? How did you come to know Otto? What are you learning from your relationship with him? How did you come to be associated with Paul Ladame, 333, myself, even Himmler? How long can a dream go on before you realize that you are dreaming it?"

He looked at the clock. "You better get back," he announced abruptly. "Habdu will take you, and it is best Otto not know about our meeting."

As the Senegalese was hurrying me out the door, Gadal added a final word. "Before you leave Tarascon," he said, "you two must visit the chapel of Notre Dame de Sabart. Pay attention for clues to the key that unlocks the door you seek to open."

The foursome was already up and in some commotion when I joined them for breakfast the next morning in the hotel dining room. A townsperson had intimated to the establishment's owner that his guests might be German spies. The innkeeper, who appreciated our party's income during his slow season, relayed the report to Steimel. I immediately suspected Gadal's intervention in the person of the informant and was awed by the speed with which he and the EC had assessed and reacted to my report the previous evening. Himmler would get his sample stone and nothing more from the cave of Lombrives.

But rather than depart immediately and risk appearing intimidated by the rumors, Steimel ruled that we would stay put for the day, allowing him time to consider the mission's next move: would they continue on to Montsegur, risking further exposure, or return home satisfied with the single specimen?

Otto remained passive during this discussion, his knapsack containing the Lombrives treasure at his side. The others knew he wanted to continue on to Montsegur but expected him to abide by Steimel's decision.

With the day of waiting on our hands, I decided to pursue Gadal's suggestion to visit the church of Notre Dame de Sabart, an innocuous activity befitting tourists to the area. Not sure if Steimel would allow the two of us to venture out without a chaperone, I asked Otto in front of the group if he wanted to join me for a walk.

No one objected until we were headed out the door. Then Steimel noticed that Rahn was wearing the backpack containing the stone. "You'll have to leave that here," he said.

Otto was about to remonstrate but then yielded. "Don't let it out of your sight," he said to his senior officer.

During our stroll along the river path towards the bridge we would cross to reach the church, he chattered about the find. "The stone's tangible evidence supporting the claim that I made an important discovery here," he said, "but it's also more personal, Raymond. For years, there's been something dead inside me. That changed the minute I felt the vibrations from that rock. The flow of warmth and energy it releases inside me surpasses any other experience on earth." He punched my shoulder. "Yes, even making love with you."

He turned for a moment and looked toward the hotel. "Even with only that small a distance between us, the effect is lessened. It sounds silly, but even now I feel the loss."

The magnitude of effect was proportional to something associated with the person touching it, I had said to Gadal. In Rahn the impact had lasted over time. "Is it something in the stone or something in you?" I quizzed him.

His head jerked toward me; his face pursed into a question mark. Then he broke into laughter. "It's not really funny," he finally spluttered, "but the way you said that reminded me of the wounded Grail King Anfortas at the point where Parzival finally asked the crucial question that healed him: 'Uncle, what is it that troubles you?'"

He abruptly sobered. "But about your question: right now all I know is that I feel bereft without the stone."

I was curious to know his thoughts about the lightning effect I had experienced in the cave but asked instead. "And you are counting on it to create some sensational effect that impresses Himmler?"

He shrugged. "The stone does as it pleases."

We came within sight of our destination: a stone church, modest despite its crenellated tower and false battlements in later Romanesque style. Several granite blocks from its Carolingian predecessor remained embedded in its façade.

"So what's this sudden urge of yours to make a pilgrimage to a church?" Otto asked. "I imagined you would have preferred to visit Bishop Fournier's country house on the other side of Tarascon, the palace from which he ordered the notorious immurement of the last group of Cathars in the caves up there. You remember that story in the last chapter of *Crusade,* I'm sure."

I recalled only vaguely but nodded anyway. Jacques Fournier's name had come up in the conversation that sent Otto momentarily out of his mind in the Mercado a few days earlier.

Suddenly he slapped himself on the temple. "The bishop's boy," he exclaimed. "Did they call you the bishop's boy?"

I was startled. It seemed as if I had indeed been called that before but could not remember when. It rang true as some unwarranted insult from the past. Was Fournier, the blood-thirsty Grand Inquisitor of the Cathar era, the bishop in that phrase?

When I looked at him quizzically, Otto only shook his head and changed the subject. "I was in the church several times when I was here before." he said. "You go on in. Meanwhile I'll poke around the tombstones in the cemetery out back."

"See if there's one for Fontaine, a priest, once pastor here in the early 1300's," I said without knowing where the name or date came from.

Pulling the heavy wooden door closed behind me, I reflexively dipped my finger into the holy water font and blessed myself. *The bishop's boy*, but that would have been later. Here I was just a little altar boy—.

I stopped myself. Nonsense was coming out of my head, and I had to quit listening to it. *Pay attention for clues to the key that unlocks the door you seek to open*, Gadal had suggested the previous night. I surveyed the present day church, unpretentious with its wooden pews, bare walls and modest high altar. Here the current congregants attended Mass and the distraught among them burned candles to relieve their guilt or pain.

I crept through the nave, abashed that my shoes slapping on the stone floor disturbed the silence. Wall plaques related the shrine's history, a legend so familiar that I had to have heard it before.

At war with the Saracens, Emperor Charlemagne is in mortal peril from an enemy ambush as he leads his army through the Ariège valley. His steed senses danger and refuses to proceed. The Virgin Mary in a vision advises the emperor to prefer his horse's instincts to his own machismo. He heeds her, halts his army, and avoids defeat. A battle never fought becomes a great victory—*Sabart*. Later his men dig on the spot of the vision and uncover a statue of the Madonna buried upside down, its face as black as the earth from which it is taken. This image is named Notre Dame de Sabart, Our

Lady of Victory, and the original church on this location becomes her shrine.

Realizing that this place once housed such a miraculous icon sent an unanticipated surge through my hardly religious body, an energy similar to what I experienced the previous day when I first approached Otto's stone. But no lightning followed. There would be no direct contact. The original Notre Dame de Sabart had disappeared during one of the French religious wars.

In its place was a statue of Our Lady of Lourdes, the White Lady of the Pyrenees as some called this composite of blue sky, white clouds, and golden sun. The ethereal opposite of the earthy Notre Dame de Sabart and a recent rendition of the Holy Virgin. Bernadette Soubirous's apparitions in Lourdes, a nearby Pyrenean village, occurred only in 1858.

I rested in one of the straight-backed pews and studied the image for some time, shifting now and then to try to catch its upraised eyes. Suddenly, my body began to sweat and my legs quivered. Eyes still riveted on the statue above the altar, I clenched my teeth and tried to breathe as a torpor pressed down on me so hard that I thought the bench might crack beneath my weight. Even though I then retained a tenuous connection to the present, I was surrounded by sounds and sights not proper to the current time and place.

At first I seemed to be seeing a segment of the Charlemagne story. There was an army and an impending battle, but since the church did not exist prior to the emperor's vision of Notre Dame de Sabart, it had to be later in history. Our group had a leader, but we were not the soldiers of a hero's army of hunters. We were about to be vanquished, the hunted. We rode no gallant steeds that saved us from impending disaster. Most of us were barefooted and clothed in rags, our disastrous destiny apparent. Unlike Charlemagne's, our foe was not an infidel force invading the valley from Spain. It was the French and Catholic armies ensconced behind us in Tarascon itself.

Our people were not devotees of the Madonna, and most regarded our having to use her church as a staging place to be an ill omen. But I cherished her shrine even with the monstrous things I knew about the church that established it. I still revered the humble Black Madonna despite the proliferation of such places solely dedicated to extracting coins from the pockets of the credulous.

A man supporting himself with a staff limped toward me. He was wearing an open black cloak. A stained white tunic embossed with a red cross showed beneath it. A gnarled old fellow with wild eyes slightly askew, he could have been John the Baptist just come down from his saintly pedestal on the church wall. He creaked into the seat on my left.

"It's settled then," he said with the graveled voice suited to a veteran warrior. "After dark we climb to the cave. You three will go well ahead of the rest. The main group will follow. I'll take up the rear with those of our fighting men who cannot hope to complete the journey. The bishop's men will eventually figure out where we went and follow us into the cave. My force will hold its position in the cul-de-sac fronting the crevice beyond the Cathedral.

"God willing, this gives you the time to cross through. It will take several days, but you are well supplied. Do not let Jean falter. In his hands are the gifts of Spirit for all mankind. Trust your own gift of memory. It will provide you with guideposts as you need them. It is an equal gift, also required by Spirit to complete its quest in the temporal realm. That's as much as has been given to me to understand. I trust you two will know what's next when that time comes."

"But Mathène, his wife?"

The warrior hunched forward and rubbed his face with his hands. "Younger than both of you and strong. She should be able to make the crossing. But—" He sighed.

"She's a woman, devout but beautiful. You are concerned that she might seduce Jean as his female companion did the last Perfect," I said, puzzled by the meaning of the script I was being given to follow.

"She will be a distraction," the older man grunted, "but is essential, so I've been told. You two will have to remain undistracted. On the other side there are a series of safe houses manned by our people: Miglos, Junac, and Montreal-de-Sos."

Bemused that he felt the need to repeat instructions I had already memorized, I said, "And in Montreal-de-Sos we will find further clues to our roles in all this."

At this point I heard footsteps coming up behind me. I shuddered involuntarily. Before I could turn, a pair of hands gripped my shoulders. "Arnaud," I gasped.

It was Jean. "Not this time," he said cheerfully, "and never again after tonight."

"Let's pray that traitor is among their troops when it meets up with us at the keyhole," the warrior said. "I've foresworn the *consolamentum* to retain my right to plunge a sword into that wretch's guts."

"God forgive you, and may the sacrament be yours in the very next lifetime," Jean said. He released my shoulders. "I'll come around."

I looked to my right. Otto was ambling up the aisle.

"Praying or napping?" he asked when he reached me.

I felt like I had just woken up but did not want to admit to being caught in an elaborate daydream. Forcing it aside for later consideration, I returned to the point we were on when we parted at the church entrance. "The bishop's boy," I said. "Seriously, Otto, what made you think of that?"

He grimaced. He had no idea what I was talking about. "I was the one out in the graveyard, but you look like the one who's been seeing ghosts," he said. "We better get back. I think the others are planning to hightail it back to Germany, and they're not going to take my stone without me."

I studied my friend, and for a moment the split in time recurred. *Do not let Jean falter. In his hands are the gifts of Spirit for all mankind.* Here I was, powerless to save Otto from the Nazis. For the sake of the stone, he would follow them back to Germany, even without visiting his beloved Montsegur. I looked towards the White

Lady. She was still gazing skyward. Antonin Gadal had framed the question perfectly: *How long can a dream go on before you realize that you are dreaming it?*

After we left the church, I asked Otto if he had found any sign of the priest Fontaine in the graveyard.

He shook his head. "Maybe he was buried here once, but after Père Clergue of Montaillou was unmasked as a heretic, Fournier assumed that all Catholic priests, past and present, were potentially Cathars, especially here in Tarascon, their last stronghold. The *perfect* disguise"—he grinned at the pun— "until Fournier caught on. He had the bodies of every last one of them dug up and burned. His strategy, like Abbot Amalric's at the battle of Béziers, was preemptive: *Kill them all and let God sort them out.*"

Chapter 13: The Carcassonne Dungeon, Late 1319

Jaques made his way through a narrow side street toward his quarters after the bittersweet encounter that had sent Arnaud Sicre, money bag in hand, on his mission to trap the Perfect Belibaste. Although the tough's threats and disdain—*Bishop's boy* indeed—diluted the achievement, Jaques could claim that he did his best as Fournier had prompted him to do. Better, in fact, than expected. He quickened his step, looking forward to a good night's rest before the wait for Arnaud's return began.

As he was about to emerge from the mouth of the dark alley into the square, he heard footsteps grinding on the gravel behind him. Before he could turn, a hand slapped across his mouth. It choked off a scream. A muscular arm gripped him around the waist. Someone else pulled a wool cap over his head and eyes.

"You're in no danger unless you fight us, Jaques de Sabart," the man holding him warned. There were at least two of them, and he was not a random target; they knew him by name. "I'll take my hand off your mouth now, but one squawk and we'll break every bone in your body. Understood?"

Jaques nodded, having already concluded that cooperating offered him the best chance to find out who his assailants were, where they were taking him, and what they wanted.

Both men were brawny, the one on his left about his height and the other taller. They moved quickly but adjusted some to his pace—

quite considerate for kidnappers.

As a boy he had practiced walking in the dark, learning to switch to alternate senses when deprived of vision. In addition to sound perception, hearing could be used to compute distance, relationship, and space, largely by noticing echoes. Feel and pressure could be used to discern elements normally left to vision: indoors or outdoors, enclosed or open, populated or isolated. And imitating the obvious capacity to see in dreams with eyes closed, Jaques had taught himself to do something similar when awake with moderate success. One had to shift his observation point from behind the shuttered eyes to a position in front of them, he had discovered

They had turned him around and were taking him back down the alley past the café where he had just met with Arnaud. Had the two of them earlier been so wrapped in discussing their own spy mission that they did not notice that they were being spied upon? An error of amateurs.

Several blocks further and into the laborers' district, they turned him left towards the Count's Castle. After several more minutes, and thus in the vicinity of the drawbridge, an abrupt right and then another left. They had to be following the castle's outer wall.

Another turn and a pause. "Watch the stairs," the shorter fellow said. With his attention occupied by the numerous landings and turns, Jaques lost count of the number of steps and the direction in which they were heading. After the first flight, the echoes told him that it was now all underground. They never stopped for a gate; if any existed, they were open. Only at what proved to be the end of the descent did the taller man let go of him to unlock the barrier. They then wound through a labyrinth of corridors obviously designed to discourage intruders. His captors were prepared to frustrate those like himself who might try to defeat a blindfold.

They halted. The tall man rapped on a wooden door. "It's thirteen twice with the Bishop's boy," came his coded response to a challenge from within.

A key turned and a door groaned open. Jaques was nudged into a room that felt spacious and of normal temperature. No cramped damp cell yet, he thought gratefully.

"Well, Joli Jaques," a familiar voice called in greeting. "We meet again. And this time, not by accident." Baldwin the Leper King. Before Jaques could express surprise, the cap came off, and his abductors slipped back into the hall.

Jaques stared around the room, bright after the blindfolding although only lit by a pair of candles. "Take it all in," Baldwin said, not unkindly.

Jaques quickly memorized the layout of the stark, stone-walled cave of a room. Probably a makeshift office from the crude table covered with papers and a few books, two open, and fronted by four high stools. A command center from the lack of personal effects. The sole decorative artifact was off in a corner: an outmoded and well-used suit of armor mounted upright on a frame. Thrown over it was a mantle, once white but now yellowed and stained. Sewn upon it was a large red cross that stretched down from neck to waist and across from shoulder to shoulder.

He glanced back at Baldwin, who still looked like the blustering vagabond of the marketplace, but a cleaner and calmer version.

"Did you guess?" Baldwin asked in a teasing tone that Jaques could not imagine the other Baldwin adopting.

"No," Jaques said.

Baldwin smiled, a grotesque gap between his teeth. "I apologize for the rude way you were brought here, but it couldn't be helped. You're a busy fellow, and I didn't want to interrupt you."

The gall, Jaques thought. He abducts me by force and then acts as if he had invited me to a mildly inconvenient business meeting. So mannerly, considerate, and even urbane. He'd had a moment of compassion during their encounter in the Mercado, but that instance of sanity passed so quickly that I took it to be a fluke. Did I have it backwards all along? The real Baldwin is this gathered individual sitting across from me; the garrulous ne'er-do-well is the act.

Despite his handicapped position as a prisoner, Jaques would have to tease the real Baldwin out. Taking a seat on one of the stools, he glanced back to the suit of armor. "What's with the Templar outfit?" he asked. "The order's been outlawed for a decade. A costume for another role you play perhaps?"

"It's complicated, and there's little time for chit-chat. We have to get you home before you're missed," Baldwin said.

"A problem you could have avoided by not kidnapping me in the first place," Jaques shot back. "But then I'm just the Bishop's boy, stuck in the middle of God knows what and no one bothers to explain."

"Perhaps I can provide some answers," Baldwin said.

Jaques looked away. "Maybe I don't need your fabricated answers. I'm not blind. Obviously something's going on between Fournier and you, with Arnaud Sicre a part of it too. But it's really none of my business. I'm just the messenger. I'm content to do that, no questions. What I can't understand—" He stopped short, realizing that what he was about to ask contradicted the noncommittal attitude he had just invoked, however sarcastically.

Baldwin sat on the stool across from him. "What don't you understand, Jaques?"

In sudden frustration, Jaques verged on tears. "Why does it have to be so complicated, so full of intrigue? You hang around, playing the fool, in front of Fournier's court in Pamiers and again here in Carcassonne. You were trying to get his attention. Well, you got it. Only now he's quizzing me about you as if we were old pals. And I don't even know who you are.

"And your connection with Arnaud Sicre. I only know there is one. You were there, so conveniently, to help arrange it when I needed to meet with him. Then all the time he's away, you are nowhere to be seen, only to show up in the marketplace adjacent to St. Nazaire's on the very day he returns. And—what a coincidence! —your thugs waylaid me this evening only minutes after a meeting between Sicre and me. Don't deny that I am sniffing in the right direction here, Baldwin."

Jaques sat back, framing his captor with piercing eyes as he had observed the bishop do to his captives.

Baldwin sighed. "You're right. And if I thought I could fool you for long, we would not be having this conversation. Even with the blindfolding and misdirection, I assume you have a good idea as to your current location?"

Jaques hesitated but then said, "In the castle dungeon area adjacent to the west wall, situated so that no one can get here from the inner city except by the way we came in. From the outside it can only be reached through a secured tunnel under the walls."

Baldwin nodded appreciatively. "And what do you suppose goes on here?"

This time Jaques refused the test. "I'm not here to be baited with silly guessing games," he said. "But I better not find out that you're Fournier's agent with this charade set up as some sort of loyalty trial. And there's reason for me to think that. If you weren't working for him, why would he tolerate your constant rabble-rousing in Pamiers and again here? Anyone else would have lost his head on the first offense."

"Excellent observation, no matter if fact or not, and further evidence of your intelligence." Baldwin pursed his lips. "But suppose I am Fournier's agent. You just criticized his methods for testing loyalty. In faulting him, are you not also faulting the Inquisition he heads and the church that instituted it?"

Jaques squirmed on his stool. He has seen similar arguments return convictions in court.

Baldwin voiced the expected conclusion. "From there I could conclude that, even though a scribe in the Inquisitorial Court, you are more aligned with the heretical cause than with the church you outwardly serve. Does that not make you a heretic also?"

Setting aside the real possibility that Baldwin might be the bishop's agent, Jaques thought to parry his captor's question with a judicial argument he had learned from Fournier himself. The legally scrupulous inquisitor once explained, Jaques recalled, that a circumstantial path of evidence like the one Baldwin had just traced out was only admissible if one or more additional witnesses could be produced to prove out the original conversation from which the charge of heresy was to be derived. If Baldwin was in fact testing him at Fournier's behest, the bishop would have told him to keep that crucial second witness present during any interrogation.

"You could try to make the case, but you'd lose," Jaques stated.

Baldwin looked quizzical. "You seem quite sure."

A mouse fighting a cat had to parlay every trick. Even though Baldwin's reaction showed that he was not Fournier's agent, Jaques chose to push on without explaining how he had figured that out. "So, if not Fournier, who do you work for? And what does it have to do with me?" he asked instead.

Baldwin propped his elbows on the table. "Let's take your second question first. I'm neither permitted nor able to answer it completely, but I will share enough for you to decide to embrace or reject your personal role in this, a destiny that from all evidence you have been preparing since birth."

Jaques smirked. It sounded too grandiose.

"Please hear me out," Baldwin begged. "It will sound incredible, maybe ridiculous, at first. I remember my disbelief when a mentor sat me down as a young man and told me similar things. But, I assure you, he was right. Are you willing to listen?"

Curious now, Jaques nodded.

"With your father's death shortly after your birth in Tarascon, Père Fontaine, pastor of Notre Dame de Sabart, became your guardian. I too was close to the priest. My family was from Miglos, on the mountainside just up the Vicdessos Valley."

"The old Knights Templar castle connected to their commandery in Junac," Jaques said. He glanced again at the shrouded suit of armor. "So you were a Templar knight in one of those outposts until the Order was disbanded."

"I served there earlier, but, just before that fateful October 13, 1307, I was reassigned to our small out-of-the-way facility in Saint-

Just-et-le-Bézu, whose chief officer just happened to be Pope Clement V's nephew. Bézu was not touched in the initial raids that closed most of our operations. But once Clement agreed to King Phillip's demand and permanently disbanded the Order in 1312, those of us at Bézu also had to disperse. I returned to the Ariège in disguise. You were already in your early teens and Père was in poor health."

"Why don't I remember seeing you there, not even in church? I thought I remembered everything."

"You did, and that's why we made sure you never saw me," Baldwin said with a wry smile. "But I also had to hide because former Templars were marked men. Phillip suspected the Order had unsurrendered treasure, and the hunt for anyone left was relentless until Grand Master de Molay, Phillip, and Clement all died around 1314.

"To complicate matters in the Ariège, the Inquisition, which had been restrained by both church and king at the turn of the century, was again operating with full force to quell the Authier revival. And, as you know well, the Inquisition's authority remains supreme to the present day. We still have to be extremely careful."

Jaques gulped. "We?" he blurted out, glancing at the cross on the tunic in the corner. "You were a Templar, a fearless crusader subject to no power other than the Pope. The opposite of everything the Cathars stand for. What did the Templars have to fear from the Inquisition, whose only business is heretics?"

"The authorities can apply the label of heretic to any group they want to deprive of rights, treasure, and lives. They used this technique to destroy the Templar Order, until then the most powerful military and commercial organization in Europe, in a single night. Charges of every sort of heresy and depravity were leveled against us. Confessions were extracted with cruel torture; retractions, once those who had confessed under duress regained their senses, were met with immediate death at the stake. This should not be news to one who sits as a witness to such proceedings every day."

Jaques reddened and looked down. "I'm not a witness in Fournier's court," he murmured. "I am only a scribe keeping the official record. I have nothing to do with the crimes or their sentences."

Baldwin rubbed his beard. "You are too aware to grant yourself such complete immunity, Jaques. And are your hands still as clean now that you gave Arnaud Sicre money in exchange for the life of the Perfect Belibaste?"

"How'd you find out about that?"

Baldwin chuckled. "I was there in the square when Arnaud first proposed it: *If I were to serve up some Cathar leftovers, one of them a Perfect, I can name it as my price.*"

Jaques felt his embarrassment turning to rage, not so much that Baldwin knew far more than he was admitting but because he himself had been fooled so thoroughly all along. He lashed out. "And I suppose you know that Arnaud threatened to squeal to the Inquisition that Père Fontaine, my mother, and other Tarasconians were Cathars heretics if I crossed him up?"

Jaques paused momentarily, his breath stopped by the thought that had suddenly entered his mind. "Now who, Baldwin, might have fed Sicre such damning information?" he asked his captor.

The older man grimaced. "It got your attention, right?"

"But it's a lie," Jaques shouted, getting to his feet and heading towards the door before realizing that he could not just walk through it.

Baldwin motioned him back to the stool. "Little here is what it seems to be. But before you can understand the current situation, you must know what led up to it."

Pouting openly to show that he was not in the mood to cooperate, Jaques sat.

"Let's go back to the destiny I mentioned earlier and to your childhood in Tarascon. As your mentor growing up, Père Fontaine taught you a way to live, learn, and believe that I trust you later found valuable even after he passed away." Jacques nodded.

"While you were growing up, you labeled him a Catholic priest. Now what if that label was changed to Cathar Perfect? Would switching role labels from priest to Perfect change who Père was?

Would switching doctrine labels from Catholic to Cathar change his teaching?"

"I suppose not," Jaques muttered, aware of the implications to admitting so.

"Père Fontaine held that labels didn't matter as long he prepared you for life by giving you the truth. He knew that both paths were equally dangerous. Catharism for all its purity was the victim about to go extinct. Catholicism with all its power was the persecutor, and the force it used to suppress would one day rebound to suppress it.

"His solution, which he had tested on himself, was to have you experience both paths. Even though he could not call it such, he instructed you early in the ways of Catharism. Then to allow you to experience its alternative, Roman Catholicism, he arranged for you to attend the Dominican school at Saint Sernin. He knew that one day you would realize he had directed you down a double path. You might believe he deceived you or at least question his judgment in placing you in such an ambiguous position. When that time came, he planned to explain why he had done what he had done.

"But when age and failing health made it clear that he would not live to see you reach that stage, he asked me to carry on for him after his death. There was no reason to intervene while you finished at Saint Sernin or immediately afterwards. You held your ground when the Dominicans tried to lure you into the priesthood and then secured a good position in the Court of the Inquisition. During this time, I stood by incognito, waiting and watching. When Arnaud Sicre arrived in Pamiers seeking revenge and reward, I saw it as the signal for action. Slowly at first, of course. A tap here, a tweak there, nothing sudden so you spooked."

Jaques got up again, thrust his hands in his pockets and began to pace. "Until tonight when you sent your thugs to pick me up. I doubt Père Fontaine would have approved of that move," he said.

"He knew I was a warrior, not a Perfect, and that our approaches would be complementary, not the same."

Still struggling with his world turned inside out, Jaques could only retort, "What authority decreed that you—or Père Fontaine—could run, or ruin, my life this way?"

Baldwin came over and tried to put his arm around the youth's shoulder. Jaques shunted him off. "At least come sit while I try to answer that," Baldwin coaxed.

Jaques again shuffled back to his stool. On taking his hand from his pocket, the slip of paper again dropped out. On picking it up Jaques read it aloud. "*The one treasure that endures, the pearl of great price.* Quoting you, ironically," he said. "I have no idea what you meant."

"You actually know quite well; far more than most."

"No more riddles, soldier," Jaques barked back. "I'm sitting on several seats here, and they're all hotter than Hell. Facts please."

Baldwin sat back and glanced toward the red cross on the Templar tunic. "I mentioned the Cathars and Templars, their rise and fall. But they are only recent chapters in an already lengthy but unfinished book."

"I know about the Gnostics," Jaques interrupted, "going back to the first centuries of Christianity and their long conflict with the Roman church. Fournier told me some about them, and I read anything I could find further. Assume my background knowledge is adequate. I'll ask when I don't understand."

"Then we can take for granted that you know this Gnostic movement evolved over the millennia to its present form, which includes Cathars, Templars, and other groups that seek spiritual awareness through direct experience rather than external authority. Also true is that the coalition is currently reeling in defeat and on the verge of extinction. What might your destiny be in relation to all this? I will stick with credible facts, as you requested. But I ask that you remain open to factors that may emerge as I proceed, elements that all but the initiated would find incredible."

"Another riddle. Are you assuming I am one of the initiated?"

"I sound vague only because I must put complex ideas into simple words. You get to decide your own status as an initiate. I only ask that you hold that decision until you have heard me out," Baldwin said. Jaques thought about it and nodded.

The man continued. "It is evident that time, place, and circumstances of birth set many of the boundaries for the course of a life to follow. You were born in 1298, near the start of the end for both Cathars and Templars. That year Pierre Authier and his brother Guillaume returned from Lombardy to organize the last Cathar revival, which served to awaken the slumbering Inquisition to renew their persecution. That same year the Templars under Grand Master de Molay conducted their last campaign against the Turks, and its failure accelerated the outcry against the Order."

"An inauspicious time to be born," Jaques replied, "but is it personally significant? Many people were born in 1298."

"Indeed, but the course of those lives would have been different had they arrived a hundred years earlier or later." Jaques had to agree.

"Your birthplace was Tarascon, the westernmost of a chain of towns along the Ariège that had become the last refuge north of the Pyrenees for Cathars dogged by the Inquisition. It was to the caves above Tarascon that earlier, just before its fall in 1244, four men from Montsegur, an ordained Perfect among them, escaped with a precious Cathar treasure. Tarascon is located at the mouth of the remote Vicdessos Valley, which contained several Templar fortresses that remained impregnable even after the dissolution of the Order. So Tarascon, at the time of your birth and since, has been a sacred region and secure haven for both Cathars and Templars. A place where their beliefs and blood intermingled."

"I admit that Tarascon affected the course of my life as no other place could have done," Jaques said.

"And that time and place produced the people close to you. To perform his ministry despite the Inquisition, Père Fontaine had to be both priest and Perfect, a requirement that led him to arrange that you too be educated in both faiths."

"I follow so far," Jaques said, "but it's still general. Any child from the area might have fit into your mold—even Arnaud Sicre."

Baldwin shrugged. "Like it or not, each human being, even those on similar courses, has a unique function. Père Fontaine and I had much in common, but I could not have travelled his road nor could he have walked mine. Also mysterious and just as marvelous: our individual functions combine to form one organization, a group operating as a unit towards a common purpose."

"It doesn't take a genius to figure out where you're heading," Jaques interjected. "But if you aim to prove that my destiny is aligned with a heretical Gnostic coalition of Templars and Cathars, you'll need more than circumstantial evidence. And if this is about my alleged phenomenal memory again, be advised that just about everyone, including Bernard Gui and Fournier, has already noticed and tried to exploit it. You are at the end of a long line."

Baldwin smiled smugly. "I am here in Père Fontaine's stead, remember. He was the first to notice your extraordinary memory, fine intelligence, and unusual gifts of internal vision. Without inciting a false pride that put you above others, he nurtured your talents as a gift from the Good God, gifts given through you to the entire coalition. Over the years, he advised me of your progress, telling me how you were advancing 'in wisdom, age, and grace,' and together we observed how perfectly your talents matched the need to preserve the essence of the Gnostic movement for posterity."

"How so?"

"Throughout its troubled history, the Gnostic tradition has been conscious of the vital role of memory for its continuance. Should the incremental record be obliterated or critically altered, the entire movement would stall. But it is equally aware of the mortality of its temporal organizations. Its facets—the Cathars and Templars being the latest—coalesce to accomplish a purpose appropriate to the period. They grow in order to accomplish that purpose and then fade away once that task is completed. The last act required of any unit before its demise is to create a permanent record to be handed on. Around the time of your birth, both Cathar and Templar leadership knew that their remaining life span was short. Your first decade of life proved them tragically correct.

"The Cathar treasure, secreted in the caves at the time of the fall of Montsegur, became a target for destruction by the reinvigorated Inquisition. Likewise, the Templars after the attack in 1307 knew that their written legacy was in extreme jeopardy. In the current decade, the situation has worsened. Few Cathars or Templars now remain alive. Our treasure and records, no matter how well hidden, are subject to the elements and loss of location. The progress both groups made in forwarding the Gnostic line seems doomed to disappear without witness or record."

Jaques let out a whistle. "Vanished without a trace. As if it never happened," he said, the finality of such an event stunning him.

"Time and place are not on our side," Baldwin said. "It may be hundreds of years before it is safe for the Gnostic way to reappear. To continue then from where we are leaving off now, we need a channel to carry our memories across the centuries."

Jaques was suddenly terrified. That anyone would think of him as the instrument to serve in this extraordinary capacity struck him like a hammer blow. A screeching swarm of frantic objections roared through his mind, battering the walls of his brain. It shoved him out the back of his head. He landed again on a hill overlooking the Temple of Jerusalem.

He watched in awed confusion, as the skies darkened, the ground shook, and an agonized cry came from the man being crucified.

Beneath the cross, like twin candles, two women stood. One, dressed in white, her face bright as the sun, gazed skyward, her eyes only for him who was dying. The other, all in black with skin color to match, looked towards him, a young man a scroll. "Write what he speaks," she requested, "so that all might remember his final words."

"Jaques, come back." Baldwin was standing over him, slapping his face lightly.

The youth opened his eyes and blinked, attempting to see in a room almost as dark as the scene from which he had just emerged. "The Temple of Jerusalem," he gasped. "The crucifixion."

Baldwin took his shoulders and held them. Jaques could only allow the waves of tears come and go as they would. Finally, their pounding against the shores of his mind subsided and an eerie silence settled in.

"What happened there?" Baldwin whispered.

"It was dark so I did not see his face, but I heard him cry out in Aramaic, *Eli, Eli, lama sabachthani. My God, my God, why hast thou forsaken me?* Then the woman, not Mary the mother of his birth, but the black Madonna, the mother of his death, instructed me to write down his words so all might remember them."

His hands still on the youth's shoulders, Baldwin stepped back and peered at Jaques. The eyes of both were wet with tears. "Even then it was your destiny," he said. "You were the witness and the scribe at Golgatha."

The two then bowed their heads and stayed in silence for a while. Finally, Baldwin said, "Come, Jaques, I will walk you home. We will talk on the way."

Chapter 14: Geneva, November 1937

For some time after my return to Geneva from the aborted junket with the Germans, the whole excursion to the Languedoc had the texture of a fevered dream, ironically excepting those parts of it that were actually dreams or dream-like events. Fragments like *the bishop's boy and pay attention for clues to the key that unlocks the door you seek to open* whirred around my brain like angry wasps unfazed by my attempts to shoo them away. And flashes of faces, some like Gadal or Habdu from the present world and some from a presumed past like the Templar or Jean, appeared to me willy-nilly awake and asleep.

Otto had been correct in assuming that Steimel would choose to return to Berlin rather than risk continuing on to Montsegur. As much as I wanted Gadal's opinion on the events in the church, there was no opportunity to report back to him. The morning after our visit to Notre Dame de Sabart, we packed back into the Citroen and returned to Pamiers, where the Germans took a train north and I headed east for Geneva. With the others now keeping closer watch, Otto and I had no chance to steal a proper hug goodbye, an omission more difficult for me than him. With his precious trophy on his back, he seemed anesthetized to the pangs of parting and the possible perils that lay ahead.

I did review the actual events of the trip as I tried to piece the adventure together in my journal, but they seemed trivial against the mysterious vision of the Cathar refugees huddled in the old shrine. That crafty wizard, Antonin Gadal, had cast a spell with his question, *how long can a dream go on before you realize that you are dreaming it?* What happened that day in the church seemed permanently etched in my brain. Back in Switzerland, I found I could replay it on demand like a film but in full color and life-like depth.

As I witnessed the scene as my present self and participated in it as a character in the medieval period, I realized that it was but a fragment of a vaster pageant that went farther back in the past and reached into the deeper future in a way beyond my ability to comprehend.

I sensed precisely who I was in the escape scene—I had allegedly lived as that person for an entire lifetime—even though I did not know my name back then. In the incident, no one had addressed me by name. Nor did I think of myself in the third person—not so odd as I rarely think of myself as *Raymond* now. A name did sit right on the tip of my tongue, so to speak, and should someone ask, I'd say it was *Jaques* with the Occitanian spelling not the French *Jacques*. And since he was from the Sabarthès, I'd give him the surname *de Sabart*. I felt quite comfortable calling this intimate stranger *Jaques de Sabart*.

Then there was the group's leader, the Templar character. He too came without a proper name, but he was a Knight Templar. The Templars were named for the Temple of Jerusalem upon the ruins of which the Order's headquarters was built. I recalled that several of the early kings from the French house of Boulogne who reigned over the Kingdom of Jerusalem, the principality created when the Crusader armies wrested the Holy Lands from the Muslims, were named Baldwin. But it was Baldwin II, also known as The Leper King after the cruel disease he had contracted as a child, whose moniker was the best fit for the hunched and disfigured Templar warrior of the Sabarthès. So Baldwin the Leper King he became.

The group's antagonist, although he was not named and did not appear in the church, was obviously the bishop. In time, place, and character, this individual matched up with the notorious Bishop Jacques Fournier. Now having Otto's *Crusade Against the Grail* in hand, I checked what he wrote about this medieval prelate in its final chapter. It confirmed that his inquisitional mop-up operation against the few remaining heretics in the area occurred a hundred years after the start of the papal crusade against the then-dominant population of Cathars in Languedoc.

The short biography mentioned, among other details, the burning of the chief Cathar revivalist, Pierre Authier, and the prosecution of a recalcitrant Franciscan, Bernard Delicieux. But most of the space was devoted to the bishop's vindictive battle to exterminate the Cathar remnant that took refuge in the vicinity of Tarascon:

> At the entrance to the Sabarthès, at the doors to the town of Tarascon, you can still see a country house called Jacques Fournier. The bishop of Pamiers directed the war against the heretical troglodytes from there; as long as the caves of Ornolac were not de-hereticized, the triumph of the cross was not complete.

Reading this my heart rate quickened. Otto mentioned the bishop's country house on our way to Notre Dame de Sabart. Tarascon as the setting and Fournier as the antagonist could be verified historically even if Jaques and Baldwin could not. But it failed to explain why everyone insisted on calling Jaques *the bishop's boy*. The bishop and the boy should have been on opposite sides.

There were, however, three people in the pageant who did come with names: Jean, Mathène, and Arnaud. I checked over the pages Otto devoted to Fournier's story without discovering any matches. His conclusion to the section, however, projected that the Tarasconian heretics did attempt an escape and may have been successful:

> It seems that the last Cathars fled to the mountains through hidden subterranean chimneys known only to them. From there, they probably emigrated to more hospitable lands, where the sun shone more purely because it was not darkened by the smoke of the execution pyre, and where the stars to which they aspired seemed closer.[31]

Otto had to know more than he put in the book. I made notes of items on which to question him further when we next got together. Our lack of communication since we went our separate ways in Pamiers was disquieting but expected. He had not objected, but he had to have been disappointed that we did not go on to Montsegur. He probably resented that I seemed to favor the decision to curtail the mission. Since I did not have his current personal address, I thought it best to wait for him to contact me.

Until we could talk, I could only conjecture about the three people named in the vision. None of the names nor what I could come up with on their personalities triggered the sense of familiarity that the Templar, the bishop, and Jaques did.

The first, Jean, seemingly a central character in the scene and the *raison d'etre* for the escape, was evidently a Cathar Perfect, perhaps the only one left, whose safety the remaining community, otherwise doomed, had entrusted to Jaques. The two did not know each other well. They had been acquainted for a few years but most of that at a distance. Nevertheless, I, as Jaques, took my responsibility for Jean as critical. Had the Templar not insisted that both our lives were equally important for the mission's ultimate success, I would have given my life to save his. Additionally, I felt a strong personal attraction to this handsome, guileless, somewhat fragile youth who seemed oblivious to both the efforts of his enemies to hunt him down and of his friends to save him. Jean and Otto had much in common.

The second person named, though not appearing in person, was the woman Mathène. Identified as Jean's wife, an incongruity for a celibate Perfect, wedlock was likely a ruse to mask Jean's status as a Perfect. Jaques knew her only well enough to wonder if it was prudent to have her along. Otto might be able to identify a historical character that fit Jean. If he came married to a woman named Mathène, we would have a ringer.

Finally, there was Arnaud, obviously a villain. Jaques, who otherwise seemed courageous, had called out his name in fear and was shaken to think of him creeping up from behind. Jean, a sanguine and forgiving sort, also wanted nothing more to do with the man. And The Templar was willing to trade immediate salvation for the chance to run Arnaud through with his sword. Certainly Otto would be aware of such a notorious individual even if I had gotten his name somewhat wrong.

Although I had faulted Otto for his excessive infatuation with the Lombrives stone, here I found myself so mesmerized for several months by the details percolating up from that daydream in Notre Dame de Sabart that I lost sight of my friend's quite perilous position back in Germany. But it only took one casual sentence from Paul Ladame at the start of a lunch to which he had invited me in mid-November to return Otto's plight back into the center of my concerns.

"You've heard, of course, that Rahn has been assigned to do military service for disciplinary reasons with the Oberbayern Regiment in the Dachau KZ," Paul said.

I gagged on the spoonful of soup I had just put into my mouth.

"Evidently not." Paul continued too blithely. "Some trouble with his SS minders after he got back from the Languedoc. Not surprised. Otto is not overly endowed with discretion."

I barely heard him. My mind had gone crazy. My personal impressions of that hellish place resurfaced along with recent news items about the horrors taking place in the burgeoning Nazi concentration camp system. Most people thought the reports too extreme, but, having been to Dachau, I could imagine the atrocities described all too easily.

"Are you sure?" I finally managed to ask. "How did you find out?"

Paul shrugged. "I can't give names, but the source is reliable. With your family business ties to Dachau, I thought you'd have been one of the first to know."

"I don't keep up with them. I'm the Perrier black sheep, remember? But Otto—he could be in great danger."

Paul finally looked a bit less blasé. "How so?"

"I haven't heard from him since France, so there's nothing recent, but the Nazis already have enough on him if they want to get him. His Jewish blood, however diluted, and his homosexual tendencies, which he barely disguises especially when drunk, are swords hanging over his head. He returned to Germany feeling all omnipotent, high on that damned stone. I should have never let him out of my sight."

Ladame sat back. "I am truly sorry, Raymond. With everyone so busy on so many other things, no one has seen to keep you informed. I feel responsible. After your mission in the Languedoc that proved to be an extremely valuable service to the EC, it was I who insisted that you not be used any further to tail Rahn. I felt it was too much to ask of you."

"You were afraid our feelings for each other might jeopardize your operations." I made no attempt to hide the hurt.

"So you know, 333 and Gadal did not agree with my assessment, but they went along, agreeing to put you in reserve for emergencies."

"And Rahn being sent to Dachau was not an emergency?"

"We thought you were in touch with him and that he had told you. After all, it's routine for an SS man, even in an administrative position, to be assigned to the camps for training and toughening up. And with the SS now in sole control over the KZ system, Himmler would want all his officers competent in camp management."

I relented a bit. "I too was preoccupied since I got back, and I don't like being Otto's tail, but our personal friendship should not exclude me either. I can do both if necessary, and I proved it in France. Otto knew nothing about my meeting with Gadal, and how it triggered the rumor that they were German spies, which then caused the mission to be aborted before he fulfilled his wish to revisit Montsegur."

Paul nodded in approval. "In a choice between Otto and the EC mission, you chose the higher good. We are in your debt. Still, it surprises me to find out that you have no idea what happened with Otto once he presented his find to Himmler."

"And you do?"

Paul nodded. "We have one agent assigned to keep an eye on Rahn, but their contact is intermittent. Another, who is working in the Deutsche Physik with Rudolf Erfurt, provides more regular information. Leaving out names and locations for security reasons and abbreviating details to save time—there is still the business I wanted to see you about—let me summarize what we assumed you already knew.

"Himmler's receipt of the stone of Lombrives was equivocal. He seemed skeptical of the science but pleased for his own purposes. He examined it carefully but from a distance. He experienced no noticeable reaction although he was careful not to touch it.

"He ordered it taken to the SS castle in Wewelsburg for safe-keeping and further examination. Rahn was in the delivery detail and was then assigned to be its primary guardian. He remained unflappable, even ecstatic, as long as he was near it. He took his typewriter into the room where it was kept, and his keys could be heard steadily throughout the day and evening. He did get nervous when Erfurt split off a piece for lab work, but our agent managed to calm him. He kept to this productive writing routine until Karl Wolff, who regarded Otto's niche too cozy for an SS officer, ordered him back to Berlin.

"His reaction on finding the stone was something we didn't count on. It was like giving an alcoholic unlimited access to liquor. But when Wolff cut him off from the source of his addiction, some sort of powerful energy emanating from that stone, Otto turned to regular alcohol. Our people couldn't determine exactly what went on with him back at headquarters, but he evidently went berserk. He was eventually reined in for some reproachable conduct that he admitted to and said he bitterly regretted. To make amends, he promised Himmler to abstain from alcohol for two years and accepted the tour of duty at Dachau as punishment."

Disturbed as I was by Otto's predicament, I was relieved that it was not worse. "Did your source have any idea how long he will have to remain in Dachau?" I asked.

"A couple of months, three or four at the most. If he behaves, he should be out shortly," Paul said.

"Then what?"

"To be determined. By Himmler rather than Wolff, he can hope. And so can we. That's what I wanted to talk to you about."

I went on full internal alert but maintained an outer calm. "I hope I can help," I said.

Paul looked around to make sure no one was eavesdropping. Satisfied we were alone, he said, "I expect that you keep up with the news and are aware of the political situation."

"You mean the Germans. They've kept their sword-rattling to a minimum since they reoccupied the Rhineland last year. Hitler has gone to great lengths to project only peaceful intentions."

"Not for much longer. Until recently we had assumed that it would be some years before the German military machine was ready to launch a war of aggression. However, we now know through reliable internal sources that Hitler, despite his public promises that Germany has no intention of breaking the peace, is accelerating the rearmament process and preparing to go to war in months rather than years.

"This past November 5th he called a secret conference in which he outlined his plans to acquire that coveted *Lebensraum*, elbow room, to which he claims the superior German race is entitled. Attending the gathering in the Reich Chancellery were Germany's two Army commanders, Field Marshal von Blomberg and General von Fritsch, Navy Chief Raeder, Hermann Göring who heads the reconstituted Air Force, Foreign Minister von Neurath, and Hitler's adjutant Colonel Friedrich Hossbach who took the minutes. He began the four-hour meeting by requiring each man to swear an oath of secrecy and then announced that what he was about to say should be regarded as his last will and testament in the event of his death.

"The Lebensraum issue, he stated, must be resolved by 1943, 1945 at the very latest, to guard against military obsolescence and the aging of the Nazi leadership. Germany must take the offensive while the rest of the world was still preparing its defenses. Although his ultimate goal was to acquire territory in the East, namely Russia, he remained focused on preliminary objectives: seizing Austria and Czechoslovakia to protect Germany's eastern and southern flanks.

"He reviewed the available options to capitalize on the military and political weaknesses of France and Britain and let it be known that he preferred to strike as early as next year. Evidently, Hitler's casual acceptance of the immense risks of starting a large-scale war in Europe shocked several in attendance, especially Blomberg and Fritsch, who strongly objected not on moral grounds but for practical reasons. In their opinion Germany was not ready for war; even by 1943 they would not be adequately armed.

"Despite Hitler's arguments for the accelerated plan, the two commanders remained opposed and the Führer was incensed. It is expected that both will soon be relieved of their command, thus depriving Germany of two of its few remaining rational voices in authority. Hitler's is a high-stakes gamble, but best guess, he will take it and win.

"To counter this radical change in timetable and to consider our response, 333 has called an emergency meeting of the EC next week. All options available to us will be discussed and all assets will be considered. Your work with Otto on Himmler's genealogy and participation in the German expedition to France, both invaluable and appreciated, gives you a unique avenue into the heart of the Third Reich through the office of the Reichsführer-SS. To make use of it or not will be decided at the meeting. We wanted to find out beforehand if you are available and willing to participate. It is likely to be more complicated and dangerous than the French venture. That's all 333 would tell me other than to say that his current preferred plan was unlikely to work without you."

It was a watershed moment and I felt it deep within my body. A wave of foreboding washed over me; what Paul proposed could end in catastrophe. I breathed in deeply, looking to find the courage to match the situation. Something refused to budge.

"One question first," I said, "and it has to do with that stone. I experienced its awesome power and saw its effects on Otto, and yet it seems ludicrous to give it so much attention. Do you know what it is made of?"

Paul shook his head.

"There are never no secrets, you once said. That again," I replied, letting my chagrin show.

"Not in this case," he said. "Even those with a scientific background can't answer that satisfactorily. I'm not sure that anyone, not even 333, knows completely, but I can tell you some things about it. The specimen your expedition turned up was curious but not unprecedented. What Rahn delivered to Himmler is an example of a peculiarly magnetized dark green moldavite, what the Russian explorer to Tibet, Nicholas Roerich, classified as a Chintimani stone. On the rare occasions these appeared in history, they were considered extra-terrestrial in origin, meteorite fragments in scientific terminology. They have played a fabled role as the source of mysterious physical, mental, spiritual, and social power. The lost crystal capstone of the pyramids, Roerich's Tibetan Treasure of the World, the power source within the Ark of the Covenant that brought down the walls of Jericho, the Kaaba Stone in Mecca, the Emerald Tablet of Hermes Tresmegistos, the alchemists' Philosopher's Stone, and Lucifer's crown jewel as defined by Wolfram von Eschenbach. All of these storied objects are said to be of this Chintimani class."

I whistled. "That would account for Otto's bizarre behavior after finding that thing. He was smitten like a schoolgirl in love. Take it from him and he lost his mind."

"Yes," Paul added, "his case proves that the specimen he found is unique, baffling, and potentially very powerful."

But not nearly as powerful as the combination of the stone, Otto's hands, and my own, I mused, remembering the lightning blast that might have killed me in the cave.

"So, may I tell 333 that you are available to work with us further on this?" Paul asked.

I breathed again, prayed the courage would be there when I needed it, and nodded assent.

Chapter 15: Pamiers, Late Summer 1320

In the beginning of summer 1320, as Jaques's trepidation over Arnaud Sicre's expected return mounted, the crowds, which gathered nightly in the Pamiers Mercado in search of diversion from the hard labor of growing season, were steeped in excitation from a different source. That year the rumors leaked from Bishop Fournier's court were unusually titillating. Béatrice de Planissoles, a noble woman formerly married to the deceased lord of the heretical mountain community of Montaillou, had been snared in the Inquisition's net. The dowager was summoned in July to answer multiple accusations. In addition to the routine allegations made against every suspected Cathar, there were charges of witchcraft and black magic, evidenced by personal items for casting spells discovered in the woman's purse. But it was the chatelaine's storied reputation for lascivious, varied, and frequent carnal encounters despite being a grandmother that buzzed through the public conversation like a swarm of cicadas.

In her initial appearance before the court, Jaques transcribing, Béatrice displayed the fire with which she allegedly conducted her sexual affairs in denying any heretical affiliation or other wrongdoing. Incensed by her disdain and convinced she was lying, the bishop ordered her back for further questioning the following week. In the meantime, she fled Pamiers accompanied by her latest priest-lover, the young Barthélemy Amilhac. Both were quickly captured, and Beatrice, now also charged with contempt of court, was brought back to face Fournier. Evidently chastened by the failure to escape, she became more cooperative. Nevertheless, her carnal proclivities, which like her heretical connections were largely stale affairs from her past, were inflated to epic tales of debauchery in passing from mouth to mouth around the town.[32]

Jaques attempted to record her convoluted trial in his usual detached manner but could not avoid noticing that the woman, despite her age and legal predicament, exerted a subtly erotic effect on the audience, himself included. To quell such reactions, he had to look away from her and filter out the seductive tones from her voice. The same allure appeared to ensnare Fournier, but he responded by locking eyes with her and becoming more aggressive. The more charm she exuded the more caustic his questions became. In the heat of one such clash with the bishop, her flashing dark eyes and quivering lips caught Jaques's attention. He thought of the Black Madonna, the mother of death, who in the Golgatha vision had bid him write the Savior's dying words. Nothing of this went into the record, of course, but he mentally wagered that Fournier might win the battle but Béatrice certainly the war.

Distracting him otherwise during the Montaillou trial, which stretched over months and involved dozens of defendants and hundreds of witnesses, was Arnaud Sicre's prediction: *Follow Fournier's current case in Montaillou. Fontaine isn't the only heretic to wear priest's clothing.* Was Arnaud pointing to the young vicar Barthélemy, who, though smitten by Béatrice whose Cathar ties remained tenuous, showed no heretical inclinations of his own? The only other cleric in the Montaillou scene was its parish priest, Pierre Clergue, but he, while mentioned in the trials by both defendants and witnesses, was not reputed to have heretical leanings.

Jaques was grateful that occasions for such speculation were rare. Enough time had passed since his abduction by the Templar in Carcassonne and the subsequent revelations about his childhood that he could perform his court duties without his other opposing role intruding.

How the Templar had explained the circumstances of his rearing made too much sense for him to argue against it further, even if some of his emotions remained offended over the obvious manipulation by Père Fontaine, Baldwin, and even his mother. In their walk back to Jacques's quarters after the kidnapping, the Templar had taken pains to delineate the changes that awareness of his dual education might make in his life.

"Now I'm further trapped in this bizarre chess match," the youth had protested then. "Père Fontaine's scheme has me in a cul-de-sac where any move puts me at odds with either one side or the other. It is as if I must serve two masters at the same time."

Baldwin grimaced. "You must—for now. But you can do it without jeopardizing your integrity. The plan was designed to make that possible."

"Not that I can see."

"Your role as a scribe to the inquisition court is neutral," Baldwin reminded him. "You record the names, words, and beliefs of the Cathars and their accusers. To preserve his legacy, the bishop will archive your manuscripts. By doing so he will unintentionally preserve the Cathar legacy for a posterity that will likely empathize with the persecuted over the persecutors. In serving the Roman Church you also serve the Cathar cause."

It made sense. "A stretch but it justifies continuing to work in the court," Jaques replied. "But what of my involvement with Arnaud? I've already paid him to set a trap for Belibaste. To back away now would stir up considerable suspicion."

"Not necessary," Baldwin said. "There too you are right where we need you to be. Continue to do what is in Fournier's best interest."

"Even if Belibaste is about to be taken and sent to the stake?"

"Especially then. It would not be the end even if it must appear to be so. Allow it to unfold. And keep in mind that you are not in this alone. Further instructions will be available when you need them."

Jaques huffed, his impatience with riddles resurfacing. "So the bishop's boy goes about the bishop's business as usual. When, if ever, do I get to quit this divided life and become the person I really am?"

"The right time to decide will be apparent when it comes." Baldwin was not about to get more specific.

"And we better hope," Jaques muttered, "it comes before the bishop gets wind of my double-dealing and sticks me on one of his infernal torture machines. You're betting that I can keep my mouth shut."

"Templars don't bet. You've heard nothing from me that must be kept from Fournier."

"The Gnostic alliance between the Cathars and Templars?"

"The Inquisition has suspected as much. The reason they went after both groups."

"Yours and Père Fontaine's connection with the heretics of Tarascon?"

"Also suspected but best kept under your hat as long as possible." Then Baldwin grinned. "Even if they forced something damning out of you, it wouldn't hold up. We would invoke Fournier's own rule: Two witnesses are required for verbal testimony to be admissible." He looked around. "Do you see any witnesses present?"

Jaques blushed. "So you knew about that rule all along. In the dungeon I thought I had that one over you. Since you kept no witness in the room, I assumed you were not doing Fournier's dirty work."

The Templar clapped him on the shoulder. "I knew, but it was a brilliant deduction nevertheless," he said. "And it performed double duty. You found out that you could trust me, and I learned that I owed you my respect."

One evening, after editing the day's transcripts, gratefully some easy tax delinquency cases rather than Béatrice or more of the Montaillou heretics, Jaques slipped down the corridor towards the exit. He didn't see Fournier's open office door before he heard his name called.

He took a deep breath and rubbed his brow to make his fatigue evident as he went in. "Good evening, Excellency."

"Sit for a moment." The bishop looked intent. Realizing it could be anything, Jaques stopped checking the possibilities. Fournier was known to read thoughts.

"It's been a long day for you, so I'll be brief. You have to know there's a lot of talk going round," the bishop started.

"Lady de Planissoles," Jaques guessed.

Fournier chuckled and waved his hands. "That woman. Everyone's talking about her. She'll eventually tell me more than I want to know. Women always do. They can't help it."

He looked down and frowned. "No, it's Bernard Delicieux. Word just came that he died in prison in Carcassonne. No one's calling it suicide, but he refused to eat for weeks before he passed. Some still think of him as a saint. They blamed me when he was sent to prison. Now they'll blame me for his death."

Fournier's worst nightmare. Jaques recalled their conversation about the monk during the trial. Brother Delicieux had become another martyred hero.

"You were there in Carcassonne, Jaques. You saw my utmost patience over the entire four months. Guilt or innocence aside, he was not willing to compromise much less cooperate. His stubbornness forced us to resort to torture and threats of excommunication before he would confess to obstructing the Inquisition even though thousands witnessed his revolt against the Dominicans in 1303. He had to be convicted of treason; his ill-conceived conspiracy to align southern Languedoc with the kingdom of Majorca was a direct affront to King Phillip II, who had earlier favored his side against the Dominicans. We exonerated him on the specious count of involvement in the murder of Pope Benedict XI and actually withheld judgment on the charge for which he was originally arrested, his disobedience in continuing to advocate the Spiritual doctrines despite direct orders from the pontiff to desist.

"For the crimes that he was convicted of, the court had no choice but to defrock him and sentence him to a life of solitary confinement in prison. But, in view of his frailty and age, we ruled to waive the usual additional penances of chains and a bread-and-water diet."

The bishop let his burly head drop. "John XXII countermanded our act of mercy and ordered that he be shackled and limited to bread and water anyway. It killed him. Still, I have to ask: why would a man endure such suffering, even surrender his life, rather than simply change his mind and say so?"

Jaques took the bishop's question to be rhetorical. "I'm fortunate," he said, "that I only have to observe and record events as they occur. To have to pass judgment, absolving or condemning those involved based on their motives, is beyond the ability of ordinary human beings."

"To avert chaos, the church and the law must delegate someone to judge. Only humans are available," Fournier said.

He then leaned forward and looked up. "Have you ever felt like you were required to be two different people at the same time?" he asked.

Jaques's head quivered uncontrollably at the pertinent question, but Fournier went on without waiting for an answer or noting the youth's reaction. "On the bench, I had to be John's delegate, there only to decide and deliver the appropriate punishment to an individual already deemed guilty by the Pope." He paused and rolled his eyes toward the ceiling.

"And who is the second person you feel you have to be?" Jaques whispered.

The bishop tapped his chest. "In here. I envied that monk, even his arrogant stubbornness. What a luxury to be able to remain true to one's deepest beliefs without fear of consequences. Few reach that state during the course of a lifetime, but they are the only ones, I fear, who can call themselves free."

The bishop's face suddenly grew brighter as if illuminated by a sunbeam coming through the window. But the moment passed so fast that Jaques thought he might have imagined it.

A gray cloud again discoloring his face, the prelate just as quickly reversed his previous statement. "*Mea culpa*, Jaques," he said with a brittle laugh. "For a moment there I spoke with the voice of the evil one. Such temptations are subtle, worming into our minds and posing there as our authentic thoughts. Delicieux's display of stubbornness was no more virtuous than Béatrice's seductions. Their tricks, curious or clever as they may be, are millstones around their necks that drag them down to the same eternal punishment." The bishop reached across the desk and placed his hand over Jaques's. "No doubt Bernard Delicieux, who preferred his own capricious insight and volatile will over God's immutable authority as revealed to His church and voiced by its vicar, is now in Hell forever."

With that the darkness around the prelate, the portent of a vicious storm, grew denser. It pervaded the room, and it pressed down as black sludge on Jaques's head, shoulders, and chest until his body seemed about to burst.

Far away now, Bishop Fournier was still talking, thanking his acolyte for taking the time to attend to an old man's remorse. But Jaques was hurtling through the gathered blackness towards a single point of starlight, the portal again, he now understood, that would explode him into the past.

The newly erected Temple of Solomon stands blazing on an island of brilliant sun in the distance. A festive procession winds through the valley towards it, but a cloud, growing darker with every beat of the timing drum, shadows the participants. Concerned heads turn skyward. The scribe appointed to record this momentous event into the sacred scrolls of the people of Israel stands on a promontory overlooking the route. Writing with an eagle feather on a papyrus roll, his hand strains to capture the words his mind frames to describe what his eyes perceive.

Spaced to allow their echoes to resolve into the sacred chords of which it is said that all things are composed, a series of trumpet blasts announce the approach of the procession's apogee. "The Ark of the Covenant, blessed be this day, is now in full sight," the scribe writes, forgoing the description of this most sacred vessel already detailed in scripture. The Ark is the eternal constant. The writer need only record the events associated with it and the people who participated in them to capture the flowing stream of its history.

Today's occasion is unprecedented. The Ark is on display to the multitude. Until now, only the High Priest was allowed to enter the Tabernacle's Holy of Holies where the Ark was kept. But when the time came to move it from its temporary home to its permanent abode in the newly erected temple, there was much argument about the way to transport it. The Ark had proved capricious in the past. Was there not danger, even sacrilege, to carrying it in the open? When the priests and elders could reach no consensus from what was written in holy lore, they turned to Solomon for a decision. After days of deliberation, the king declared, "The God of Israel is the God of all the people. Let His Ark of their Covenant with God be transferred so all can view it."

After a rigorous selection process, four men were chosen to carry the rectangular wooden coffer sheeted in burnished gold, each man holding an end of two poles slipped through a pair of rings on either side. To touch the Ark directly was to summon instant death. Atop the box, a pair of golden cherubim, the tips of their wings touching, arched over the sealed opening, the only point of access to the sacred contents within.

As the Ark reaches the promontory where the scribe is standing, a shattering crash of thunder booms from the cloud above him and the passing procession. People scream, and the two bearers on the left side of the Ark stumble, their knees buckled by the detonation. Their burden sways and lists. The Ark is about to fall to the ground, the ultimate desecration. One of the trumpeters marching alongside the porters sees what is about to happen. Dropping his horn, he sidesteps quickly and reaches towards the falling Ark. With each hand on one of the cherub's wings, he catches the heavy container in midair. Pushing upward with all his might, he stops its fall. The bearers recover their footing and rebalance the Ark in an upright position.

Applause for the trumpeter's agility begins among the witnesses. At that same moment, a blinding flash of lightning seethes not from of the cloud above but from the Ark itself. The trumpeter, whose hands had clutched the angels' wings, gags and drops to the ground, his body blackened to charcoal by the punishing bolt.

"If anything you heard here has marred your innocence, my son, let it be a lesson to you," the bishop was saying. He pulled his hand away as Jaques strained to blink past the scorched sight and smell of sacrilege and sacrifice.

"None, save the pope, is immune to temptation." The bishop raised his right hand and traced the sign of the cross. "With the power of my office as an exorcist of the church, I now consign the demon Delicieux to the eternal flames with the words of our Lord, Jesus Christ: *Get behind me, Satan.*"

Groping to regain a sense of his surroundings after the bewildering journey into antiquity, Jaques was further startled to realize that he had been staring right through the bishop the whole time. He had to have looked like a corpse. It felt like hours, and any thread of thought should have been lost, but Fournier's words now followed those previously as if no time had elapsed.

"You have been given many gifts, my friend, and because of that I fear for you. Before making use of any of them, ask yourself where this power comes from. If you can't be sure, forgo its use."

Fournier sighed and then smiled. "Of course, this conversation is strictly confidential. Should anyone ask, it never happened."

He winked and moved on. "I doubt there will be any envy when that randy old goat Belibaste is on trial before us. His high-minded Cathar principles, I understand, crumble to the most common temptations. Telling that the last of the Perfects is such an imperfect example. I assume there's been no word from our man in Catalonia yet."

Jaques shook his head, vigorously this time to disguise another oncoming quiver. Arnaud had spoken of his brother Bernard, also a Perfect, as still alive. Should he not warn the inquisitor that Belibaste might not actually be the last Perfect? *My brother too was a traitor to the family. I will find him and, after that, Belibaste will be the only Perfect left.* Arnaud had added.

"Just as well," the bishop went on, saving Jaques the need for a decision. "My hands are full with Lady Planissoles and her accomplices. She may look like a dried up crone, but there's more juice to be squeezed from her, some of which may be useful against Belibaste and company. There's traffic between the heretics on this side of the Pyrenees and those in Spain. We'll pinch them from both sides, the quicker to be rid of these rodents forever."

Steeling his body against any movement that might betray his revulsion, Jaques said, "You will be the first to know when I hear from Arnaud."

"Any recent sign of that loud-mouthed vagabond you call Baldwin?" Fournier asked as the youth rose to leave.

Jaques shook his head again. Only a partial untruth. The Templar was not a vagabond, and Jaques had not seen him since the abduction in Carcassonne almost a year ago. Hardly recent. When he had asked the Templar what to do if he found himself in a position where a lie seemed appropriate, Baldwin had said, "A Perfect takes a vow to speak the truth regardless of consequences. As far as I know, you are not one of them—at least not yet."

"Rest assured, Arnaud, that you will have your audience with Bishop Fournier when, according to legal procedure, you enter the Court of the Inquisition shackled as primary witness to your prisoner. Accolades and money will then be yours in abundance."

Once again Jaques found himself soothing Arnaud Sicre's indignation at having to deal through him rather than with the bishop directly. Arnaud had returned incognito to Pamiers in early October, a year on the nose since he left for Catalonia, and surprised Jaques as he was strolling the Mercado on a Sunday afternoon. The scribe led his visitor to his private office in the tower across from the cathedral, Arnaud shouting throughout that he only wanted to speak with the bishop.

"Damn your legal procedures," he spat in response to Jaques's attempt to pacify him. "I've been out among those wolves for a year, my life in jeopardy every day, and I'll be hanged, Joli, before I deal through any bishop's boy. I've got Belibaste. Fournier wants him. Fournier speaks to me."

Jaques took a deep breath and tried again. "I understand the difficulties of your mission, Arnaud. But protocol requires that a judge not meet with the accused or witnesses against him before the defendant is in custody and arraigned. Why not outline what you have found and how you plan to proceed? I'll take that to the bishop, and he'll decide if your situation warrants an exception."

Arnaud snickered. "Did it ever cross your simple mind or the bishop's or those Dominican black-and-white skirts' that this bloody crusade would have been over a hundred years ago if you had dropped the hypocritical rules and ritual trials and just tossed the buggers into the fire on the first sniff of an offense?" He got up, kicked back his chair and began pacing the length of the room, stomping and swearing as if fighting through a conflict between pride and greed. Finally, he pulled up and, fists on the desk, he arched over his seated nemesis.

"As much as it disgusts me to have to deal with you at all, Joli, I'll grant you this: you've weaseled your way into the bishop's ear and purse, and I need both. Go then and tell your master this for me: it won't be overnight and not without a lot more gold, but I will deliver the Perfect Guilhem Belibaste to him just as surely as Herod delivered the head of John the Baptist to his dancing girl Salome. Only I will hand over Belibaste alive for his Excellency's later roasting pleasure."

"Where is he? How will you get him here?" Jaques asked.

"No names or places except what you need to set the trap. Nobody's trusting anybody here, but"—he straightened up and thumped his chest— "you are looking at the man who knows more about the Catalonian Cathars than they know about themselves. Information enough to implicate every last one of them."

The fellow's braggadocio irked Jaques enough that he threw out a whimsical if ill-advised challenge. "Like what?" he asked.

Licking his lips and grinning, Arnaud circled the table twice before settling back into his chair. "A curious development in Belibaste's so-called celibate relationship with Raymonde. As you know, he got her pregnant and they had a daughter in 1313. After that he was on good behavior or they took proper precautions until, during the time I was there, the old goat lost control and did it a second time. His people, he knew, might have forgiven once, but they would not be so kind the second time. He needed an alibi."

Jaques leaned in, feigning interest in what sounded like gossip.

"Of the lot, Piere Maury is the only one I'd consider a friend, but he has a blind spot bigger than the sun when it comes to Belibaste. He reveres the man and pampers him like a grandfather. And Belibaste is shameless in taking advantage. So, realizing that Raymonde was with child and how she got that way and how it would destroy his position as their leader, Belibaste talked Piere into marrying the girl without revealing her condition. He performed the wedding ceremony himself."

Arnaud's leering grin widened. "But in conceiving the plan, Belibaste overlooked an important item: for the ruse to work, Piere had to copulate with Raymonde. That happened, and the new couple had such a good time that they repeated the act quite often in their few days of wedded bliss. At least once within earshot of the Perfect. Forced to endure such carnal pleasure from a distance, Belibaste turned jealous and went pouting about and refusing to eat for days. Piere noticed his mentor's distress, figured out the cause, and allowed Belibaste to dissolve the marriage, thus returning things to the way they were before, although now the child to be born could be said to be Piere's. Piere went along with the divorce and the subsequent paternal responsibility as docilely as he had entered the marriage."

Jaques had to chuckle. "Such carrying on among the so-called *pure ones*. Belibaste I can understand. But Piere?" He tapped his temple. "Does he have something loose?'

"Only when it comes to Belibaste," Arnaud said. "Otherwise

Piere's the brawn and brains of the bunch. He manages the group's scarce funds so well that Belibaste lives in the style to which he thinks he's entitled. Without Piere the colony would have bellied up years ago."

Jaques was incredulous. "Makes no sense. Is he so enthralled by their beliefs and the role of the Perfects within their system that he just let Belibaste pull so obvious a stunt?"

Arnaud shook his head. "Piere's no fanatic. He's extremely tolerant, which explains how he gets along with so many people, even me. When they asked him to curb his brother Jean, who had openly criticized Belibaste as a hypocrite, he defended Jean's right to express his views with quite the sermon on tolerance. Very convincing coming from a man who practices what he preaches."

"A rare fellow of character—" Jaques started to comment, but then checked himself. He had to keep after Arnaud for the substance of his plan.

"Before you left, you mentioned your brother Bernard was also a Perfect," Jaques said. "I assume he didn't show up to complicate matters."

"Nor will he," Arnaud sneered.

"So sure? Last you told me he was headed for Majorca. As I've seen during their trials, these people maintain tight communication even between groups in different countries."

"Bernard's dead," Arnaud said.

Jaques frowned. "The records of the Inquisition have him as missing for some years but not confirmed dead."

Arnaud grinned, showing his teeth. "He's dead. I know."

Had it been any other human being in front of him, Jaques would not have even dared to think what he asked Arnaud next. "You killed him?"

"He's dead. You don't need details."

Jaques felt the blood drain from his face. He gasped and leaned back. Now was not the time to lose control.

"You're horrified, Joli," Arnaud jeered. "Fratricide, you're thinking. Cain and Abel. So what if I killed him? More merciful than the fiery death to which Fournier would have condemned him, while you, the bishop's boy, wrote it down as just another sentence in your bloody record book. The bishop should be thanking me with a bonus. It's one less Perfect to capture, adding value to Belibaste as the last of the bastard breed."

Jaques breathed in, silently demanding that his squeamish self get behind him as the Bishop had ordered Satan to do.

He straightened up. "So that leaves your aunt in the Pallars and her daughter. Also from Ax if I understand correctly. Known to the Maurys and others. What if—?"

"Joli, Joli, you worry your pretty head too much. Many more questions and I'll have to remove it from your shoulders. Auntie Alazais and her daughter won't be making appearances any time soon. The colony's suspicions, now calmed by the coins I returned with the last time, will be kept in check by an even more generous donation from Auntie Alazais, which you will again put up. I'll treat them to the richest Christmas celebration in their memory. Given the generous dowry involved, Arnaud Marty has already agreed to marry Alazais's daughter sight unseen.

"When I get back, I'll tell them that Alazais is now too ill to travel, and her daughter, of course, won't leave her side. An endowment generous enough to fund the colony for years will give Belibaste the incentive to risk travelling to the Pallars to console the sick woman and perform the wedding. It's been scheduled for early spring, when travel is easier. Nothing can look rushed. Despite his greed, Belibaste can be skittish and superstitious. He has to go on his own accord. The journey will take us through Tirvia, a border town open to the bishop's troops. My father, who has already conducted several successful operations against the Cathars, will let you know our final schedule. Have the arresting party positioned according to his directions."

Jaques could barely hear what Arnaud was saying. This man had virtually admitted to killing his brother and intimated that he had done likewise to his aunt and her daughter. The bishop's hired spy was a criminal without a conscience. How would his own over-seers, one a bishop and the other a Templar, respond to hearing that Arnaud had killed three times without warrant or trial while conducting a mission they either sanctioned or permitted? Fournier would take it in stride: they were Cathars. *The verdict follows the facts*, he had said. *They did or said so-and-so, which is deemed heretical, and so are guilty.* And Baldwin's final instructions had been unambiguous: *You are right where you need to be. Continue to do what is in Fournier's best interest.*

Arnaud suddenly got up, his chair chattering backwards over the stone floor. "I'm going to make this easier on you, Joli," he announced. "I'll forego any audience with his Excellency for now. I imagine I'll enjoy encountering him for the first time in his court room, triumphantly dragging his trophy Perfect behind me in the style of imperial Rome. You now have all you need to finish this up on your end. Let's have the funds. Then leave the details to me and go poke your nose up someone else's asshole."

Jaques removed a large sack of coins from his desk drawer and gave it to his henchman. If Arnaud Sicre was a traitor and murderer, what of the one who handed him the means to betray and murder? If Arnaud Sicre was Judas Iscariot taking the thirty pieces of silver for the blood of the Christ, was not he the Pharisee who paid out the blood money?

"Until we meet in the spring, Joli," Arnaud said as he left. Jaques could hear him whistling as he jostled through the Sunday after-noon crowd in the Mercado.

Chapter 16: Dornach, December 1937

A couple of weeks after the conversation with Ladame in which I learned that Otto was serving in Dachau, I was summoned to meet with 333 in Dornach again. As I got out of the car to begin my second visit to Rudolph Steiner's Goetheanum, the sound of a flag flapping in the brisk wind caught my attention. Looking up into winter sun, I became momentarily mesmerized by the red and white Swiss national banner thrashing noisily above. The colors seem backwards, I thought. It should be a red cross on a white field, and the arms of the cross should be flared not squared. I caught myself and chuckled: how strange to be rearranging our country's flag in my head with so much else on my mind.

333 was waiting for me inside the main entrance with extended hand and welcoming smile. He ushered me into the same office where we had met the previous time, served coffee, and initiated a conversation that recapped the year since our last visit.

"Antonin Gadal attended our general meeting," he remarked at one point. "His folks are now watching the Montsegur area as well. All the recent publicity, Otto's books included, about the Cathars and their hidden treasure has increased the tourists to the area. Many come armed with maps, picks, and shovels, mostly amateurs but a few knowledgeable and with more sophisticated methods. Since your expedition with the Germans to Tarascon, a service for which the EC owes you a debt of gratitude by the way, no Nazi agents have been obvious in the area so far. Gadal sends his personal regards and said he was gratified that you took his cue and visited Notre Dame de Sabart. He hopes it was worthwhile."

I nodded, wondering how much of the extraordinary experience in the Tarascon church I ought to share with this virtual stranger, but 333 left me no immediate opening.

"More on that later," he said, "but first some preliminaries. This is now your second visit to the Goetheanum, Steiner's second temple, so to speak. If I may ask, Raymond, what struck you first upon your arrival this time?"

The noisy flag jumped into my mind and I smiled. 333 nodded. "Silly, with all the dramatic history, science and architecture going on here, but it was the Swiss flag flapping in the wind. And I had the odd thought that—" I stopped. So childish.

His expectant silence forced me to go on. "I thought that the colors in our flag are backwards like—"

"Like that?" He pointed out a large painting that I had not noticed before. It depicted three men with the center figure a knight with a red cross on his white tunic.

"The standard of the Knights Templar," I said.

"What the psychologist Carl Jung called a synchronicity. Excellent," he applauded as if I had passed a critical test. Then he waited again.

"There was a Knight Templar—well, an ex-Templar since the Order had already been disbanded—in this daydream or vision I had when I visited Notre Dame de Sabart."

I had to blink. 333's smooth face with high forehead and cropped dark hair suddenly turned into the gnarled and scarred visage of the hobbled John the Baptist character from that same vision.

I gasped. The face across from me flicked back to normal. "Does the name Baldwin mean anything to you?" I blurted out.

"As in Baldwin II, King of Jerusalem during the Crusades, also known as the Leper King?" He smiled wryly. "It wasn't my real name. I was petty nobility, not royalty, but others insisted on calling me that. Perhaps a tribute to my profound ugliness in that lifetime."

"You were a Knight Templar then."

He put his finger to his lips. "Still am, but it's no safer to admit now than it was then."

I rolled my head to clear my mind. It was becoming too bizarre. "I think I was named Jaques then."

"Jaques de Sabart," he completed, coming around the desk to embrace me. "It's been a long time, my dear friend."

I remained quizzical. "Was our planned escape through the cave successful?" I asked after he sat back down.

He shrugged. "I don't know. I stayed behind to hold them off while you went on. We gained time for you but then were overwhelmed. That coward Arnaud never showed. I'd hoped you'd be able to tell me the ending."

I heard the wind pick up. The windows began to rattle. The room grew dark as if the power had gone out. I gripped the arms of my chair and held on.

"Congratulations, Raymond," I thought I heard him say as I was being carried off. "You've discovered the portal and opened it."

A meteorite, blinding green, screams through a blackness broken only by distant streaking stars. With eyes blinded by the brightness and ears deafened by the din, we cling to the rock as it careens towards a distant blue-white planet, its destination and our destiny. It screeches to a flaming stop on striking Earth's atmosphere and explodes. Most becomes dust that spreads and disperses, but a few shards hold together and continue their fiery journeys towards the land and sea below. With fierce determination I grip one such piece, sensing that two others are accompanying me. We strike the planet's surface with such impact that our stone vehicle burrows into the earth, only grinding to a halt deep within a mountain's belly. Bruised and exhausted, we huddle and sleep for I don't know how long.

I wake to the sound of the other man's frantic voice. "Mathène, Mathène," he is calling. "Where are you?"

I prop myself on my elbow, my eyes following the light cast by my fellow traveler's torch. I smile; he actually cares for this woman even though she is his wife in name only.

A way off, Mathène laughs triumphantly between heaving breaths. "I found it, Jean," she calls. "I can't believe it. I'd hoped with all my heart. It's heavy. Help me. Over here."

"Coming," Jean says, his voice measured again. His lamp disappears.

I wait in the dark, not quite ready to get up yet. Then I see a green glow—certainly not Jean's torch—coming from the tunnel through which he had just disappeared. They are not talking but panting and giggling like lovers in the midst of intimacy.

The sounds get closer. The singular green glow gets brighter, infusing their faces and clothes. It all appear to be a single flame, but green.

"Jaques," the woman shouts to me. "We found the Grail. It lights up from the inside."

"Mathène found it." Jean corrects her as they approach carrying the large rock between them. They lift it gently, as if it were a sleeping infant, onto a flat-topped stalagmite in our camping area. "She had another of those dreams, only this one showed her where the stone actually was."

I get up and approach it, my quivering hands outstretched to determine what I can sense without touching it.

"I too had a dream," I tell them. "It was the end of the great war in Heaven. An emerald larger than the moon broke loose from Lucifer's crown. The three of us rode a piece of it after it exploded passing through the atmosphere. That fragment burrowed into this cave in the heart of the Sabarthès Mountains."

I stretch both hands toward the stone, my left to the place where Mathène holds it, my right to where Jean grips it. At the moment of contact between the three of us and the stone, the glowing green turns to a brilliant gold. A searing shock hurls me backwards. I strike a jutting crag and crumble to the ground.

Jean and Mathène shiver only slightly, and then both laugh. "Is it so, Jaques, that you are still afraid to ask the question?" Mathène says.

I am embarrassed. She is right. It might kill me. Then suddenly I freeze in panic. Even if I wanted to ask the question, I no longer remember what it is.

I opened my eyes, or maybe they were open all the time and I was now looking through them again. 333's chair was empty. I could not stop shivering. Hands tightened on my shoulders from behind. "You went into the portal," he whispered.

"But I didn't see if we made it through the cave. The woman found the stone. The thing almost killed me."

"You made it into the portal and returned with a piece of that memory. You proved that the channel is open. That's enough for now."

The shaking intensified. "If it opens too wide," I tried to explain, "I'm afraid it will all come flooding in. Beyond the opening is another complete lifetime running parallel to this one. Sometimes it threatens to overwhelm what is now. I've recorded pieces, like bits of a book, but didn't know where they came from or how they fit together. At first I thought it was imagination. But sometimes that life turns more real than this one." I rapped hard on the desk with my knuckles. "You have to see it to believe it."

333 returned to his chair. "I did not feel what you felt, but I saw it all like I was watching a movie," he said. "The three of you were back in Lombrives long ago all holding a large incandescent rock. At the end, the woman was laughing because you were afraid to ask the question."

"I couldn't remember it. And that made me more afraid. I didn't know what it was like to not be able to remember. With that I had to come back. I didn't get a chance to see what happened next."

"Enough for now," 333 repeated. "The portal is open, and you can go through again when you need or want to. Knowing the road is there is more important than what you see each time you take it."

I was not willing to be put off so easily. "You were the Templar then, and I suspect Otto was Jean, and perhaps Gabriele was Mathène. Others that I know now had to have been there then. Who is the tyrant Fournier or the traitor Arnaud?"

333 leaned back and beamed the benign smile that said he knew much more than he was telling.

"Mathène called that stone the Grail," I said. "I must let Otto know as soon as possible. He is the Grail hunter."

333 held up his hands in warning. "He will get to know in time, but there could be a problem if he learns too much too soon."

I frowned. Sometimes neither he nor Paul understood where my deepest loyalties lay. "Otto's immediate situation is already critical," I protested. "It's unfair to hold back anything from him that might give him a better chance. Sometimes I feel that both sides here—the EC and the Nazis—are playing Otto for their own purposes."

333 sighed. "Likely so," he said, "but our side remains extremely cautious because we are aware that we are working with something that is only poorly known. Do you recall how Wolfram von Eschenbach defined the Grail in *Parzival*?"

I repeated the line of the poem that I had recited for Ladame in our conversation prior to my joining the German mission to Languedoc. "'There was a Thing that was called the Grail, the crown of all earthly wishes, fair fullness that ne'er shall fail.' Paul and I discussed it as *the one treasure that endures. The pearl of great price.*"

I stopped and looked closely at the man across from me. A bright glint came into his eyes. Again my head jolted, and that disconcerting sensation of slipping sideways came on. I gritted my teeth and leaned in the opposite direction to stop the slide. "I first heard those words from you as the vagabond in the Mercado. Before I knew you as the Templar," I said.

"The door is opening wider on its own," 333 said approvingly. "But back to von Eschenbach. The Grail is the crown of *all earthly wishes*. Whatever its holder wants will come to fruition on the physical plane, and this happens indiscriminately: *fair fullness that ne'er shall fail.*"

He waited for me to absorb the intended point. I struggled with it. "The Grail's compliance with the bidder's wish is absolute. It produces fairly and fully what is requested regardless of the character of the petitioner. Is this why the Nazis want it and the EC can't let it fall into their hands?"

"Exactly," he said, clasping his hands. "The power of the Grail, whatever that word represents essentially, is activated by the intention of the suppliant. *Ask and you shall receive,* Jesus said without limiting what one could ask for. He was citing a basic principle, one that *ne'er shall fail.*"

I shuddered. "It sounds so absolute," I said. "Like the Midas touch. The king asked that everything he touched be turned to gold. His wish was granted literally, even to the food he picked up to eat and the daughter he reached out to caress."

333 concurred. "The Grail is neutral, not necessarily benevolent as is sometimes implied when it is called the Holy Grail. Who knows what the Nazis might ask of it? What horrors might it produce for those bent on mass destruction?"

"So why was Otto allowed to lead the Nazis to the stone at Lombrives only to have them take it back to Germany?" I asked.

"The Grail is like fire: essential for human progress but fatal when misused," he replied. "It cannot be kept secret forever. Depriving all humanity of its benefits is worse than what the Nazis could make of it. Our purpose now is to limit the damage as best we can and thus secure its beneficence for a more appropriate time in the future." He then leaned forward and held my eyes. "And it is to enlist your help with this that I asked you here today."

"Why me?" I fairly squealed.

He then explained how I was the one best qualified, as if by divine design, for the task he had in mind. How events, impossible to construe as sequenced by chance, had me meet Otto in Berlin in 1928 as he was forming his theories about *Parzival* and the Cathars, had me become involved intimately with him while he was researching and writing *Crusade Against the Grail*, and now had us perfectly positioned to serve as a bridge between a belligerent Germany and the rest of Europe still seeking peace. By working with Otto on Himmler's ahnenpass, I had gained rare access to the Reichsführer-SS, a fortuitous liaison Rahn had achieved earlier with *Crusade*.

But all the time the man was speaking, I could also hear this same individual as the Templar briefing Jaques de Sabart along the same lines. I found myself swinging like a pendulum between 333's office with the painting of the Knight Templar on the wall and a dungeon below a medieval city with the soiled mantle of another Templar on a stand in the corner. When he spoke of the Nazis, I thought of the Inquisition. For Heinrich Himmler I heard Jacques Fournier. The motives he attributed to the secretive EC applied also to the esoteric Gnostic coalition. I took for granted that my part would be largely supportive rather than operative in what was about to transpire; my earlier role had been to observe and record rather than to participate in the action directly.

I threw out my hands to let him know that I was having trouble keeping up.

"The parallels are by design," he said gently. "Our meeting in Carcassonne prepared you not only for your role in that lifetime but also for your similar and more difficult mission now."

"Which is?" I pleaded.

"We need someone close to Heinrich Himmler who can get his attention without arousing suspicion. Otto is in that position if he does not blow it by indiscretion. And you, as his close confidant, can steady him there and pass on our instructions."

"Whoa, whoa." Again I held up my hands. "I'm to be Otto's handler while he handles the Reichsführer-SS? I'll have to know a lot more about this before I commit either of us to any such thing."

"Nor would I have broached the idea until I was sure you were well connected to the channel that will supply you with the information and assistance you will need in addition to what I can tell you."

"And you are now assured of that?"

"Indeed. There was Notre Dame de Sabart, the opening of the portal, the meteor and cave vision a bit ago, and direct memory of our conversations in Pamiers and Carcassonne. What you need to know will be revealed as this unfolds."

I ran my hands over my face and through my hair. "Visions that leak as they will from some mysterious past hardly seem adequate against the harsh reality of Nazi Germany, but tell me what you have in mind."

He opened a folder on his desk and scanned its contents as if he were conducting a business meeting. "Ladame informed you about Hitler's Chancellery conference with his top military leaders and his decision to go on the offensive in the near future, also that the few voices of reason among them, men we counted on to keep Hitler in check, will be purged shortly. In our emergency meeting two weeks ago, we considered all options we had to counter the Führer's expedited timetable to start a war for continental domination. Given the lethargy of the western governments, which would rather appease than oppose the dictator, we decided to form a response of our own. Not military of course, as we have no army, and Hitler is so firmly entrenched that replacing him democratically has become impossible.

"But change can be made at a deeper and more pervasive level, one that most politicians and almost all historians ignore because they don't believe, despite solid evidence, that it actually exists. It is beneath and fundamental to all major changes in the human condition. Most important visible manifestations—revolution, political upheaval, or war—for better or for worse, have to be activated at this subliminal level. A vital role of the Emerald Club, an alliance of prequalified initiates, is to guard this level against intrusion by those who would employ its resources for selfish individual or group purposes rather than for mankind and life as a whole.

"In the early '20s, Rudolf Steiner became aware that Adolph Hitler had tunneled into this power source with negative intentions. That story has yet to be told, and it will be a long time before the general public has the stomach for it.

"No doubt that Adolf Hitler, a lackluster Austrian foot-soldier and second-rate artist then, was initiated into this Dark Side soon after the end of the last war. A man with negative attractiveness, low self-esteem, and weak will was transformed into a charismatic speaker and messianic leader who turned defeat and imprisonment into absolute control over one of the world's most advanced nations. Pre-existing conditions primed him for this transformation, but something else, something extraordinary, was invoked.

"He was in contact with several of the occult wizards of the immediate pre-Nazi period—Guido Von List, Jörg von Lieben-fels, Dietrich Eckhardt, Rudolf von Sebottendorff —and their secret brotherhoods—the Ariosophists, the Germanenorden, and the Thule Society. Eckhardt claimed that he not only initiated Adolph Hitler but possessed him. On his deathbed, he said, 'Follow Hitler! He will dance, but it is I who have called the tune. We have given him the means of communication with Them. Do not mourn for me; I shall have influenced history more than any other German.' Tellingly, Hitler, who habitually ridicules those who would presume influence in his early development, reveres Eckhart. He dedicated *Mein Kampf* to him and later an Olympic arena.[33] Eckhart's *Them* is working through the Führer, who remains surrounded by the old occult teachers' disciples: Karl Haushofer, Alfred Rosenberg, and Hitler's deputy, Rudolf Hess."

"Like Goethe's Dr. Faust," I said. "Hitler sold his soul to the devil."

333 clucked and nodded. "But unlike Faust who ultimately found redemption, Hitler is hell-bent on a course of destruction. With his iron will, he intends to wreak maximum mayhem until he meets his own end by force. Our task is to limit the havoc he creates for the world on his road to perdition."

"So the maniac at the top is incorrigible. Since you sent for me, the EC must have another option," I said, my voice trembling.

"To persuade one or more key characters in the German govern-

ment to oppose Hitler, we have to rely on resources already in position and any esoteric power we can legitimately employ. Ideally, our
target would be someone already tapped into this deeper level but
not invested in using it selfishly. We've studied the Nazi hierarchy
for a fit. Rudolph Hess, Hitler's Deputy Führer, has had an abiding
interest in occult phenomena and has at times defended Steiner's
views against detractors. But his influence within the hierarchy is
narrow and his character unstable. Others have similar deficiencies
or are less accessible, making them too risky to approach. And only
one has a semi-independent army of sufficient strength under his
control to manage an internal takeover."

I gasped as his drift dawned on me. "You can't be thinking about
recruiting Heinrich Himmler and the SS for this," I exclaimed.

"I know, I know. Preposterous. What the majority of the EC also
thought initially. But the situation is dire, so the response must be
creative. Hitler already has the capacity, material, and occult skills
to achieve his destructive objectives, and he will not deviate as long
as he breathes. Himmler, in his dual role as Chief of German Police
and Reichsführer SS, is the only man in Europe capable of opposing
Hitler. He is now devoted to the Nazi cause, but he is an opportunist
who calculates several steps in advance, keeping his options open
to compensate for the inevitable misstep. His primary computation
is, however, non-negotiable: Himmler always does what he sees as
best for Himmler. As long as Hitler is winning, Himmler is with
Hitler. Should he perceive that Hitler is losing or could lose, he will
unhitch his wagon from Hitler's star.

"We have no direct evidence that Himmler aspires to succeed
Hitler much less overthrow him. Nor would he admit to such an
ambition even in private. However, following the pattern of the
Night of the Long Knives operation in 1934 that resulted in his gaining control of the SA, two-million strong, he continues to build the
numbers, powers, and influence of the SS. The Waffen-SS, its military arm, is now comparable to the Wehrmacht, the regular army,
and infinitely more cohesive. In other words, he has the firepower

to take and keep control on the material plane.

"At the same time, even though he keeps it under wraps, he has a profound if somewhat superstitious regard for occult powers and is on constant lookout for paranormal manifestations."

I thought of the dinner in Berlin at which I was first introduced to Himmler. Even then his occult connections were pronounced: his eccentric runic wizard Weisthor, Gabriele alluding to his past life as Henry the Fowler, and the veiled mention of Wewelsburg, his Aryan version of King Arthur's Camelot.

"That's what led him to track down and employ Otto in the first place and then risk letting him return to Lombrives more recently," I noted.

"Although a prudent skepticism keeps him from being consumed by them, his occult ambitions are subtler than those of Hitler, who is enthralled by the sheer coercive power of conjury. Himmler looks beyond gaining territory and material goods to acquiring elements capable of overturning the predominant Judeo-Christian world view. Weisthor's Aryan runic scriptures would replace the Bible, and the Teutonic temple unearthed at Externsteine would supersede the Temple of Jerusalem while Wewelsburg Castle would trump St. Peter's in Rome as a religious center. Further, and more to the point regarding Otto and the Lombrives stone, Himmler is aware of the value of talismanic objects that emit energy from an inner source, thus potentially giving the holder access to super-human powers."

"The Grail," I gasped.

"A talisman of the highest order," 333 said with a nod, "and Himmler, like every power-seeking human being, would like to get his hands on it. But he seems to have a personal problem. Like Steimel in the cave, he felt nothing when he came in direct contact with the stone. Evidently a certain type of person lacks sensitivity to the active ingredient in such items even though it affects others strongly and instruments registers it dramatically."

"Would that not be a worrisome indication of core character?" I asked.

"Possibly," 333 said. "But in this case it's to our advantage. Since he cannot perceive something he is convinced exists, Himmler is a blind man who needs a seeing-eye dog."

For the first time in the long discussion, I grinned. Without Otto Rahn to guide him to it, the Reichsführer-SS could not gain what he desired most: *the one treasure that endures. The pearl of great price.* And for the first time since the French expedition, I felt a leap of hope about Otto's chances to escape his current predicament alive if not triumphant.

"If the Lombrives stone is indeed a golden egg, Himmler won't sacrifice the goose that laid it," I said. "Perhaps what Otto is referring to when he says he is carrying the Dietrich with him."

333 was less enthusiastic. "In locating the stone, Rahn showed Himmler, and us too, that his claims are genuine. But his subsequent intoxication by it points to a certain immaturity, an unexpected inability to transcend to the next level. He had the key to unlock the treasure chamber, but then in the excitement of the moment he left the key in the door. That's why we had to have the mission in France aborted before it reached Montsegur. Had Rahn discovered a further piece of the puzzle there, only to have it fall into German hands, our task of containment would have been exponentially more difficult."

"So you already know what is hidden at Montsegur?" I asked.

333 shook his head vigorously. "Of course not! And it would do no good if I did. It's not so much a thing to be found or the place where it is concealed as the people ordained to find it."

I sighed. Another riddle. "So this comes down to a treasure hunt between the EC and the Nazis. You both need Rahn to lead you to the Grail."

"Perhaps he will lead us eventually. For now, we have only to make sure he does not lead the Nazis there first."

He paused and looked off before he continued. "Some of our people are concerned that Rahn does not have the mettle to withstand Nazi pressure. A few think he is already a Nazi at heart. The anti-Semitic comments in his latest book did not help."

Rather than object to such assessments, which I was prepared and inclined to do to defend my friend, I took quick stock of my own reservations about Otto's suitability for the type of strenuous task 333 was intimating. Minor deprivations made him panic. Simply misplacing his cigarettes could make the brilliant writer frantic. Some people can have their heads in the clouds and their feet on the ground simultaneously. Not Rahn. Once he got going in a particular direction, there was no stopping him without a lariat. Had the bouncers not intervened that evening in the SS officers' club during the Olympics, Otto would have baited the whole platoon into beating him bloody. He is so enthralled with his ideal of a united Europe that he thinks his words alone will convince the wolfish Führer to lie down in peace beside Jews, gypsies, homosexuals, and the world's non-Aryan peoples.

If I, my judgment colored positive by my deep affection for him, could have such doubts about the dear man, how could I fault others for questioning his courage or stamina, even his loyalty? When we visited Dachau the previous year, had he not blithely suggested that I envision the positive potential of a place obviously designed to be a slave labor camp?

"Like many highly gifted people," 333 responded as if I had spoken my thoughts aloud, "Otto seems to suffer from an unusual form of blindness, one caused by too much light rather than too little. Look straight at the sun and you can see little else after you look away. A condition often found in otherwise advanced souls who rush through physical existence with insufficient attention to the seemingly petty lessons it was designed to teach."

His point took a moment to absorb and apply. If Otto was Jean the Perfect and I was Jaques his protector, as we seemed to have been related in Notre Dame de Sabart, then Otto too should be aware of our earlier lifetime and relationship. As one known to see things that other people do not, why did he never speak to me of our past together? Perhaps he already knew who Mathène was. And Bishop

Fournier and Arnaud the traitor. Did he not trust me enough?

"And yet," I said to 333, "he's making the same mistakes now so that he'll be lucky to get out alive. It can be infuriating. He wanders around blinded by the light and then wonders what hurt him when he crashes into solid objects. I love the man but am afraid for him. And I don't know that there is anything I can do to help him."

"But you do know," 333 asserted. "You've been through all this before."

That stopped me. I scanned my mind and found nothing that fit. "My memory is quite good," I said, "but I can't recall anything similar."

"You're looking at the wrong lifetime," 333 stated with a grim smile. "But don't force it. Trust that it will come as needed."

Then, as if just remembering it was there, he reached into his desk and brought out a small wrapped package about two inches square and a half inch high. "Antonin Gadal left this for you with the instruction that you open it only with Otto. It's meant for both of you, I presume."

Curious, I put the parcel heavy for its size into my pocket.

333 glanced at his watch. "You will then undertake this mission in tandem with Otto Rahn?" he asked.

"I'll agree to it for myself on your word, but I can't vouch that Otto will do the same."

"Getting him aboard and keeping him there has always been a part of your role. I don't doubt you will come through with colors flying again." He closed the folder on his desk, then rose to bid me goodbye.

"But the details. What am I supposed to do from here? Otto is still in Dachau," I stammered.

He smiled as he extended his hand. "Our next step could not be fully devised until your participation was confirmed. I'll check into that now. An agent will be in touch with you shortly with further instruction."

I flashed my middle fingers three times to reconfirm the contact signal.

He shook it off, then made a fist, flipped only the index and adjacent finger, held it for a moment, and then returned to the fist. "The code for your mission with Otto is 020," he said.

Chapter 17: Tarascon, Autumn 1320

Jaques wiped his eyes and then dug his tear-stained hands into the loose soil piled over his mother's body recently buried in the graveyard of Notre Dame de Sabart. Why had he not been told she was ill sooner? Why had he not been given a chance to say good-bye?

A courier had arrived in Pamiers with the message that his mother had passed away on the night of October 1 from a sudden illness. The funeral was to be held on October 3, the same day Jaques received the news. It was too late to attend the ceremony, but still he requested leave to go to Tarascon.

Bishop Fournier expressed his sympathy, promised to remember the scribe's mother in his masses, and insisted that Jaques stay at the episcopal mansion on the outskirts of Tarascon during his visit. With Arnaud Sicre not due back for several months, Fournier noted, and the Montaillou trials in recess after the sentencing of Beatrice de Planissoles to prison—her damning revelations about the Cathar affiliations of the local parish priest, Pierre Clergue, having saved her from the stake—it was an opportune time for Jaques to take a break to grieve and rest. The lavish property on a promontory overlooking the Ariège was amply staffed and guarded, its library well-stocked to keep the youth occupied.

He might find the locals hostile, Fournier cautioned. The region remained resistant to "the occupation," as its citizens referred to French rule, and still provided a haven for heretics fleeing Montaillou and other towns up the valley as the Inquisition's cleansing campaign moved downriver. Several squadrons quartered in the camp adjacent to the episcopal complex stood ready for action.

"You are known as one who serves in my court. Don't venture too far from the villa without a bodyguard," the bishop warned. Jaques expressed doubt that he would need such precautions among his own countrymen.

"Of course, your own will welcome you," Fournier said. And then added with a wink, "They might invite you to some of their secret heretical activities. Keep an eye open. Let no good evidence slip past unnoticed."

Still on his knees, Jaques bent and kissed the soft earth blanketing his mother's body. He then pushed himself up and made his way through the scattered and skewed monuments, mostly crosses, toward the cemetery entrance. An obelisk, taller than most of the head stones, caught his attention. *Père Richard Fontaine* it read. The tears, which had not quite stopped, burst into a fresh stream and momentarily blinded him.

Maybe he was buried here once, but after Père Clergue of Montaillou was unmasked as a heretic, Fournier assumed that all Catholic priests, past and present, were potentially Cathars, especially here in Tarascon, their last stronghold. The somewhat cynical voice in his head was familiar, but the words came from afar as if in the distant future. *Kill them all and let God sort them out.* Jaques shook himself to return to the present. How long would they let Père's remains rest in consecrated soil before they dug up his bones and tossed them into the flames? A painful howl rose from his gut. He grabbed the obelisk for support.

Fournier would have his way. He had badgered the haughty Beatrice into confessing not only her adultery with Montaillou's vicar but also his pillow talk that invoked Cathar teachings to justify his lechery. The priest had indeed fingered some Cathars in his congregation for prosecution by the Inquisition in the earlier raid, but only those, it turned out, who opposed his family's iron-fisted control over the town.

Clergue too had trod the path of Catholicism blended with Catharism but without devotion to either. Beatrice, outfoxed by Fournier, betrayed him. Now the priest was rotting in prison, having escaped capital punishment only by betraying several more of his fellow townsmen in turn. Death, Jaques thought, had mercifully rescued Père Fontaine, but for how long would he be left in peace? That Père had served two masters with a purpose nobler than Clergue's would not save his body from final insult at the hands of the rapacious bishop.

His heart sickened at the stench of a future bonfire consuming the unearthed bones of many of the cemetery's current occupants, his mother and Père Fontaine among them. He struck the flank of the monument with his fist, kicked at the pebbles under his feet, and made his way towards the miserable little church.

Somewhere off in the trees that fronted the river in the valley below, a bird insisted on singing—as if the scene could again be the idyllic village he knew as a child.

The young boy makes his way up the hill at dawn to serve Mass for his Père. The Ariège, foaming with snow-melt from the blinding white glaciers on the distant Pyrenean peaks, roars between cliffs honeycombed with caves. Later he will climb to his special hideout where, a knight in armor, he will slay the many dragons certainly lurking there. He laughs. But that will only come after Père and he perform the Mass for the few people who come out this early, after his lessons in Père's office behind the altar. He still hasn't decided which his favorite place is: the private classroom with Père or his personal cave on the hillside.

Serving Mass, even though it is a special privilege rarely shared with the other village boys because they do not like to get up early, is certainly not his favorite. Sure, there is something mysterious about the rituals done in an ancient language by a man dressed in robes that change colors with the feast days and seasons. He too gets to wear a cassock with a white knee-length surplice over it. His dress is not as elegant as the embroidered vestments that he helps Père Fontaine put on but special enough that he does not mind getting up early and washing his hands to prepare. But the Mass is long and complicated. The altar boy is expected to move precisely: stand, kneel, sit, ring the bell, pour the water and wine, move the book—all exactly on time.

In the beginning there was the matter of the words. Like everyone else he spoke two languages: the native Occitan, the langue d'oc, and French, the langue d'oui. *But Mass was in Latin, which, other than the priest, no one else spoke beyond the short phrases like* Deo Gratias *and* Et cum spiritu tuo. *An altar boy was expected to recite long prayers like the* Confiteor *and the* Suscipiat *fluently and with meaning. When Jaques wanted to be an altar boy, even his mother was worried that he would not be able to speak the Latin parts properly. He did not know how it happened, but when the time came to try out, he found he knew all the right words and could translate them into both of the languages he spoke.*

Seeing this, Père Fontaine seemed more amused than amazed. "You have a gift, Jaques" was all he said about it at the time.

Coming around from the graveyard, Jaques now approached the church entrance. The right half of the double doors scraped against the threshold as he pulled it open. Inside the place looked abandoned, smelling of dust and mold rather than incense and flowers. The holy water font was dry. The candle that normally burned next to the high altar to indicate the presence of the Holy Sacrament was out. Evidently no priest had been sent to replace Père Fontaine after his death.

Jaques walked up the center aisle towards the altar. It was stripped of its linen and candlesticks and the empty tabernacle stood open. Passing through the sanctuary, he went into the room where he once met with Père each morning for lessons. The books were gone, but the desk at which they had studied was still there.

He brushed the layer of dust from his old chair and sat. He imagined his mentor sitting across from him.

The priest beams with proud approval for his former student even though Jaques is about to chide him for having put him in so precarious a position. "Your well-intentioned plan, Père, now has my countrymen shunning me like an enemy, even in my time of sorrow. Because of your teachings, the son is judged unworthy of his mother. You set me on a dual path that led to opposing destinations. In Catholic Pamiers, I am a heretic in mind and spirit and thus a hypocrite in word and deed. Here in Cathar Tarascon, I am the hated bishop's boy residing in the house of their oppressor. I yearn to have a home, but as a result of your plan I am divided and alone."

Père Fontaine responds with a wise sad look that says he understood. He too had been in a similar position and there is nothing to do now but endure. He then holds up a small book, the Secret Gospel of John, a volume Jaques heard mentioned in the courtroom as the sacred book of Cathar Perfects. Père places the tome on Jaques's head, his lips silently moving with a blessing, the act of confirmation administered by a Perfect to a fellow believer, a Good Christian. Père's presence then fades with a gentle smile but without the traditional Catholic parting gesture, the sign of the cross.

Jaques was left shaken. Arnaud Sicre's threat was founded on fact: Père Fontaine was both priest and Perfect, and just now he had demonstrated the preference with which he had died. The thought left Jaques less desperate but still desolate.

I must find my mother, he thought. Père had told him the story of Our Lady of Victory to whom this shrine was dedicated. Back in the church proper, he ducked past the image of the Virgin in white located to the right of the main altar and sought instead the small niche towards the rear where the original wooden image of Notre Dame de Sabart was placed. She was there, seated with the child on her lap, her face in the low light even darker and more somber than he had remembered.

The kneeler on the prie-dieu before the image had two dust-free spots where someone had knelt recently. Perhaps his mother was the last one here, paying a final visit to her patroness before she died. For her devotion to the Black Madonna would not have been a contradiction even if her beliefs otherwise were heretical. He lowered his knees, carefully matching them to the spots left by the previous supplicant, and propped his elbows on the rest that would have supported his mother's arms. Fresh tears fell into the dust around him.

No comforting words came with which to pray, no sublime thoughts to pierce the darkness that weighed him down like a cloak of mail. He slowly raised his eyes to meet the ancient ones of the dark woman. He gazed through the tears and waited, barely breathing for he did not know how long. Waiting, just waiting.

The statue did not turn aglow nor did his own beloved mother appear out of the darkness. No vision at all, just a small voice that came not from the image above but from within his soul, "Home is not any church. Go to your cave above the river where you played as a boy. There you will learn what you now need to know."

Jaques stole down the carriage road that followed the Ariège, burbling through the jutting rocks, its peak flow of summer runoff now depleted. Although the route was familiar, something about it now felt forbidding. The overhanging woods, once populated in his imagination with gallant knights and lovely ladies, seemed to crackle with the furtive footsteps of spies prowling for both sides: the bishop's men to see if he would lead them to a heretics' lair and Cathar agents guarding against intrusion by a traitor.

To buoy himself, he tried to commune with the birds by whistling, once an effortless art, but the attempted trill caught on his dry lips and petered out. Fighting the impulse to run back to the safety of the bishop's house, he urged himself forward, one foot in front of the other, a forced march to the beat of crunching leaves.

With the underbrush thickened over the years and some of the most familiar trees grown over or gone, he was lucky to spot his old path up the mountainside. Checking around to make sure he was not being followed, he plunged into the brush and followed the trail's faint trace upward, ducking beneath low branches as weeds whipped his legs and spattered his trousers with burrs.

He reached the ledge where the main trail branched right to the famous Lombrives. He turned left towards the less spectacular cave he had claimed for his own. Its opening was hidden by a thicket of scrub. He pushed through the tangle and was about to step across the threshold when he smelled smoke coming out of the cave. He froze. Someone was in there. He turned to run. A pleasant enough called voice after him. "Hello, Jaques. I've been expecting you."

He stood paralyzed. Cathar or Catholic? Whoever it was knew him by name. Going back along the narrow ledge would be risky; there might be accomplices. He wheeled around, his face as fierce as he could make it. "Who are you? How do you know me? Nobody knew I was coming here. What do you want?" he shouted.

The man, very slight, bearded and dressed in a clean simple robe corded at the waist, extended a hand. "I didn't mean to frighten you," he said. "I made the fire to let you know in advance that I was here. I bring greetings from Baldwin. I also knew your mother, God rest her soul, and Père Fontaine."

Jaques went past the man and entered the cave. "So are you Cathar, Templar, or spy for hire?" he asked, disappointed that he would not have the cave to himself.

"A bit of all but indentured to none. They call me Timekeeper, a journeyman historian of sorts, although I include the present and future in my purview as well as the past."

"We have something in common at least. I work as a scribe in the Inquisitional Court—as if you don't already know that."

Despite the man's geniality, Jaques was irritated to find his every move being monitored. "So Baldwin sent you, eh?" he snorted.

"Not a word from him since Carcassonne. I have to thank him for sending me back to Hell to manage for myself."

"You no longer need a guardian. Fournier suspects that he is a Templar. He has assumed a role more appropriate to his knightly calling. You will meet again," Timekeeper said.

"I have some questions for him."

"And we have some further instructions for you."

It was not the words or even the man's tone of voice but the underlying presumption that made Jaques tense further. He gripped his hands, the black soil from the cemetery still under his nails, and said, "I came here from my mother's grave to find the solitude to grieve. Isn't there a better time for delivering orders?"

Timekeeper looked apologetic. "It was our only chance. Inappropriate as it might seem given your recent loss, these are otherwise the right circumstances—this town, your staying in the bishop's house, your mother's death, your childhood sanctuary— to advance the plan and your part in it."

Jaques allowed his smoldering anger to flare. "What plan? Whose part? I'm sick of jumping around like a puppet with others pulling the strings. Worse, I'm two puppets at once with dueling puppeteers pitting one of me against the other. Have you ever been split down the middle like this? When Baldwin told me that I was intentionally raised in two faiths, I reluctantly agreed to stay on as the scribe in Fournier's court even though I then considered myself as guilty of heresy as those whose cases I was recording. At the same time, I agreed to continue to liaison with Arnaud Sicre in the plot to capture Belibaste.

"But neither Fournier nor Baldwin informed me that my agent in the field had the license to kill innocent people. No great matter to Fournier. All of them— Arnaud's brother Bernard, his aunt and her daughter—were fair game as heretics. But does Baldwin know that the blood of three of our own is on my hands? Or that Arnaud, that clever bastard, would get his nose into the business of every Cathar on the far side of the Pyrenees and into plenty about those on this side also? Haven't you learned any lesson from Montaillou? In only a few months, Belibaste will be trapped and brought in so Fournier can sentence him to the stake. Does Baldwin understand the urgency?"

Timekeeper sat in a silence too smug for Jaques to stomach. "I asked you, does Baldwin know what's going on? Do you?" he demanded.

The other man slowly nodded, his eyes unblinking.

Jaques grew more incensed. "You know and are allowing this to happen? Some Knight Templar that Baldwin, hiding in dungeons and caves while our people are murdered. No wonder we are going extinct. How long before Fournier orders his army to enter Tarascon and murder every last Cathar there?" He stamped the packed earth between his feet and howled into the damp cave air. "I hope you have some answers for me, Sir Timekeeper. Right now I'm tempted to ditch both bloody plans, yours and the bishop's, and take up my own."

Timekeeper finally looked down as if studying the ground. When he looked up and caught Jaques's eyes again, he said, "It's time for you to know more, Jaques. This is the point where the decision about what comes next is put into your own hands."

Jaques was not appeased. "Too late for that," he muttered. "The ground is already littered with Cathar corpses and the jails filled with them starving. The last Perfect is already on his death march. What good is a scribe recording their story for posterity when you need an army that can take on both France and the church, and all you've got is a ragtag once-Templar for a commander and a fistful of pacifists?

"Or do you assume, just because I have been given some gifts, that I also have magical powers, as Bernard Gui and Fournier once suspected of me? Do you suppose that I can, from the alleged ocean of human history in my mind, recall some arcane battle cry that will summon an angelic host to smite the enemy? Or do you expect that I can utter an incantation, perhaps from some ancient Book of Shadows, that will conjure up a demonic horde from the bowels of the earth to bring the bishop's forces to its knees?"

Timekeeper smiled at first and then broke into laughter. "Nothing quite that dramatic, my friend. We seek not to hasten Armageddon, but to forestall it. We need your memory only to keep an accurate accounting of the history of the Grail."

Jaques did not understand the strange word Timekeeper had used, but he felt his anger ebb. "What is this Grail you speak of?" he asked.

Then even as he dropped his eyes and focused on the cavern floor, a part of him, like a shadow broken loose, slipped upwards and outwards and hung afloat above a boundless expanse of space, a motionless mirror gleaming golden like the reflection of an enormous invisible sun.

After what seems an infinity, there arises from the molten ocean a shaft, brilliant, metallic, but silver in color. Comes the thought, "The Grail is the uplifted sword, the penetrating phallus."

On cue the column's pinnacle erupts, spewing fire and ice that bleeds down to form around the base of the shaft a glowing mountain of shimmering emerald, an island of green in a golden sea. "The Grail is the magma that forms the emerald, the primordial stone," it is said.

Threadlike veins break out on the flanks of the crystal cone. Through them trickles of sparkling fluid from the ocean below flow upward and pool at the apex into a lake that vibrates with mounting intensity. Reaching its bursting point, the body of molten gold explodes and expels a billion lightning bolts into outer space, impregnating that empty womb with the embryos of galaxies, stars, suns, and planets. "The Grail is the seed of the Universe, its energy source" comes the refrain.

Dusk settles in, and the endless ocean loses its luster, first waning green to reflect the mountain, then blue, and finally black. Taking the place of the receded waters is an endless bowl of sand under a dusty dome impervious to sun or stars. At the center of the desert is a pyramid formed from gray granite. Atop it is the sole light source for the dreary scene: a glowing green capstone fed scarce life-giving energy through fine threads that trickle down from the distant stars. Living creatures, animals and men, are crossing the desert and swarming up the monument's flanks towards the apex. "The Grail is the pyramid's capstone, an oasis for all that would live in the desert," it is revealed.

Then from the west riding monstrous beasts comes a thundering horde clad in steel and brandishing weapons intended to maim and kill. The pilgrims to the pyramid retreat in panic for the open desert, running over the less agile on their way past and leaving them to die under the clubs and axes of the attackers. The triumphant invaders clamber up the monument's slanted flanks. They drive anchors into the capstone's base and pull with ropes to tear the crystal loose. The huge but brittle jewel slides forward and tumbles down the granite slope, shattering like fine glass into a blizzard of fragments. The falling shards kill many; more succumb in the frantic scramble to gather the treasured remnants. From the silence that now covers the field of blood, it is said, "The Grail shattered is Death."

Jaques moaned and, as if waking from a monstrous dream, felt his faculty for remote viewing settle back to ordinary vision.

"And that was the end of it?" Timekeeper asked.

Trying to see more, Jaques rubbed his eyes, but the vision did not continue. He could only speculate. "There was no longer a single crystal of sufficient size, when positioned correctly in relation to the heavens, to draw down enough of the substance of life to sustain the entire body of consciousness created originally," he said. "As long as living beings could derive energy from the capstone, there was enough for all. After its fall and fragmentation, the distribution became uneven, vastly too much for the few who possessed its larger pieces, hardly adequate to sustain the rest.

"Significant fragments of the capstone survived through time, several of sufficient size and shape to channel sufficient etheric power to do dramatic good or harm. Moses acquired one such and placed it in the Ark, where it enabled the formation and prosperity of the Jewish nation, bringing manna from heaven and felling the walls of Jericho. But the emerald stone in the Ark was only a part of the whole. Informed as it was to serve a specific group in a specific era to the exclusion of other peoples and times—made to play favorites, one might say—it proved hostile to anything other than Mosaic Judaism. Once times changed and the Jews diverged from Moses' teachings, the stone in their Ark turned hostile. A high priest who entered the Holy of Holies improperly was struck down; a potential ally that sought peace with Israel was instead infested with plague. And so the Ark had to be entombed deep beneath the Temple to shield the people from further destructive emanations. But that act also deprived them of their power source and left them prone to attack and persecution ever since."

"And other fragments?" Timekeeper asked.

Jaques had to strain to continue further. Trying to retrieve consciously what came automatically in the trance or sleep state led to a dreadful headache. "There have been sightings throughout the ages and many stories about them, some factual, some partially true, others absurdly false. Famous is that of the emerald cup that the high priest Melchizedek presented to Abraham to initiate the Abrahamic race. This chalice was passed down through the Jewish priestly line, arriving in Jesus' hands at the Last Supper. Joseph of Arimathea took it to Calvary the next day and filled it with the blood of Jesus during the crucifixion. He later carried it to Britain, to Glastonbury, where its story merges into the Celtic tales of King Arthur and the Knights of the Round Table. This object, as distinguished from the other fragments of the capstone, has become known as the Holy Grail."

The hammering and ringing in Jaques's head now prevented him from going any further. He barely noticed the bliss that suffused Timekeeper's face.

"So our Gnostic forefathers were correct," the ecstatic man said.

"Every transformative movement comes from a single source. For Jews it is the Ark of the Covenant. For Christians the Cup of the Last Supper. For Islam the Kaaba in Mecca. Each religion has its separate sacred stone, but it still remains for them to recognize that their separate pieces are part of the same rock. It is one. Thank you, Jaques. Your memory confirms our ultimate intention."

Still somewhat dazed, Jaques shook his head. "Ultimate intention?" he asked. "The capstone was shattered beyond repair. The grail is now death. I didn't remember anything about an ultimate intention."

"You wouldn't. Memory, your gift, is a perfect impression of the past. It is intention, another's gift, that predicts the future. And yet there is a thin sliver of time between past and future that is common to both. The present, the precise moment that is only right now. And that's when, my friend, the decision before you has to be made."

Jaques grimaced. "I'd almost forgotten. The decision about what comes next that you are leaving to me."

Timekeeper placed another log on the fire and poured two cups of tea from the battered pot. "Before you make that decision though, there is more to understand," he said.

Anticipating a long explanation, Jaques sat on a log, his back against a rock.

After a deliberate sip of his hot brew, Timekeeper started. "You were concerned earlier about having a direct hand in Guilhem Belibaste's capture and death. Did Baldwin not explain this earlier?"

Jaques thought back to the conversation with the Templar in Carcassonne. "He told me that such a fate for Belibaste would not be the end but must appear to be so and advised that I allow it to unfold. This I have been doing. But he made no mention of a rescue plan, if there is one, and nothing about Arnaud's relatives getting killed along the way."

"Their sacrifice may sound callous, Jaques, but death to a Cathar is not the end but a doorway. Even if they die without the *consolamentum*, which would elevate them to a higher form of existence, they believe they will return here, usually the wiser, with another chance to finish what they left incomplete. Père Fontaine, your mother, and Arnaud's victims all departed with this confidence."

Still unwilling to accept the man's cursory summary of mortality, Jaques squirmed a bit. "If Belibaste is to die at the stake," he finally asked, "has he been informed of his fate or is he walking into our trap blindly?"

Timekeeper shrugged. "I can't answer that because I don't know. I doubt Baldwin knows either."

"Does anyone?"

"Someone has to know. Whoever it is should be in position to inform Belibaste. Maybe he will, maybe not. A necessary security arrangement. The Inquisition's interrogation methods are formidable, as you know."

Jaques sighed. "So complicated and secretive," he said. "If your people know what Arnaud is up to, why not have the whole community, Belibaste included, just move further south out of Fournier's reach?"

"If only it were that simple. As you know, the Gnostic guardianship of the sacred truths has spanned centuries, remaining constant despite the rise and fall of its various branches. After flourishing for two hundred years, the Templar Order no longer served the coalition's basic purpose, and Philip IV was allowed to bring it down in a single night. Its complete demise was then certified with the death of Jacques de Molay, who intentionally retracted his earlier confession, thus obliging the Inquisition to execute him."

Jaques shivered. "You make it sound like the Order brought on its own destruction and de Molay committed suicide."

"It was required to convince the Templars' enemies that they were indeed obliterated. Once the hunt was called off, the Order could be reconceived in the new form required by a new generation."

Jaques felt some pieces shifting into place. "And so now it must be with the Cathars. The Inquisition will continue its harassment until Fournier is certain that every last heretic and their relatives have been eradicated. Belibaste will act as their Grand Master, his death proof that Catharism is permanently defunct, never to rise again." Jaques sipped from his cup and looked away. "Is Belibaste aware that he has been designated the Cathars' final martyred hero?"

Timekeeper shrugged again. "He understands that the Cathar movement's time has passed and knows his death would become its tombstone. Long dry as a spiritual fountainhead, the Roman church as a temporal power will claim victory."

Jaques recalled his conversation the previous year with Fournier about Belibaste: as the last of the Perfects, he presented an opportunity for the Roman church to break into Gnostic line and reclaim the treasure it lost not long after the time of Christ.

"Fournier will not allow him to die in peace," he told Timekeeper. "Counting on Belibaste's weaknesses, he plans to pry from him the keys to spiritual knowledge and power that his church lost shortly after the death of Jesus. He wants Belibaste to be brought in alive so he has the opportunity to take them back."

Timekeeper smiled thinly. "Foolish man. He believes that spiritual power exists in some external form that can be lost and found, given and taken back." He tapped his fingers on his temple. "Still we had to account for Belibaste's shortcomings. His infidelity to his vows by having intercourse with his woman in essence nullified his status as a Perfect. He knows that the sacrament he now administers has no benefit. What Fournier wants from him, the power of the *consolamentum*, is no longer his to impart. Without another Perfect to absolve and reordain him, Belibaste realizes that only voluntary martyrdom will restore his status."

Jaques whistled. "Arnaud told me about Piere and Raymonde. A disgrace. Do you suppose Belibaste has the courage to become a martyr?"

"Only Belibaste can respond to that and only when that time is at hand."

Jaques's mind raced ahead. "If Belibaste is the last Perfect and he can only regain the power to administer the *consolamentum* through death, does not the power then die with him?"

"We are not so careless about safeguarding the sacred knowledge. That's why, despite the occasion of your mother's death, it was so urgent to meet with you here and get your decision now."

Jaques remained perplexed. "I'm still not sure what I'm supposed to decide."

"It's straightforward," Timekeeper replied. "So far in your life you have played a double role—half Cathar, half Catholic—with others deciding which to portray when. Now you must go forward under your own power. You will choose if you want to continue on this risky dual path or take another that's safer. We are ready, despite all you know about us, to release you from all obligation. You may continue on as the scribe and intelligence agent to the Inquisition if you wish. Or we can arrange a safe haven beyond the bishop's reach."

Jaques had to smile. "It looks like you've given me all the details I am allowed to know prior to my commitment. Understood. And you would not have taken the trouble to groom me for this role if it was not essential to a successful outcome. You might have other options were I to bow out, but my role is part of the preferred plan. Possibly the plan will collapse, at least this time around, without my participation. Baldwin already told me how memory is vital to the preservation of the Gnostic record.

"The vision of Grail history I saw here a short time ago proves that I am not a novice. Evidently I have long been an initiate—to answer the question I once put to Baldwin that he deftly evaded. Staying on Fournier's side now would make me a traitor, choosing to escape a coward. The decision you are asking me to make has, in fact, already been made. Of course, I now choose to continue to do on my own volition what I have been doing ever since I served as Père Fontaine's altar boy. If it requires that I remain the bishop's boy for a while longer, so be it."

"Even if you must bear witness in silence to the shedding of innocent blood?" Timekeeper asked.

"Like my mother and Père Fontaine, I can choose to see death not as the end but as a doorway," Jaques said.

Rising to his feet and motioning Jaques to stand also, Time-keeper reached into his robe and pulled out a round object. Extending both hands, he solemnly presented it to Jaques. "A gift from Baldwin and the Knights Templar Order to commemorate your courageous acceptance of destiny. As Père Fontaine proclaimed when you were still a child, 'You are one of us.'"

Jaques studied the medallion in his hands. Etched into the thick bronze was the image of two armored men riding back-to-front on a single horse.

"The Templar emblem," Timekeeper explained. "Their warriors rode into battle saddled in pairs, one knight with the sword in the right hand, the other with it in the left to cover both flanks. Cathar Perfects also travelled and taught in pairs, sometimes a man and a woman working together. Jesus had directed his disciples, the original Gnostics, to preach in pairs. *Two to a horse* now becomes your watchword."

Jaques rubbed the image with his thumb. "Should there not then be another to ride with me?"

"There has always been another, even at the times you felt most alone. However, the one specifically designated to team with you in carrying the Grail to a later generation is yet to be revealed. To protect the plan, he still remains paired with another in proxy. When the time is right, you will be introduced to each other with the watchword, 'Two to a horse.' Listen for it."

Chapter 18: Konstanz, Schliersee, January 1938

A pale and pregnant Gabriel Winckler-Dechend ushered me out of the winter wind blowing from Lake Konstanz and into her comfortable new home on a January morning early in the new year 1938.[34] After her hurried greeting that showed I was expected but not quite welcome, we sat close to the blazing fireplace with cups of hot tea. "I understand from your letter," she began, "that you're on your way east to meet with Otto. He was here a few days after Christmas. What do you want to know about him?"

Her curtness, more typical of a middle-age matron than the whimsical young woman I had known in Berlin, threw me off balance.

"He showed up in that uniform—he rarely wears it—and only stayed a few hours. A short holiday leave from training, he told me. I understand he's through at Dachau now."

"So I've heard. We're to meet in Munich and then head down to Schliersee for a few days, hopefully to ski. He said his health was poor—"

"Really? He looked better than I've ever seen him. Barely smoked. For Otto, miraculous. He credited the discipline of the training, all enthusiastic like a fresh recruit. Overdone, in my opinion. I've snooped through my husband's SS handbooks. Otto has the lines down. 'My honor is loyalty' and with such conviction. Who's he trying to impress? He's already got Himmler in his pocket. How he gets away with some of his outrageous antics. Always so dramatic."

She frowned but continued breathlessly. "I was surprised he came to see me. He dropped off the face of the earth after the trip to Languedoc. Never visited; barely wrote. He didn't even know Himmler arranged Winckler for me, that we married, or that I was pregnant." She patted her stomach and, for the first time, looked pleasant. "At least he agreed to be the child's godfather."

I smiled at that, but an awkward silence followed. Counting on our prior acquaintance to glean some advance insight into Otto's state of mind did not look promising. I could sense her suspicion but could think of no way around it.

She got up and went toward the kitchen. "Some lunch?" she asked.

Her time hustling about in the adjacent room gave me time to wonder whether I had already made a fatal misstep in executing my assignment. 333's emissary, it turned out, did not have to introduce himself. When a man hailed me on a Geneva street a few days after the Dornach meeting, I was surprised to recognize him as Adolf Frisé, the publisher I had only met briefly in the SS club during the Olympics, the person Ladame had called "Otto's guardian angel." I was further flabbergasted when over coffee he flashed me the 020 sign that designated him privy to our mission. Without attempting to explain his role with the EC, Frisé informed me about Rahn's visit with Gabriele in Konstanz, the date his Dachau stint would be completed, and his request that we get together for a short vacation before he returned to Berlin.

"The plan will evolve in stages, each further step adjusted to the results of the previous one," Frisé explained. "First things first then. While on holiday, re-establish good personal contact with him. Have him tell you about his time in the camp. Notice his attitude, any changes in loyalty, and his current relationship with Himmler. Use mutual acquaintances for additional information and to verify as possible. If this step leads you to suspect that Otto has turned true Nazi, ease out and come back."

"It won't," I asserted despite a bit of doubt.

"If things prove positive, proceed to inform him in general terms that there is an operation afoot that strongly supports his vision of a united Europe. He knows from earlier contacts with the Polaires in Paris and Gadal in the Languedoc that various organizations have been promoting such ideas since the end of the last war. He should be familiar with Count Coudenhove's Paneuropean Movement as well as Steiner's Three Folding.

"Then to specifics. Swiss minister Jean-Marie Musy revealed that Otto was present at a Nobel Restaurant gathering in Berlin earlier this year that included himself and the Swiss Doctor Riedweg, plus several Nazi bigwigs, including Himmler and Karl Wolff.[35] Use Musy as evidence with Otto that our movement enjoys Swiss government support.

"Swing the conversation around to Franz Riedweg, a former adherent to the Paneuropean movement but now Nazi sympathizer, and his professed ambition to join the SS."

Frisé then explained how Riedweg's addition to Himmler's inner circle would pose a possibly fatal threat to the EC plan to swing the Reichsführer-SS away from Hitler. Rahn's first task would be to persuade Himmler to refuse Riedweg admission to the SS. Success here would neutralize the traitor and signal that a further attempt to recruit Himmler was in order.

Of my own accord, I had added the Konstanz visit to Frisé's given agenda and now was having second thoughts about the wisdom of that improvisation. An Otto Rahn reformed by the rigors of Dachau, as Gabriele had described him to be, reduced the odds for the mission's success before it got started.

"Otto is no more suited to be a soldier than I a shoemaker." Gabriele seemed to have thawed a bit as we started on our sandwiches. "Why do they want them all to be the same? Otto's a poet and mystic, and when he tries to march to the beat of another drum, he's as out of place as a nun in a beer hall. He's not a politician but an idealist. He's more European than German. He sincerely believes that Germany, France, Britain and even Russia can unite as a cooperative community rather than war eternally as enemies. He's no National Socialist; he's a Cathar. He just wants to return to his beloved Languedoc to continue his research and writing. He's enchanted by whatever he discovered there and won't rest until he can show it to the whole world."

"He told you that when he was just here?" I asked, my hopes rekindled.

She smirked. "Of all people, you should know that about him. You were there when he found his darling rock. Once I drew him out of being the soldier boy, he glowed with something unearthly when he talked about the stone's effect on him." Again she patted her pregnant tummy. "He was so beautiful in that state that I actually wished he was this child's father."

Jaques, we found the Grail. It lights up from the inside.
Mathène found it. She had another of those dreams, only this one showed her where the stone actually was.

I blinked several times to stop from slipping back into the reverie I had experienced with 333 in Dornach.

Gabriele caught the reaction. "You alright?"

"Does the name *Mathène* mean anything to you?" I asked before I could catch myself.

She thought a moment, then shook her head. "It's pretty and French and somehow reminded me that Otto promised to take me to see his stone now enshrined in Himmler's castle in Wewelsburg. Why do you ask?"

I hesitated. She already had Otto's inclination for fantasy to deal with. "The name just popped into my head," I said.

But my hands had started to shake so noticeably that I slipped them into my pockets. The right one came into contact with the package from Gadal. The tremor immediately subsided.

"Otto will know about Mathène," Gabriele said as she began to gather the dishes, signaling that it was time for me to leave.

The farther we travelled from Munich with the nightmare of Dachau on its northern fringe the more Otto Rahn released the soldierly posture so pronounced when we met at the Munich Marienplatz station the previous day. As the short train fled the city and the scenery expanded into the panoramic Alpine foothills, Otto eased back. Once the number of passengers thinned to only those headed for a holiday at the train's destination, Lake Schliersee, he stopped checking around every few minutes to see if someone was watching us.[36]

Eventually he turned and spoke directly to me rather than facing forward and talking out of the side of his mouth. "I hope I'm not presuming, Raymond," he said, "but I wrote to Himmler about your visit and asked permission for us to continue working together on the remaining details of his ahnenpass."

I immediately sensed this as an opportunity to forward the mission but also recognized the risk in having the Reichsführer-SS aware of our renewed association. And as Ladame would advise, I should be alert for a trap. "Do you think he will be agreeable?" I asked.

"Why not? He likes you even if you are a Swiss who speaks French and hardly a Nazi. His views are broader than most of his associates." He punched me playfully on the arm. "Maybe he'll bet that you'll be a good influence and keep me in line."

"From what Gabriele told me, your stint in Dachau has already made you straighten up considerably."

"Can't say I'll miss the place," he whispered. "One more push-up, and I'd have dropped dead. Thank God it was Ullmann keeping score. He must have been under orders from Himmler to pass me if I showed enough effort even if I lacked the strength and skill. Still it was eight weeks in hell."

"Does every SS officer have to go through such training regularly?" I asked. "You're no recruit."

"I hope not. You know I have trouble following rules. Theirs are proving to be a lot more than I bargained for. Every day more orders." He shrugged. "They take this notion of making us into supermen too damn literally."

Despite trying to stay focused, I found myself getting confused. Was Otto telling me what he thought I wanted to hear just as he might have told Gabriele what he wanted her to take back to her SS connections, Himmler included?

My mind slipped a bit further. I caught a glimpse of a face not familiar to my current consciousness: A hollow-cheeked monk telling me how to conduct myself: *Adhere to the discipline of body, mind and soul that you have learned here among the Dominicans. See and record all without adulterating what you observe with anyone's opinion—including your own.* The voice of an exacting mentor but one with my well-being at heart. The advice fit, whatever its source, so I resolved to heed it even with this man who was my lover.

The next morning, we took to the powdered slopes early. Otto showed no signs of physical fatigue nor did he restrain his smoking. At one point around midday, he attempted to light up even though we were cruising close together down an open trail. Poles in one hand, he pulled out his pack with the other, popped a cigarette into his mouth, and was flicking his lighter when a mogul popped up in front of us. Before I could veer off, we hit the bump and were tossed into a snowy tangle of bodies, clothes, and equipment. My eyes cleared to us lying side by side, his face only inches from mine. He was panting. We stayed there looking into each other's eyes, our breathing getting faster. Then he laughed, slid forward, and kissed me hard on the lips before he pushed away and let out a howl of pain.

"You hurt?" I asked.

He grabbed his left ankle and grimaced. "Pulled it," he said.

Leaving our equipment to pick up later, I draped his arm around my neck so we could maneuver down the hill and back to his hotel room. While I attended to the leg, which showed no sign of swelling, I imagined his mind tossing between his duty to be the upright SS man and the desire to satisfy the need for intimacy. I kept to the role of neutral nurse, solicitous about his injury but impervious to any sexual overtures.

After I wrapped his ankle and settled him into bed, I went towards the door. "Let me check in the village for a doctor in case we need one," I said.

He burst into tears. "Please don't go yet, Raymond. Please. Just sit with me and hold my hand for a little while," he cried like a child about to be abandoned.

I returned to his bedside. "It's safe here," I said as his grief abated. "I saw your need to kiss me out there, but also felt its opposite, the obligation not to. Should we talk about it?"

Wincing at the effort, he turned away and stared out the window. It was several minutes before he spoke. "What's becoming of me, Raymond?" he sniffled. "I don't know how much longer I can go on being two people. One on the outside. The other, its opposite, on the inside."

I remained silent, inviting him to go on. He did not. "Is that what you think is needed, that you be two different people at the same time?" I finally asked.

He glanced back towards me. "Not at all. The Nazis only want me to be that first person, the one that conforms to their idea of a good SS officer. They want to obliterate the inner me. And I'm afraid they are succeeding."

My chest contracted. I grasped his hand. "No, Otto. You can't let them. You know who you are. You can't be someone else."

He grimaced. "Try to hold that thought through eight weeks in Dachau."

"Do you want to tell me what happened there?"

"Not so much what happened there, but what happened that got me sent there. Had they let me stay in Wewelsburg with the stone and my writing, the ugliness in between would not have happened, and I would never have seen the inside of that camp."

"Why did they send you there?"

"Karl Wolff had me called back to Berlin. For all his hauteur, he simply hates me. He goes out of his way to make my life miserable, perhaps because he knows I'm not his kind of tough guy. I admit I went nuts without the stone. It was like some amazing drug too difficult to describe."

"I remember from Tarascon."

"In Berlin I felt like an addict who couldn't get his fix: irritated, angry, and impossible to deal with. I tried anything to feel better: chain smoking, hard drinking, even—"

"Even what?" I prompted after a pause.

He looked away. "If it's a sin at all, it's a sin against you."

"You had sex with another man," I suggested.

"Two," he confessed, "but I only got caught with one." He looked away. "It wasn't love. It was desperation. Drunk both times and neither was worth it. But the second one got back to headquarters. Himmler would have let me off with just a warning. He thinks homosexuality is an illness to be cured, not a perversion to be punished. But Wolff insisted that an officer violating the SS code of conduct without penalty would send the wrong message about discipline to the ranks. So I had to sign an agreement not to drink alcohol for a two-year period, promise to refrain from homosexual activity, and accept probation pending successful rehabilitation in Dachau."

To lighten the mood, I said, "It doesn't look like Dachau cured you of your queerness, my friend."

"Like you thought it would! But it's no joking matter, Raymond. Some of the sadistic ones in the corps would love to catch me *in flagrante* so they could toss me to the other side of the KZ fence. Among all those Jews with yellow stars in Dachau, there were several homosexual prisoners wearing pretty pink triangles."

I shuddered. "The camp's potential has matured in a different direction than you expected when we visited there a year ago," I said, fully meaning to remind him of his earlier positive appraisal of the KZ operation.

He tossed his head away. "It's been greatly enlarged, especially the area for prisoners, many of whom are mistreated, malnourished, and overworked. No one talks about it, but more die now."

"And it is operated by the SS with Himmler in charge?"

He grimaced. "Why I must get back into his good graces right away. He'd stop the excesses if he knew about them. He'd remove the current commander, Oberführer Loritz, posthaste like he did that criminal Wäckerle. But I must inform Himmler only in strict confidence. Ranking officers don't take kindly to being reported by their juniors."

Despite my resolve to stay detached, I feared that Otto's confidence in Himmler's integrity might be an instance of his being blinded by the light. But, I also realized, I had to hope that he was right; our mission's success depended on a less-than-evident level of rectitude in the Reichsführer-SS's character. We had to hope that Himmler knew little or nothing of the atrocities committed in the camps despite evidence to the contrary and that he would intervene and end such wrongs immediately on being informed.

As if intuiting my concern, Otto tightened his grip on my hand. "You might think I can't measure up to someone so powerful," he said, "and your doubt is legitimate. I've been dishonorable enough times to deserve to be taken for a gullible weakling. When I realized that the address, 8 Albrechtstrasse, on the telegram I received in 1935 was that of SS headquarters in Berlin, I should have turned away. But I went into that building, and ever since it's been a series of compromises that now have me locked in this cul-de-sac. Most were easily justified, some blatantly selfish. 'A man has to eat,' I told Ladame to explain away my wearing an SS uniform during the Olympics.

"But I am the author of *Crusade Against the Grail,* a tale of tyranny, religious and political. I know abuse of power unless I close my eyes to it. I sensed from the start that National Socialism could turn as sinister as the medieval Inquisition. Warning signs were everywhere. And yet, I confess that, to secure physical survival and comfort, I overlooked or gave alibi to several things I knew were wrong or could go wrong. I, who wrote about the sacking of Béziers by the blood-thirsty Crusaders and the fiery immolation of the Cathars after the fall of Montsegur, even tried to convince myself that human beings were incapable of the evil some were attributing to the Nazis.

"I am now paying for my selfish naiveté. Despite his trust in me earlier, Himmler's agreeing to my sentence to Dachau shows that it is waning. Support for research such as mine from the scientific community was lost when tests on the Lombrives stone revealed no apparent properties that would help the Nazi effort to develop new weaponry. Interest in my work as history and literature is passé; writing is only valued if it serves as Nazi propaganda. The original purpose for which my unit, the Ahnenerbe, was founded—archaeological and cultural research—has now been supplanted by medical and biological experimentation in which I have no expertise or inclination.

"My homosexuality is now on record; and worse, my genealogy will reveal racial impurity. No coincidence that Wolff is pressuring me to deliver my overdue Certificate of Racial Origin."

He looked at me intently and said, "Heinrich Himmler truly believes that he is the reincarnation of Henry the Fowler, the founder of the German empire, and that he is destined to restore the nation's greatness. Along with crazy Weisthor and perhaps Gabriele, I am among the few who are privy to his master plan to accomplish this. As his new SS central headquarters, he is reconstructing the old castle at Wewelsburg, an allegedly magical site consecrated by the blood of witches murdered in its dungeon during the German stage of the Inquisition. In its North Tower, which he touts to be the center of the world, he plans to enshrine nothing less than the authentic Grail. Above any political, military, social or personal ambitions embodied in his Black Order modeled from a clever combination of the Knights Templar and the Jesuits, Himmler's burning ambition is to find and recover the Grail.

Otto abruptly sat up and swung his legs, sprained ankle and all, over the side of the bed. His face went from pale to suffused, and his eyes glistened as if suddenly feverish. "Besides the work we are doing on his ahnenpass," he said, "it is only Himmler's belief in the existence of the Grail and his conviction that I can and will produce the genuine historical artifact that keeps him protecting me. He is counting on me to provide the *piece de resistance* for his version of Camelot in Wewelsburg."

"I'm not sure that you can understand," he said, his voice becoming distant and dreamy. "Himmler must have known before we even met that I possessed the gift of Heinrich Schliemann, who used his talent to divine and discover the historical city of Troy via Homer's *Iliad and Odyssey*. For me *Parzival* is the map to the Grail that Himmler seeks. Recovering it is my destiny." His breathing grew heavier. "This is why I could write in the closing of *Lucifer's Court*, 'I am carrying a Dietrich with me!' It is literally true."

He exhaled and slumped over. I expected him to break into tears, but he held still and let his breath subside. That haunting scene from the vision of the glowing green stone again came to mind: Mathène mocking me for being afraid to ask the question.

I had forgotten the question then, but I knew what I must ask him now. "What is this Dietrich, Otto? What is this key? Why are you looking for what you are already carrying with you?"

He looked up, his eyes bolted wide. His head started to shake so violently that I had to hold his face with both hands to keep him from cracking his neck.

"I don't know why," he finally murmured, "I know I am carrying it with me but feel I must keep looking for it. I've been over it a thousand times. Insane."

He limped to the window and stared at the light snow dusting the courtyard. "It seems that I can't do this alone," he muttered through clenched teeth. "I'm only half a man or one with a split down the middle. When I'm on one side, I can't hear or see the other. When I go over there, I lose touch with me back here." He whirled around, his fists balled. "I don't mean to blame you, Raymond, but somehow I feel it's your damned fault. I may have the key, but you're supposed to remember where I put it last." His eyes filled up and his body sagged into a nearby chair.

You're looking at the wrong lifetime, 333 had told me when I was similarly confounded.

"Do you remember coming into Notre Dame de Sabart from the graveyard in Tarascon last June?" I asked Otto.

He looked puzzled. "Of course."

"What did you see when you first came through the church door?"

"It was pretty dark. You were hunched in a pew in front of the shrine of the Black Madonna. I thought you were meditating or asleep, so I tip-toed up and touched you on the shoulder."

"And then?"

"You flinched because I caught you unaware. You called out a word, a name, Arnaud, I think."

"A case of mistaken identity on my part, but the name is still important. Who was Arnaud?"

"You were the one who called it out, not me."

"From your research into the Cathar period."

"A common name then."

"Someone notorious. Perhaps connected to Jacques Fournier of Pamiers. You wrote about the bishop in *Crusade* but don't mention any Arnaud. I checked."

He looked off for a moment. "Ah, the brief Cathar revival under the Authiers decades after the fall of Montsegur. Early 1300's. You must mean Arnaud Sicre-Baille, a notorious turncoat who trapped the last Perfect Guilhem Belibaste and handed him over to Fournier to be burnt at the stake. That Arnaud might fit. He'd cause any heretic a fright if he crept up from behind. I studied that period briefly in the Register of the Inquisition; the National Library in Paris has a French translation. But it was their clever secular leader, a shepherd named Piere Maury, that impressed me the most in that account even though he couldn't save Belibaste in the end."

"Piere Maury," I repeated. "Arnaud told me that Piere was the only Catalonian Cathar he considered a friend but that the shepherd for all his cunning had a blind spot bigger than the sun when it came to Belibaste."

Otto's eyes suddenly popped.

"What?" I asked.

He began to laugh. "Do you know what you just said: *Arnaud told me?* Like you two had a little chat the other day. Arnaud Sicre and Piere Maury lived in medieval times. And people say I hear and see things that other people don't!"

I gulped. I had slipped into some remote past without catching it. "Sorry," I said. "Doesn't that happen to you sometimes?"

"Too much." He grinned. "But not in the Sabart church. I was just being plain old Otto Rahn there. Who did the man you mistook for Arnaud turn out to be?"

"I never actually identified him, but I called him Jean during the daydream or whatever it was. Another common name. He seemed to be the central character in the story, the real last Perfect. From an earlier discussion, I understood that the two of us as a team were to escape using a secret passage through the cave to a safe location, carrying the Cathar treasure with us. A group of fighters, led by a former Templar Knight I call Baldwin, were to form a protective barricade against the bishop's troops that were giving chase."

He whistled. "The Templars and Cathars in cahoots. Makes sense. In *Parzival* von Eschenbach uses the word *Templar* to describe the elite guardians of the Grail Castle, which we know is Montsegur." He thought for a moment. "Your setting feels right although I don't know that period's history well enough to verify it. But no Jean jumps to mind. I'll have to research that further. And who did you see as yourself there?"

"Does the name Jaques, without the *c*, ring a bell?"

"Ah, Jaques. Why does that make me instantly think *the bishop's boy*? Isn't that what you accused me of calling you in Tarascon?"

I nodded.

He frowned. "But that makes no sense. The bishop had to be

Fournier, and this Jaques was on the Cathar side."

I had already noticed that discrepancy. I tried to force my memory back, only to encounter blackness and the beginning of a headache. "I can't figure that out either." I shrugged. "So who was Mathène? Gabriele said you'd know."

"Mathène? I don't know any Mathène. Sounds like a woman's name. A celibate Perfect wouldn't have anything to do with a woman."

"Belibaste had one. Not quite a wife, but she bore him two children."

"Raymonde Piquier. I remember her from the Register. Belibaste conned Piere Maury into marrying her to cover his own indiscretion. Didn't last long. The old lecher got jealous and unmarried them again so he could have Raymonde back. So are you're insinuating that our Jean was no more faithful to his vows than Belibaste? That Mathène was his wife?"

"A common arrangement made to camouflage a Perfect's identity. They didn't have to know each other in the biblical sense."

He went very quiet, and then as if close to tears again he murmured, "Mathène, Gabriele. All these poor women with only bit parts then and now except for Esclarmonde of Foix."

I could not follow either his thought or emotion. "Esclarmonde of Foix?" I queried.

"A digression, but you must read more carefully," he chided. "In *Crusade* I write about the great theological debate between the most learned Cathar Perfects and the Roman clergy held in Pamiers in 1207, two years prior to the start of the Crusade. The Catholics were indignant that the Cathar contingent included a woman, the countess Esclarmonde of Foix. 'Madame, stay with your spinning wheel! You have nothing to say here,' an infuriated priest is said to have shouted at her when she started to outwit their brightest scholars. Nothing quite galled the Roman patriarchy like the Cathar practice of ordaining women right along with the men."

He immediately turned introspective again. "With all I've written about the Cathars," he said, "I've never placed myself into their story. Now it seems to be turning personal. For the sake of argument, let's suppose I was Jean and you were Jaques. What happened to us after that scene in the church, Raymond?"

There was pain in his voice as he asked the question, a heartfelt plea for an answer. I had already tried to get beyond the mouth of the cave to see how it turned out but without results so far.

Don't force it. Trust that it will come as needed, 333 had advised. "I don't know yet either," I told Otto, "but we'll find out when we need to know." I glanced at my watch. "It's been a long day already although it's only three o'clock. Why don't you lie down and rest that leg for a bit?"

He moved toward the bed. I thought of the package in my pocket. Gadal had asked that it be opened when we were together.

"I have a gift for both of us from an old friend of yours," I said as he shuffled to make himself comfortable.

"What? From whom?"

"From Antonin Gadal. He was in Geneva and left this for us with Paul Ladame." I allowed myself the lie of convenience; I was not yet ready to introduce him to 333 and the Emerald Club. I handed him the packet. "Open it."

He pulled off the wrapper and unclasped the silver plated jewelry box inside. I looked over his shoulder. Etched into a heavy bronze medal was the image of two armored men astride a single horse.

"The Templar emblem," I explained with words that seemed to come from someone explaining the object to me. "Two to a horse. Templar warriors rode into battle saddled in pairs, one with the sword in the right hand, the other with it in the left to cover both flanks. Cathar Perfects also travelled and taught in pairs. Christ's disciples likewise preached in pairs."

He flashed me a genuine Otto grin. "Two to a horse," he repeated. "If I didn't know better, I'd say it was the motto of some ancient fraternity of homosexuals."

"Not far off," I said as I headed for the door. "The Inquisition did charge the Templars with being a bunch of queers. Now put it under your pillow, a talisman for pleasant dreams, and take a nap. We'll meet in the dining room for dinner at seven."

Calling the break proved to be inspired. The confident fellow who strode across the chalet restaurant without a limp and flashed me a warm smile upon arrival at the table was a different man from the somber individual I left in the hotel room a few hours earlier. After glancing around to ensure that our privacy was adequate, Otto went through the meal without looking over his shoulder.

"Had our earlier conversation not been so beneficial," he began, "I'd owe you a profuse apology for my pathetic behavior. However, since it brought me to understand the gravity of the current situation and work up the courage to reach some difficult conclusions, I'll simply express gratitude for your assistance. Raymond, I now see that my country and all of Europe is in a state of critical emergency. With what I saw at Dachau, the somewhat negative intimations I sensed when I joined the SS in 1935 have become high probabilities. Nazi Germany intends to conquer this continent and exterminate all elements outside the pale of their concept of Aryan superiority.

"The skiing on Spitzingsee was superb today," he quipped as the waiter brought our plates to the table. Remarkably, Otto passed on the wine.

"But you are aware of all this," he continued once the server moved on. "You didn't come here to take a vacation with me any more than you joined our group in the Languedoc just to keep me company. I'll let you get to your agenda in few moments, but first allow me to make a couple of points.

"Heinrich Himmler remains the only wild card in the deck of the German hierarchy who might derail Hitler's infernal machine of destruction. I believe I may be able to influence him in that direction if two conditions can be met.

"First, I must regain his complete confidence, which I can do by showing him that Dachau shaped me into the ideal SS man. I have several ideas beyond my meager acting experience for accomplishing that. Second, my assessment that Himmler is more decent human being than devoted Nazi must prove true. Once he understands what is going on in the camps, he must be outraged and order a permanent halt to such activities.

"Beyond that is the Dietrich. He knows I have it, and he desperately wants it. That tug-of-war has been going on for a long time, and he knows that too."

I whistled softly, surprised that his thinking was so close to 333's. It saved me lengthy explanations. "We are not only on the same track but on the same train," I exclaimed before reviewing the case for the Pan European Movement and the other efforts to achieve continental unity through peaceful means.

"I am familiar with the work of Count Coudenhove and admire Rudolf Steiner's political thought although both their organizations are now banned in Germany," he said after I had made my statement. "But that doesn't matter. No political philosophy is going to stop the Nazi military and police machines. I imagine your people have something more substantial in the works."

It was my turn to cite the limits to information I could divulge. "I can't get into the details because—"

He cut me off. "No preambles necessary. Every SS man is taught the basics of espionage: no one agent is to know more than he needs to know; no one knows more than we can afford to lose at one time; and so forth. Just tell me what I need to know to do the job."

Again he handed me the opening I had spent hours trying to concoct. "My associates understand that a few months back you attended a dinner in the Nobel Restaurant in Berlin. Jean-Marie Musy, the Swiss politician and filmmaker, was present along with Himmler and Wolff."

"Also Dr. Franz Riedweg, oozing charm in Himmler's direction, obviously intent on securing a ranking position in the SS."

I nodded. "Riedweg's the target. A former member of Coudenhove's PEM and a Swiss political insider, he's privy to a lot of confidential information. He's become aligned with the Swiss party that

aims to incorporate our country, at least its German-speaking can-
tons, into the Greater Third Reich. Further, as a medical doctor, he
is privy to some controversial research in the field of eugenics, which
could prove disastrous in Nazi hands bent on racial purification."

"And, let me guess." Otto said. "You want me to wield my influence on Himmler so he denies Riedweg's application."

"Correct."

"I fooled them before. I'll fool them again. They had the power
to seduce me; it's time to turn the tables on them." He pursed his
lips, pulled the medallion from his pocket and rubbed the image
with his thumb. "Two to a horse," he murmured. "Since it looks like
I have to wade in deeper than you in the next act, I'll hang on to this
for now." We got up from the table together.

"We better get busy then." Otto was irresistible when he assumed control. "Get on with Himmler's ahnenpass. Find something
intriguing that I will just have to present to Himmler in person.
Leave Riedweg to me."

Chapter 19: Pamiers, March 1321

The stomp of mailed boots and clank of chains behind the door that led from the prisoners' dungeon to the courtroom signaled the arrival of the accused and his accuser. The buzz of conversation in the overflowing gallery settled into an expectant silence. Seated at his usual desk, Jaques shifted back into a more obscured position.

Bishop Fournier in ceremonial purple strode into the courtroom and took his place in the center of the raised table around which were arrayed the full complement of clergy and lawyers even though this was only a preliminary indictment. It was the most significant Cathar trial since that of the revival's mastermind, Pierre Authier, in 1310.

"Your Excellency and honored members of the Court of the Inquisition," the bailiff intoned. Jaques bent to record the official's words even though he had transcribed this opening ritual hundreds of times, "I present to you for trial and judgment, the alleged heretic, Guilhem Belibaste, and, as required by ecclesiastical law, the primary witness against him, Arnaud Sicre-Baille."

Jaques glanced up to get his first look at the notorious prisoner, the hot tempered Languedocian shepherd accused of murder in his youth who later converted to Catharism and was then admitted into its clergy. Dressed in the blue-black robe cinched with the white cord customary for a Perfect, evidently featured here to mock the man's heretical priesthood, the tall and stocky Belibaste looked impressive. Head high, he stepped briskly toward the dais despite the heavy ankle chain fettering him to Arnaud Sicre-Baille, who, despite a feigned bravado, could not keep his eyes from darting about like those of a panicked puppy.

As the pair approached the bench, Arnaud caught sight of Jaques. To mark his moment of triumph, he leered and mouthed "Joli Jaques" in greeting. When the arresting party arrived in Pamiers the previous day, Jaques had requested a preliminary debriefing with Arnaud, but the man refused, insisting that this time he would only deal with the bishop.

The business of the indictment moved on. Jaques duly recorded the usual pledges for justice and warnings against perjury even though the prosecution would ignore any mitigating evidence from the defense and proceed posthaste towards the preordained conviction. Nevertheless, the scribe could not quell the exciting sense that he was about to observe an important historical event from his unique dual vantage point. The single record he would make of the proceedings that would presently stand as evidence of the Catholic Inquisition's administration of justice towards heretics would later, perhaps hundreds of years hence, serve as equal proof to its cruel oppression of worthy dissidents.

Fournier's approach to this trial quickly proved that he too considered this case extraordinary. With unaccustomed and conspicuous disdain for his star witness, the bishop bullied Arnaud Sicre whenever he dallied or preened in his presentation of the immediate causes for Belibaste's arrest.

"On the journey here, which I had to make shackled to his heretical body, the accused called me an endless stream of vile names: *Judas, son of a viper*, even *bastard* although he knows I am the legitimate son of his friend, Sybille Baille—"[37]

"Name calling is not evidence of heresy. Facts. Just facts," the bishop goaded.

Arnaud hung his head momentarily. "How about this then?" he finally said. "On the way here we were kept shackled together in the main tower of the fortress of Castelbó. While standing before a window high above the ground, he tempted me, 'If you can redis-cover your moral conscience and repent of what you've done to me, I will console you before we plunge from this tower together. Both our souls will ascend at once to our Heavenly Father, where we will have crowns and thrones waiting for us.'" Arnaud stared hard at the bishop. "Does that meet your standard for evidence, Excellency?"

"Quite enough," Fournier said with a wave of his hand. "Un-shackle the witness. He's dismissed."

"But there's much more against this villain." Arnaud bawled as the attendants dragged him from the courtroom.

While Jaques was still suppressing a grin over Arnaud's humili-ation, Bishop Fournier abruptly stood up, a posture taken by a court official only when addressing one of his betters. The accused alone seemed not to notice the sensational gesture.

"At last, Guilhem Belibaste, we meet face to face," Fournier be-gan, pleasure evident in his tone. "Welcome back to Languedoc. You are quite the celebrity, you understand, here in your homeland. And not just among your own Cathar brethren. The Archbishop of Narbonne attempted to claim the privilege of trying you based on an outstanding murder indictment in his diocese. To persuade him that your later and more egregious activities as a heretical leader superseded any adolescent offense, I had to cede him the right to hold your eventual execution within his boundaries. Thus I was able to relocate the proceedings from the Narbonnese criminal courts, where you would have been ignominiously beheaded for murder, to this ecclesiastical court where the charges merit a more spectacu-lar form of execution, death at the stake." For a second Fournier smiled, amused, Jaques thought, by his own grim humor.

"Now, just because I'm curious and to get past it," the bishop added, "let me ask: did you actually attempt to lead Arnaud Sicre into suicide with you?"

It was Belibaste's turn for a wry smile. "Dispense with the cat-and-mouse game, Jacques Fournier. I contest no evidence. Do what you must do and be done with it."

Looking chagrinned that his opening bit of theater had failed to ruffle the prisoner, the bishop retook his seat. He turned toward the scribe and said, "Strike that last about the suicide. We'll not consider it further. The less I see the insufferable Sicre in my court the better."

He banged the gavel and dismissed the audience. "Guilhem Belibaste's trial will start at a date still to be determined," he growled.

Nor was the bishop's mood improved when Jaques later complied with Fournier's request for a meeting.

"Sit, Jaques. This one is between us and confidential." Fournier did not look up from his papers. "Evidently Belibaste has decided not to cooperate. We can't tempt him with gold and luxuries like the Sicre fellow did to get him here. He's strong and stubborn, so we could torture him to death before we got anything by duress. He's obstinate enough to become one of those martyred heroes, another Bernard Delicieux."

He finally looked up. "But that's no longer my greatest concern. With the movement now in tatters, the Inquisition and the army can wipe the whole lot of them out. It is the other matter we discussed earlier, why I wanted Belibaste to be brought in alive. Do you remember?"

Jaques nodded. "The Gnostic line, the *consolamentum*, the lost keys. Belibaste gives the church a final opportunity to reclaim the knowledge and power it lost shortly after the time of Jesus," he said.

"Of course you remember it word-for-word. I sometimes forget who I am talking to. All will be ashes if Belibaste dies without giving me what I must have. The Cathars get another martyr, the church remains sterile, and that nitwit Arnaud Sicre walks away with our money."

"You really dislike him," Jaques said just to gain some time to think.

"What's in him to like? A Cathar by blood who betrayed his own. A Judas Iscariot." Fournier leaned forward. "But he's all we've got right now, and he was cunning enough to walk Belibaste into our trap in the Pallars. Perhaps he knows something else we could use to induce Belibaste to talk. That type always reserves some choice pieces of information for use in further extortion."

"And I'm to pry them out of him even though he insists on dealing only with you directly?"

Fournier made a face. "I can't stand him in my sight. Take lots of money and get what you can for it."

Jaques was tempted to ask the bishop whether he knew about the murders Arnaud had committed; perhaps his revulsion for the murderer came from guilty complicity in his crimes. He checked his curiosity and asked instead, "Can I promise that his mother's property will be returned to his family? That should make him talk."

Fournier flushed. "It was sold and the funds went to the Bishop of Ax. To reverse that deal would set a dangerous precedent. Hundreds of such properties have been confiscated in the Languedoc." Then he grinned. "But promise, if you must. We can always dispose of Arnaud once we are finished with him."

Jaques checked a gulp and tittered to disguise his shock. "Arnaud dislikes me as much as you dislike him. But I'll see what I can do."

As he got up to leave, the bishop came around and grasped his shoulders. "I rarely admit this to anyone," he said, his voice choked, "but I am going into debt with you again. The Roman Catholic Church's future depends on our success here. And I am powerless against a resistant Belibaste without some assistance. Find a key that will unlock the treasure taken from us by the Gnostics centuries ago. Belibaste may be our last chance."

When Arnaud Sicre accepted his latest invitation to meet without any argument, Jaques raised his readiness for chicanery to high alert. He became further suspicious when Arnaud greeted him not with the anger or resentment expected from a proud individual who has just suffered public humiliation but with the insouciance of an experienced card player holding the winning hand.

Once across the table from each other, Arnaud was in no rush. "Here by order of the bishop, I presume," he said to open.

Jaques had to adjust his approach on the fly. Since he need not offer money just to start the conversation, he decided to satisfy his own reasons for wanting this meeting, leaving the bishop's agenda item for later.

"I'm also here for myself," he said. "Even though my role in your recent achievement was minimal, your bringing the Languedoc's most wanted criminal back alive reflects to my credit also. For that I want to express my gratitude. Your cleverness and persistence alone made Belibaste's capture possible. As one who works with him closely, I understand how the pressure of his position turns Bishop Fournier brusque on occasion, causing him to sometimes wound his friends along with his enemies. Since his office does not allow that he apologize in person, I do so on his behalf, adding ten gold florins to your reward money to compensate for any unintended harm."

Arnaud's eyes tightened. "If you toy with me, Joli, I'll strangle you with my own hands, but not until you're made to watch them dig up your mother and that false priest Fontaine and smell the stench of their heretical bodies being burned to ash." He grinned. "Yes, we passed through Tarascon on the way here. I heard that your mummy died. Condolences."

Jaques held back a swallow lest it betray his disgust. "Thank you," he said, pushing on. "When we last talked, you asked me to leave the details of the operation up to you. A necessary security measure then, but now that it's over, I hope you'll tell me something of your exploits. Such valorous deeds, which may not make it into the record during the hearings, should not be lost to history."

Arnaud stared for several moments. Jaques waited. Finally, the other man chuckled. "That the scheme worked at all is enough to make one believe in Divine Providence," he said. "Only Belibaste's enormous greed and Piere Maury's extreme gullibility saved me numerous times from getting caught and hurled over a cliff as has happened to other spies despite the Cathars' claim to nonviolence."

"So when you returned to the colony, they swallowed your story:[38] Aunt Alazais was too sick to travel and her daughter Raymonde wouldn't think of wedding without her. Belibaste proved willing to risk the trip to the Pallars to console the sick woman and marry the pair. The groom came along easily, a wife and dowry as bait. Piere Maury, usually quite bright but never smelling the rat in this case, tagged right along."

"Not that simple, Joli," Arnaud barked. But he then launched into the details for which Jaques was fishing. "There were obstacles galore. Belibaste wanted Piere's brother, Jean, to come to the Pallars as well. Why I don't know. The kid constantly tries to embarrass the old man and regularly expresses his distaste for their faith. With my own ears I heard him cursing a donkey that was giving him trouble, calling it a 'filthy heretic.' Piere and I wanted him left behind although for different reasons. Piere thought he would be too disruptive and I felt we'd end up carrying his lazy ass. That got settled when Jean took ill and couldn't travel.

"Then on the day we were scheduled to leave the enclave in Morella, Belibaste saw a soothsayer who predicted that he would never return to Catalonia. Luckily, Piere Maury talked him out of his fright, and I solidified the schedule by having the parties sign a binding contract for the wedding on the set date.

"Belibaste then turned skittish when two magpies crossed his path in the back country, a bad omen, I understand. Again Piere, who might as well have been working for us, talked him out of his conviction of doom.

"But the most serious challenge came on the third night of the nine-day trip. We spent that evening in the village of Asco. Both Belibaste and Piere got leery and decided to run me through the *in vino veritas* ploy, getting me drunk before putting a test question to me. I caught on quickly but played along. They plied me with wine, and I pretended to grow drunker while pouring out my goblet as fast as they filled it. Finally, faking fall-down inebriation, I let Piere lead me to the bed we were to share. I pulled out my cock and started to piss on his pillow. He dragged me outside to finish my business. As I was thrashing in the weeds for a place to go, he suggested that we betray Belibaste to the authorities and collect the bounty on his head. To which I asserted, slurs and all, 'I can't believe you'd do such a thing. I'd never let you get away with it.' I then staggered back to bed and pretended to snore, but not so loud that I couldn't hear Piere tell Belibaste what had happened outside, assuring the old man that I was nothing to worry about."

"Brilliant, Arnaud," Jaques cheered. "And so it went smoothly from there until our men surrounded the hostel where you bedded down in Tirvia and made the arrests."

Arnaud nodded with a triumphant leer.

"What happened to the other two men in Belibaste's party?"

"I had the commanding officer release them."

"But why?"

"You only paid for Belibaste. The bridegroom did his job as decoy and got no woman or dowry for the effort—punishment enough. And Piere Maury—" Jaques saw Arnaud's eyes soften. "I couldn't let him be taken in even though there was a large bounty on his head. The Cathars call themselves *bonhommes*. Piere is actually a good man. I hope he has sense enough to make himself scarce because I may not feel so benevolent next time."

Jaques was struck with an unusual wave of admiration for this Piere Maury. It would be an honor to know a man with enough charisma to touch a heart as black as Arnaud's. He experienced a moment of yearning. In the cave in Tarascon, Timekeeper had predicted that he would be given a partner with whom he would accomplish his destiny. *To protect the plan, he still remains paired with another in proxy. When the time is right, you will be introduced to each other with the watchword, 'Two to a horse.' Listen for it.* Could this Piere Maury be the man of whom Timekeeper spoke? He could only hope.

But he wrenched his attention back to the task at hand. "You were then shackled to Belibaste, and the incident in Castelbó occurred."

"Then all the way here across the mountain pass. Imagine being tied two to a horse with that filthy bastard for days," he snorted, swiping under his nose.

Two to a horse. Jaques instinctively reached for the medallion he kept in his pocket ever since Timekeeper had given it to him. That the watchword cropped up twice in the last few moments was beyond chance. This realization came with that peculiar shift that signaled an oncoming vision, but this time it did not absorb his consciousness completely. He never lost sight of Arnaud or control of the conversation with him. He seemed to be able to operate in both dimensions simultaneously or at least to swing rapidly enough from one to the other that Arnaud did not notice his absences. Prior visions appeared to be a series of fixed images of past events. This was more fluid in presentation: drifting smoke forming a shape, erasing itself, and then reorganizing into something else, as if whatever was trying to evolve could not make up its mind. The future perhaps, he figured, or alternate interpretations of the past generating possible futures.

Piere Maury, the dedicated disciple, and Belibaste, the Perfect. Piere was Belibaste's second, the one Timekeeper meant when he said: *Someone has to know. Whoever it is should be in position to inform Belibaste. Maybe he will, maybe not. A necessary security arrangement.* Piere adulated Belibaste but was not oblivious to his flaws. He played along with the charade that made him the man's mistress's husband briefly and surrogate father to his child permanently. He understood that Belibaste had to give his life to recover his Perfect status but would only do so reluctantly. Thus he did not tell Belibaste that Arnaud was a traitor. With the *in vino veritas* test, Arnaud thought he was gaming Piere, but Piere, a step ahead, saw that Arnaud was pouring out the wine rather than drinking it. The spy who thought he had fooled his targets was himself fooled. He became the instrument that kept Belibaste on the path to his redeeming fate, which awaited him with the bishop's posse in the border town of Tirvia in the Pallars.

"Even more galling than his crude name-calling after he was captured," Arnaud continued, "was Belibaste's hypocritical switch to righteousness once he realized that his death was inevitable. He actually believed he could convert me back to the 'true faith of my mother and brother.' When he was trying to talk me into jumping from the tower, his words were so convincing that for a moment I was tempted. I had to cross myself to expel the devil he planted in my head. Black magic," he snorted.

Jaques observed the wispy vision reshape itself. *He's obstinate enough to become one of those martyred heroes, another Bernard Delicieux,* Fournier had said of Belibaste. Had the fallen Perfect somehow acquired the courage to endure a martyr's death, the one position against which the bishop was defenseless?

"You mentioned a sudden change in Belibaste," he said to Arnaud. "Did you notice anything peculiar that might have caused it?"

Arnaud hesitated. "You mean something freakish that would turn a greedy lecher into an actual Perfect like my mother was?" He thought for a moment. "After he realized he had been tricked and captured, he started snarling like a chained lion and damning me all to hell. At some point later, he took the coins he had in his pocket and gave them to Piere, the settlement of an old debt, I heard him say. Piere did lean in and whisper something to him. Whatever it was, Belibaste looked surprised and then far too pleased for the circumstances. They embraced and Piere left. From then on the old buzzard seemed different."

The smoke began to dance as if coiled by a whirlwind. At the moment Arnaud had described, Piere told Belibaste something that put the Perfect at peace. *We are not so careless about safeguarding the sacred knowledge,* Timekeeper had said. Whatever Piere whispered served to assure Belibaste that the work would continue beyond him, that he was now free to redeem himself through death. The Perfect's promise to console Arnaud as they fell to their deaths was not unfounded; that act of faith in leaping from the battlement would have restored his power to administer the sacrament before they hit the ground.

Jaques sighed with a secret sense of satisfaction. Other than the identity of his future partner, he had learned what he needed to know to continue in the role he had embraced with his vow to Timekeeper.

As the bishop's boy, however, he had to continue to prod Arnaud for clues that might lead to the key that Fournier coveted. "While in Catalonia," he said, "you must have heard talk about the famous Cathar treasure that many have sought for since the four heretics escaped with it just prior to the fall of Montsegur in 1244."

Arnaud snorted. "Got your nose up the wrong ass again, Joli. So it's treasure that Fournier sent you for. Believe me, the Cathars in Spain are paupers, all living on the pittance paid to the few shepherds, weavers, and carders among them. If it's treasure he wants, have him look around your hometown, in the cliff caves above the Ariège, or in the Templar commanderies like Miglos, Junac, or as far up the Vicdessos Valley as Montreal-de-Sos. But beware: the ghosts of old Templar legionnaires guard those places. Otherwise, I'd be out there hunting myself. Point him in that direction. I dare you."

He poked at Jaques. "But you won't, Joli. Your people are in Tarascon, and you wouldn't set Fournier's dogs on them. Or would you?" He held out his hand for the expected payment.

Jaques pulled out the purse containing the bounty and laid it on the table. He then counted out ten more florins to compensate for Fournier's rudeness in court. "Your reward for bringing in the last Perfect, my friend," he said.

Arnaud sniffed while snatching up the money. "There are a lot more heretics in the hills where Belibaste came from. The church still holds my mother's property in Ax. Inform His Excellency that if wants the rest of them, he knows the price: my deed."

Chapter 20: Muggenbrunn, Wewelsburg, June 1938

The bravado with which Otto had announced at Schliersee that he would work solo to prevent Dr. Riedweg's admission to the SS left me somewhat concerned for both his safety and the success of the endeavor, an apprehension that only increased as weeks without communication turned into months. Meanwhile, the collision between Germany and the rest of Europe loomed larger daily. Shortly after our meeting at the ski resort, a coup engineered by Himmler and Heydrich ousted the moderate army leaders von Blomberg and Fritsch from the German High command. Then throughout February 1938, the world press screamed of dire consequences should Germany attempt to annex Austria in direct violation of the Versailles Treaty. And yet, when on March 12th Wehrmacht troops marched into Austria and consummated the forbidden *Anschluss*, the western allies mouthed only meek protests and kept their guns holstered. The swastika had barely risen over Vienna before an emboldened Hitler announced that Czechoslovakia was next in line for annexation to the Greater Reich.

Throughout, I tried to focus on the tedious and seemingly trivial task of tracing Heinrich Himmler's relationship to the Passaquay family of Savoy; but my mind—awake, in reverie, and in dreams—obsessed instead over the details of the life of Jaques de Sabart. I learned to catch hold of a promising subliminal clue, tug on it gently, and then pull any new content attached to it into consciousness.

I kept notes of gaps and confusions encountered to sort out later with Otto. Thus I put together a reasonably complete biography of my subject from his birth in Tarascon through his service as scribe in Bishop Fournier's court prior to the 1321 trial of Guilhem Belibaste, the purported last Cathar Perfect.

Once certain that we could confirm the Passaquay connection to Himmler's satisfaction, I advised Otto via SS Headquarters in Berlin that I had confidential information I needed to deliver to him in person. I received no response until mid-April and then indirectly via a letter from Gabriele Winckler-Dechend in Konstanz.

Rahn had stopped for another unannounced visit in early April,[39] she wrote. Her first child had just been born, and she reminded him that he had agreed to be the boy's godfather; but Rahn absent-mindedly left before the christening, leaving her quite upset. He was headed for the summer to the remote mountain village of Muggenbrunn in the Black Forest north of Freiburg supposedly to complete his long-promised book about the German heretic hunter, Konrad von Marburg.

> While he went on to me about his accomplishments, including a well-received lecture on the Cathars at the Dietrich-Eckart Club in Dortmund, he seemed hurried and secretive. He mentioned that General Karl Wolff was hounding him to complete his long overdue Certificate of Racial Origin. He complained that his duties keep him too busy to research it correctly. Were we still working together, I'd have just done it for him. I feel artists and writers should be barred from the SS; they lack the basic discipline the organization requires.

She mentioned that Rahn had received my message and asked that she extend an invitation on his behalf to meet him in Muggenbrunn as soon as possible. Her letter ended with a bombshell:

> As he was walking out the door, he announced this startling bit of news: "Now that the Reichsführer-SS has married you off to Herr Winckler and you have a child, I suppose it's my turn," he said.

I was stunned. "You are getting married?"

"To Asta Baeschlin, a Swiss woman with a four-year-old blond blue-eyed boy, a perfect Aryan. She will be spending part of the summer in Muggenbrunn." I was so dumbstruck that he got away before I could get any details. I thought you'd want to know in advance that the Otto who awaits you in the Schwarzwald is not alone.

Indeed! Once I caught my breath, my sympathy was more for Gabriele than for myself. I imagined the lovely Mathène trailing after the Perfect Jean Maury, her brow creased with chaste dedication to duty while inside she burned with carnal desire. *All these poor women only had bit parts,* Otto had said in Schliersee. Pity Asta Baeschlin.

U ltimately though, my personal distress over his putting a woman he was incapable of loving in my place sent me running to Muggenbrunn. The EC's concern relayed through Ladame that Rahn in his zeal might be mismanaging the Riedweg's case provided the necessary impersonal alibi to cover for the wounded lover.

Spring blooms late in the rolling hills of the Black Forest so Muggenbrunn still danced with fresh blossoms, cool sunlight, and rushing streams when I arrived there in early June. Despite recent complaints to his superiors about a chronic bronchial condition, no doubt aggravated by his chain smoking, Otto exuded health and ease as he waved me up the drive to the small but comfortable cottage he had rented for the summer.

Once the driver left my luggage, he grabbed hold and hugged me.

"So, she told you," he said, suddenly stepping back and eyeing me hungrily.

"Who told me what?" I asked, knowing exactly what he meant.

"Gabriele—that I was getting married. I wanted to tell you myself. Damn woman, can't keep her mouth shut."

"How did you know I knew?"

He grabbed hold of one of the vertical pillars supporting the porch. "When I hugged you, your body was as inflexible as this post and the part of you that should have been stiff was barely evident." He pointed to chairs overlooking the town and the ragged hills beyond it. "You aren't taking this seriously, are you?"

"It's not true then?"

"Of course, it's true. At Schliersee I said I had to show Himmler that Dachau had turned me into an exemplary SS man. I even volunteered for stud service at one of those horrific Lebensborn camps and may have managed to seed a few compliant *fraulein* with future Aryan warriors that will look like me."

"Those Nazi baby farms actually exist and you participated?"

"Distasteful, but it confirms one's reputation as a real man. And now I'm getting married like every other proper SS officer. Even though she is Swiss and a divorcee with a young child, Himmler was sufficiently impressed that he offered to preside at our wedding ceremony."

"And Asta, the bride—what does she say to all this?"

He looked away. "They'll arrive this weekend and stay at the chalet in town. I'll have to play it suavely. She's from a wealthy Swiss family, and her parents are already miffed that her first marriage went bad. I have to appear to be the accomplished writer of considerable means, which is not a lie, just a matter of time. An SS salary alone, even an officer's, won't impress Asta or her parents. My masterpiece, *Sebastian*, now stands at two thousand pages. A little polish and then we publish."

"You haven't asked her, and yet you told Himmler you're engaged?" I had to whistle.

He clapped his hand over mine and squeezed. "Trust me, Raymond. It will work. It's got to. It's part of my master plan. So far so good. After our meeting in Schliersee, I invoked my poor health to obtain leave and permission to travel to Switzerland for a cure. Luck had it that I ran into our Jean-Marie Musy, who pointed me to connections with information about Riedweg. The details are complicated and unimportant. Musy introduced me to a knowledgeable clique at *Der Kreis*, an influential gay journal dedicated to the ideas of the poet Stephan George and the novelist Albert Rausch. There—good fortune again—I encountered Dr. Alfred Schmid, the chemist and founder of the German youth movement, the Grey Corps, which the Nazis banned in 1934. We'd met earlier and have tried to remain friends. The Party held him objectionable but could not blacklist him because, as a leading chemist indispensable to several leading industrial companies, he enjoys a certain immunity. Gabriele and I were warned for sending him Christmas cards last year. He is watched.

"I couldn't just blurt out what I wanted, but Schmid got the idea when I mentioned Riedweg. They are bitter rivals. He casually dropped some information, leaving me to come to my own conclusions. I even wondered if he might be an EC agent himself."

"If so, not something they think I need to know. But how does Schmid's information about Riedweg help with Himmler?"

"Since he is known to be an insider to homosexual circles with no reputation to lose with the Nazis, his gossip is as good as gold. If Schmid infers that Riedweg is homosexual and involved with the Pan Europeans, the SS will want to have nothing to do with him."

I had to smile. Otto was a cleverer agent than I expected. By visiting the Lebensborn and getting married, he had built himself the he-man platform from which he could finger Riedweg as gay.

"And that's the case you made to Himmler?" I asked.

"The case I am trying to make. So far, I fear my dossier on this is being held up in the administrative jungle. I first voiced my suspicions about Riedweg to Ullmann, who suggested I report them via Wolff to Himmler. Wolff took his time to read what I submitted and then asked for clarification on a counter-allegation, probably from Riedweg's supporters, that I had propositioned sex with an unnamed Luftwaffe officer. Wolff, of course, knew of the earlier indiscretion that got me sent to Dachau and is less prone than Himmler to believe I have reformed. Ullmann believes Wolff is not taking the new charge too seriously, especially as the officer allegedly involved is no longer in the service, but my report has yet to reach

Himmler, and I believe the delay is intentional. I must get past whoever is holding it up and speak to Himmler in person. I certainly can
convince him about Riedweg and probably about our larger objective. But I need something more to get in the door, and we are about
to go and get it."

"We?"

He patted my hand again. "You've finished your part of the work
on the ahnenpass, I understand."

"Yes, Johann Michael Passaquay[40] of Savoy was, indeed, Himmler's
great-great-grandfather. One correction: he was born in 1739 and not
in 1736 as was originally recorded. Hardly sensational though."

"Our genealogy project is confidential. On it I report to Himmler directly. I need something too big to put in writing, something
that justifies a personal audience. Passaquay helps some, but—and I
don't want to get too excited too soon—there is another piece that if
confirmed will assure me a meeting." He smirked, rose, and picked
up my luggage. "As soon as I get Asta and her son settled for the
weekend, you and I are going on a trip—to Wewelsburg and Heinrich Himmler's Castle Camelot."

I only caught a glimpse of the 27-year-old Asta Baeschlin—
pretty, petite, chestnut hair pulled back, facial profile not unlike
Otto's—as Rahn shepherded the Swiss woman and her four-year-
old son from the taxi to the hostel located on the main street down
from the cottage. Otto had summarily excluded me from the arrival
scene, asking me instead to complete preparations for a predawn
departure the next morning. Wewelsburg was a six-hour drive to
the north.

"We'll all have plenty of time to get to know each other when we
get back," he said to brush aside my concern that Asta might likely
feel slighted if we left so soon after her arrival.

"Since we are passing right through town, let's make a quick stop
to visit the Marburg cathedral," Otto said after several hours of
relative silence on the road. Given that our destination was an SS in-

stallation, I should have expected it, but I was taken aback when Otto appeared that morning in uniform, its swastika armband the first reminder of Nazi rule I had seen since arriving in the remote mountain town. Travelling in a government car with an SS chauffer, who had arrived out of nowhere to pick us up, restricted even casual conversation. We only spoke freely after the driver dropped us in front of the twin-spired sandstone St. Elizabeth Church in central Marburg.

Maintaining the rigid posture expected of an SS officer in public, Otto strode towards the building's ornate main entrance. "I know this place well," he said. "One chapter in *Lucifer's Court* focuses on Queen Elizabeth of Hungary, for whom it was named. But it barely touches on the beastly character of her confessor, Conrad of Marburg, who literally whipped his royal penitent to a saintly death at age 24. He was the German prototype for the French inquisitors who terrorized Languedoc for two centuries after his time."

Merely entering the great cathedral was enough to reactivate the vortex that drew me back to the enthralled Jaques de Sabart walking through the grand houses of worship in Pamiers and Carcassonne. To resist the lure, I had to keep talking.

"Those clever masons," I said to Otto, "built these churches as memory machines to record in space and stone both the grand themes and minute details of the period of their construction. Without the cathedrals we would know very little of the medieval period."

As if he had not heard me, Otto replied, "Obviously this wasn't here when the fanatical Conrad was rampaging through Hesse hunting heretics. He was, however, the impetus behind its construction starting in 1235, the year of Elisabeth's canonization and only four years after she died. With his dominant will, he made her a saint, and this church was built to commemorate his accomplishment more than hers."

"Typically Gothic," I remarked. "The male vertical trumping the female horizontal of the earlier domed Romanesque style."

Otto frowned as if I was the one going off subject. "I must complete the Conrad work and get it to Himmler. Zealots infest the Corps and the Party. Like Conrad they will cause much death and destruction. Only the Reichsführer-SS can check them. Like ourselves, he knows that he has lived before. I was at Quedlinburger Dom last year[41] where he presided over the ceremony to reinter the remains of King Henry the Fowler in a special crypt built to Himmler's specifications. He was moved to tears by the sight of bones he considers his own. His relentless energy, I have to conclude, comes from the lofty vision for this nation that he shares with its founder Henry I, called *the most German of all Germans*.

"From the rabble that was Rohm's brawling Brownshirts, Himmler is forming the elite Schutzstaffel, designed in the image of the warrior monks that were the Knights Templar, of the gentle Good Christians that were the heretical Cathars, of the Grail seekers that were the Knights of the Round Table. To present the history and continuing mission of these three groups and their heroism in the face of tyranny, he made my *Crusade Against the Grail* required reading for SS recruits.

"Your people in Switzerland are correct: he alone in the German leadership has the rank and resources to save this nation from the Conrads among us, from the new inquisition that would exterminate those vast sectors of the population deemed inferior."

I shuddered. In talking to 333 about the *dramatis personae* around Jaques de Sabart and who they might be in the current lifetime, I had glimpsed Heinrich Himmler as Jacques Fournier, Conrad of Marburg's doppelganger. If, in addition to Henry the Fowler, the bishop of Pamiers belonged on the Reichsführer-SS's past-life genealogy chart, he was indeed a character of historical magnitude but hardly as beneficent as Otto took him to be.

Not a subject for discussion in public. "Refresh my memory," I said instead. "For all his atrocities, how did Conrad accrue such power in the first place and how did he end up?"

"He was an educated German monk whose zeal for Christian doctrine came to the attention of Gregory IX, the pope who later established the Inquisition in France. Gregory made Conrad his personal emissary to this heresy-ridden region of Germany and commissioned him to cleanse it of all but orthodox Christian belief. In the end he became the victim of the hatred he instigated with his fanatical and indiscriminate prosecutions. He was ambushed and murdered in 1233 between Mainz and Marburg, on the very road we just travelled to get here. He had many enemies; his mere presence in an area could set off panic. His actual murderers were never found."

As we walked through the church, other visitors seemed to scurry off as we approached. Otto too noticed that others were avoiding us. "Do we smell bad?" he asked.

"Your uniform, my friend."

He looked down at himself and then removed his peaked cap and stuck it under his arm. "I'd forgotten I was wearing it," he said. "We better get going then."

I had expected something more spectacular, perhaps along the lines of the gleaming marble facades and delicate spires with which King Arthur's Camelot was usually depicted. So the bulky slate-grey structure that loomed atop a modest hill above the Alme Valley, through which we drove on approach to Wewelsburg, was a disappointment even from a distance. More like the ugly Castle Klingsor in *Parzival*, I thought, than the Grail Castle. Unique, however, was its three-sided shape. As we got closer, its southern face could be seen as flanked by two domed turrets that fronted its eastern and western wings, which converged into the wider flat-topped North Tower at the triangle's peak.

"A work in progress," Rahn explained as we walked from the parking area towards the guardhouse that fronted a bridge across a moat surrounding the building. "It belonged to the prince-bishops of Paderborn for centuries and then to the Prussian state. The local district acquired it in 1925 and renovated part of it as a museum and youth hostel. Weisthor brought it to Himmler's attention as a site important in ancient German history and heritage. In AD 9 the native warlord Hermann defeated the legions of Varus in the battle of Teutoburger near here, effectively stopping Roman expansion. And those strange rock formations, Externsteine, that Weisthor and his Irminists claim to be the Irminsul, the sacred tree of the world, is also nearby. Legend claims that the Battle of the Birch Tree, a future event in which the armies of the West will defeat the armies of the East in an apocalyptic struggle, will occur here."

That shift occurs inside my head again, but this time not to the left, the past, but to the right, the future.

It turns violent. I look for cover.

Now smeared in camouflage paint, the building is in flames. Rapidly spaced explosions, set off from the inside, blast through sections of the blazing walls and belch the castle's occupants, looters perhaps, into the moat. Then from the west comes the roar of aircraft, huge bombers and darting fighters all screaming towards the burning castle. From their tail markings, the planes are English and American, the armies of the West. The Battle of the Birch Tree is underway, but, contrary to earlier expectation, the retreating Nazis are the armies of the East. Bomb bays open and winged-tailed capsules streak towards us. I grab Otto's shoulder and try to pull him to the ground. "Cover your head. Get down," I shriek.

"I have a hat on, and not here, Raymond," Otto said with a quick grin as he moved my hand aside.

He had evidently already checked in, and we were crossing the bridge. Too shaken to try to explain what caused my bizarre behavior, I followed silently. Even though he had to be known here, we were stopped once more at the entrance to the west wing. Rahn again displayed his papers and signed me in as "a genealogy specialist with the office of the Reichsführer-SS."

Inside was the model of efficient German industry. The stripe-suited prisoners lifted and hammered in concert with regular laborers, the entire team responding in unison to the construction manager's orders barked over the clatter of heavy equipment.

Rahn steered me towards a narrow window overlooking a

wooded slope with peaceful farms below. "Pretend to enjoy the scenery," he whispered, "while I explain what we are doing here. A short while ago, Wewelsburg commander SS-Sturmbannführer von Knobelsdorff[42] forwarded documents to Himmler's Berlin secretariat that showed that Wilhelm Himmler, a plumber of nearby Bergburgheim, is the Reichsführer-SS's cousin six times removed. To this he added a further curious note: his source, the Vicar of Bergburgheim, also mentioned that there exists a mutual ancestral line between Himmler and the family Rahn Bergburgheim."

He paused, waiting for my response, which was too slow in coming. "Don't you get it, Raymond? Heinrich Himmler and I are likely blood relatives. We've come to verify that claim from the archives."

Finally realizing the implications, I gasped. If Rahn was related to Himmler, it would certainly help him in making the EC's argument to the Reichsführer-SS. From there though? Himmler could refuse to turn and Rahn, relative or not, could be charged with treason. Or Himmler could agree to conspire, only to have Hitler discover the plot prematurely with the same fatal outcome for Otto. For Rahn to survive, it had to be all or nothing, and he was already in too deep for the latter.

I followed Otto down a dusty corridor and into a freshly painted room filled with desks, filing cabinets, and clacking teleprinters. A clerk retrieved the documents he requested, and Otto sat and studied them for some time before he closed the file and managed a meager grin.

We left the room and headed north in the corridor before he delivered his verdict. "Enough to make a case, but too far back to determine an exact relationship. Not for his official ahnenpass, but worth bringing to his attention. Even a remote blood relationship would impress Himmler. But later for that. The walls have ears here," he said.

I breathed easier. Something unofficial and not in writing would be less damning if discovered later under adverse circumstances.

We went on past doors labeled with names to evoke Camelot—

Gral, King Arthur—and German mythology. At the one marked *Henry I the Vogler*, Rahn abruptly stopped. He stood in front of it for several moments as if straining to hear something through the sounds of the construction. He shook his head and focused in turn on each door, glancing down one side of the corridor and back the other.

"I felt its presence, but weakly," he finally said.

When I looked puzzled, he added, "The Lombrives Stone. It used to be in a safe in the *Gral* Room, but they moved it after I left. I don't dare ask directly, but I was hoping to establish some contact with it."

I tensed. I had seen him lose his bearings after discovering the stone in Tarascon and heard about his withdrawal reaction. Another sip from that cup would not help.

"Whatever happened to that scientist, the one with the Geiger counter in France?" I asked to distract him.

Rahn glared at me, evidently annoyed that I had broken his concentration. "Rudolph Erfurt? Pfft. What didn't fit his formulas was useless to him. He granted that the stone was more than plain rock but sided with the others who claimed that uranium and other materials had higher weapons potential. Had Himmler not stepped in, Erfurt would have tossed the Lombrives stone into the landfill. He's been reassigned to some top secret military facility, designing bigger bombs most likely."

He put his hand over his mouth and glanced around. "I forget where I am sometimes. Let's go."

Relieved to have diverted his attention from the addictive item, I followed him to the North Tower. "I've seen the blueprints," he said as we surveyed the massive chamber that occupied the entire ground level floor of the circular structure. Although no work was going on at time, there was evidence of construction and refurbishment from the domed ceiling to the partially paved marble floor. "It's proceeding according to the latest plan," Otto observed. "Originally, it was only to be an SS training facility called the SS School House Wewelsburg. Then Himmler had a grander vision. It is now becoming the nerve center of the entire Order, a secure central meeting place for the SS's highest brass. In this room, the *Obergruppenführersaal* or SS Generals' Hall, with the sacred sun wheel embedded in the center of the floor, inductions to the corps and the SS sacraments—baptisms, wedding, funerals—will be celebrated."

Sacraments. Try as I might, I could not resist the shift. This time, again, to the right.

The light from the twelve windows spaced equally around the room dims. Flaming torches, one on each of the twelve pillars around the perimeter, replace the sunlight. Between each pillar is a high-backed leather chair, each with a name plate affixed to it, twelve in all.

But only ten men in SS ceremonial dress advance single-file to the center of the room. There each bows profoundly to the north, straightens, clicks his heels on the sun wheel, raises his right arm and shouts Sieg Heil before proceeding to his seat.

Lastly, the eleventh, the Reichsführer-SS, advances to the center, raises his arm and slowly wheels full circle.

The officers return their leader's greeting with another salute and Sieg Heil.

"Tonight again there is an empty chair among us," the Reichsführer-SS intones without emotion. "Before it can be refilled to again bring our number to twelve, we pause according to custom to remember the one who once filled it. Some we remember as heroes, brothers who have given their lives for the glory for the Fatherland, the forever blessed. Others we remember as friends, warhorses exhausted by age or injury who have proceeded to the placid pastures of retirement, their bliss still incomplete. Finally, and rarely, there are the few we remember as traitors, the occasional Judas Iscariot who dons the uniform of the Black Order only to disgrace it, the forever damned."

He pauses and scans the faces around him. "Status as blessed or damned must be reached by unanimous vote," he then says. "In the case of the one missing tonight, consensus could not be reached. To decide his eternal fate then, we will consult the stone."

A murmur of voices arises at the suggestion, several objecting to the unusual method of arbitration.

"We will process to the vault," the Reichsführer-SS orders sternly.

"Himmler does everything in twelves," Otto was saying as I shook myself back into the present, a nauseating bitterness lingering in my nose and mouth. "Twelve windows, twelve columns, twelve seats, and twelve members of the SS synod. Tradition: the twelve signs of the Zodiac, the twelve Apostles, and the twelve Knights of the Round Table."

He then moved toward a narrow downward staircase.

"Where does that go?" I asked, chills racing through my spine.

"To the vault," he said.

He started down without looking back. I forced myself to follow.

"Himmler regards this tower to be the center of the world," he said, chattering away below me. "And he's gathered evidence that supports him. Geo-surveyors like Gaston de Mengel claim it is positioned on the precise intersection of the two most powerful ley lines on the planet. The castle in the shape of an arrowhead points due north. Around it Himmler wants to build a vast complex, which will eventually engulf the entire town."

"The center of the world," I murmured. "Doesn't the Führer claim that honor for his chancery in Berlin or his lair in Berchtesgaden?"

Otto stopped and allowed me to catch up. "Hitler knows about this place, of course, although he's never come here. I assume they have some agreement between them like the separation of church and state in America. Hitler in Berlin is the Aryan Emperor and Himmler here is the Aryan Pope."

"Convenient," I muttered, although more concerned about what we might find now that we had reached the bottom of the stairs. I peered into a rough-hewn chamber, more like a large cavity in an underground mine, dimly lit by a single bulb dangling in the center of it.

I shivered with a deepening chill. My mind strained as if trying to shift in both directions at the same time. On the right were the officers from upstairs who preceded us here. They gathered around the rim of a pit at the center of which was an enshrined object. The stone.

But Otto's narration of the dungeon's history pulled me away from what had to be a future event to the left, to the past.

"Long after Conrad of Marburg and the extermination of the Cathars, the Inquisition retrained its investigations on those who practiced the black arts. In 1630 in this castle, they conducted several witch trials, all of women, usually the poorest and most unsightly in the area. Once convicted as witches, the women were imprisoned in this dungeon before being led to death at the stake in the central courtyard."

I inched toward the stairwell. "Why would Himmler then choose this place for his mother church?" I asked

Oddly unfazed, Otto smiled. "He took me down here himself. It was like the Cave of Lombrives. 'The stone you brought back from France will reside here,' he said. 'A placeholder to attract the Grail Stone itself. At the center of the room, the precise center of the world, there will be a specially designed pit. The stone positioned properly with the appropriate ceremony will be electrified by the unique convergence here of the conduits of energy that flow across and through the entire planet. It will accumulate a reservoir of power unlike any before known to man. Not only the walls of Jericho, but those of Moscow, Paris, London, Washington, Rome, and Jerusalem will come tumbling down should the trumpets of the Black Order sound in the presence of this powerful array.'"

I chuckled uneasily. "Do you believe any stone has such potential?"

He shrugged. "There's science to support the theory. A crystal radio receiver is just a lump of lead until it is tuned to the proper frequency. Then, without an external power source, it plucks vibrations from the air and produces intelligible sounds. The right stone, the right environment, and the right vibrations, who knows what magic might come out of it?"

I started up the stairs. "Shouldn't we be starting back soon?" I asked, my voice quivering.

He looked at his watch, "Yes, if we want to make it back to Muggenbrunn before midnight."

Chapter 21: Episcopal Chambers, Pamiers, March 1321

After his latest meeting with Arnaud Sicre, Jaques was in no rush to report back to Bishop Fournier. While he had satisfied himself about the details of Belibaste's seduction, arrest, and change of heart, he had gleaned little to slake the bishop's thirst for a key that would unlock the nebulous treasure supposedly taken from the Roman Church by the Gnostics some centuries earlier. Arnaud's suggestion that Jaques advise Fournier to seek the Cathar treasure in the caves and castles around Tarascon was fraught with dilemma. If not designed to mislead—a definite possibility—Arnaud was assuming the treasure was material, a premise Jaques felt to be incorrect.

And even if the key was a discrete object that could be sought and found, the bishop's need was immediate. The trial could not be delayed while a hunt for an undefined item in an unspecified location was conducted in hostile territory. It could take years. Plus, focusing the bishop's attention on the Tarascon section of the Ariège would undoubtedly increase the risk for the Cathars there. As he had learned when he visited the town after his mother's death, the area was already under heavy surveillance with troops poised to pounce at a moment's notice.

He also contemplated the advantages in fingering Tarascon as Arnaud suggested. It might delay the pursuit of the remaining Catalonian enclave, giving Piere Maury time to return there and move the colony south to safety. Further, his informing on his own countrymen would confirm his loyalty to the Catholic cause and increase his chances to learn about any attack planned against the Ariège, which would then allow him to forewarn the community of the impending danger.

Arnaud had suggested that the former Templar commanderies in the Vicdessos Valley were possible hiding places for the secrets of the Cathars. Other than his occasional question about Baldwin, Fournier seemed oddly unaware of or unconcerned about the former Knights' connection with either the remaining heretics or the Gnostic coalition. Would Arnaud's intimation that a Templar remnant now guarded the Cathar treasure in that remote valley serve as a sufficient clue to satisfy Fournier for the time being without jeopardizing any vital interest of the coalition?

So many possibilities but no clear path to follow. It was a time when Jaques would have appreciated Baldwin making an appearance. He even made some additional passes through the Mercado just in case, but there was no sign of the vagabond stirring up the crowds.

However, all Jaques's internal debate proved unnecessary. When he called for his scribe the next day, Bishop Fournier had already devised a radically different approach to the Belibaste case. Before Jaques could mention the meeting with Arnaud, the prelate announced that there had been a change of venue for the formal trial. It would take place, after all, in the Archbishop of Narbonne's jurisdiction: in the castle of Villerouge Termenes in the Corbières region, halfway between Carcassonne and Narbonne. This arrangement, he explained, freed himself from canonical restrictions while interrogating the Perfect.

"The questions I need to ask him are too sensitive, as you might have surmised, for an open hearing," he explained. "I'll meet that stubborn mule in my private chamber as an equal. There will be ample fruit and wine available and only a single witness—you. I will present you as an impartial observer and allow Belibaste to accept your presence. You will write nothing down. He needn't know, of course, about your phenomenal memory. It's your golden opportunity to put every mind trick from Cicero to Llull into good use."

Positioned to the side where he could observe the faces both of the participants, Jaques breathed deeply as the two guards led the prisoner into the spacious conference room and then to the chair across the table from the already seated bishop.

"Take off his chains and wait outside," Fournier said to the men. Although hesitant to leave their muscular charge unshackled, the soldiers complied and departed.

"I did state in my offer to meet with you that this was to be one-on-one affair," the bishop said to Belibaste, who sat motionless with his hands and feet positioned as if he still wore chains. "And so it is, in effect." He pointed towards me. "Jaques de Sabart, whom you saw in court as the scribe, here has no pen and paper to record this session. As his name indicates, he is from the Sabarthès, which, I understand is more Cathar than Catholic. He was born and raised in Tarascon and is fluent in Occitanian. Will you allow his presence as an impartial observer to our meeting?"

Slowly, as if noticing a third person for the first time, Belibaste turned his large head. He eyed the young man for several seconds before he replied. "If I endured several days shackled two to a horse with Arnaud from Ax, I can tolerate a Tarasconian who scribes for the Inquisition."

Two to a horse. Jaques noted the expression. He bowed slightly towards the Perfect. He thought Belibaste might see the gesture as a recognition of his use of the watchword. The man, however, turned immediately back towards Fournier without anything further.

The bishop went to fill Belibaste's glass with wine. The Perfect shook the offer away.

"Grapes then? I understand prison fare is poor." Again Belibaste motioned no.

"So, it is then true that you have refused all food and drink since you've been in custody, my friend? Have you entered the *endura* customary among your people for those who are about to die?"

Belibaste nodded.

Jaques shivered. This man was starving himself to death. Fournier clucked. "You call yourself a good Christian, but suicide is an ungodly act."

"Is that so?" Belibaste asked, speaking for the first time.

"I respect your preparing for it, but death is not inevitable. We have the power to condemn, but we also have the power to let you live."

"Only the Good God, which you and your church do not serve, has such power. You would not have taken me were it not his will."

Fournier pursed his lips. "Casting aspersions on each other's faith becomes neither of us. Nor is there any benefit in arguing the fine points of theology as was done between Cathars and Catholics prior to the Crusade. Those debates led only to war where the strongest army rather than the strongest argument prevailed. Can we not talk civilly one religious leader to another?"

Belibaste looked down at his hands and wiggled his fingers. "Our brotherhood vows to allow no falsehood to cross our lips, but your smooth tongue shoots out words that contradict your mind and heart. What do you seek from me that you feign respect in court and fellowship now?"

Fournier sat back, his eyes narrowing. Belibaste was refusing the bait; the bishop was changing tactics, Jaques surmised.

"Like your predecessor *perfecti* now long reduced to ash," the prelate intoned, the sarcasm evident, "you scorn our ornate cathedrals, elaborate ceremonies, and complex canons, perhaps with good reason." He leaned across the table as if to crack through the prisoner's façade with his eyes. "But unlike your forefathers, who practiced a routine of rigorous poverty, stringent chastity, and tireless service to their flock, you, Guilhem Belibaste, worship mammon, impregnate women, and satisfy your personal comfort while your sheep are attacked by wolves like Arnaud Sicre."

Belibaste nodded. "It is so. I have sinned."

Fournier smiled. "So we understand each other for the imperfect shepherds we are, both mortals despite the pedestals of our offices. I too must strike my *mea culpas*."

"Our sins are not of the same order." Belibaste saw right through the bishop's affected humility. "Have you ever loved a woman?" Jaques wondered where the Perfect intended to take this unexpected question.

"Well, not really," the bishop said. "What does that have to do with it?"

"I have lain with a woman and made love to her, but my greater sin, even among my own people, is that I don't see that loving the wonderful gift of God that is woman as a sin at all."

For the first time the Perfect showed some emotion; a flash of pain cinched his face. He cherishes his Raymonde, Jaques realized, as a true partner. They rode *two to a horse*.

"Would that you and yours could sin likewise," Belibaste continued. "The Catholic Church builds magnificent temples dedicated to the Divine Feminine—Hagia Sophia in Constantinople; Notre Dame in Paris, Chartres, and the Sabarthès—but reduces the human woman to an inferior status, one unfit to enter the sanctuary of the Most High as an ordained minister. What is the greater sin: to make love to one woman or to demean all women?"

The bishop suppressed a smirk. "Your reputation for earthy homilies precedes you, Belibaste, as does your skill to rework already heretical precepts into teachings more suited to your base instincts. Nevertheless, women's role in our respective faiths is not germane to this conversation, and I will not indulge in theological speculation."

But Belibaste plowed past the bishop's objection. "I honor and revere my forefathers who gave their lives for our faith. Without their laying on of hands, through which I inherited the gift, I would still be an ignorant shepherd in the Corbières or worse. But, in accordance with the very gift they gave me, I am not obliged to adhere blindly to their set teachings and rules. Did not Christ break old laws when Love, the one immutable law, dictated that they be dispensed with? Unlike your church, whose evolution has been fixed to a past era—

not that of Christ or his Apostles, but to the time of the early Christian Roman emperors from Constantine to Justinian who mandated teachings that suited their specifications—the Cathar community sees itself as a human institution, which over time must evolve as do all things. Mistakes are made; correction must follow.

"Thus I have preached against the strict dualism, which our elders adopted from the Manicheans, that pitted the Good God against an equal, the King of the World, in an eternal battle for human souls. In the course of my training and ministry, I recognized a principle superior to this duality: there is only One God, God the Good. All evil—illness, misfortune, even death— is apparency, absence, a state that, like darkness, dissipates when light is shone upon it."

Tapping his fingers bejeweled with the episcopal ring, Fournier seemed to be losing patience. "By what authority do you alter the teachings of your predecessors even as they defied the teachings of the church?" he challenged.

"On the ultimate authority of which Jesus taught when he said, 'The kingdom of God is within.' In my inner temple before my personal altar, I came to understand where my elders went astray. Afterwards I could preach nothing but the Good God, the sole substance from which all creation springs."

The bishop yawned but caught and covered it. Belibaste, his face aglow, seemed not to notice.

"Fine theological distinctions, like how many angels can dance on the head of a pin," Fournier muttered. "Matters we won't settle anytime soon."

"So be it. What then do you want from me?" Belibaste asked.

Jaques felt Fournier trying to press towards the one agenda item that mattered; but doubt, so alien to him, seemed to have crept in. The collected but cagey Belibaste was demonstrating willpower, like Bernard Delicieux earlier, stronger than the prelate's. He would not break as did Beatrice de Planissoles.

Fournier pursed his lips and took in a deep breath. He's decided to risk everything, Jaques reckoned, to gain the treasure Belibaste has or knows about.

Fournier glanced around and lowered his voice. "That I am now about to tell you certain things, Guilhem Belibaste, might well seal your fate. No one hears them and stays alive unless they are utterly beholden to me."

The Perfect nodded towards Jaques. "That young man has ears."

"I've spoken to him about these matters, and he's kept them to himself. He knows the consequences."

"All right then. Let my curiosity kill me." Both bishop and scribe had to snicker at the quick quip.

Fournier cleared his throat. "I will begin with an unprecedented confession on behalf of the Roman Church to a minister of a heretical faith. For centuries, the inner council of the church has known that the spiritual gifts of some dissenting groups are more authentic than its own; that their reading of the Gospel is closer to the Christ's teachings than our orthodox interpretation; that the blood of martyrs, once the seed of Christianity, now waters the fields of alien faiths while our church has become a desert. Even as a bishop of this church and its chief prosecutor of heretics, I remain objective enough to agree with the high council."

Belibaste allowed a slight smile. "When did the church first become aware that it had lost the keys?" he asked.

Jaques leaned in, goading his mind to a higher level of attention and impression. From the mere words about to pass between these two men, he would later have to color in all the images and inferences from past memory and future vision that this momentous encounter between the dual traditions, in both of which he had been initiated, would encompass.

"Time, translation, and intentional misdirection have obscured the precise point at which the church lost the keys Jesus presented to his apostles," the bishop replied. "It happened gradually, perhaps starting when Peter and Paul divorced Jerusalem, the holy city of the Chosen People, and embraced Rome, the debauched capital of a worldly empire. At that time, they likely released the keys to other followers of Jesus: James, his brother; or, in the Grail tradition, Joseph of Arimathea; or, as the legends of Provence suggest, Mary Magdalene. Perhaps to all three and others as well.

"As a Gnostic, you would know better than myself the history of the suppressed sects, its leaders, and the manner in which the keys were passed through the generations. I am only versed in the church's efforts to retake them.

"The Holy Land was only of minor interest to Roman Christianity as long as European influence over Palestine was unchallenged. That complacency was disturbed when the Muslim Seljuk Turks invaded and captured Jerusalem towards the end of the 11th Century. Europe's military response was swift. The First Crusade was organized, and Jerusalem was retaken in 1099.

"With Christianity's place of origin back under Western political control—how long it could be held was uncertain as the Muslim armies had merely retreated—Europe rediscovered the spiritual significance of Jerusalem. It was not only the city where Jesus Christ lived and died but also the cradle of Judaism, the rich history and traditions of which are encoded in the Old Testament. Realizing that its thousand-year religious monopoly in Europe was crumbling under the weight of bureaucracy, infighting, impiety, and heresy, the church saw Jerusalem and the nostalgia it aroused in both nobles and commoners as an opportunity to restore its own supremacy.

"Ironically, the reconquered Holy Land also afforded the hierarchy an opening through which to reveal the bad news that the keys had long gone missing since it was now able to counter with the good news that they had been found again in Christianity's place of origin. I don't pretend that the church's leaders at the time of the early Crusades where men of great faith or charity. On the contrary, they were pragmatic schemers who understood that maintaining control over a continent rapidly evolving into strong secular nation-states would require a spectacular manifestation of supernatural authority to be kept in the church's orbit.

"Such a production was not left to chance. Some twenty years after the recapture of Jerusalem, Hugues de Payens founded the military Order of the Knights Templar with headquarters in Solomon's Temple in Jerusalem. While supposedly established to protect pilgrims travelling to and from the holy city, the original band of nine knights remained within the Temple confines for several years, exploring the caves and tunnels below its foundations for artifacts and treasure to be shipped back to Europe as evidence of the church's revitalized authenticity. In 1129, ten years after its founding, the Order's results were dramatic enough that Bernard of Clairvaux, the enormously influential Cistercian monk, became the Templars' advocate, writing the Order a rule that made it independent of all authority other than the pope. Its elite status was approved by the Council of Troyes that same year.

"The Templars' subsequent military and material success is legend even though many details of their operations remain obscure. They had to have happened upon a considerable cache of precious metals and stones to fund their function as Europe's international banker. They retrieved enough lost information to revolutionize European art, architecture, and education. The Gothic cathedral is a testament to their inexplicable technical prowess. But they also acquired some form of potent spiritual knowledge, evidently at odds with established Christian belief, that they intentionally withheld from church authorities. It is suspected, however, that they did share such findings with the church's rivals, among them the Cathars."

To Jaques, following along, little of what the bishop said was novel until he spoke of this direct connection between the Templars and the Cathars.

The revelation also confounded Belibaste, and he challenged it. "So that is how the church justified its brutal suppression of the Templars. Branded them as being in league with heretics. A flimsy concoction at best. What would the Cathars, a people committed to turn the other cheek, have in common with a violent army of murderous thugs and thieves like the Knights Templar?"

The Perfect, Jaques quickly understood, was not dissembling. He obviously had no knowledge of any alliance between the groups. He had never been informed. He did not need to know.

"Is it mere coincidence then that a third of all Templar preceptories were located in the Languedoc, where Catharism grew its deepest roots in the century following the Order's founding?" Fournier retorted. "Despite all the Templars legions in the area, none ever fought on the side of the church during the Albigensian Crusade. We know that Cathars were sheltered in Templar preceptories and buried in their cemeteries against ecclesiastical law. And what of reports that the Templars received extensive Cathar treasure, even that of Montsegur, for safe-keeping?"

Jaques was astounded by the amount of detail Fournier already possessed about the alliance. Neither Timekeeper nor Baldwin had intimated that their nemesis was so well informed. Fournier would have greeted Arnaud's suggestion of a Templar-Cathar connection with a yawn.

Belibaste allowed himself a short belly laugh. "Ah," he said, "the Cathar treasure again. I held a higher opinion of you, Excellency. Are you a gold digger like the rest of them?"

Fournier showed no sign of offense. "Look around you, Belibaste. The church has accumulated material treasure in excess of that of Rome and Jerusalem in their heyday. You underestimate the church's objective in launching the Crusades to the Holy Land. Its leaders circulated the tales of fabulous booty there only to raise an army led by Europe's noble houses. Canon law forbade it to have one of its own. The troops that entered Jerusalem alive were permitted to pillage any surface treasure as reward, and their leaders were granted title to the land. The church's inner circle had no desire for material gains. It was only interested in recovering the keys that Jesus gave to Peter, which were last evident in Jerusalem."

"And you believe that the Templars during their excavations found those keys in the form of some occult knowledge. Then, contrary to their prior agreement to deliver such discoveries to the church, they entrusted them to the Cathars instead."

The bishop nodded. "The Templars became suspicious of the motives of the church leaders, so they gave what they found to their enemies, speculating that some such group would then grow powerful enough to overthrow or replace the Roman Church. The Cathars certainly posed such a threat."

Belibaste grew silent, closed his eyes, and remained with his head bowed for several moments. Then he said, "Your theory, though foolish, makes a certain sense. I would amend it though to posit that the Templars did not hand over the keys to the Cathars. Rather they aligned the Order with the Cathars and other groups that already possessed the keys. They rightly feared that the Catholic leaders would keep such sacred knowledge for themselves and fashion it into a weapon to subdue their opponents rather than disseminate it to all people as was intended."

Fournier leaned forward, his hands suddenly shaking. "So, the Templars aside, you too possess a set of the keys?" he blurted out eagerly.

The Perfect wagged his head slowly. "I am beginning to understand something here. The church—you—lost the keys long ago. You finally figured that out and started looking around for them. During this search, you decided to hunt down every last man, woman, and child with beliefs different from yours; not just Cathars, but Waldensians, Beguines, sorcerers, Spirituals, and Templars as well. You did not so much want to eliminate us as to take from us what you thought was rightly yours alone."

He paused and studied the bishop before he asked, "If I do have the keys as you allege, what warrants that I, an already condemned man, hand them over to you?"

The bishop sat back, a sudden sadness creasing his face. "I have long been a student of church history and regrettably have had to accept that the tables have turned. In the first centuries after Christ, ours were the martyred heroes who stood against the false gods of Rome, choosing torture and death rather than deny what they knew to be the truth. Such courage does not come from shallow belief, illusion or self-deception, all of which crumble under duress, but from conviction derived from genuine experience.

"Now that same church, once flourishing in the blood of its martyrs, has become the persecutor, making martyrs of those who worship God as they understand Him rather than God as decreed by the church of Rome. Day after day with all my learning and cleverness, I've been attempting to undermine that faith in men and women, old and young, learned and simple. I succeed with the weak, but what victory is that? The rest—those buoyed by an indefinable fortitude even if bent by torture—will not break. I have to admire them, envy them, even as I condemn them to prison or death. In the end, they defeat me. By martyring them, I anoint them heroes who will inspire a new generation of their own kind."

Belibaste again nodded slowly. "I underestimated you, Jacques Fournier. You do know—even with so much blood on your hands. Personally you yearn for what the Christian martyrs had; what we, the few of us who remain, still have and will sacrifice our physical lives to keep."

"The Catholic Church could well afford to have that spirit alive again in its ranks," Fournier said.

"Spirit is infused into the members through the head. That is why the Perfects among us commit to practice and demonstrate a more rigorous faith than is required of the *credentes*, our laity."

Jaques caught the glint in the bishop's eyes. Like a jungle cat he was poised to pounce. "So a Perfect has some supernatural power, what you would have used to impart salvation even to your betrayer had he joined you in jumping from the tower of Castelbó. Through what means—rite, words, initiation—is a Perfect so infused?"

"Through constant meditation, prayer, and fasting, a Perfect molds himself into a more conscious reservoir of Spirit, the Good God, the omnipresent and omnipotent substance beneath all that exists. While a believer may be distracted by other concerns, Spirit within him does not diminish. In laying on the hands during the *con-*

solamentum, the Perfect serves to reawaken the willing recipient to full consciousness of Spirit, which is already and always within him. Had Arnaud joined me in jumping to his death with the belief that all was forgiven, it would have been his faith, not mine, that saved him. In the Gospels Jesus always consults the supplicant thus, 'Do you have faith that you can be healed?' God, who created us with free will, cannot cure someone who does not want to be cured."

"So, right here, right now, you could lay your hands on me and I would be saved?" Fournier asked.

"Do you sincerely want to receive the *consolamentum* then?" Belibaste raised both hands, palms outward. "Will you then join me in the *endura*, refusing all food and water to prepare your body to be consumed by the flames designated for heretics?"

The bishop quivered and then sniggered. "Suicide is a sin in my religion, and I'm certainly not ready to embrace yours. But"— he pointed his right index finger at Belibaste— "I still want to know the source of the power that imbues your people with the courage to choose the flames rather than say the few words required to recant."

"Do you not know the Lord's Prayer? Have you not read the Gospel of John?" Belibaste asked.

Fournier flushed. "What's that got to do with it?"

"Say it with meaning often enough and you too will regain the grace to console and be consoled. The Good God has made the sacrament available to everyone. No one robbed the church of the keys to the kingdom of Heaven, Excellency. It tossed them away for the keys to the Roman Empire. That we, so-called heretics, have held on to them and used them across the centuries does not make them unavailable to you. Nor do we have to be deprived of them for your members to have them also. If, by the grace of God, the Gnostics and Cathars were chosen to preserve what the church wantonly discarded, what right does the church have to take that away from us? The Good God's treasure does not exclude; it includes. In the end none will be damned; all will be saved. All is God's creation so it cannot be otherwise. The one treasure that endures, the pearl of great price, is hidden in plain sight. He who has ears to hear, let him hear."

Fournier shoved his large body back from the desk and stood, blood flushing his face. "I will not tolerate the words of the Savior coming out of your blasphemous mouth. No more sermons from a heretical simpleton," he gasped. "You want to be a martyr? So be it." Out of breath he leaned on the desk. "Guards," he shouted.

"I welcome death. My consolation is in the flames," Belibaste said calmly even as the soldiers entered and moved toward him rattling the chains. The Perfect held up his hands, motioning for them to stop; they froze as if turned to stone.

"One final thing, Bishop Fournier. Despite what you refused here today, the Good God regards you with mercy and will offer you another chance. One day you will occupy the papal throne. Through you, for the last time in many generations, it will be within the papal capacity to unite all faiths in the peace Christ intended when he prayed: 'That they may all be one; even as you, Father, are in me and I in you.'"

Fournier was taken aback. "Are you a prophet?"

Again Belibaste lifted his hands, palms outwards. "You ask with incredulity. Nevertheless, what I say will be so."

"And when I reach that lofty office, how do I go about doing what you suggest?"

"I will answer in truth despite the cynicism in your mouth and heart: Abolish the Inquisition. End the church's persecution of all people everywhere. All are God's children: Christians, Muslims, Jews, heretics, agnostics, pagans, and even non-believers. Let the church heed the rule: Judge not. Declare with papal authority that the trials, tortures, imprisonments, stigmatization, hate, and killing of anyone no matter how different are anathema. Expand the church to the vast and welcoming dwelling that Christ intended when He said, 'My Father's house has many rooms.'"

"Just open the doors and let everyone in?" the bishop asked. "How long would I be on the papal throne if I suggested that?"

As if released from a spell, the soldiers were suddenly able to move again. Jaques watched them reshackle the prisoner, but, when they tried to move him towards the door, they became immobilized again.

Belibaste continued to address the bishop. "You have wanted to know what makes a martyred hero. You will be given the supreme opportunity. As Pope you will have access to the Vatican archives that certainly contain copies of the so-called heretical works, from the suppressed gospels of eye-witnesses like the apostle Thomas and Mary Magdalene to our Cathar text of the original Gospel of John. From these learn what the Christ actually said and did, and then proclaim the Good News as he proclaimed it."

"You are another crazy dreamer, Belibaste," the bishop scoffed. "Just like the 200 of Montsegur, the Authiers and Bernard Delicieux. Your vision is fantasy. The church must survive and operate in the real world. Your beguiling recipe would only result in anarchy and chaos." Fournier flapped his hands wildly. "Get him out of here."

The guards were able once more to move the powerfully-built prisoner, but only to a position halfway across the room between the fuming Fournier and Jaques. There again, they stood paralyzed. Looking through the window, the Perfect fixed his eyes on a leafless laurel tree out in the courtyard.

"It will be written in official histories," he proclaimed, "that the Cathar heresy was eradicated with the execution of its last Perfect, Guilhem Belibaste, in the courtyard of the castle of Villerouge Termenes in the spring of 1321. My ashes will be scattered, the last remains of the laurel tree that shaded Languedoc for two centuries."

Jaques was mesmerized, as if Belibaste was speaking directly for the recording of the event he was making in his mind. For just an instant Belibaste cast his full attention on Jaques. Without a word or gesture, there was recognition.

"What happened today was not put on paper. To the current world this meeting never occurred. Nevertheless, hear this: nothing is lost. Every word and gesture, even the intent in the hearts of the participants, has been indelibly preserved."

The Perfect then returned his eyes to the laurel tree and said. "For the Cathars, it is no more over with me than it was for the Knights Templar when their last Grand Master, Jacques de Molay, met his death in Paris seven years ago. Bodies can be killed, but truth cannot. Mark these words: In seven hundred years, the laurel tree will root again and flourish in the Languedoc. The Good Christians and the Knights Templar will be vindicated as prophetic voices that cried in the wilderness of intolerance for liberty, equality, and kinship for all humans of good will."

"Get this heretic out of my sight," the bishop screamed.

"We can go now," Belibaste said to the soldiers. They hauled him off. Bishop Fournier left through a side door, slamming it behind him. Jaques sat marveling that all that he had just witnessed was written word-for-word in his mind.

Chapter 22: Muggenbrun, July-August 1938

U pon our return from Wewelsburg, Otto submitted a request marked "Urgent" to meet with Himmler to discuss the latest results of our research on the Reichsführer-SS's ahnenpass. The more days that accumulated without a response, the more Rahn obsessed over the reasons for the delay and the more apprehensive I became about the outcome of our mission and the fate of Europe. From the bellicose propaganda pumped over the radio, I gleaned that Hitler's drumming for the annexation of the Sudeten region of Czechoslovakia had the other European nations, led by Prime Minister Chamberlain's Britain, leaning towards appeasement to avoid war.

Only Asta Baeschlin and her little boy seemed able to enjoy the abundant summer pleasures of the Black Forest as if it were a tranquil enclave cut off from a continent hell-bent for chaos. Oblivious to Otto's impending marriage proposition, which he said he was postponing until he received a positive response from Himmler, Asta frequented the cottage as a guest for meals and evening entertainment and joined us for hikes in the hills. Otto so conspicuously avoided any amorous overtures towards her that I had to coach him. "Good God, man, you're too polite for a suitor. At least touch her now and then. I think she likes you, but keep up the aloofness, and she'll think you're gay."

He blushed at the remark and afterwards tried harder but only by increasing the affection he showed for her son with whom he now chatted and played over-exuberantly. Otherwise he passed the time looking like he was writing *Sebastian* or talking about its plot but with his attention always on the postman. When would he show up? Would there be a letter from headquarters? What would Himmler have to say? Would he invite us both to the meeting in Berlin or would he have to go alone? After a month of such speculation without a response, he began to have graver misgivings about the delay, which he previously attributed to the Reichsführer-SS's busy calendar.

In mid-July he received a letter from Ullmann that said nothing about the requested meeting. It further devastated Otto, though, by mentioning that Himmler had recently asked Ullmann to expedite getting Riedweg's application to his desk.

"Someone around Himmler is blocking my communication to him," Rahn said after reading the letter. "They may have something personal against me, but it may be bigger. With so many internal factions fighting for position, I'm a dispensable pawn caught in between. Even my last letter may not have made it to Himmler's desk."

This additional disappointment affected his behavior adversely. Although it seemed impossible, his smoking increased; he would light the next cigarette before snuffing out the previous one. He would sit trying to write while drinking glass after glass of wine, and he spurned invitations from Asta and me to walk or dine in town.

If Otto was blinded by the light as 333 and I had discussed, Paul Ladame's observation about him was equally true: "Otto Rahn is utterly amazing. You can't nail him down because, I swear, there are two of him." Ullmann's letter drowned his remaining optimism with such a dreary depression that I began to consider advising the EC to scrap our mission and get Rahn out of Germany without delay. Knowing that Asta's family was well-connected in Switzerland, I probed a bit to determine if she might serve as a means by which Otto could leave the country without alerting German intelligence. She had noticed his radical withdrawal, but, still oblivious to his intent to marry her, she took it to be a passing mood and went on to talk of her own imminent plan to return to Switzerland, which certainly did not include him. Just as well, I realized, as no arrangement to spirit him to safety would work without his cooperation.

Several times I tried to suggest that Himmler might not have the requisite idealism we projected as necessary at the start of the mission. "Our friends in Switzerland might not consider the additional risks you have to take as worth it," I said to him one evening. "Since Schliersee, several political and diplomatic doors, still open then, have closed. Hitler is on the march, and Himmler seems to be marching right behind him."

He sprang up and stood grasping the porch railing. "Are they losing faith? Are your people capitulating to this madness too?" He swung around. "Well, I haven't. Himmler can still be brought over, and with the SS he can topple Hitler and save Germany and Europe from the horrors of another war." He came close enough that I could feel his breath on my face. "Look, Raymond, I am personally responsible for what has happened to my beloved country. *Crusade Against the Grail,* my book, is now a vital part of SS training. Himmler had a leather-bound copy of *Lucifer's Court* sent to Hitler as a birthday present. It's now on his shelf next to *Mein Kampf.* The Führer may never read my work, but Himmler has. I do not write about war and hate but about peace and love. My books"—he beat his chest— "mine, can save Germany from this. They must." He returned to the railing and slumped over it. "If we fail, history will pass a cruel judgment on me: I was one of them."

A couple of mornings later after some additional failed attempts to have Otto look at the deteriorating political situation more realistically, I woke up with 333's advice again resounding in my head: *You're looking at the wrong lifetime.* In Schliersee the application of those words to the situation had miraculously induced Otto to switch his dual persona from despair to enthusiasm.

With a cup of coffee in hand, he was sitting on the porch in a cloud of smoke when I went out to say good morning.

"It's a beautiful day, Otto. Get your hiking boots on," I said.

"Where to this time?" he asked flatly.

"There." I pointed east to the tallest hill on the far side of the valley beyond Muggenbrunn. "To the caves up there."

"Lombrives is that way," he said, pointing south.

"Technicality," I muttered.

Fortunately, he played along. After breakfast we took off through town. He stopped in front of the stone village church and studied it for several moments before saying, "Notre Dame de Sabart."

"Where we were when we left off that time in your room in Schliersee. The Templar Baldwin, you as Jean, I as Jaques de Sabart, and your wife Mathène—Gabriele we can safely presume—huddled in that little church," I said to reorient him.

"Planning an escape through the secret and dangerous passage that started at the mouth of Lombrives and ended on the other side of the mountain near Miglos." He smiled for the first time since Ullmann's letter. "So this hike is to be a reenactment, a way of re-membering by feeling and doing what might have happened there. A technique I use when writing scenes that prove difficult."

There were the missing pieces to the story that I felt he could provide, so I said, "I wonder how we got to the church of Notre Dame de Sabart to start with. The last I know for sure, I was still the bishop's boy, the sole witness to the final interview between Jaques Fournier and Guilhem Belibaste." I briefed him on that dramatic encounter. Also how I had assumed that Piere Maury had returned to Catalonia after the Perfect's arrest to shepherd the remaining community to safety further south.

We started up the road that led to a path into the hills.

"Piere did come back, I seem to remember," Otto began. He was looking off into the distance. "He cried when he told us that Beli-baste had been taken but not until he ordered everyone to pack their things. He then took me aside to discuss what we would do next."

"Was your name Jean?" I asked eagerly.

"Of course," he said. "Jean Maury, Piere's brother."

"But I thought *that* Jean was a rebellious youth who took every opportunity to insult Belibaste and anything Cathar."

"Entirely staged by Piere for Arnaud's benefit, a performance required by an unfortunate slip of the tongue by our aunt Guillemette Maury. During Arnaud's second visit to Catalonia, she happened to mention in his presence that I was in training to become a Perfect,[43] and when Arnaud probed further, she revealed that my initiation had been underway since 1314, some six years earlier. She immediately regretted her indiscretion and informed Piere, who then had to manufacture the elaborate cover-up to keep Arnaud off the track."

"Was Belibaste in on the ruse?"

"We couldn't allow him to know about Aunt Guillemette's slip. To him Piere excused my disaffection as a temporary lapse. Thinking it might help to bring me back to my calling as a Perfect, Belibaste wanted me to come to the Pallars as his assistant to the wedding ceremony, a role I had served several times before. Piere made me stay behind to keep me safe. Belibaste only learned of the elaborate deception when Piere whispered in his ear after the arrest in Tirvia."

"So when he was face-to-face with Fournier he knew he was not the last Perfect but made sure the bishop thought he was," I said with a chuckle. The scenes I had witnessed and retained now began to mesh with those proper to Jean Maury alone. "Brilliant, and Piere was behind it all. A mastermind so adroit that even Arnaud considered him a friend enough to request his release in the end."

Otto cleared his throat to let me know that I had interrupted him. "Sorry," I said. "So Piere took you aside in Catalonia—"

"He reminded me that there was still a price on our heads. We both were on Fournier's list when the Montaillou investigation was reopened in 1318. Arnaud would be back for us once he spent Belibaste's reward money. If we were caught and put on trial, Arnaud would remember Aunt Guillemette's indiscretion. I would be proven a Perfect with death at the stake inevitable.

"However, Piere told me, we could not just run with the others.

I was not destined to minister only to the remaining congregation as Belibaste had done. When I asked why not, he explained how, shortly after his own release in Tirvia, he was approached by a thin bearded man. He informed Piere that he knew of my ordination but the secret was safe with him. Something of a prophet, he explained how the Cathar church was predestined to extinction, but as its last Perfect I had been chosen to carry the seed of its next incarnation into the future. This mission would require me to partner with another I was yet to meet, someone specially trained for his own unique role in the transmission of the seed. The thin man said that we would only meet in Languedoc, and our route into the future would follow the traditional path of initiation through the Sabarthès caves."

"And the prophet's name?" I asked.

"He called himself Timekeeper."

I gasped. "I figured so," I said. "Go on."

"He said that as the team would ride together in the tradition of the Templars. Piere would learn my partner's identity in advance and present us to each other at the appropriate time with the watchword, *Two to a horse*."

We both smiled, remembering how that same phrase had come into our conversation when we opened Antonin Gadal's gift at Schliersee.

Otto continued. "For two years we plotted the return to Languedoc. Piere arranged that I marry Mathène Servel,[44] a Cathar woman who accepted that I had no desire to consummate the relationship although we dared not explain why. She may have assumed I was gay. In the meantime, the wolf got hungry again and began to prowl. Arnaud began tracking us. In the spring of 1323, Piere, Mathène, and I were reconnoitering along the border for a way to cross. Fate would have it that we got careless, and Arnaud's men grabbed us while we were sleeping in the hills and dragged us back to Pamiers."

"That bastard!" I exclaimed. "Belibaste wasn't good enough for him."

"Piere knew his own goose was cooked, but he had to protect me. Since I could not lie to the court, he lied for me. I was the deranged little brother who had no respect for Cathar beliefs or traditions. He painted me as an incorrigible skirt-chaser whom he desperately paired with Mathène, an equally lascivious woman despite her strict Cathar upbringing. He described our frequent copulation in such raw detail that the bishop had to order his descriptions deleted from the record. Under oath Arnaud had to admit that he had heard me mock Belibaste as a hypocrite and fornicator. He also had to tell the court that he heard me call my donkey a stubborn heretic in a fit of anger—an event Piere had me stage for Arnaud's benefit."

"Piere's ruse evidently worked," I said. "Neither of you were burnt at the stake, a certain fate had Fournier suspected either of you were ordained Perfects."

"Only because of Piere's cleverness in creating my rogue reputation all along. At one point in the trial Arnaud Sicre did testify that he had heard my aunt say that I was a Perfect in training."

"But the bishop didn't believe Arnaud," I said, remembering how Fournier loathed the traitor.

"Guillemette Maury was already dead. Piere said truthfully that he witnessed no such incident, and Fournier, convinced perhaps that I was a fool, never asked me directly. Without a corroborating witness, Arnaud's testimony was invalid. Nevertheless, in August 1324, Piere, Mathène and I were sentenced[45] to *murus strictus*, a severe prison regimen of bread and water but without shackles."

We had begun to climb, Muggenbrunn falling away in the valley below. I was puzzled. "As Fournier's scribe and the man with the perfect memory, why don't I recall your trial like I did Belibaste's and everything else?" I thought out loud.

"Because you weren't there. Fournier must have excused you." Otto said

There was a slight dizziness, a stumble in my step. Something shifted. If I was not recording the trial, I too must have been under suspicion. I tried to explain what I was sensing to Otto. "Arnaud finally got his private tête-à-tête in which he tattled to the bishop that Père Fontaine, my mother, and just about everyone in Tarascon were Cathars or sympathizers. Fournier had to remove me from the case," I guessed.

"And yet you were able to do all that maneuvering afterwards on our behalf. How did you manage that?" Otto asked.

I've spoken to him about these matters, and he's kept them to himself. He knows the consequences, Fournier had said of Jaques to Belibaste.

"The bishop got caught in his own trap," I said with a grin. I then summarized the great secret that Fournier had revealed in that last meeting with the Perfect. "He confessed that the church had lost Peter's keys to various heretical groups, what became known as the Gnostic coalition, the Templars and Cathars among them. He acknowledged that the church's enemies possessed and practiced a more authentic Gospel than Rome's.

To conclude, I said, "Such statements made Fournier himself a heretic, and I was witness to it. Belibaste also predicted that he would be pope someday, as did happen. It was his ultimate ambition, and he couldn't have me in a position to jeopardize his chances. I knew too much for him to risk crossing me. He could have had me killed—Arnaud would have gladly obliged—but he may have felt that he still needed me. He'd staked so much on my memory. He may have hoped I'd eventually turn back and be of service in his lofty future.

"It became a cat-and-mouse game. He excluded me from the trial but allowed me access to the prisoners, with someone tailing me of course. Perhaps he thought I would hear or say something that proved that either Piere or you were a Perfect after all. Failing to extract the precious keys from Belibaste still rankled him, and he would have relished a second chance."

"I understand you could visit Allemans prison where we were kept, but what drew you, a privileged citizen, to that terrible place?" Otto asked.

"Piere," I answered without hesitation. "I remembered what Arnaud had said about him: *The Cathars call themselves 'good men.' Piere is actually a good man.* When Timekeeper told me about my future partner, I had hoped it would be Piere. When I first approached him in his miserable cell, he appropriately distrusted me, but he was neither rude nor groveling. I brought in food from time to time and carried messages among the prisoners. I got to know you and Mathène although you both remained distant. One day Piere told me that another visitor had vouched for my trustworthiness despite my still being the bishop's boy."

"Timekeeper again?" Otto asked.

"Piere didn't say. Him or Baldwin, I'd guess. This person suggested that Piere let me help to arrange for your group's escape. Throughout the planning and even after the date for the breakout was settled, Piere never claimed to be my designated partner, although I kept hoping he would do so, nor did he inform me of your identity."

Otto filled in from there. "Even in prison I had to hide in Piere's shadow. I had to remain the mystery man, the invisible one, efficient Piere's dumb little brother. I had to stand by and watch our people die without raising my hands to perform the *consolamentum*. I complained to Piere, but he reminded me that mine was a future destiny and begged me to bide my time. I was on the verge of defiance, so many souls departing without consolation, when he came that night. He told me to secure my few possessions, stand close to the rear prison exit with Mathène, and be ready to run on signal. Almost as an afterthought, he reminded me that should anything happen to him, I was to cleave to the one whom he identified with the watchword, *Two to a horse*.

"We heard the lock release and saw that it was you opening the door. Piere waved his arm and we rushed into the alley. An armored knight was mounted on one horse and had another in tow. He swept up Mathène and perched her in the saddle behind him. Piere motioned you to mount the second horse and then with a kiss hoisted me up behind you. Just as we began to move, there was the sound of other horses running. We had been spotted.

"The knight tossed Piere a sword. Before he took his fighting stance, he looked up at us and shouted, 'Two to a horse.' He slapped our horse on the flank. 'Now go. Follow the Templar to Lombrives.' As we raced away, I heard him scream. The mounted guards had run him through."

"*Two to a horse.* Timekeeper's watchword. It was then that I knew that you were the partner I had been waiting for. Not Piere, but Piere's brother," I said.

"During that night's hard ride from Pamiers to Tarascon, my dying brother's cry echoed all the way in my ears," Otto said. "I had no thoughts about the man who had become my partner; I could only mourn the man who had always been so. All I knew about you as we rode together that first night was that you were the bishop's boy, you'd set us free, Piere's final act was to confirm you as his replacement, and I better hang on tight. When it came to running horses, you were not Piere."

Pushing up a steeper portion of the path, we went silent, each alone with his thoughts although I suspected they were quite similar. When the trail leveled out to a platform area near the top, we stopped. I sat on a rock to catch my breath while Otto stood precariously close to the edge of the cliff.

"Your relationship with Fournier was a lot like mine is with Himmler," he finally said. "A different time, but—" He tailed off just as I hoped he would go on.

Pacing back and forth while peering down towards the town below, he assessed our position. "If we were on the cliff above the Ariège, Muggenbrunn would be Tarascon and the entrance to Lombrives would be behind us. Do you remember?"

Scenes from the various visits I had made to the cave by myself and with him in both lives flipped through my mind like cards shuffled by a practiced dealer. "Which time?" I asked.

I don't know if he heard my question. His gestures became animated as only Otto's, on the verge of insight, could do. "*Parzival*," he exclaimed. His shout left an echo.

"Wolfram von Eschenbach's poem did to me what the painting of Troy in flames did to young Schliemann: it forecast his entire lifetime. After that he had no choice but to invest everything to find Troy. When my father gave me that copy of *Parzival*, he handed me my life plan. By reading it, I was anointed an Arthurian Knight, one compelled to seek the Grail. It was my star. I had to follow it to Paris and the Polaires, to Tarascon and Gadal, to Montsegur and Esclarmonde, and then to Berlin and Heinrich Himmler. Once I embraced my destiny, the entire universe—every person I met, every place I went, every situation I encountered, and every idea that rose in my mind—carried me towards the Grail. Even actions I took to escape my sometimes onerous fate had a way of twisting back towards the appointed goal rather than away from it."

He turned and looked at me, his left eye squinted. He suddenly wilted. "That is, until I found the Lombrives stone," he said mournfully. "If *Parzival* was an infallible guide, that rock was a painted whore. When I first touched it, it embraced me back and suffused me with exhilarating energy. I was the swooning schoolgirl being kissed by the prince of her wildest dreams. It felt like the Grail itself, *the crown of all earthly wishes, fair fullness that ne'er shall fail.*

"Only later did I discover that my prince was a bully to children and a boor among the nobility. What for me was a keyhole through which I glimpsed a glorious future—peace on earth and good will to men—was for others a doorway leading to more hellish type of war or, worse, to nothing at all."

I saw his surging tears. "Something's still missing, Raymond. It's still like I said at Schliersee: I am carrying the Dietrich with me but I can't remember where I put it." He turned and started down.

Following, I reminded him, "At Schliersee, you also said that it was I who was supposed to remember where you put it last."

He paid no attention. "It has to be on Montsegur," he murmured, already several steps ahead. "I must get back into Himmler's good graces. The way this country's going he's the only one with the power to allow me to go back there."

We walked for several minutes more before he added, "Maybe I should contact Gabriele. If the request comes from her rather than through the SS chain of command, maybe Himmler will grant me the few minutes I need with him."

His abrupt return to the present crisis seemed like a fruitless detour. I used his cue to steer the conversation back to the earlier life. "Gabriele should be on this hike with us. As Mathène she set out with us to traverse the cave while Baldwin and his men stayed behind to hold off the bishop's army."

The tactic seemed to work. "So many paid a terrible price to allow us to escape," he said. "When I wrote that last chapter of *Crusade*, I never suspected I had a personal part in the scene, but I viscerally hated Fournier for that fierce final campaign in which Tarascon was leveled, its inhabitants murdered, and so many graves opened with the remaining bones defiled. Then the ultimate cruelty: walling in the remnant of people hiding in the caves to slowly die of thirst and starvation. Does it not hurt you to think about the people who suffered so horribly while we scooted through the cave to safety?"

His question, however gruesome, lent clarity to scenes that had been vague or missing so far. "Yes," I said, "and, as the bishop's confidant, I could have made choices that would have saved some of them had I not agreed to do otherwise. I, as Jaques, came to see death not as the end but as a doorway. My role was to remain quiet and observe. It was hard, but I learned to watch others go on to their destiny, honoring them only by recording their passage."

I permitted myself to slip back momentarily. The last of our party to do so, I felt myself being lifted up to the narrow keyhole behind Baldwin's barricade that led into the bowels of the mountain. I put on a brave face and waved farewell to the beloved vagabond turned Templar, but inside I was quaking. In all my time exploring caves, I had never dared to go that deep before. Why had they not chosen a more experienced guide to accompany the last Perfect on so critical a journey? *We need your memory only to keep an accurate accounting of the history of the Grail,* Timekeeper had said of my appointed role. But where was this Grail I was supposed to be tracking?

I was tempted to ask Otto if he, as Jean, recalled having some precious object in his possession as we started out. But I checked myself. I could see the three of us there. Jean's hands were empty. He knew then, as Otto did now, that something was missing and he was expecting me to help him find it. The Grail, which we were to bear into the future, had to lie somewhere in front of us in that darkness, in the unknown. My role was not to ask questions but to record events as they unfolded.

Still there was impatience. Why did my memory refuse to yield anything beyond the black hole that faced us as we began our journey into the mountain? *Don't force it. It will come as you need it,* 333 had advised. I also recalled Jaques conversing with Bishop Fournier about the memory techniques Cicero and other classical orators used to memorize their lengthy speeches. First, they imprinted a list of a building's significant features in a fixed sequence in mind, then assigned a pertinent image to each feature, and finally associated the exact words of the text to each image. To deliver the speech, the orator walked mentally through the building, approached each preset feature in order, recalled its image, and declaimed the words that went with it.

Suddenly a simple insight exploded through my mind. I had to laugh out loud. Once set, the sequence had to be followed. The technique would fail if the speaker was thinking about the words attached to location 9 when he was in fact at location 5.

Could it be that a thread of events in the current lifetime was intentionally synchronized with a similar thread in a previous incarnation? As the current thread unwound, did its noteworthy details serve to remind the person of correspondences in the former life? Was our trip to the mountain here in the Black Forest above

Muggenbrunn a scene designed to evoke a parallel scene on a mountain in the Ariège above Tarascon in 1323?

Otto turned when I laughed. "What's so funny?" he asked.

"I'm not sure yet," I said, "but I think I'm starting to understand something here. Our lives now and the Cathar period—it's as if the two lives run side by side to form a single track. The train requires both tracks, separate but parallel, to cross the present space to reach its destination."

A smile flickered on Otto's lips. "I fear you too are becoming a poet, my friend."

"More like an actor who recites from a script someone else wrote. Just now I was at a point where I felt paralyzed because I'd forgotten my lines. I laughed when I understood why."

He grimaced. "Why?"

"The play is not yet at the place where I am supposed to speak. The words only come at the point where they fit."

He grunted. "Possibly. But of our two parallel lives, I have a damned good idea about our situation in this one. How does it correspond with the saga of Jaques and Jean?"

We were approaching the bottom of the hill. The chalet where Asta and her son were staying was in sight down the slope and across the road.

"Precisely where we left off at the top there. We, with Mathène, are about to face the unknown, the dark passage through the mountains that should lead to safety in Miglos."

"One discrepancy though in your parallel theory," he said. "Gabriele is not here to play Mathène. Should she not be?"

As if on cue a door of the hotel in the distance swung open, and Asta came out, spotted the hikers, and starting waving.

"Your bride-to-be summons you, Otto," I needled. "Lacking Gabriele, who better to fill in as the chaste wife of a Cathar Perfect? Isn't it time, my friend, to propose and give her a proper role in this script?" He scowled.

Little Johann in tow, Asta came running towards us. "I watched for you to come down as I didn't want to miss you," she said, out of breath. The boy cozied up to Otto, wrapping an arm around his leg. Otto patted him on the head.

"There's been a change in plans," the woman continued, "and we are to leave tomorrow morning. But we want to thank you for your hospitality and friendship before we go, so I've arranged a small party in your honor at the best restaurant in town, the only one. Seven o'clock. I've also invited a few of the other people who have been so nice during our vacation here."

She turned back towards the hotel. "Come, Johann. Otto and Raymond don't have much time to get cleaned up before dinner. They certainly can't show up like that, all sweaty from their hike, right?"

"Right," the boy echoed. "Go take a bath together like Mom and I do."

Asta blushed. "See you at seven."

"That wasn't comfortable," I said when out of earshot.

"Do you think she suspects?"

"What does it matter now unless you intend to actually propose before the evening is over?"

When we reached the cottage, Otto checked the mailbox. He flinched at the official brown envelope he found there. "It's from General Wolff," he said, tearing it open. I stood aside as he read, his face telling me that it was not good news.

"He starts by announcing that the new president of the Ahnenerbe, Dr. Walter Wüst, who took over from its founder, Dr. Wirth, last year, has initiated a major reorganization of our unit, a move long-expected as Wirth was a historian and Wüst is a scientist previously with the Security Service. Wolff says that the process requires that my rank and function be reviewed. Not positive for staff like Weisthor and myself. Wüst has been vocal in his disdain for what he calls the privileged scholars in the Ahnenerbe.

"Then more strong words about my failing to file my ahnenpass by his deadline. Says he must now report my delinquency to the Personnel Office. Bad enough, but then he summons me back to

Berlin immediately for a hearing on a legal matter brought to the attention of the Reichsführer-SS's office."

"Any idea what that's about?" I asked.

He shrugged. "Probably backlash because I opposed Riedweg's appointment. Maybe new life to the allegation that I propositioned sex with that Luftwaffe officer."

"But didn't Wolff tell Ullmann that rumor was inconsequential?"

"Not if it's in his or someone's interest to bring it up again." He shoved the letter back into the envelope. "Not a word about my request for an appointment with Himmler."

He wheeled around and strode into the house. He slapped the letter to the table. "Why, Raymond, do I always have to come down from the mountain?" His voice was breaking. He looked away. "Up there I can breathe. Down here it's always this shit." He stalked into the bedroom and slammed the door behind him.

I stood in for both of us that evening, excusing Otto as having had a sudden attack of asthma, probably caused by weeds we walked through on our hike. Asta accepted his absence nonchalantly, but Johann sulked for much of the evening. Fortunately, mother and son were quite popular with the townspeople, so the event was not the washout that Otto's tantrum might have made of it.

Otto had little to say until an hour before the SS car that would take him to Berlin was scheduled to arrive.

When I came out to the porch, he was sitting atop his packed trunk in full uniform. "I am sorry, Raymond," he said while exhaling a cloud of smoke. "I never intended it to end this way."

I dared to place my hand on his arm. "Nothing's ending, Otto. You really don't know what's in store. It might turn out to be minor."

His eyes filled with tears. He gripped my arm. "Why then do I see darkness everywhere I look? I have enemies hidden in those shadows, powerful enemies, some even posing as friends. I feel like Arnaud Sicre and his cronies have returned and are closing in."

My turn to shiver. "Do you suspect someone, Ullmann perhaps?"

"Not Ullmann. He's a decent man and a friend. Besides, he is not influential enough."

"Weisthor?"

He smirked. "A drunk and irrelevant. He won't survive Wüst for long."

"How about General Wolff himself?"

Otto paused for a moment. "He never liked me. He ordered me back from Wewelsburg and then insisted I be punished in Dachau when Himmler would have been more lenient. A fellow Hessian but old school with a cruel bent towards discipline. As Himmler's Chief of Staff, he is powerful but not enough to overrule his boss. In fact, as the chief liaison between the two leaders, he was the one who presented the leather-bound copy of my book to the Führer for his birthday. So I don't know."

Time was growing short. "You should still have Himmler on your side, whatever this turns out to be. You are blood relatives, remember?"

He took a breath. "I'd forgotten that. Perhaps it will help."

"Play that card if you have the need and opportunity. Remember how I, as Jaques working in Bishop Fournier's office, had to serve a double role; it's your turn now. Remember what Himmler wants deep down and be there to help him get it when given the chance. And keep in mind that you are not alone. I'll stop in Konstanz and visit Gabriele on the way back to Geneva. I'll be discrete but still clue her about your situation. She cares for you deeply, Otto."

"I know."

"Then I'll get word to Ladame and 333. The EC is keeping tabs. Frisé is our open man here, but there are also others, resources ready to intervene should the situation warrants it."

He managed a smile. "Thanks, Raymond. Even if no one else comes through, it's a consolation to know you are watching my back. Be careful yourself. I may wind up where I can't watch yours in return."

He reached into his pocket and pulled out the Templar medallion I had given him in Schliersee and pressed it into my hand. "*Two to a horse.* You take this now for us. It may be in jeopardy where I am headed."

After a long embrace that only ended with the sound of an approaching motor, I handed the medallion back to him. "You will need it more where you are going," I said. "It will be dark for a while as it was deep in the caves of Lombrives. We won't be able to see each other, but we are still travelling side by side. Trust we'll make it through to Miglos."

Chapter 23: Buchenwald, September-December 1938

"We will not allow mystically-minded occult folk with a passion for exploring the secrets of the world beyond to steal into our Movement. Such folk are not National Socialists, but something else—in any case something which has nothing to do with us," Adolph Hitler was reported as saying in a speech in Nuremberg that week.[46] Ordinarily, I had little time for the German dictator's rhetoric, but knowing that Otto, a ranking member of Himmler's paranormal research corps, was in Berlin for re-evaluation made me sit up at such a specific anti-occult statement. Was this another ploy to further justify the persecution of astrologers, Freemasons, Theosophists, Anthroposophists, and other esoteric groups, or did it signal an ideological rift between Hitler and Himmler, who, as Wewelsburg demonstrated, was deeply invested in such views and practices? Regardless, such a pronouncement indicated a Nazi policy change that could only be negative for Otto.

Travelling back from Muggenbrunn to Switzerland, I had visited briefly with Gabriele Winckler-Dechend. Our conversation was again cautious on both sides, but she did voice an opinion on Rahn's relationship with Himmler. "Uncle Heinrich is a man of ambition," she said, "but extremely circumspect. Otto, bless his naiveté, should not be overconfident. While we may not endorse the prevailing view on homosexuality, Otto's past behavior in that regard leaves him vulnerable to anyone with the intent to harm him."

Then after stating that her long absence from the SS made it unlikely she could be of any assistance should Otto get into legal trouble, she made it a point to add, "Beware of the wolf who serves two masters." She followed this enigmatic statement with an artless stare that told me she had given me all I was going to get and I better heed it.

While now reviewing the conversation with Gabriele in my Geneva study, my mind went back to the Cathar Mathène. The woman's role had varied little over the course of 700 years, a *bit part* Otto had called it at Schliersee. To me it seemed quite important although subtle like that of the appearing and disappearing Black Madonna.

The three refugees—Jean, Jaques, and Mathène—had plunged into the bowels of the mountain. The emphasis—*two to a horse*—was on the men, and yet the woman's presence could not have been accidental. Despite her current retreat into the anonymity of the German *hausfrau*, it was Gabriele who brought Otto and his *Crusade* to Himmler's attention, thus catalyzing both his subsequent fame and current peril. Mathène had acted as the good wife to protect Jean, a Perfect, from the Inquisition. But for what purpose did she accompany the men on the perilous passage through miles of underground tunnels fraught with yawning abysses, slippery sills, and teetering boulders?

I recalled my earlier vision about the stone and the cave, which I had had with 333 the previous December. In it Mathène located the glowing green stone, a fragment of a meteor we had ridden from the heavens. She then summoned Jean, and together they brought it back to me, who was still trying to sleep. "*We found the Grail. It lights up from the inside,*" she told me. I was so paralyzed by its power that she then asked, "*Is it so, Jaques, that you are still afraid to ask the question?*" Only later with Timekeeper, was I able, like Parzival in the final scene in King Anfortas's castle, to remember and voice the pivotal question: "*What is this Grail you speak of?*" The answer that came was a vision of the primordial stone's journey, the length of history itself, from the beginning of time to the fragmented capstone of which it was said, *The Grail shattered is Death.*

Was this mystical scene with the green stone in a cave a missing segment from our initiatory journey from the mouth of Lombrives to Miglos? No sooner had that thought occurred to me than a woman's scream shattered the autumn morning in the adjacent courtyard. I rushed to the window, expecting to see a tragic accident, but all was quiet outside. I returned to my desk, sickened to realize that the shriek was Mathène's. It had crossed from the earlier lifetime.

I dig in my fingers to keep a grip on the slippery handhold, the only anchor that allows me to balance on the narrow ledge. I hold my breath and strain to catch any sound from the deep crevasse into which Mathène has just tumbled. Using the light of the flickering torch in my other hand, I keep an eye on Jean, dreading that he might move rashly to try to rescue his wife.

"We've got to get off this sill first," I whisper. "We'll figure it out on the next platform."

Staring downward where one cannot see, he doesn't budge. I sidle forward enough that our bodies are in contact. One misstep from either of us and the mission is over. He is sniffling.

"I know, Jean," I whisper. "You loved her. She found the stone for us. Her work is done. Ours is not."

He starts forward. I dare to exhale. We inch across the ledge, the most precarious one so far. Once off it he slumps to his knees, facing back toward the crevasse into which Mathène had just fallen. He remains so for a long time. Then he stretches into a full prostration and recites The Lord's Prayer thrice. Finally he rises, and drawing a small book from his vest pocket he stretches it, the Secret Gospel of John, towards the abyss.

"Let us adore the Father and Son and Holy Spirit," he chants, again three times. He then prays, "Holy Father, welcome thy servant in thy justice and send upon her thy grace and thy holy spirit"—the closing words of the consolamentum, *a sacrament*

meant to be administered before the believer actually dies.

This ceremony was the first official act I had seen Jean perform in his role as a Perfect. I fall to my knees and place my palms on the ground, the customary act required of a believer approaching a Cathar minister. "Bless us, Lord, and pray God for this sinner that he deliver him from an evil death and lead him to a good end," I say as prescribed by the ritual of the melioramentum.

Rather than place the Gospel book on my head and deliver the traditional blessing, Jean lifts me to my feet. Embracing me he says, "Between us, Jaques, there is no prostration of one before another. Mathène led us both to the Grail. With it and in her blood, we have been jointly ordained in a new covenant. As woman and mother, she birthed the child and delivered it to us. We are its father and mother now. Our unique mission, one foreseen and overseen by the unbroken line of our wise predecessors, is to raise this child for a destiny that lies beyond death in the centuries ahead."

Without looking back towards the woman's grave, we join hands and walk forward side-by-side.

I heard the receding crunch of gravel under heavy boots coming from the courtyard as my study came back into focus. I did not need to go to the window. Instead, I reached for pen and paper and wrote down all that I had witnessed, stopping only when the two men walked away after Mathène's death.

What happened next? I could see nothing further. I laughed ruefully as I remembered what I had learned on the mountain in Muggenbrunn: *The line only comes to me at the point where it fits.* The parallel lives of Jean-Jaques and Otto-Raymond were up to date. The present now had Rahn in Berlin and me sitting in my office. The present then had two men travelling side-by-side through darkness into the mountain, into the greater unknown. For now, that was all I needed to know.

It was another month before 333 was available to meet with Ladame and me to discuss what could or should be done about Otto Rahn. In the meantime, Adolph Frisé, who had a contact within the SS Personnel Office, reported that Otto's situation was neither secure nor desperate. Peculiarly, since he was still awaiting the outcome of the hearing on his alleged affair with the Luftwaffe commander, Rahn was promoted in mid-September to the rank of SS-Obersturmführer, indicating that he was well regarded by at least some of his fellow officers.

But in early October, Frisé advised us that Rahn had been ordered to extended training similar to the disciplinary assignment in Dachau the previous year, only this time in Buchenwald,[47] a concentration camp near Weimar that housed about 3,000 prisoners. Informants had reported increased construction activity at this site: new barracks, additional guard towers, and other preparations that signaled a large influx of new detainees. The SS overseers and guards stationed there had swelled in disproportion to the current population. Was Otto Rahn's sentence part of this buildup rather than just a penalty for some untoward behavior uncovered during the hearing? Frisé's reports were not clear on this point.

333 looked harried and haggard when he invited us into his Dornach study in mid-October. After initial greetings, Paul acknowledged the other man's fatigue. "Not a good month for our cause, sir," he said. "Chamberlain's capitulation to Hitler's demands for the Sudetenland bodes badly for the rest of Czechoslovakia. A wolf is only appeased by a good meal until he gets hungry again."

"I too am concerned by the German appetite," 333 said, "but we'll keep this focused on Otto Rahn. He's been sent to Buchenwald, I understand. Can he provide us with any information about what's going on there?"

I was taken aback. I thought we were going to talk about getting Otto out of Germany, not what intelligence he could pass to us from inside.

333 noticed my consternation. "We suspect the Nazis are gearing up for a major push against their internal enemies, mainly Jews. We've

already allowed Hitler's political expansion without a fight. To also do nothing when he moves against the unwanted peoples within his borders would make us accessories to potentially cataclysmic crimes against humanity. We must sound an alarm that the world hears before it is too late. We have to use every resource available to gather evidence. Your friend is right where we need a pair of sharp eyes."

"Has he been informed about this change in mission? Last I knew he was to keep Riedweg out of the SS and attempt to win over Himmler," I said.

333 said, "Riedweg is now an SS medical officer, and Himmler's staff is running and manning the concentration camp system. The Ahnenerbe's mandate has been revised from digging up prehistoric Aryan artifacts to digging graves for the Fatherland's non-Aryan populations. Hitler has openly castigated all occult activities like Grail hunting as foolishness. Before he sets out to conquer Europe, he has to disable any perceived enemies within, and he won't waste time or effort in getting the job done."

"So recruiting Himmler is off the table?" I asked.

333 looked at Ladame. Paul said, "Hitler is winning. The rest of Europe is unwilling to take a stand against him. Himmler will stay with the winner."

"But Otto remains convinced that there's still a chance and is operating on that assumption. Shouldn't he be told of the change in agenda?"

333 grimaced. "Too dangerous. If Otto is caught and forced to reveal what he knows about us now, it will be old news. No sense burdening him further. After Dachau he played the good SS man well enough to merit a promotion. The slap on the wrist that finds him in Buchenwald can be turned to our advantage. He can observe firsthand what we expect to happen soon and provide us with an adequate account of what transpires afterwards."

Paul touched my arm. "Frisé and others are keeping a close eye on him. Should his situation turn critical, we'll spring him."

I groaned, remembering that Otto had suspected an Arnaud Sicre among his fellows. "He may still enjoy Himmler's protection, which too could change quickly, but he was concerned that someone or several with considerable power have a vendetta against him. He could be betrayed," I said.

333 leaned forward, that weary lack of luster gone from his eyes. "Hitler and Himmler may have dropped their belief in the chivalry of the Templars and the way of the Grail," he said, "but we have not. That they are falling back to military weapons and prisons camps as their standard mode of operation is not to our liking, but it can work to our favor. It will, however, be costlier and take longer. You and Otto, riding together, have already served admirably. Your efforts revealed what was not possible, thus freeing us to try other options. Remember, we have millennia invested in this. The current life, while valuable, is worth no more than the many lives we have already lived and left behind."

"I'm sorry. It's so hard to hold that viewpoint when—" I hung my head and choked up.

"When you love each other." 333 finished my sentence. "Look at me, Raymond." I did. He was beaming benignly, wise old Baldwin the Leper King who had covered our backs with his life so we could escape through the Lombrives labyrinth. "You two could not do what you have to do if you did not love each other."

On the morning of November 8, Paul telephoned me to set a breakfast meeting. He wanted to discuss an urgent matter about to break in the French newspapers.

Once we settled in with coffee, his serious look forecasting bad news, Paul said, "Yesterday a young German-born Polish Jew named Herschel Grynszpan walked into the German Embassy on Rue de Lille in Paris and asked to see an embassy official. The clerk on duty showed him into the office of Ernst von Rath, the junior of the two staffers. Grynszpan then pulled out a gun and shot Von Rath several times in the stomach. According to the police report, he shouted 'You're a filthy *boche*' as he fired.

"Von Rath is being treated in the hospital by French and German doctors but is not expected to survive for long. In Hershel's pocket was a postcard addressed to his parents that proves that the shooting was a premeditated act to protest the recent deportation of 12,000 Polish Jews from Germany, Hershel's family among them. On checking further, we found that a large group of Poles living in the Reich were indeed arrested, stripped of their property, and herded onto trains. They were dropped at the Polish border and are stranded near Zbąszyn. Poland refuses to repatriate them. It was from there that Herschel's father wrote to his son, himself a destitute illegal alien in France, telling the boy what happened and pleading for help."

"Terrible for Von Rath," I said, "and also tragic for the assassin, his family, and the homeless Jews. But, from your concern over what seems like a lesser incident compared to the world-shaking events you usually deal with, I suspect this has broader implications."

He sipped his coffee and looked off. "It is precisely the kind of incident the Nazis have been praying for. In the disinformation business where conspiracy is more the rule than the exception, we suspect a set up. If Von Rath dies, the dire event designed to suppress Germany's Jewish population would happen soon, perhaps within days."

"Any details on what they are up to?"

He shook his head. "They've kept a tight lid on this one. We do know that Goebbels's Propaganda Office has been running a nationwide media campaign designed to drum up hatred for the Jews among the general population. Von Rath's murder might well be the match they need to set off the explosion."

Although Ladame had predicted the reprisal, I was unprepared for the speed and savagery with which it was launched. Ernst Von Rath died on the morning of November 9th. Fortuitously for the Nazis, the date of his death was also the fifteenth anniversary of the Munich Beer Hall Putsch of 1923, the *"Tag der Bewegung"* or Day of the Movement, a Nazi high holy day. That evening Joseph Goebbels took the stage in the famed beer hall and delivered an inflammatory speech to a frenzied crowd of veteran Nazis. It would not be surprising, he said, if the German people were so outraged by Van Rath's assassination by a Jew that they took the law into their own hands and attacked Jewish businesses, community centers, and synagogues. While the Party and its armed forces should not be seen as openly organizing such 'spontaneous outbursts,' he said, neither would they oppose or prevent them.

Only hours later, crowds took to the streets and invaded Jewish communities throughout Germany and Austria. That night of pillaging, destruction, arrests, and murder became known as *Kristallnacht*, the Night of Broken Glass, after the shards from shops and synagogue windows left in the wake of mobs running amok through Jewish communities while the police stood by. The next day tens of thousands of Jews were rounded up and transported to the readied concentration camps. The justification, endlessly repeated to quiet a foreign press critical of such mass incarcerations, was that Jews now required government protection from an outraged German citizenry.

With security impenetrable around the Buchenwald facility located in a forested cleft in the hills above Weimar, it took Adolf Frisé a week to glean some information on Otto's status after Kristallnacht. The publisher managed to find himself in a Weimar restaurant at a time when several SS officers, Ullmann among them, were dining there. He used the opportunity to ask Rahn's associate about their mutual friend.

Ullmann expressed concern. The author was not equal to the rigorous duties of a field officer. As at Dachau he had performed well in training, even leading the drilling of recruits. But when the swollen prison population demanded that he work in the detainee area and participate in its administration, something cracked. "He became withdrawn and uncooperative with constant complaints of ill health," Ullman said. "As his senior officer, I had to adjudicate his fitness to continue." At this point, Frisé said Ullmann became vague, intimating he was trying to get Otto reassigned to a more appropriate position but that the decision was now in the hands of those above him.

"Otto seems to have taken Kristallnacht personally," Ladame said as we discussed Frisé's report. "He can no longer playact the model SS man. It's been estimated that Buchenwald's population multiplied from 3,000 to 20,000 overnight; and even with the new construction they can't handle such an increase without jeopardizing the detainees. Prisoners who can't be squeezed into the barracks will be kept in open pens. Food and sanitation have to be nightmarish. Deaths have been reported, although the Nazis minimize the number, attributing those they are forced to admit as due to natural causes, accidents, or inmate infighting. Tough as he might try to be, Otto doesn't have the stomach to absorb such brutality."

I nodded. "He was already disillusioned. Now he has to digest that Himmler is the designer and manager of the tragedy he is witnessing."

Ladame clucked. "We can only hope he finally gets that."

Although I shared Paul's concern over Otto's naiveté, I ignored the barb. "In case Ullmann gets him out of the camp and someplace where we can whisk him out of the country," I said, "we should be getting something ready now. Perhaps Gabriele or even Asta Baeschlin—"

"No," Paul said abruptly. "We wait. If Ullmann's plan works without our interference and Otto's cover remains intact, he may be of further use in Germany."

In the first week of December, Frisé reported that Ullmann had succeeded in arranging Rahn's reassignment. Such special treatment met with considerable resistance within the SS hierarchy. General Wolff suggested that Rahn's physical condition amounted to malingering and that the cure was stricter discipline. The final decision came from Himmler though, and Rahn was on the way back to Muggenbrunn to continue writing his sequel to *Lucifer's Court* but this time under orders not to leave the country. Frisé promised to visit Rahn once it was confirmed that he was resituated.

Adolph Frisé met with Otto in Muggenbrunn shortly after Christmas. Contrary to the expected warm welcome, he found the man apathetic. Otto offered no explanation for his assignment to Buchenwald or details about his experience there other than the repeated exclamation, "I can't fathom what has become of my country."

Otto did hint to embarrassment over his failure to keep up the performance as a proper SS man because it had both jeopardized his commitment to the EC and made him look weak to his fellow officers all the way up the line to Himmler. He admitted shame that his books were being used as Nazi propaganda, a situation that was now paralyzing his productivity even though meeting strict deadlines was a condition of his reassignment. He still maintained that Himmler could not be aware of the intolerable conditions at Buchenwald or the inhumane treatment of internees held for their own protection. On only one point did he become passionate: it was his duty as an SS member, a German citizen, and human being to report what he had seen directly to Himmler, and he vowed that he would make the opportunity to do so if one was not given to him.

The rest of their conversation, so Frisé summarized, was the disjointed ramblings of a man crazed by the horrors he had witnessed. While time might restore his balance, the continuing pressure to write intelligibly while under surveillance made it improbable. Frisé recommended that we continue to ready an escape plan but could not guarantee Otto's cooperation, which might then require a more drastic alternative.

Before I could get Ladame to explain to me what this *drastic alternative* might involve, there came a follow-up dispatch from Frisé: when he attempted to check back with Rahn in Muggenbrun, he found out that Otto was on his way to Berlin.

Otto's abrupt departure for the capital put the EC on high alert. 333 rearranged his travel schedule to meet with Paul and me in Dornach once again. Ladame did not restrain his annoyance over Rahn's reckless risk-taking.

"Why Berlin?" he voiced on our way to the meeting. "From Muggenbrunn, out of the way and close to the border, we had a chance, but how the hell do we get him out of Berlin?"

333 was also displeased. "While we can monitor his movements in the open city," he said as the meeting got underway, "once he's inside SS Headquarters, he'd be on his own."

"Given that he stubbornly believes that Himmler's hands are clean," Paul said, "our greater concern is that he might reveal what he discovered at Montsegur, perhaps even the treasure's location. Himmler might seduce it out of him with a promise to let him travel there to retrieve it. Otto may not be able to resist the fulfillment of his fondest dream."

"He's not that naïve," I countered, allowing my disgust to show. "Anyway, Hitler has squashed all occult research. Himmler will hardly risk his position by continuing his pursuit of the Grail."

"Disinformation, Raymond," Paul replied. "Hitler and Himmler already know the fruits of practicing the dark arts. The official prohibitions are designed to keep everyone else's fingers out of the occult till, leaving only the privileged inner circle with access to it."

333 tapped his fingers on the desk. "Paul is right," he eventually said. "There is much more to the whole story, but I don't need to tell you that. You felt the lightning when you both held the stone in the cave. And that was a mere fragment, a single depleted facet of the power of the whole that you encountered in your reveries. *The Grail is the uplifted sword, the penetrating phallus.* You remember that."

I thought for a moment. That line had come from the vision in the cave in Tarascon with Timekeeper. I had not spoken to anyone in this lifetime about it.

333 smiled. "As Baldwin I also worked with Timekeeper then. We too were a team although with a different specialty than yours and Jean's."

I glanced at Ladame. "Do you still work as a team now?" I asked 333.

The other two men looked at each other, a moment of levity. "Not me," Paul said. "I'm a recent recruit. The EC needed some young blood infused into its hoary veins."

"Then who is Timekeeper?" I asked. They just looked at me. I answered my own question "I know, Paul. There are never no secrets, right?"

"Back to current business, gentlemen," 333 said. "It's not firecrackers we are dealing with here, and the Nazis mean business. Thank goodness they sent Albert Einstein and his cadre of Jewish nuclear scientists packing for America, but they know enough on their own to understand the potential for harnessing the tremendous invisible energies of the planet, forces previously the province of mystics and occultists, to tinker with turning such power into weapons of unimaginable destruction. We know that Himmler employed the services of serious but unconventional scientists like the French mathematician and alchemist Gaston de Mengel. He advised in the construction of several Nazi projects, including military installations, so that they were positioned at the intersection of the magnetic grid lines that crisscross the earth."

At Wewelsburg, Otto had mentioned de Mengel and his role in defining the North Tower as the future "center of the world." I told what I learned there.

"Wewelsburg and other such redoubts must be leveled before Germany is to be defeated in the coming war," 333 said.

The Battle of the Birch Tree, where the armies of the West will defeat the armies of the East. "They will be," I assured him, recalling the vivid premonition of British and American planes bombing Himmler's Camelot.

"As Einstein discovered with his theory of relativity and Nicolai Tesla demonstrated practically with his inventions," 333 continued, "certain esoteric principles have practical applications that can either bring enormous benefit or extreme destruction to humanity. *As above, so below,* the primordial Hermetic rule. The Ark of the Covenant, with its Chintimani fragment, was a lethal weapon as well as religious artifact. If the Nazis were to retrieve certain occult formulas, their scientists could develop arms with which they could hold the entire planet hostage."

"Would Otto's discovery at Montsegur give them that capacity?" I asked.

333 shrugged. "Not an experiment we can risk letting them attempt."

I shuddered. "Is that where Frisé's 'drastic alternative' comes in?" The two men nodded.

"But we are getting ahead of ourselves," 333 quickly added. "All we know so far is that Rahn went to Berlin to inform Himmler about the Buchenwald atrocities. We'll find out shortly if he gets his audience, then whether he survives his cheeky protest against Nazi policy and is allowed to return to Muggenbrunn."

A vivid precognition flashed through my mind: Rahn and Himmler, both with hands folded leaning towards each other across the Reichsführer-SS's massive desk. A staring match, neither man blinking.

"He got his meeting," I said. "He'll return to Muggenbrunn but will be closely followed. He wants more time to decide. He'll get it, but not much."

333 nodded. "I figured you'd know what was happening with him. Ride *two to a horse* long enough and you become joined at the hip. All is unfolding according to the plan. The EC has promised its protection. Now he needs someone he trusts more than Frisé, someone the Nazis won't immediately suspect. Someone who can reach into his soul, evaluate the situation from deep down, and decide the best course of action on the spot."

"You would trust my objectivity when he is my closest friend?" I asked, understanding that he intended to send me.

333 said, "Only you can rightly decide if his lifetime as Otto Rahn should continue or terminate. And only from you would he accept the right decision."

Chapter 24: Freiburg, March 8, 1939

Following the instructions I received from Adolph Frisé before I left Switzerland, I arrived in Freiburg on March 8, walked from the train station to the venerable Schwarzwälder Hof, took the side entrance, climbed the back stairs, and tapped on the door to room 214 at precisely 6:00 p.m. "Two to a horse," I said softly.

"Come in," a voice almost too husky to be Otto's responded. "And close it behind you."

I entered the large but dimly-lit sitting room of his hotel suite. He pointed to a chair in the near corner, across from him. "Keep away from the windows. They have binoculars," he said.

I did as directed, all the while trying to assess his condition from a face hidden in shadows. After six months apart, our greeting felt awkward and understated. I would have to get used to us being watched.

"Not that it matters what they think of us anymore, but they know I came here to meet with my publisher, Otto Vogelsgang, this afternoon," Otto said. "But not about you. Best to keep them off your trail as long as possible."

"Who are *they*?" I asked. I noticed no tobacco smell in the room, and he was not smoking.

He shrugged indifferently. "Who knows? SS snoops for sure, but several factions in and outside the government seem intrigued by my personal life. Some are spies spying on the other spies. Welcome to Nazi Germany." The despondency Frisé had reported earlier was hardly evident.

"A few weeks back, when I was sick with indecision, I visited Kurt Eggers in Dortmund," he said. "Van Haller, my former publisher was there. Hearing of my predicament, he mentioned that he had a set of counterfeit papers that I could use to get out of the country. Eggers vetoed the idea, pointing out the men in raincoats stationed across the street from his house. We'd all get arrested if they detected any move to escape on my part, he argued. That was the point where I knew I was trapped."

"So your meeting with Himmler didn't go as well as your current freedom of movement might indicate?" I asked with a pang of anxiety.

His voice flattened. "Perhaps I should have listened to Frisé and not gone to Berlin. But I had to. After Kristallnacht in Buchenwald, I had to find out what Himmler, my benefactor for the last four years, knew and didn't know." He threw out his hands. "Too late now."

"Himmler didn't take kindly that you objected to the mistreatment of the Jews. Then why did he let you return to your writing?" I asked.

"Two points you have wrong there. I never got the chance to voice my protest. And I am not allowed to do my own writing. I'm a Nazi propaganda hack. Nor was it ever appropriate to mention our possible blood relationship."

I frowned. He leaned towards me. "Let me take you through it quickly. It won't make the history books—unless you put it there."

The parallel between Jaques mentally scribing the final confrontation between Bishop Fournier and Guilhem Belibaste with my now taking in the details of Rahn's last meeting with the Reichsführer-SS was obvious to both of us. Another stab of dread: had Otto Rahn, like the Perfect, entered the endura? Was his not smoking evidence of resignation to a death he considered inevitable?

"I arrived at headquarters without an invitation, but Himmler acted as if he expected me," Otto began. "He greeted me heartily, old friends, and asked about my writing progress. I started to comment on the book about Conrad of Marburg and the novel *Sebastian*, but he brushed past those.

"'The sequel to *Lucifer's Court* is what I want to see next,' he said. 'Pick up the key threads you barely touched on there and expand on them. Hit the Roman church and their Jesuit mafia with a hammer. Word is that Eugenio Pacelli, our former nuncio, is about to become pope. We want him to remember that Nazi Germany can either be ally or adversary—his choice and the church's fate. And the Jews. Too light on them in *Lucifer's Court* even after we edited in some facts to make it publishable. You weren't long in Buchenwald, I understand, but long enough to paint some shocking word pictures of those hairy vermin posturing as human.'"

I said, "A self-indictment. He knew and expected you to be on board. It doesn't seem like he left you any wiggle room. And yet he let you go."

"The Reichsführer-SS tends to speak more than he listens. Here it was to my advantage. Before I could respond, he was already off, pals again, informing me that Hitler's prohibition against occultism was for the *hoi polloi*. True, the Ahnenerbe proper was redirected towards scientific experiments designed to increase our soldiers' durability under duress and our enemies' vulnerability to it. Also true that Dr. Wüst had offloaded several of the old hands from the prehistory research days, Weisthor among them. The old pretender, Himmler told me in confidence, had been committed to an insane asylum before joining the SS, a career-ending tidbit uncovered by General Wolff during a fact-finding mission to Austria. Himmler did, however, retain an elite group of researchers, explorers, scientists, and writers to pursue his occult projects. And I was to be one of the chosen. Now—and here he was insistent—he needed me more than ever. This puzzled me, so I asked where he saw me as still fitting in. 'In one word, Montsegur,' he said."

I tensed. "He wants you to go back there?"

"He never said as much. But he requested that I assemble every scrap of information—notes, maps, sketches, material from memory—about my discoveries there and hand it over to him for review. He hinted that I might get to lead a future expedition there, perhaps once France was in Germany's orbit, but cautioned against holding anything back, intimating that others, mainly Wolff, thought that's what I'd been doing all along."

"And you agreed to do that?"

"I certainly felt trapped, but dire as the immediate situation was, I managed to get distracted. I kept seeing scenes from that Inquisition courtroom back in Pamiers while Piere and I were on trial before Fournier. I was scared silly then too, but one look at Piere and I knew that we would make it through. So while bouncing back and forth between Himmler and Fournier—they are the same, you know—I reached into my pocket and took hold of the Templar medallion. I was amazed to feel the same sensation of comfort and peace that I'd gotten from the Lombrives stone. I immediately knew I had to consult with you before reaching any decision. It was simply a matter of buying time."

"Which you did," I said. "But how?"

"At first I tried tossing a red herring. No lie; it may contain some truth. I explained how a new lead placed the Grail treasure in the German convent of St. Odelien, and that St. Odile, the convent's namesake, was the matriarch of Europe's chief dynasties, thus making certain royal houses here the proper guardians of the Grail mysteries."

"And he wants you to pursue that clue?" I asked.

Otto laughed. "He didn't get his job by being easily fooled. He caught the attempted detour and retaliated swiftly. Without raising his voice, he ticked off the major counts against me: homosexuality, Jewish ancestry, malingering at Buchenwald, and opposing the Riedweg appointment. He then piled on several more that could incriminate me further: making critical comments about the party, fabricating the engagement to Asta Baeschlin, and showing sympathy for non-German nations like France and Switzerland. And all along I thought I was getting away with much of this."

"So the rumors about his encyclopedic mind are true," I said,

"Details on everyone. And calculating. He held everything, especially the dirt, in reserve, choosing to act or not as he saw fit."

"He then mentioned that my assignments in Dachau and Buchenwald were warnings. He was doing his best to prevent it, but I had enemies who thought I belonged inside the KZ fence."

"There's an Arnaud Sicre in every group," I said, remembering Gabriele's ominous warning: *Beware of the wolf who serves two masters.*

Otto pushed on with the narrative. "Then his tone radically changed again. The shift felt premeditated. He turned personal, even emotional. He had befriended, supported, and even fathered me when I was down. He arranged to bring me into the corps and made me a writer recognized throughout the country. We had been soul mates across lifetimes as Teutonic Knights and Grail seekers. Destiny had brought us together again, this time to recover the Grail and properly enshrine it in Wewelsburg for the duration of the gloriously dawning Thousand-Year Reich.

"Honestly, Raymond, the stolid Reichsführer-SS was close to tears. 'Without your inspiration,' he said, 'I would not have embraced my noble past as Henry the Fowler. Without your dream of a united Europe, I would not have started to build its future capital in Wewelsburg. Without your stone for its centerpiece, I would not have conceived of the North Tower as the beacon at the center of the world.'"

Otto's body visibly quivered. "Here he stopped and held me in his gaze, a giant cobra intent on bending me to do his will. I clutched the medallion tighter to counter his pulsing hypnotic power. His voice softened even further. 'I have a confession to make,' he said, 'that must never go any further than this room. From the moment I first lay hands on your book, *Crusade Against the Grail*, I knew you had the critical talent that I was lacking to reach my godlike dreams. You were my Heinrich Schliemann, one who could access the past and future in a way that ordinary mortals could not. Your finding the Lombrives stone and bringing it home confirmed your ability, even though I personally felt nothing from your talisman. Your power, the power I require, is not in a single demonstration of ability or the product of that demonstration but in the possession and control of the skeleton key, the talent itself that can be used to open door after door in the esoteric realm."

"Fournier wanted Peter's keys from Belibaste so that he could become the Roman pope. The Reichsführer-SS wants the Dietrich from you so he can become the Nazi pope," I said.

Otto reached into his pocket for a cigarette only to find no pack there. "His argument almost worked," he said, his hand shaking. "For a moment, Dachau, Kristallnacht, Buchenwald, the hollow-eyed Jews in prison stripes marked with yellow stars slipped from my awareness. Instead, I saw beautiful blue-eyed, blond-haired German legions marching across Europe, the swastika flying everywhere, the bodies of the *untermensch*—Jews, gypsies, Freemasons, Slavs, defectives—left behind in mass graves." He paused for a breath.

"You said almost, so it didn't happen. How then did you answer him?"

"I didn't. I remained silent, which he took that as an act of defiance. And like the cobra, suddenly crossed by his intended victim, he struck with venom.

"'You are no Templar warrior or Cathar martyr much less your noble Lucifer, Rahn,' he hissed. 'For all the noble sentiments you preach in your books, you are a whining sissy, a quivering girl posing in an SS uniform. Take away your creature comforts—food, bed, cigarettes, liquor—and you'll be on your knees begging to spill everything I want to know.' He leaned in, his attitude slightly less menacing. 'Admit it, Otto. I bent over backwards to accommodate your faults. I knew about your homosexuality from the beginning and paired you with Gabriele, thinking she might cure you. But you spurned her advances and she went to Winckler instead. I included your Swiss friend Raymond so that you would have a companion of your own kind but one who followed the celibate Stefan George and thus was likely to help you check your perversion.'

"He allowed our association to continue, he said, even after Wolff discovered that you were aligned with anti-Nazi factions in Switzerland. Ironically, Himmler hoped that our relationship would turn you while we were plotting how to turn him. 'Without my intervention, your SS comrades would have expelled you, or worse, some time ago,' he concluded. 'I rescued you then, and only I can rescue you again. Give in, Rahn.'"

Jacques Fournier, the inquisitorial wizard, had only improved with time, I thought. "How did you get out of that?"

Rahn grinned. "I let him be right. I played the sissy he took me for. A weak, distracted woman unable to make up my fickle mind. In the most pitiable tone I could conjure, I pleaded for more time to decide."

"And he gave it to you?"

Otto nodded. "But not much, and not without close supervision. And not before he spelled out the stark alternatives. I could hand over all that I knew about the treasure of Montsegur and then settle down and write according to his prescription. Or, if I could not bring myself to do that, I was to proceed to a certain mountain just across the Austrian border near Soll, a place designated for disgraced SS men to end their lives with a modicum of respect. Any attempt to do otherwise would result in immediate arrest, incarceration, torture until I told all, and finally a slow and brutal death. With that ultimatum, he let me walk out of his office with barely two weeks to decide."

I clenched my lips to squelch my grief. The worst fears for my friend and lover were realized. Any words that might have comforted him were stifled along with the tears. I could only look at him with a fierce longing that it had been different. I thought of my prophetic vision in the General's Hall in Wewelsburg's North Tower. There the spectral Reichsführer-SS had declared: *Status as blessed or damned must be reached by unanimous vote. In the case of the one missing tonight, consensus could not be reached. To decide his eternal fate then, we will consult the stone.* Rahn could have been the missing member in question. They had gone down to the vault to determine his destiny.

Otto finally spoke again. "I know, Raymond, but we can't waste time on blame or pity. I know too much. The Nazis cannot afford to let me escape. Even if I gave Himmler all he asked for, he would take the gift and dispose of the giver. Nor would the EC allow me to give him what he requests. If you were to conclude here that I might comply with Himmler's order, you would issue my death warrant and perhaps execute it.

"I didn't come here just to fill you in on the story up to this point, although that too had to be done. We came here to plot our story's ending. We have come to a fork in the road. I won't choose which route to take without your advice and agreement. It's our decision and we can only make it together."

With that he looked at me so intently that I felt he expected me to untie this Gordian knot. We sat in silence, staring at each other. I felt powerless to offer a solution. Then 333's admonition came back to mind: *You're looking at the wrong lifetime.*

Chapter 25: Montreal de Sos, Autumn 1365

The two elderly men, the weaker supported by the stronger, wind their way up the slope that borders the crumbling outer wall of the once formidable Chateau de Montreal-de-Sos. Like the leaves falling around them, they quiver to the autumn breeze already tinged with the scent of winter that blows down from the white-capped Pyrenees glistening in the morning sunlight to the south. It is not far from their secluded quarters in the village to the highest point of the promontory, but their ritual walk, done most mornings for the forty years of their sojourn here, now takes almost an hour.

"Our bench, Jaques," the younger man says, breaking the traditional silence they ordinarily maintain prior to prayer and contemplation; both men know this will not be a normal day. He helps seat his wheezing companion on the stone slab slick from their regular use.

The older man catches his breath and then says to the younger, "It is right, Jean, that today we contemplate with our eyes open. I wish to ponder the Peak of the Grail for the last time as we talk."

"Are you in great discomfort, my friend?" Jean asks.

Jaques sighs. "I am well, but this old body is worn out. But before I give it up, I want to make sure that I have everything that I must take with me." He slowly scans the mountainous landscape before him. "It didn't take Arnaud Sicre long to come poking around Castle Miglos after our initiatory journey through the caves of Lombrives. So we came here, ten miles deeper into the mountains, a stronghold still under the Count of Foix's control then and garrisoned by knights in the old chivalric tradition. Montreal-de-Sos has been our home ever since. We have remained blessedly untouched in this eagle's nest."

"Watched over by the Templars, if that's what our hosts actually are," Jean says.

"We don't ask. They don't tell. They may be angels. Baldwin vouched for them."

"And he was right. They have provided everything, even the necessary news from outside, but otherwise let us go about our lives, no questions about our past or our spiritual practices. They even turned a blind eye to our propensity to bury things in the caves in the hill below us."

Jaques chuckles. "Digging around like a dog you did. So all the artifacts have been secured?"

"Right down to my Gospel book, the last to be interred. And you have committed the locations to memory?"

Jaques pats the top of his head. "All buckled down. According to Belibaste, it will be seven hundred years before the laurel again blooms in Languedoc."

It is Jean's turn to smile. "Seven hundred years, the 1900's, the century before the second millennium. It will be here in the blink of an eye."

"So say you who can't remember yesterday. A lot can happen in seven hundred years."

"For yesterday, seven hundred years ago, seven thousand years ago, I have your incomparable memory. Holding the future in my head is much easier. Nothing has happened in it yet, so there's nothing to remember."

Jaques grimaces. "All this time together and we remain a paradox to each other, complementary but opposite. From the same central position, you look forward while I look backward." He glances off for a moment. "Do you even remember your wife Mathène?"

"I don't re-member her, as in putting the pieces of her shattered body back together. I have only to touch the fragment of the precious stone she left with us to feel her presence. No matter what form she chooses in the future, I will know her."

"Her stone," Jaques says. "I have encrypted clues to its location in several of the buried manuscripts, and there are others embedded in features of the churches in this region, reminders in case I catch amnesia along the way."

"Unlikely. You can't even forget the things you ought to," Jean jibes.

"And you'd be the first to criticize if I miss a single jot or tittle."

Jean lets loose a ripple of laughter. "You're dying, and we're having a lovers' quarrel. Perhaps we should have followed the Templar model literally. It was said that they rode two on the same horse so they could bugger each other as they galloped along, you know."

"Hah," Jaques snaps back, "Beware. Every thought becomes a future reality."

Jean puts his arm over his companion's shoulder. "Would that be so bad? I do love you, Jaques."

Then he gets up and begins to pace in front of the bench. "But I must admit that I am extremely anxious about our coming separation. I know it won't be long before I follow you out of this life, but there's that time in between. On my own, I am like a balloon. I tend to float above the trees and into the sky, bobbing along without watching where I came from or where I am going. But should I want to land, I can't get down on my own. I have relied on you to remember where we came from. Without you I fear I will lose track of where we are going."

Jaques chuckles as hard as his failing condition allows.

"What's funny?" Jean asks.

"The paradox we are again. Like any ordinary human, I start at the beginning and read forward page by page through to the end, taking events in the order presented. You jump right to the last page, read the book's conclusion, and leave the details that make it a story to someone else."

Jean shrugs. "Why not? Why read for hours when someone can tell me what I need to know in a few minutes? Why be concerned with the tedium of transcription when I have you to record it all?"

"The answer I expected and have accepted throughout my life. The scribe's lot is humble compared to the roles of an event's participants, but I take consolation in knowing that, without the scribe's record, any affair, no matter how important, might as well have not occurred."

Jean returns to his seat and links arms with Jaques's. "I have not been properly appreciative. I have carried the Book of the Gospel of John close to my heart and held it aloft to concentrate the presence of Spirit while administering the *consolamentum* but paid scant attention to the words it contains and less to the writer who wrote them."

"You need not apologize. He who consciously carries spirit in his heart has no need of the words or the book that contains them. He is his own writer, constantly recreating the book through his experience, reshaping, revising, and improving it through the process of living it."

Jean sighs. "Only in the ideal world, which we were privileged to visit only once. But here the tendency is to forget, even those truths most conducive to our permanent happiness. John the evangelist faithfully recorded the words of the Master: 'Very truly I tell you, whoever believes in me will do the works I have been doing, and they will do even greater things than these.'[48] And yet this ineffable promise penetrated few hearts. Rather than believe in him, the vast majority, including the Roman church, ignored or vilified his words, preaching instead that Jesus was the supreme exception, God's only Son sent to save the rest of us sinners, rather than the supreme example, a divine being demonstrating that our divinity is on par with his own. In another place, the authentic Christ countered those who criticized his claim to divinity by invoking the divinity of all: 'Has it not been written in your Law, *I said, you are gods?*'"[49]

Jaques picks up the theme. "The first and master key lost by the early church leaders who abandoned Jerusalem for Rome: man's inherent divinity. The reason Belibaste asked Fournier if he had read the Gospel of John. The key was hidden in plain sight in their own Bible. The bishop and his church did not have the eyes to see it.

"Nor could they grasp the second key, which proceeds logically from the first: a divine being cannot be anything other than what he conceives himself to be. A mirror can only reflect that which is front of it. If a being conceives itself to be divine, it is so. If a being conceives itself to be a miserable sinner, it is that. With our thoughts, we create ourselves.

"One who wants to control another must seduce the subject into thinking that he can be controlled by something other than his own thoughts. The Roman church adopted the mechanics of control from the Roman Empire, and its followers became sinful slaves who worshipped an imperial Jesus who bore no resemblance to the Jewish teacher of the same name.

"The Gnostics and similar communities, soon to be declared heretical, retained the keys of the authentic Christ, and thus the knowledge of humanity's inherent divinity and self-determination. Theirs remained the community of love while the Roman church became the church of fear, a fear that drove it to hate the ones who loved."

"But love, by its very nature, cannot die," Jean says. "Its external manifestation—organization, rites, priesthood, and practice—can be driven underground, buried in essence, but even suppression only acts to replant love. Love is the grain of wheat that Jesus meant when he said, 'Unless a grain of wheat falls into the earth and dies, it remains alone; but if it dies, it bears much fruit.'"

"The Perfect Belibaste understood that. Fournier could not," Jaques says. "It was the seeds of love lost that the Templars located beneath the ruins of the Temple of Jerusalem. They replanted them and brought them back to flower. Thus, during their watch Europe enjoyed a material, mental, and spiritual prosperity not known since the Dark Ages. The Cathar community was able to reconstitute the seed from the suppressed written and oral remnants of the original Church of Jerusalem, the Paulicans and Bogomils among others.

In the salutary environment thus created, Languedoc became the affluent, diverse, and creative hub of southern Europe. Even as he condemned our last known leader to death, Fournier confessed that Belibaste possessed the seed the church needed to restore itself. Unfortunately, his observation did not extend from his mind to his heart and actions. In his eight years as Pope Benedict XII, he did nothing to meet Belibaste's prescription for recovering the keys."

Jean again jumps to his feet and resumes pacing. "I fear death less than having to continue without you, Jaques. What if something had happened to you as it did with Mathène, and I'd had to continue that initiatory journey through the cave of Lombrives alone? Had I even the courage to go on after the loss, I would not have made it far through the physical darkness and hazards of the passage without succumbing to accident or mental paralysis.

"As for the spiritual trials we encountered there—the phantasms and delusions too grotesque for the human soul, the visions and ecstasies too sublime for the human spirit—I could not have endured without your constant goading. Sometimes pushing me forward, sometimes cheering me on, sometimes cajoling, and often enough just ordering me to keep moving. How many times when I thought I had lost my mind did you remind me that you were tracking all that was occurring and that there would be the opportunity to review it when we reached our next landing? Time after time you proved right, and I learned to trust you even though I knew you had not been through there before any more than I had been."

He wheels and faces the older man. "You never did tell me how you managed to do that."

Jaques grins like a child proud of an accomplishment. "I'm glad you finally asked. Very simple. I had a map."

Jean grimaces. "I never saw you with any map. And, from what I understood from Piere when he explained that I had to return to the Ariège despite the danger of capture, there was no written information about the initiatory route or process."

Jaques taps his right temple. "It was in here although I didn't

realize it until we left the others behind and entered into the unknown. Once on our way, I recognized that the route was chosen
because its natural features conformed to the ancient blueprint for
initiation that has been used to plot labyrinths at least as far back
as the Egyptians."

"Black magic," Jean murmurs.

"Not at all. Mnemonics, memory technique. Classical orators like
Cicero used a version of this method to guide them through lengthy
speeches. I once tried to explain it to Fournier, and he too thought
it might be sorcery. Every initiatory labyrinth is constructed with a
given set of fixtures. In a cave the architectural features of a building
are replaced with natural ones. A raised flat rock can stand for an altar. The preset image attached to the altar stands for a set of instructions. A seven-branched candelabra on the altar would translate into
a steep ascent, with a pause at the apex to receive a vision, followed
by an equivalent descent. Such details informed me about both the
physical and spiritual landscape in the darkness ahead. The sequence
of fixtures may change from one labyrinth to another to accommodate the process required by the specific initiate."

Jean lets out a dry whistle. "Too complicated for me. I'd have
gotten lost around the first bend."

"That's why they had me go along with you, my friend. As Baldwin said, you had the gift of Spirit and I the gift of memory. As we
first learned during our joint initiation in the caves, our unique experiment and experience is in the combination of two into one, two
riders on one horse."

"Given that you were using a pattern as ancient as the signs of the
Zodiac, how was it possible to evolve something so new by following such a well-worn path? To my knowledge, other initiates—the
disciples, the Perfects, and the Templars—worked in pairs without
developing the deep communion that we have. How did we, who are
certainly of the same substance, achieve so different an outcome?"

Jaques turns inwards and then replies, "I have asked myself the
same question and reached no definite answer, but I have an in-

kling. The initiation process not only affects the initiate, but each initiate has a unique effect on the process as he passes through it. Process and initiate interact with each other. The process changes slightly with every initiation. And so each subsequent initiate has the advantage of the experience of all those who preceded him. An intelligent design that retains the past without petrifying the process at any point, thus allowing continual progress. Our individual characteristics aside, we could not have achieved what we did without the cumulative experience of all who preceded us in passage through initiatory labyrinths everywhere. And now our imprint too has been added to the process so that others who pass through will experience what we did and improve upon it."

"I don't grasp the mechanics, but the overall idea of interactive evolution is elegant," Jean says. "Despite criticism including mine, Belibaste was inspired to revise Manichean dualism, spirit opposed to matter, to accommodate the evidence that both spiritual and material universes were created by a single Divine Principle."

"And in his wisdom Père Fontaine arranged that I studied both Catharism and Catholicism, not to embrace one and oppose the other, but to reach a synthesis that includes both."

Jean resumes his pacing. "It's wonderful in theory, but what is there to show for our years of effort? The Cathars have been annihilated, all evidence of their existence destroyed. The Knights Templar have been abolished with only these few anonymous stragglers who serve as our protectors. And we, the last representatives of the Gnostic tradition, are old men on the edge of the grave."

Jaques coughs to catch Jean's attention. "In my only meeting with Timekeeper, an event so contrived that I felt he was an entity from another plane, he reminded me, when I was unduly concerned about Belibaste's fate, to see death as not the end but a doorway."

"I know, I know," Jean says, "but that doesn't make it easy to open the door. Here we are facing the most crucial test, and so much remains incomplete."

Jaques smiles serenely. "As it should be. A chapter is not the entire book. Our joint role is not the full cast of characters. A lifetime is not life." He winks. "The security setup is intentional, remember. Each gets to know only what he requires to play his part. The rest is revealed as the drama unfolds. We are hardly the last remnant of the Gnostic coalition, merely the only ones we know about now. Our mission requires that it seem like we are working in isolation. We are a team of two, which is a level above each of us alone, but we are not the whole Order of the Knights Templar or the entire Cathar church or the full coalition. Just as we will one day return to complete our mission, so they will come back—from the bloody battles in the Outremer, from the battered walls of Béziers, from the flaming pyres of Montsegur—to continue their appointed tasks."

Jean stands still. "We have been on our own for so long that I sometimes forget the others. This is why I need you to tether me, my friend."

"Even after I was somewhat apprised of the larger plan by Baldwin and Timekeeper," Jaques says, "I had to sit day after day in court transcribing trials. The task seemed tangential to the main effort until I learned that Fournier placed my transcripts into the Vatican Library when he became pope. What I thought inconsequential thus becomes the means by which the truth about both the Inquisition's crimes and Cathar heroism is transmitted to posterity. I became the means through which Bishop Fournier will eventually defeat himself.

"Truth is persistent in sustaining itself. After the fall of Montsegur and against all logic, the conquerors granted the defeated force just enough time before they took over the fortress to permit four men to escape with the invaluable Cathar treasure. The Templar commandery at Bézu was miraculously left untouched until the Order's precious goods and records were moved to safety. Troubadours and Grail raconteurs encoded forbidden Gnostic knowledge into sensual love songs and fantastic tales, innocuous forms that allowed our truths to slip past the church's censors. And in the structure and design of the great Gothic cathedrals, the Templars' most arcane secrets are publicly displayed, impressed into stonework by adepts trained as masons.

"The various components of the truth have been secured in place, many redundantly as a hedge against inevitable loss. As it has been written in scripture, 'The time is coming when everything that is covered up will be revealed, and all that is secret will be made known to all.'[50] Centuries hence, there will come those who will read the remaining foundations of this fortress, the labyrinth on the floor of the Notre Dame de Chartres, or Wolfram von Eschenbach's *Parzival* and from them discover the hidden nature and location of the true Grail."

Jean kicks at the gravel beneath his feet. "Your faith in humanity is greater than mine, Brother Jaques. The thirteen hundred years since Jesus delivered his message of love and peace have produced many more murdered innocents than ascended saints. How can we presume that the lives and deaths of this generation, ours included, will fare better?"

He looks towards his companion whose half-closed eyes are drifting into repose. "Don't you dare go yet," Jean fairly shouts. "Your records of the past show no more proof for optimism than do my dire premonitions of the future. Your Grail vision ended with the great capstone of the pyramid in fragments of which it was said, *The Grail shattered is Death.* Jesus denounced the Pharisees as whitened sepulchers that entombed the spirit of the Mosaic Law. But the church founded in his name to rejuvenate that Law not only undermined Judaism but itself has become a funereal institution administered by like hypocrites. Fournier spurned Belibaste's offer to share the lost keys with the Roman Church. During the rest of his tenure as bishop of Pamiers, he continued the inquisition unabated, preferring the spoils—Piere, Mathène and myself among them—of Arnaud Sicre's treachery to God's all-encompassing generosity. Even when he became pope as Belibaste prophesied he would, he spurned the supreme opportunity to reveal what the Christ actually said and did and thus return ownership of the keys to all men.

"Truth is thus ignored without a price. As I look into the future, I see mobs composed of both clergy and laity warring against Rome's tyranny and further fragmenting Christianity. Rebellious sects will supplant papal power in much of Europe, but these in turn will war against each other, creating more hate and slaughter but not more life, peace, and love. The secular monarchs, who have risen to pre-eminence over harsh ecclesiastical rule in our lifetime, will likewise be toppled by the commoners over whom they lorded for so long. But replacing royal rule will not result in the equality and brother-hood for which the downtrodden will have rushed to arms, but in more brutish dictatorships. At the end of the future given to me to foresee, mad leaders and their equally mad mob of worshippers will twist the very cross of Christ into a dizzying vortex of violence, fill the cup of the unwanted with noxious substances that will poison millions, and fuse the very elements of the earth into unnatural con-figurations that will destroy whole cities in a single blinding flash.

"In the midst of such insanity, who will remain to decipher records from a long-forgotten inquisition written in a language no longer spoken? As fire rains down on Europe's cities, who will shield the sacred knowledge etched into the weathered stones of its cathedrals? With desperate hordes of the homeless roaming the countryside, who will venture into these hills to seek the secrets we have secured here? With mayhem on all sides, who will care enough to study *Parzival* to unravel the way to the Grail?"

His head now resting against the stone wall behind him, Jaques pats a place on the stone beside him. Jean reluctantly sits.

"Dear Jean," Jaques says in a barely audible whisper, "from the moment we first embraced each other riding two to a horse, as your blessed brother Piere enjoined us to do that night of the flight from Allemans Prison, through our ritual journey inside the mountain, and throughout our years of retreat in this fortress, we have been preparing ourselves to perform the very mission you just described. Who will channel the Grail, *Fair fullness that ne'er shall fail*, to that future time of consummate chaos? Who, indeed, but us?"

His breathing becomes more labored, but he struggles on. "By then the once monolithic Grail will have been ground into grains of sand, each particle detached from all others, drifting at the prompting of the prevailing wind, restless, groundless, and bereft of foundation. Who will then show by example that this deterioration can only be reversed by reversing the process of separation itself? Who, indeed, but we who have spent a lifetime learning to ride two on one horse?"

Jaques takes a deep breath and releases it with a sigh. Jean grips his arm and prays he will draw in another. Jaques continues to speak, even slower now. "In keeping with my talent for memory and my calling as a scribe, the map...the locations...the images...the words...I take them with me. For us, this entire life was initiation, the beginning. Your gift is Spirit... your vocation the Perfect." He coughs and clutches his chest. "There is that point at the apex of our initiation that words cannot contain. Tell me one last time, Jean, of that moment in the caves when we became one."

The younger man bows his head and closes his eyes. He descends into that pulsating core of light and energy in the center of his body although unbound by physical contours.

"Mathène had passed on and left us with the stone," he relates. "I consoled her with the Book. You went to your knees as if to offer me the *melioramentum*, but I would not have it. 'Between us, Jaques, there is no prostration of one before another. Mathène led us both to the Grail. With it and in her blood, we have been jointly ordained in a new covenant. As woman and mother, she birthed the child and delivered it to us. We are its father and mother now,' I said as I lifted you to your feet. We then took the stone, Mathène's child, and continued the journey. At one point it became impossible to squeeze it through a certain narrow passageway. We realized that we would have to leave the stone behind. I was distraught. Mathène's gift seemed essential to our success. I turned stubborn and refused to leave it, and you rather sternly instructed me to chip off a small piece to take with us. You then found a proper place to bury the rest of it. After we knelt together and lowered the stone into the hole we had dug for it, I stretched out my right hand and placed it on your head. You stretched out your right hand and placed it on my head. Then on the top face of Mathène's stone, we both placed our left hands side by side and touching."

Both men's eyes are now moist. "Yes," Jaques says. "That was the instant. Lightning struck. The moment of fusion. Separation ceased. The new covenant. This is the treasure we carry together into the future."

"And we sealed it with a kiss, our sacred marriage," Jean reminds him.

With enormous effort Jaques opens his eyes and fully cups Jean's hand with his own. "You asked, 'Who will care enough to study *Parzival* to recover the secrets of the Grail?' Do you now have your answer?"

"Yes, brother, I know. We will."

"No," Jaques says. "You will. You are the one carrying the key within you. Without a doubt I'll be riding along to remind you should you forget where you put it. And, of course, I will be there, pen in hand, to record the best part of our story: how we channeled the Grail from here to there."

With his free hand Jaques fumbles with the clothing around his neck. Thinking he is choking, Jean jumps to his feet to assist. Jaques points to a worn leather string that runs beneath his shirt. He motions for Jean to pull up on it. Attached to it is a heavy medallion, aged and stained by the many years he has been wearing it.

His eyes again fluttering, the dying man prompts Jean to take the medal and place it around his own neck. "A gift from Baldwin the Templar. Timekeeper gave it to me a long time ago. It will keep you grounded until it is your time. A talisman to remind us when we return."

Jean puts the medal on and rubs the image with his thumb. "Two to a horse," he murmurs reverently.

Jaques's eyes close. "This chapter is done," he says.

Jean bows his head and reaches into his pocket for the Gospel of John. It is not there; it had already been buried. The fragment of Mathène's sacred stone that he had retained all these years has also been buried. He has only his hands with which to administer the *consolamentum*. He brings them to rest on the crown of Jaques's head and feels a flutter as his companion's departing spirit passes through them.

"Go through the doorway in peace, Jaques de Sabart," he says, and he concludes the sacrament with a kiss to his partner's now lifeless lips.

Chapter 26: Geneva, 1946

The war with Nazi Germany had been over for almost a year, but the appalling horrors of its perpetration and execution still oozed from every pore of Europe's mutilated countenance. The arch-villains of the tragedy—Hitler, Himmler, and Goebbels—had escaped judgment by taking their own lives. Thus it was up to lesser notables to bear the brunt of the Allies' wrath in the wake of the known atrocities, with even more hideous ones emerging daily from the proceedings of the International Military Tribunal in Nuremburg.

Sitting in my office in gentle Geneva, the capital of neutral Switzerland, a nation that escaped the ravages of war by riding it out in the hurricane's neutral eye, I felt no vindication over what was wrought by mere insulation. From the window I could see the columned Palace of Nations, once the headquarters for the now defunct League of Nations. After World War I, the international community entrusted Switzerland to house the institution intended to make war obsolete. It was empty now, a shame on our idyllic mountain country and damning evidence that human nations prefer war to peace.

In the mere five years since 1939, when Otto Rahn had disappeared and Adolph Hitler had ignited the global conflagration with his invasion of Poland, the continent had endured infinitely more death and destruction than in the fifty years of the Cathar Crusade. And it could have been much worse. Had the European war continued a few more months, American atomic bombs would have obliterated

Berlin and other German cities along with Hiroshima and Nagasaki. Or the Nazis might have perfected their own nuclear weapons and sent them on V-2 rockets to destroy London and other allied cities.

The thought of what might have been had the dice fallen differently set me doodling on my desk pad, a habit I had adopted to pass the long stretches of impotent idleness, my normal lot during the conflict. Unlike 333, who spent those years as an undercover advisor to the Allied leaders on the art and science of occult combat, or Paul Ladame, so besieged for advice to counter Goebbels and his crafty Propaganda Ministry that he rarely had time to share a glass of wine or bit of news with me, I was mostly sidelined by the EC after my service with Otto Rahn. Other than an occasional invitation to a social function where I was humored like a relic of some long-concluded campaign, I was given nothing of substance to do.

When I thought I spotted 333 with Winston Churchill in a late 1945 news photo taken at the Nuremburg trials, I asked Ladame if he was there to testify about the occult activities that had occurred on both sides during the war. He seemed irritated that I mentioned it and said, "The shooting war is over and our limited objective is accomplished, Raymond, but the real war has just begun. On the highest orders, evidence to esoteric events on either side will be quashed or ridiculed at Nuremberg and afterwards. The German leaders, solely as human beings, will be held responsible. For public consumption, Nazi occult activities, Otto Rahn's included, are fables."

Any vow of silence to the EC did not, however, prohibit me from trying to disprove the one public document that would eventually emerge to blacken Otto Rahn's reputation, the damning obituary that appeared in *Völkische Beobachter* dated May 18, 1939:[51]

> SS - Obersturmführer OTTO RAHN died tragically in March of this year in a snow storm in the mountains. We mourn the loss of our comrade, a decent SS-man and creator of outstanding historical-scholarly works.
>
> SS Chief of Staff, SS-GruppenFührer Wolff

Two months after Rahn's disappearance into the Austrian foothills, the SS considered him dead enough by whatever method that they felt free to attribute his passing to an unfortunate mishap befallen one of their own. But I knew that Otto had not perished by accident nor did he commit suicide to atone for alleged violations of the SS code of conduct. I had directly witnessed that Wolff's fawning obituary was false either way.

After the joint vision of ourselves as two old men awaiting death on the summit of Montreal-de-Sos in the autumn of 1365, we returned to present consciousness in Otto's Schwarzwälder Hof guest room on that evening of March 8, 1939. Despite the spies outside the windows, Otto had crossed the room and was sitting in the chair next to me. Our hands had been joined during the bittersweet finale to our Cathar lifetime and remained so as we faded forward towards the denouement of our tenure together in Nazi Germany.

Otto spoke first, his voice somewhat musical. "Our next step is self-evident, my friend." He took a handwritten letter from his breast pocket. He passed it me. "A copy of what I sent to General Wolff about a week ago," he said.

It was dated February 28th and read:

> GruppenFührer! Unfortunately, I have to ask you to ask the Reichsführer-SS for my immediate dismissal from the Schutzstaffel. The reasons for that are so deep and serious that I can explain them only orally. For that purpose, I will come to Berlin in the next days and report to you. Heil Hitler, Otto Rahn.[52]

"Wolff already replied that Himmler had simply scrawled 'Yes' to approve the resignation and added that there was no need for me to come to Berlin. Himmler had already informed me of my options," Otto explained.

I was stunned. "You sealed your fate by making it official. No one resigns from the SS and lives. This makes it almost impossible for the EC to execute an escape plan."

"I accepted the mission from the EC on my own determination," he said. "I knew the possible consequences. They must not jeopardize their operation further for my sake. I also cooperated with the Nazis earlier to my shame. I won't compound that error by letting them claim that I gave my life to compensate for some trumped up sins against the Nazi state: homosexuality, impure blood, or whatever. Germany will only be redeemed by those who see the truth, however long it takes to do so, and have the courage to speak it. If I must give my life for my country, I will give it for the Germany of the Odenwald, the land I was born to love, not for the Germany of Dachau and Buchenwald, the dictatorship I have come to despise."

The instant I read Wolff's obituary for Rahn, obviously written at Himmler's behest as Wolff would have let Otto slip into oblivion without mention, I resolved to correct the record.

During the war there was little I could discover further about his fate. I followed Himmler in the Swiss, Allied, and German presses, aware that each news outlet was biased beyond credibility. Only after the war, when pictures of the grotesque heaps of emaciated corpses found in the Reichsführer-SS's concentration camps were published, did the heinous side of the character Otto trusted, Gabriele adored, and I regarded indifferently emerge as the epitome of evil. On hearing of Himmler's arrest two weeks after Germany's surrender, I thought I might get a chance to question him, but any information he may have held personally about Otto was lost when he swallowed cyanide shortly after his capture.

SS General Karl Wolff, who signed the obituary, still remains alive in an Allied prison cell. "Beware of the wolf who serves two masters," Gabriele had said of this haughty Hessian. Prior to the war and during its early years, Wolff, as liaison between them, played Hitler and Himmler against each other to his own advantage. When he fell out with Himmler in 1943, he had enough of Hitler's confidence that the Führer made him commander of German forces in Italy. From this position and contrary to Hitler's order to continue the war to the last man, Wolff negotiated the surrender of his troops through Swiss intermediaries and ordered his men to lay down their arms six days prior to Germany's final surrender on May 2, 1945. He then attempted to trade duplicity for immunity, claiming that he had saved Allied lives and Italian property by capitulating early. He was imprisoned for a time but escaped prosecution at Nuremburg by providing evidence against his fellow Nazis. Wolff would serve any master as long the advantage accrued to Wolff.

But asking for the truth about Otto's death from the former SS personnel chief was akin to seeking compunction for the Cathar deaths he had caused from Arnaud Sicre, Wolff's 14th century counterpart. I would only get what I paid dearly for and that too would be suspect.

Like Arnaud who lived out his days in a comfort extorted with the blood of his countrymen, Karl Wolff would likely skate past any responsibility for the Nazi carnage[53] despite occupying the seat directly behind its two chief architects. Inevitable as his exoneration seemed, I was not about to hasten it by bartering for Otto's vindication. Nevertheless, I would not allow Wolff's epitaph, "a decent SS-man," a cynical lie couched as a compliment, stand to mark Rahn as one of them. Wolff might have been the only other living witness to Otto's courageous resignation from the SS, but I sought other routes to clear his name.

Gabriele Winckler-Dechend, who had to know more than she revealed during our last meeting immediately after Rahn's death, still resided in Konstanz, but I hesitated to contact her. Her close ties to "Uncle" Heinrich and other Nazi leaders prior to war and her husband's tenure as an SS officer made her bait for the denazification courts. Even if she wanted to speak frankly to me, she would not risk her child to do so. As we had shown reverence for Mathène who had fallen into the abyss through no fault of her own 700 years earlier, I felt it honorable to allow Gabriele her anonymity.

I could not locate any information on Willy Ullmann or Adolph Frisé after the war; they may have perished. Himmler had banished

Karl Maria Wiligut into retirement in August 1939, where he weathered through the war in poor health of body and mind. Had he not died in a refugee camp in January 1946, any memories he might have retained about Otto would have been too muddled to be of value. The German government had accrued acres of records that the Allies recovered and stored despite the Nazis' effort to destroy them as the war came to a close, but it would be years before a layman like myself would be permitted to peruse sensitive SS personnel files. Rahn's relatives still lived in the Michelstadt area and probably possessed or had access to some of his papers and manuscripts, but they too would need time to heal before they might be willing to reveal anything even to me, Otto's closest friend.

So I spent the better part of that first year after the war stymied in my quest, doodling at my desk, waiting for the dust and passions of war to settle into the tedium of redrawing maps, rebuilding infrastructure, holding trials, and resettling the displaced before the next conflict, already threatening between the Soviets and the West, restarted the cycle of destruction once again.

I had to bide my time. Given the serenity with which Otto boarded the train that would take him to his death on the evening of March 8, I was likely more concerned about his reputation than he would have been. Displayed face-out on my bookshelf were his two published works, copies of each in German and French, an obvious extravagance that drew questions from the curious.

"An author friend from before the war," I would reply. "A good German—there were some—who also cherished France and claimed to have found the Grail there." I would then point to his photo on my desk. "His name was Otto Rahn."

A well-thumbed copy of von Eschenbach's *Parzival*, Rahn's copy from his student days given to me as a gift, was on that same shelf. The afternoon on the mountain above Muggenbrun he had said: *When my father gave me that copy of Parzival, he handed me my life plan. By reading it, I was anointed an Arthurian Knight, one compelled to seek the Grail. It was my star…. Once I embraced my destiny, the entire universe—every person I met, every place I went, every situation I encountered, and every idea that rose in my mind—carried me towards the Grail.*

I could hate that volume of abstruse lore so intensely that I wanted to shred it. It had set his course, consumed his life, and killed him. And I, merely a planet in orbit around his sun, was sucked along, pen in hand, simultaneously serving as his devoted lover and remote observer, a dual role without purpose for me apart from him.

To the side of his framed photo on my desk was a stone the size of half a fist, another item he had left to me that evening in the Freiburg hotel. "Immortalized in the final pages of *Lucifer's Court*," he told me with an impish grin, "as the stone I found at the heretical castle of Montsegur. Keep it in memory of me, but don't do as I did at Lombrives and mistake the stone, the talisman, for the Grail itself."

I did not ask him what finally he had concluded the Grail to be. Nor did I ask him about the Dietrich, which, on that same page of the book, he wrote that he was carrying with him. It didn't matter though. He would have tapped me on the chest and chided me for asking about what I already knew.

Blindsided by the emotions such thoughts would evoke, I could only throw a kiss towards his image. And, should tears well up, I'd tell myself that I don't miss Otto because Otto is not missing. As his lover I have his heart. As his scribe, I have only to get his obituary revised and our joint task is done.

On a May afternoon that year after the war was over, it was in such a frame of mind that I somewhat idly picked up the stone. I was reprimanding myself for again acting as if Otto were actually dead. I fondled the stone, and there came the thought: If he is here with me now, what does he most want to do?

Chapter 27: Montsegur, 1946

Montsegur: the Town

I remain amazed that an unprompted inkling can become reality with merely a nudge of the will. After realizing that Otto's most cherished wish, often expressed in his last years, would be to return to Montsegur, I spent the rest of the day settling my immediate affairs in Geneva and was on the road the next morning counting down the seven hundred kilometers to our destination. Neither the dramatic scenery nor the lure of history along the way tempted me to diverge.

Upon crossing into France, I proceeded to Valence and then south through Avignon, where Fournier reigned as Pope Benedict XII. After an overnight in Arles, this morning I headed west, following the curve of the Mediterranean coast through Béziers, where the first brutal massacre of the Albigensian Crusade occurred, and Narbonne, whose archbishop ordered the execution of Guilhem Belibaste, and reached the heart of Cathar country just after noon.

Otto quietly occupied the passenger seat beside me throughout; conversation is superfluous between two minds in phase. Just past Carcassonne, with its memories of the heroic Count Raymond-Roger de Trencavel and the pugnacious Brother Bernard Delicieux, I took a secondary road through Mirepoix and Lavelanet, towns Otto featured as chapter titles in *Lucifer's Court*. After a final turn south on a road little more than a hard-packed trail, I chugged up and down through the Pays d'Olmes, the promontory of Montsegur popping out at intervals on my left.

I am now pulled over to the side of the road beneath its towering bulk. Behind it the setting sun is staging a light show of shifting rays and colors. I turn to the passenger seat and announce, "We're here. Tomorrow we go up."

It is dinner time when I reach the town's single hotel, a cozy auberge that Otto frequented when he explored the area in the early '30's. Its proprietress, Madame Couquet, is ecstatic when I mention that I am a friend of Rahn's. "Ah, Raymond," she coos over my name on my registration card. "He spoke fondly of you." Her face glistens redder as she reminisces about him, but she turns incredulous when I inform her that he died prior to the war.

"Otto's dead? Then I must be too," she says, pursing her ample face. "And he's no Nazi despite the nasty rumors around here. He's a true Cathar, a Perfect no doubt, coming back like so many of the old ones, many as writers to tell the world what really happened." She winks. "Right on time. Belibaste said that in seven hundred years the laurel would re-root and flourish again in Languedoc."

A chair scrapes back from a table in the dining room off to the right. Its occupant approaches us. My jaw drops.

"Raymond," Antonin Gadal says, embracing me in a bear hug.

"Monsieur Gadal, you are here," I gasp.

Madame Couquet chuckles. "I was about to introduce you two. Not necessary, I see. You shouldn't be surprised that he got here before you, Raymond. Timekeeper always arrives first for important events." She comes around the counter and takes my valise. "Otto's old room, of course. You talk with Antonin. The kitchen will send out your meal."

Still in shock, I sit, and blurt out, "Madame Couquet called you Timekeeper. That can't be coincidence."

"No coincidences, Raymond," he says with an indulgent smile. "It just wasn't right for you to know earlier. Only here, in the shadow of Montsegur, Muntsalvaesche, in that singular zone between two worlds where the spirits of Good Christians rub shoulders with grubby treasure hunters picking for the trinkets they left behind centuries ago."

Uneasy with ghosts of any sort, I cast a glance around the room. He goes on. "The diggers were here during the war too. Himmler's ambition to obtain the *piece de resistance* for Castle Wewelsburg didn't end with Otto. They watched this place throughout the occupation, but only in '44, perhaps because they feared that they'd soon lose France to an Allied invasion, did they move aggressively. In March, at the time of a locally planned 700th anniversary celebration of the fall of Montsegur, a troop of commandos, allegedly headed by the daredevil Otto Skorzeny, moved in, sealed off the mountain, and began excavating furiously. Several containers of material were carted off to the Fatherland."

"So Otto's discovery has been compromised?"

Gadal shrugs. "If Himmler had whatever they found here taken to Wewelsburg as we suspect, it was moved to a secret location before the SS blew up the place as the Americans closed in."

"The Battle of the Birch Tree," I whisper, recalling the vision that came in the Wewelsburg parking lot in 1938. "So Otto's discovery may be lost forever. Could not the EC have prevented that?" I frown. "Or is its fate beyond what I need to know, part of the real war that has only just begun?"

"During the war, we had to ensure that the Nazis did not get hold of enough of the secret knowledge to do irrevocable damage," Gadal says, smiling incongruously to my annoyance. "333 claims that the power of the Grail is activated by the intention of the one making a request of it. *Ask and you shall receive.* The Midas touch. The Grail is unerringly neutral, not necessarily benevolent.

"Jacques Fournier intuited the power behind the *consolamentum* well enough to achieve the Papacy. Heinrich Himmler grasped the power of the occult sufficiently to vault himself into the role of Reichsführer-SS. However, neither of them could take the critical leap required to activate its potential further. In deciding to use it as a weapon against their perceived enemies and contrary to the universal good, they triggered the built-in failsafe that trumps the Grail's otherwise foolproof effectiveness: The Golden Rule or the Law of Reciprocity. *As you do unto others so shall it be done unto you.* This law requires that any ill-effects from the selfish use of this sublime energy be returned in kind to the perpetrator. The church's disintegration with the Protestant Reformation in the 16th century was hastened by the omissions of Benedict XII's papacy. The Thousand Year Reich lasted less than two decades.

"The seed of the divine, the source of this power, is in every one, Himmler included. This principle motivated the EC to take a calculated gamble and send Otto to offer him an option to Hitler. There was also a karmic connection between Himmler and Rahn, and this was their opportunity to resolve that. Both knew the Grail's potential, although Otto carried the key to unlock it. Himmler remained dependent on intermediaries and talismans. Ultimately, as was just, he wasted the very one who held the Dietrich to the vault containing the treasure he most desired."

As he talks so candidly, I have to wonder who and what this eccentric Frenchman from Tarascon, also known as Timekeeper, really is. An inhabitant of the earth like the rest of us or an advanced soul that embodies and disembodies at will, some mysterious guide or muse who might be caught whispering key verses of *Parzival* into von Eschenbach's allegedly illiterate ear?

As I should have expected, he picks up my thought. "*In this world, but not of it,* John the Evangelist wrote," he says. "There are many levels of consciousness above the merely human but well short of the ecstasy of the beatific vision. The realm in-between. Some who have entered there return for another complete human experience as I have chosen to do this time. Others, including several from the Cathar period have not reincarnated quite so fully: Esclarmonde de Foix, Père Fontaine, Piere Maury, and Guilhem Belibaste among them."

In another place or time, such talk would have left me incredulous. In the waking dream that is Montsegur, it feels quite normal. However, I must still question perceived inconsistencies. Thinking of Otto and the millions of victims of the recent cataclysm, I ask Gadal, "I understand that lessons can be learned even from this tragic war, but was the terrible cost worth it?"

The eyes of the aging self-appointed custodian of the Cathar legacy mist over. His face shifts to that of the thin, bearded Timekeeper of centuries ago. Solemnly he says, "Most of mankind will have to face that question in the years ahead, but neither Otto nor you need question the value of your contribution. Otto indeed carried the Gnostic charisma across the centuries in his heart. You transported the details of its history and function over the same period in your mind. But ultimately it was your mutual love, your sacred marriage, that permitted you both to know to merge your separate gifts, Spirit and Memory, when the proper time came."

Something in my head began slipping to the left. To balance myself, I reached into my pocket for the Templar medallion Otto had left with me on that night in March of 1939. Too late.

Freiburg, March 8, 1939

With Otto carrying a knapsack containing a few personal belongings and me holding a small bag with the several items he had bequeathed to me, we leave his room, pass through the lobby of the Schwarzwälder Hof, and exit through the main door. With little effort to keep cover, two men emerge from the shadows and follow us. Turning right on Herrenstrasse and then left through the Münsterplatz, we stop at the main entrance to Freiburg Cathedral, its single Gothic spire piercing the night sky behind us.

"They'll trail me to the station and board after me. It is time for us to part," Otto says.

There is no need for a prolonged farewell. Before we left the hotel, Otto told me what he planned to do and why.

"I'll pay a final visit to the Lauermanns in Schliersee[54] and then take the bus across to Kufstein in Austria and then on to Soll. I'll hike up the mountain the Reichsführer-SS has designated as the place of self-immolation for SS penitents. I am already in the endura. I will not take my own life, but I will give it if necessary."

When I remonstrated that his lack of nourishment would hobble any chance to escape through the mountains, he calmed me. "You're too concerned, Raymond. I have almost completed what I was born to do as Otto Rahn. My books have been published for future readers, no matter how the Nazis and others might misconstrue them. They contain the truth as I observed it. My other manuscripts are in a relative's safekeeping to be released only after this scourge has passed."

He then turned more pensive than he had been all evening. "The Cathars held that death was not the end but a doorway," he said. "The martyrs of Montsegur were so convinced of this that they leapt joyfully into the flames. Belibaste, once he was cleansed, so anticipated his end that he baited Fournier into condemning him. Such conviction is contagious enough that worldly men like Fournier and Himmler are tempted to risk their careers to attain it."

Tears sprang to his eyes. "Death is every person's fate, and a man can die many times and still fear it. He reaches the doorway but does not walk through it voluntarily. There was much of the imperfect Belibaste left in me this lifetime. I chose the SS uniform over deprivation. Others chose to lose their homes and lives rather than surrender their integrity. Had every conscientious German done the same from the beginning, the Nazis would not have had a chance. My selfishness contributed to the current appalling state of this country, which now threatens the world. Letting go of my life now will not prevent the catastrophe—it is not my creation alone—but it will mitigate the outcome intended by the Nazis if only eventually. I go to the mountain of Soll consciously. With eyes wide open, I will locate that doorway, open the door, and walk through. I do this so that I will never again face death with fear."

"I will go with you," I said.

He shook his head emphatically.

"'Two always practiced the endura together,' you wrote in *Cru-*

sade," I protested. "After sharing lifetimes of effort, 'only together could the Brothers decide to co-participate in the next life, the true life of the intuitive beauties of the Hereafter, and the knowledge of the divine laws that move worlds.' Your words, Otto Rahn."

He continued to shake his head. "You died without fear on Montreal de Sos. I witnessed it. Prior to your lifetime as Jaques de Sabart, you had already crossed the river of forgetfulness and retained your memory without being bound to it. No, my friend, you needn't cross that way again. This is the key you possess. It's what induced Père Fontaine, Baldwin, and Timekeeper to choose you as a partner for me, a blithe spirit from a higher realm but one so blinded by the light that I could not make my way through this one.

"On Montreal de Sos, you were not afraid to die, but I was still afraid to see you do so. By going through that experience without fighting it, I discovered that I could allow your body to go into the ground and your soul to depart without fear, loss, or sense of separation." He paused and held my gaze.

"And now the tables are turned," I said, wiping my eyes. "For you, what needs to be completed is there. For me, what is unfinished is here. It is still one horse with two riders, one looking forward while the other looks back."

He took both my hands and pressed them firmly. "Mine is the easier part this time, Raymond. What you will have to witness here and put into words in the next few years, things I have seen only in their malignant infancy, will make pale my descriptions of the cruel Crusade against the Cathars. It will be terrible, but less terrible because of my forewarning. What you will see will seem unbearable, but look and report so that the unbearable becomes unrepeatable. My death and your life in combination will continue to nurture the next great human emergence."

He reached into his bag and took out the Templar medallion I had declined to take before he departed for Berlin and Buchenwald. "We now carry the Dietrich together, but this symbol of it, precious though it is, belongs to the earthly realm. You keep it for both of us."

I accepted, pressing it first to his lips and then to my own before pocketing it.

Thus, now in front of the Freiburg Cathedral of Our Lady, there is no need for further words of farewell or final embrace. We face each other, no tears in our eyes, as the famed sixteen bells in its spire start to chime.

I raise my right hand and place it on the crown of his head. "Be consoled, Otto. All is well," I say. The night around us glows golden.

He then raises his right hand and places it on my head. "Be consoled also, Raymond. All is indeed well," he says. The light around us quivers and sparkles. We lower our arms and kiss each other on the lips. He turns and walks towards the train station. The glow and the spies follow him.

Montsegur: The Church

Without noticing that I had closed my eyes earlier, I reopen them. I have to blink to see that I am in Madame Couquet's auberge in Montsegur, and that it is Antonin Gadal, Timekeeper, across the dinner table, his head bobbing to show that he saw what I had just revisited.

Still in solemn mode, he continues where he left off. "In the name of all who throughout the ages who have pledged to preserve, protect, and propagate the most sacred knowledge of the Grail, we commend you two for your valiant services during the Cathar crisis in the fourteenth century and in the most recent crisis with Nazism.

"Others have also contributed in both events in which the Gnostic heritage was under threats as well as in others like them. However, until now, the lack of a reliable method to transmit our sacred knowledge from generation to generation across the millennia has been hampered by the barriers posed by physical death, the between-lives area, and subsequent rebirth. Loss of unbroken consciousness by initiates and direct witnesses has required us to depend on imperfectly written documents and word-of-mouth transmissions that have diluted and polluted the pristine truths of our corpus of truth.

"The potential for living witnesses to cross the trifold barrier between one life and the next without losing consciousness, and thus memory, has been evident to initiates for some time. There have been some rare individual successes such as Heinrich Schliemann, but his memories were subject to skepticism because he lacked that crucial second witness to corroborate his recollections. A single witness is subject to the normal distortions of perception in both the life where the experience is seen and in the one where it is reported. As was evident in the practice of the original Christians, the Templars, and the Cathars, the solution to this dilemma was to travel and labor in pairs, one person to perform and the other to observe and record. The roles were interchangeable over time; but in the course of a single event they had to remain discrete, the one active and the other passive. Two to a horse.

"But as is also easily observed, it is a rare team that can remain in tandem for the duration of a single life. To retain a partnership that also survives death, between lives, and rebirth requires a supernatural fusion between the parties that can withstand the vicissitudes of Heaven and Hell as well as those of human coexistence. You two, Raymond and Otto, have accomplished this, and for this singular feat we applaud you most highly. By actual experiment and its verification, each of you the witness to the other and all of us witness to your achievement, you have demonstrated that the mutual love binding two souls as one is a sufficient channel to conduct the sacred knowledge, which will eventually embrace us all in the unity that was intended from the beginning, across the barriers of time, space, and mortality without loss of memory of what we were or consciousness of who we are. For this inestimable feat there is no award worthy of you other than the fruit of the deed itself."

Overawed by the import of his statement and somewhat embarrassed by its lavishness, I pull the Templar medallion from my pocket and drop it on the table. "Will this do as our prize?" I ask.

Gadal picks it up and caresses it with his fingers. He then flashes a broad grin and presents the medal back to me. "Indeed. The medal you have already bestowed on each other."

He then wags his finger. "This is not a final discharge. There is still much to be done, and the two of you, with centuries of preparation and experience behind you, are too valuable to be excused quite yet."

Before we part for our rooms, he stops me a final time. "You will climb the mountain tomorrow to the castle of our lovely Esclarmonde," he says, "but before you go, stop into the village church across the road. It will be open early. Pay attention for clues to the key that unlocks the door you seek to open." The same words, obviously intentional, with which he had invited me to visit Notre Dame de Sabart in 1937.

A shiver runs through me. Earlier Madame Couquet had said, "Otto dead? Then I must be too."

Gadal evidently felt my consternation. "Montsegur is in Otto's realm. Here we all tend to see things that most people don't," he says.

In the early morning light, clouds scudding across the sun struggling to rise, Montsegur's tiny church could have been Notre Dame de Sabart. Not the refurbished shrine that Otto and I visited in 1937 but the fourteenth century chapel where I as Jaques served as Père Fontaine's altar boy. I open the wooden door and enter, prepared for my mind to play its now familiar tricks with time, sliding left and right in synchrony with something beyond the normal calendar. It is dark and empty like the church in Tarascon would have been in early morning. A few votive candles burn before the right side altar over which stands a statue of the Virgin in sky-blue and white, her empty arms extended, and her sad eyes searching the heavens for something lost.

Antonin Gadal had declared the mountain of Montsegur to be the shrine of Esclarmonde. Otto referred to this noble woman as the White Lady of the Cathars. If as a troubadour he had a lady love, it would have been this noble Perfecta. I glance at the statue again: Notre Dame, womanhood perfected according to Roman Catholicism, in which Père Fontaine had initiated me simultaneously with heretical Catharism. But I cannot gaze at her too long. Otto was enchanted by the unapproachable; aloofness makes me queasy. It is the Black Madonna that attracts me. Unlikely that a village chapel would have such an image. All those known are now housed in famous churches and touted as tourist attractions. I move up the right side aisle, pause for a moment before the main altar, and then turn down the left.

Nothing strikes me. Perhaps I am not awake enough to see in the way that Otto did, or Gadal was somehow mistaken. The medallion in my pocket is comfort enough, and I am eager to start for the mountain. A single candle burning in an alcove at the rear of the church catches my attention. I go to it. The image ensconced above it makes me gasp. It is the Black Madonna. Not standing proud and remote like the Virgin in front but sitting serenely, the child on her lap, and yet regally, the cross-crowned globe aloft in her left hand. Mother and child's skin is dark, their forms primitive. Elemental creatures risen from the womb of the inner earth rather than ethereal beings descended through the dome of the distant sky.

There is a prie-dieu here as there was in the Sabart church. As Jaques I had knelt there in grief over the loss of my mother. I am about to kneel again when a voice ripples the air: *Between us, Jaques, there is no prostration of one before another.* Otto's voice.

Startled, I remain standing. A spray of sparks burst from my heart.

Mathène led us both to the Grail. With it and in her blood, we have been jointly ordained in a new covenant. As woman and mother, she birthed the child and delivered it to us.

I lean in to see the face of the Black Madonna more clearly. Tears come to my eyes.

We are its father and mother now. Our unique mission, one foreseen and overseen by the unbroken line of our wise predeces-

sors, is to raise this child for a destiny that lies beyond death in the centuries ahead.

I look at the child in her lap. He is grinning. "You're no longer afraid. Ask the question," he says.

Otto is now close, side-by-side like the two old men sitting on the stone bench atop Montreal de Sos. *The Grail shattered is Death.*

"Go ahead," the child prods.

"What then is the Grail?" I ask.

"*San Greal.* The Holy Grail. The sacred cup. The vessel of Life," the woman replies.

"*Sang Real.* The royal blood. The fruit of the womb. Life itself," the child says.

I gaze at the image: mother and child together. The woman, the chalice, fills to overflowing. The child, flesh and blood from her body, comes forth and sits on her lap.

"We also rode two to a horse," the impish infant adds. "*The Flight into Egypt.* Giotto painted it famously. Mother and I on our steed, father Joseph in front. We outran old Herod and his army."

I grin. He shrugs like any child caught in an exaggeration. "All right, then. *Two to a donkey.* Works like a horse, only slower," he says, resuming his more serious pose.

"Now you are hearing and seeing things like I do," Otto whispers in my ear.

Out of such banter, there comes an insight. This icon tucked in the corner of a Catholic chapel in the most sacred of Cathar holy places is the symbol of an archetypal event that happened before the beginning of time when *the earth was a formless void and darkness covered the face of the deep while a wind from God swept over the waters. Then God said, "Let there be light,"*[55] *and there was light.* The mother, the matrix, was the face of the deep, the child the light that came forth from her.

The flame within me sputters like a candle catching. This dusky image of the Black Madonna and Child was another of the lost keys: they tore the son from the womb that nurtured him and subordinated the mother to the child. *"Madame, stay with your spinning wheel! You have nothing to say here,"* a Catholic priest had shouted to silence the learned Esclarmonde. The Grail stone had been cleaved in two and the evidence of the breakage was hidden in these shadows. But for us, who had passed through the doorway of death and returned as one, the answer to the question had changed: The Grail reunited is Love itself, and Love must start with two.

The sparks from my heart burst into flame within my chest and spread upward and outward throughout my body. At the end of von Eschenbach's tale, the purified Parzival cannot go to the Grail castle alone. He first meets and reconciles with his long-lost half-brother, Feirefiz, a Muslim of mixed race, and then together they ride to Munsalvaesche where both men, despite their different mothers, faiths, and races, are received with honor. Only now is Parzival able to ask the critical question, "Uncle, what is it that troubles you?" that heals Anfortas, the long disabled Lord of the Grail.

The fire within gains strength as if fanned by a wind. At the same time, as if watching myself in a mirror, a like conflagration explodes in the center of the body of my reflected counterpart. Both flames burst their physical bounds and fuse into a dazzling orb glowing green in the narrow space between our bodies. The two have become one in the womblike form of the resurrected stone given to us by Mathène and buried along the path of initiation.

The blazing emerald star waxes hotter, larger, brighter. It consumes the wooden image of the Madonna and child, then travels into the little church, its pews now filled with those who walked with us in Cathar Languedoc: Raymond-Roger de Trencavel, Jacques de Molay, Jaques de Sabart's mother, Père Fontaine, Baldwin the Leper King, Timekeeper, Piere Maury, Beatrice de Planissoles, and Bernard Delicieux. They joyfully welcome the fire that embraces them and their legions of Pure Ones and Knights Templar. The inferno then reaches towards those whose role then was to oppose us: Simon de Montfort, Abbot Arnaud-Amaury, Conrad of Marburg, Bishop Fournier, Arnaud Sicre, and Bernard Gui with their armies of Crusaders and inquisitors. They shy from its brilliance, but it sweeps over them. They yield to its unexpected delight.

A tidal wave, it moves outward, breaking through the streets and sweeping upward toward the mountain that hovers over the town. From the flames, a brilliant cloud plumes skyward forming the image of the noble White Lady. She raises a golden vessel: the shattered Grail restored.

Montsegur: The Mountain

We cast only one shadow as we traverse the Camp de Cremat, the now flowering meadow where two hundred and twenty consoled Cathars died for their faith on a cold March morning in 1244. A simple stele stands to commemorate these martyred heroes. We pause and press a hand to the stone monument to bless and receive their blessing.

In his concluding chapter of *Crusade Against the Grail,* Otto said of this sacred burial ground:

> Perhaps the last Cathars lie there, dead through endura in defense of the heretical treasure, whose mere contemplation gave their brothers sufficient courage to advance to their deaths and shout in the last moment, as the flames of the pyre began to consume them, "God is love!" If God is more benevolent and understanding than mankind, shouldn't he concede to them in the Hereafter what they so ardently desired and pursued with total abstinence, consequential strength, and unparalleled heroism? The divinization of the Spirit—the apotheosis! This is what they wanted. The anxiety of mankind consists in reaching the kingdom of the heavens, which is to say, to live on after death.
>
> What happened to the Grail, the Occitan Mani? According to a Pyrenean legend, the Grail moves farther away from this world, and upward toward the sky, when humanity is no longer worthy of it. Perhaps the Pure Ones of Occitania keep the Grail on one of those stars that circle Montsegur like a halo, the Golgatha of Occitania. The Grail symbolized their desire for Paradise, where

mankind is the image, not the caricature, of God—an image that is revealed only when you love your fellow man as yourself.[56]

Leaving only a single set of footsteps, we take the trail that snakes up the south face of the incline. The village below with Madame Couquet's auberge and its tiny church fall away as we ascend.

The incline is too steep to take straight up. The path corkscrews back and forth, each loop a new lifetime positioned atop the previous one. The leaven of love is the updraft that counters the stagnation that would leave us pacing horizontally or the desperation that would drag us back to the bottom.

We reach the top. Around us the earth unfolds in all directions. Far to the east glints the Mediterranean coast that fronts Narbonne and Béziers. To the north the Aude Valley that runs through Carcassonne. Gentle foothills to the west show the roads to Toulouse and Pamiers. To the south, crowned by the snowcapped Pyrenees in distant Catalonia, are the hills that formed the last Cathar refuges along the Ariège.

In front of us is a wooden bridge that leads to the remains of the last fortress of the Good Christians atop the summit. In counterpoint to Himmler's sacrilegious center of the world that he would have set in the North Tower of Wewelsburg, the mount of Montsegur marks true north, the basilica of the New Covenant built upon the shoulders of the Temple of Jerusalem, the Gnostic chapels in the desert, St. Peter's in Rome, the Templar round churches, and the humble Cathar meeting houses.

At the end of the bridge, an arched doorway leads into the heart of the mountain to a secret chamber that is said to contain the Ark of the Covenant, and within it the sacred stone that attracts all things to itself, the one treasure that endures, the pearl of great price, the Grail.

Riding two to a horse, our heart contracts with expectation. The scribe is about to experience directly what he dutifully recorded from a viewpoint apart. Riding two to a horse, our heart eases with content. The journeying spirit has traversed the valley of the shadow of death and returned home.

> *There was a Thing that was called the Grail,*
> *The crown of all earthly wishes,*
> *Fair fullness that ne'er shall fail.*

ENDNOTES

[1]Rahn, Otto, *Crusade Against the Grail,* Translated and annotated by Christopher Jones, Inner Traditions International, 2006, p. 90.

[2]Piere Authier was a Cathar Perfect in the Languedoc, a leader of the Cathar revival in the early 14th Century. Originally a notary from Ax-les-Thermes, he travelled to Lombardy and Piedmont with his brother, Jacques, in the 1290s to study Catharism. During the winter of 1299-1300, he returned to Languedoc to revive the Cathar church. He was arrested by the inquisitor Geoffroy d'Ablis in August 1309 and burned at the stake for heresy on April 10, 1310.

[3]The Nibelungenlied, translated as The Song of the Nibelungs, is an epic poem in Middle High German. The story tells of dragon-slayer Siegfried at the court of the Burgundians, how he was murdered, and of his wife Kriemhild's revenge. http://en.wikipedia.org/wiki/Nibelungenlied.

[4]Graddon, Nigel, *Otto Rahn & the Quest for the Holy Grail,* Adventures Unlimited Press, 2008, p.90.

[5]Irminism: A Germanic neo-pagan denomination; the term comes from the Irminsul pillar, which represents the world axis in old German lore. Karl Maria Weisthor considered Irminism the original belief of the old Germanic peoples. http://en.metapedia.org/wiki/Irminism.

[6]Goodrick-Clarke, Nicholas, *The Occult Roots of Nazism,* New York University Press, 1985, p. 180

[7]George, Stefan Anton (12 July 1868 – 4 December 1933) was a German poet, editor, and translator. George and his writings were identified with the Conservative Revolutionary movement. He was a homosexual yet exhorted his followers to lead a celibate life like his own. In 1933 after the Nazi takeover, Joseph Goebbels offered him the presidency of a new academy for the arts, which he refused. He also stayed away from celebrations prepared for his 65th birthday. Instead, he travelled to Switzerland, where he died near Locarno. The group of writers and admirers that formed around him were known as the *Georgekreis.*

[8]The penal code of the Second Reich formed in 1871 included paragraph 175 that punished homosexuality with imprisonment and the loss of civil rights. The Nazi Party amended paragraph 175 to close what they saw as loopholes in the existing law. http://en.wikipedia.org/wiki/Persecution_of_homosexuals_in_Nazi_Germany_and_the_Holocaust

[9]Geoffrey d'Ablis was a Dominican who led the Inquisition in Carcassonne against Cathars such as Piere Authier from 1303 to 1316. He collaborated with Bernard Gui, the inquisitor at Toulouse.

[10]Matthew 5:18

[11]The Externsteine is a distinctive rock formation near the city of Detmold, Germany. The formation is a tor consisting of several tall, narrow columns of rock that rise abruptly from the surrounding wooded hills. During the Nazi period, the site became a focus of nationalistic propaganda. In 1933, the Externsteine Foundation was established with Himmler as president. Interest in the location was furthered by the Ahnenerbe division within the SS, who studied the stones for their value to Germanic folklore and history

[12]Rahn's experiences with an SS expedition to Iceland are chronicled in his *Lucifer's Court*, Part Three.

[13]Ernst Röhm was an early Nazi leader. He was a co-founder of the *Sturmabteilung* ("Storm Battalion"; SA), the Nazi Party militia, and later was its commander. In 1934, as part of the Night of the Long Knives, he was executed on Heinrich Himmler's orders.

[14]Heinrich Schliemann was a German pioneer in field archaeology. He advocated the historical reality of places mentioned in the works of Homer. He excavated Hissarlik, now presumed to be the site of Troy, along with the Mycenaean sites Mycenae and Tiryns. His work lent weight to the idea that Homer's *Iliad* and Virgil's *Aeneid* reflect historical events.

[15]The Polaires were a group of French esoteric seekers centered in Paris in the early 20th Century. The medieval Cathars of Languedoc attracted their interest. They sponsored a research expedition led by Otto Rahn to southern France in 1932.

[16]Maurice Magre (1877-1941) was a French writer whose historical novels publicized the persecution of the Cathars. A Polaire, he influenced Otto Rahn's viewpoint of Cathar history and influence.

[17]The mysterious Countess Pujol-Murat was a spiritualist who lived in Languedoc with connections to the Polaires. Rahn considered her a personal friend, and she likely provided him funds during his time exploring in southern France.

[18]Arthur Caussou (also known as M. Rives) was an old Ariegois whom Rahn held in great esteem. Caussou told Rahn the legend of Esclarmonde de Foix and reinforced his belief that Montsegur was the Grail Castle.

[19]Graddon, p. 129.

[20]Graddon, p. 33.

[21]Costen, Michael, *The Cathars and the Albigensian Crusade.* Manchester University Press 1997, p. 121.

[22]Montaillou is best known as the subject of Emmanuel Le Roy Ladurie's work of microhistory, *Montaillou, village occitan.* It analyzes the town in great detail over a thirty-year period from 1294 to 1324. Montaillou was one of the last bastions of Catharism. The then local bishop, Fournier, launched an extensive inquisition involving dozens of lengthy recorded interviews with the locals, all of which were faithfully recorded, such as the arrest of the entire village in 1308. When Fournier became Pope he brought the records with him and they remain in the Vatican Library.

[23]The International Paneuropean Union is the oldest European unification movement. It began with the publishing of Count Richard Nikolaus von Coudenhove-Kalergi's manifesto *Paneuropa* (1923), which presented the idea of a unified European State. Coudenhove-Kalergi, was the organization's central figure and President until his death in 1972. The movement is still active in European politics today.

[24]A detail based on the biography of Walter Johannes Stein (1891-1957), Austrian philosopher, Waldorf teacher, Grail researcher, and one of the pioneers of anthroposophy, whose Grail researches culminated in 1928 with his book *Weltgeschichte im Lichte des heiligen Gral. Das neunte Jahrhundert (The Ninth Century and the Holy Grail).* Stein moved to London in 1933 and is said to have served the British government in an intelligence capacity during the Second World War and as a lecturer on anthroposophy and related subjects afterwards.

[25]*Urban and Rural Communities in Medieval France: Provence and Languedoc,* edited by Kathryn Louise Reyerson, John Victor Drendel, p. 312.

[26]*New Revised Standard Version,* Exodus 20:5

[27]Rahn, Otto, *Lucifer's Court,* translated by Christopher Jones, Inner Traditions 2004. Prologue, p. xiv.

[28]Bonner, Anthony, *The Art and Logic of Ramon Llull,* Brill Academic Pub, 2007.

[29]Rahn, *Lucifer's Court,* p. 199.

[30]Rahn, *Crusade Against the Grail,* p. 191.

[31]Rahn, *Crusade Against the Grail,* p. 187.

[32]For the full story of Béatrice de Planissoles, see Weis, René, *The Yellow Cross,* Vintage Books, 2002.

[33]https://en.wikipedia.org/wiki/Dietrich_Eckart

[34]Graddon, p. 95.

[35]Graddon, p. 116.

[36]Graddon, p. 118.

[37]Weis, René, *The Yellow Cross*, Vintage Books, 2002, p. 313

[38]O'Shea, Stephen, *The Perfect Heresy*, Profile Books, 2000, p. 243-4.

[39]Graddon, p. 95.

[40]Graddon, p. 108.

[41]Yenne, Bill, *Hitler's Master of the Dark Arts*, Zenith Press, 2010, p. 117-24.

[42]Graddon, Ch. 8, p.109

[43]Weis, p. 268-9, 314-5.

[44]Weis, p. 361

[45]Weis, p. 363

[46]*The Speeches of Adolf Hitler*, April 1922-August 1939, Volume 1, Edited by Norman Hepburn Baynes. University of Michigan Press, p. 396.

[47]Graddon, p. 140.

[48]John 14:12.

[49]John 10:34.

[50]Luke 12:2.

[51]Graddon, p. 146.

[52]Graddon, p. 141.

[53]While Karl Wolff did serve some prison time for his part in the Nazi atrocities, he pleaded ignorance of any direct knowledge of the holocaust. Sentenced to fifteen years' imprisonment in 1964 for organizing the deportation of Italian Jews in 1944, Wolff served only part of his sentence and was released in 1969 due to ill health, with his full civil rights restored in 1971. He died on July 17, 1984.

[54]Graddon, p. 145.

[55]Genesis 1, 2-3.

[56]Rahn, *Crusade Against the Grail*, p. 189.

Cast of Major Characters

Cathar Period

Baldwin (Fictional) Named after Baldwin "the Leper" King of Jerusalem during the Crusades.

Belibaste, Guilhem (Birth date unknown- 1321) Said to have been the last Cathar Perfect in Languedoc. Pupil of Pierre and Jacques Authier. Mentor to a community of Cathars in Catalonia who had fled persecution in the Languedoc. He was captured and burned at the stake in 1321.

Bernard Gui (1261-1331) Inquisitor of the Dominican Order and one of the most prolific writers of the Middle Ages.

De Sabart, Jaques (Fictional) Scribe in the Inquisitional Court of Bishop Jacques Fournier of Pamiers.

Delicieux, Bernard (1260-1320) Franciscan monk of the Spiritual (strict) faction who also protested the excesses of the Dominican Inquisition. He was accused of treason and disobedience and tried and convicted in Carcassonne in 1317. He died in prison in 1320.

Fournier, Jacques (@1280-1342) (Pope Benedict XII 1334-1342) Cistercian monk, who studied at the University of Paris. In 1311 became Abbot of Fontfroide Abbey and in 1317 bishop of Pamiers, where he undertook a rigorous hunt for Cathar heretics. His trials were carefully recorded in the Fournier Register which he deposited in the Vatican Library.

In 1326, he was made Bishop of Mirepoix in the Ariège. A year later, he was made a cardinal. Fournier succeeded Pope John XXII (1316–34) as Pope Benedict XII in 1334, being elected on the first conclave ballot.

Maury, Jean (Birth/death dates unknown) Brother of Piere Maury. The records of the Inquisition are ambivalent about his heretical leanings. In 1324 was imprisoned with his brother and wife, and there is no record of him past this date.

Maury, Piere (1282-unknown) Born in Montaillou, a Cathar shepherd, who joined the Catalonian exile group in 1311. Skilled at his trade and comparatively wealthy, he was a strong supporter of the Perfect Belibaste.

Père Fontaine (Fictional) Pastor of Notre Dame de Sabart. Jaques's mentor as a youth.

Roger (Fictional) Jaques de Sabart's schoolmate at Saint Sernin Abbey School in Toulouse.

Servel, Mathène (Birth/death dates unknown) Cathar woman who was married to Jean Maury in 1322. She was arrested with Piere and Jean but there is no mention of her sentence or death.

Sicre, Arnaud (Birth/death dates unknown) Son of Sybille Baille, Cathar Perfecta from Ax, and Arnaud Sicre Sr., a Catholic notary. Served as a spy for Fournier's Inquisitional court.

Timekeeper (Fictional)

Twentieth Century

333 (Fictional) Head of the anti-Nazi Emerald Club, sometime operating from the Goetheanum in Dornach, Switzerland. His character is partially modelled on the clandestine role that Walter Johannes Stein (1891-1957), Austrian philosopher, Waldorf school teacher, Grail researcher, and one of the pioneers of anthroposophy, played before and during World War II.

Baeschlin, Asta (Dates unknown) Swiss divorcee with a young son, around age 27 in 1938 when Otto Rahn advised Himmler that he was engaged to her. Although there are photos of the couple and child together in Muggenbrunn, Ms. Baeschlin later claimed, "I was never engaged to Rahn, he just wanted everybody to believe that."

Frisé, Adolph (1910-2003) Journalist and writer, known as editor of the works of Robert Musil. First met Otto Rahn in 1934, and, according to biographers, the lives of the two men intersected until the last months of Rahn's life at Muggenbrunn.

Gadal, Antonin (1877-1962) French mystic and historian who dedicated his life to the study of the Cathars in the south of France, their spirituality, beliefs and ideology. Gadal grew up next to the Tarasconian historian Adolphe Garrigou who saw himself as a preserver of the memory of Catharism sect and, seeing a kindred spirit in Gadal, made him the inheritor of his knowledge. In addition to his work as custodian in the Ariège, Gadal lectured worldwide on his findings and theories about the Cathars. His books include *The Inheritance of the Cathars* and *On the Path to the Holy Grail*. He died in 1962.

Habdu (Dates unknown) Mysterious Senegalese barman that Rahn associated with while living in Tarascon. Later served as Rahn's manservant.

Himmler, Heinrich (1900-1945) Reichsführer of the Schutzstaffel and a leading member of Germany's Nazi Party.

Ladame, Paul Alexis (1909-2000) Professor at Geneva University on the "methodology of information and disinformation," journalist, radio man and author of several books in French, two on Otto Rahn. Friend of Otto Rahn from 1928-1939.

Perrier, Raymond (1909-1998) Aside from the few remaining references in Otto Rahn's correspondence, little historical detail is known of the life of Raymond Perrier. In a letter to the author Albert Rausch in November 1928, Rahn first mentions Raymond as the new love in his life: "19 years old, beautiful, even very beautiful, and from Geneva." Five years Otto's junior, Raymond's relationship lasted for the rest of Rahn's life. Rahn introduced Raymond to Himmler, who warmed to the Genevan. The novel depends on extant documents as the basis for their private relationship but adds fictional details on aspects not in historical records. Perrier died in Nyon in 1998.

Rahn, Otto (Feb. 18, 1904-Mar. 13, 1939) German writer, medievalist, philologist and member of the Nazi SS, who researched and wrote about the Grail myths and Catharism. He wrote two books linking Montsegur and the Cathars with the Grail: *Kreuzzug gegen den Gral* (Crusade Against the Grail) in 1933 and *Luzifers*

Hofgesind (Lucifer's Court) in 1937. His first book came to the attention of Heinrich Himmler who was already fascinated by the occult. Rahn became a full member of the SS in 1936.

Ullman, Willy(?) (1899-?) SSObersturmbannführer and Stabführer of the Personnel Department RFSS. Only historical detail known is from existing correspondence with Rahn, who at times confided in him as a friend. His role in having Rahn released in late 1938 from Buchenwald is documented.

Wiligut, Karl Maria (Weisthor) (1886-1946) Austrian occultist, Wiligut was inducted into the SS (as "Karl Maria Weisthor") to head the Department for Pre- and Early History within the SS Race and Settlement Main Office (RuSHA). In the spring of 1935, Wiligut was transferred to Berlin to serve on Himmler's personal staff. He contributed to the development of Wewelsburg as the order-castle and ceremonial center of SS pseudo-religious practice. He designed the prestigious SS Totenkopfring. He was retired in February 1939 on the recommendation of Karl Wolff, survived the war, but died in 1946.

Winckler-Dechend, Gabriele (1908-?) Secretary to Karl Maria Wiligut during his SS service. She was the first who read Rahn's book and showed it to Wiligut. She became a good friend of Otto's. As recently as 1998, Gabriele granted limited interviews of her experiences with Himmler, Wiligut and Rahn.

Wolff, Karl (1900-1984) High-ranking member of the Nazi SS. Chief of Personal Staff to the Reichsführer-SS and SS Liaison Officer to Hitler until his replacement in 1943. He ended World War II as the Supreme Commander of SS forces in Italy.

Time Line: The Cathar Revival Period

1119		Hugues de Payens founds the Order of Knights Templars in Jerusalem.
1208		Crusade against the Albigensians (Cathars) launched in southern France by Pope Innocent III.
1209		Massacres of Beziers, fall of Carcassonne to Simon de Montfort.
1244		Last Cathar stronghold at Montsegur falls.
1285		Start of reign of Philip IV of France (the Fair).
1292		Jacques de Molay elected 23rd and last Grand Master of the Templars.
1299		Franciscan Frater Bernard Délicieux leads a revolt against Dominican inquisitors of Carcassonne.
		Return of the Cathar Perfects led by Pierre Authier to Languedoc.
1305		Pope Clement V (1260-1314) moves the papal residence and administrative offices to Avignon to escape the political turmoil in Rome.
1307	Sept. 14	Philip IV issues secret orders calling for the arrest of all Templars across France.
	Fri. Oct. 13	Templars all across France are arrested and imprisoned on orders from Phillip IV.
1308	Sept. 8	First major raid at Montaillou by the Inquisition.
1309		Guilhem Belibaste breaks out of prison after capture and escapes to Catalonia.
1310		The leaders of a Cathar revival, Pierre and Jacques Authier, are executed.
1314		Jacques de Molay, the last Grand Master of the Templars, burnt at the stake in Paris.
	April 20	Pope Clement V dies.
	Nov. 29	Philip IV dies in a hunting accident.
1317	Mar. 19	Jacques Fournier becomes bishop of Pamiers.
	April	Pope John XXII orders the Spiritual Franciscans to Avignon to answer for their disobedience. Bernard Délicieux arrested upon arrival.

1318	Oct.	Arnaud Sicre arrives in Sant Mateu in Catalonia, encounters Guillemette Maury and meets Piere Maury and Guilhem Belibaste.
1319	Sept.-Oct.	Arnaud Sicre returns to Languedoc and visits Jacques Fournier at Pamiers.
	Dec.	'Marriage' in Morella of Piere Maury to the pregnant Raymonde, Belibaste's companion. Belibaste divorces them a few days later.
	Sept.-Dec.	Delicieux's trial in Carcassonne runs from 1319. He is sentenced to life in prison in solitary confinement.
1320		Délicieux dies in prison.
	Late summer	Second visit by Arnaud Sicre to Jacques Fournier in Pamiers.
	Jul. 26	First appearance of Beatrice de Planissoles of Montaillou before Fournier.
	Aug. 7	Beatrice implicates Pierre Clergue in her testimony. He is arrested, tried and imprisoned.
	Dec.	Arnaud Sicre, Belibaste, and the Catalonian Cathars celebrate Christmas in Morella.
1321	Mar. 8	Sentencing of Beatrice de Planissoles at Pamiers.
	End of Mar.	Arrest of Belibaste at Tirvia.
		The last known Cathar Perfect in the Languedoc, Guillaume Belibaste, is burnt at the stake in Villerouge Termenes.
1323	May	The Inquisition arrests Piere Maury, Jean and Mathène.
1324	Jun. 25	First appearance of Piere Maury in court before Fournier.
	Aug.	Piere and Jean Maury sentenced to prison. No further record of theirs or Mathène's fate exists.
1326		Fournier made bishop of Mirepoix in the Ariège. Made a cardinal the next year.
1334		Fournier succeeds Pope John XXII (1316-34). Takes the name Benedict XII. Dies in 1342.
1342		Benedict XII dies.

Time Line: Otto Rahn

1904	Feb. 18	Otto Rahn born in Michelstadt (Hesse). Parents Karl and Clara (nee Hamburger).
1910-16		Junior school at Bigen.
1916-21		Secondary school at Griessen.
1924		Receives Bachelor degree in Philology and History.
1928	Jan.	Rahn leaves the family home to live in Berlin.
	Nov.	Returns to Lorsch to live with his parents, attending Heidelberg for his doctorate studies in Philology. Raymond Perrier staying as a houseguest to learn German.
1929		Rahn's thesis titled "The Research of Master Kyot of Wolfram von Eschenbach" dedicated to the author of Parzival, to Wagner and to the troubadours.
	Nov.	After eight months in Heidelberg and two months at Raymond's parents' house in Nyon near Geneva, Rahn and Perrier move to Berlin, sharing accommodation in Martin Luther Street. Here Rahn meets Paul Ladame and the pair become close friends.
1930		Rahn begins his European travels (Paris, Provence, Switzerland, Catalonia, Italy), residing for periods near Geneva.
1931	Beginning	Resident in Paris in Rue de Lille for six weeks where he makes contact with Maurice Magre and the Polaires. Then back to Switzerland for a time before making his way to the southern French Pyrenees.
	Nov.	Rahn arrives in the Languedoc. Explores the Montsegur area and the caves of the Sabarthès, notably Ornolac and Lombrives. Meets Antonin Gadal.
1932		Rahn leads a Polaires expedition in Pyrenees. Ladame accompanies him as guide.
	Sept.	Rahn Departs Languedoc leaving various unpaid bills and travels to Saint-Germain-en-Laye near Paris. Returns to Tarascon for legal reasons in Dec.
1933	Jan. 30	President Paul von Hindenburg appoints Hitler Chancellor of Germany.
	Early	Rahn in Germany and living in Berlin-Charlotten-

berg. He capitalizes in his home country on his activities in the Pyrenees.

	Autumn	In Heidelberg completes *Kreuzzug gegen den Gral (Crusade Against the Grail)* two years after beginning the work. Published by Urban Verlag in Freiburg.
	Dec. 13	Joins the German Writers Association.
1934	Feb.	Introduced to the publisher Adolf Frisé.
	June 30	Night of the Long Knives. Putsch against Ernst Röhm and the SA led largely by Himmler and the SS.
	Nov.	Karl Maria Wiligut (Weisthor) and Gabriele Dechend go to work for Himmler in Berlin.
	Fall	Rahn living in Brixen, Italy; wants to return to France; writes to Gadal: "it is impossible for a tolerant and generous person to stay for long in this country which used to be my wonderful homeland."
1935	Early	Gabriele reads *Kreuzzug*, gives to Weisthor, who gives it to Himmler. Himmler wants to bring Rahn to Berlin. Gabriele contacts him thru Rahn's publisher. Rahn travels from Freiburg to Berlin and meets with Gabriele. (There is some controversy about the details and timing of these events.)
	Early	Appointed to personal staff of Heinrich Himmler, working with Weisthor and Gabriele. Living in basement apartment on Tiergartenstrasse in Berlin.
1936	Mar. 12	Rahn formally admitted to Allgemeine-SS, member 276 208 and is attached to Weisthor's department.
	April	Himmler requests Rahn's help on his ahnenpass (genealogy).
	June	Visits Iceland with 20 men on a research assignment.
	Aug.	Seen in uniform Paul by Ladame at Berlin Olympic Games.
		Gabriele leaves Berlin, but keeps in touch with Rahn by letter.
1937	April	Publishes *Luzifers Hofgesind. Eine Reise zu denguten Gelstern Europa (Lucifer's Court in Europe)*.
		Sent back to Languedoc, visits Montsegur, and says he will return in 1939. (Some biographers contest the timing of this event or that the visit to France actually occurred. Available records not clear on it.)

	Apr. 20	Promoted to sub-lieutenant (Untersturmführer)
	Nov.-Dec.	Military service for "disciplinary reasons" with Oberbayern Regiment in Dachau KZ. Visits Gabriele in Konstanz around Christmas.
1938	Jan.	Lecture in Dortmund to Dietrich-Eckhardt Society, introduced by Kurt Eggers.
	Jan.	Skiing at Lake Schliersee in Bavaria with Raymond.
	Jan.	Granted permission to travel to Switzerland for health reasons.
	Jan.	Rahn and Perrier worked together on Passaquay family tree research for Himmler's ahnenpass.
	Feb. 29	Karl Wolff informs SS Office of Racial Questions that Rahn is unable to produce a certificate of racial origin.
	April	In a letter to Ullman, Rahn says he had interrupted his stay in Switzerland to resolve things in his absence that had gone wrong; mentions trying to see Musy.
	April	Gabriele's first son is born and she asks Rahn to be the boy's godfather. Rahn agrees but then leaves for Muggenbrun without attending the event.
	April	Rahn makes an oral statement against the admission of Dr Franz Riedweg, Musy's former secretary, into the SS. Later he is asked to provide a written statement.
	June	Settles in Muggenbrun to write sequel to Lucifer and the novel Sebastian.
	June 17	Writes to Himmler about marrying Asta Baeschlin. On June 27 Himmler replies that he is pleased about the wedding.
	June-Aug.	Perrier with Rahn in Muggenbrun.
	Summer	Civil action brought against Rahn.
	Sept. 11	Promoted to lieutenant (Obersturmführer), his final promotion.
	Oct. 1	Called up for an SS Autumn reserve duty training exercise.
	Nov. 9	A letter to the head of the concentration camps, Eicke, confirms that Rahn was serving in Buchenwald on the day of the Reichskristallnacht.
	Early Dec.	Ullman letter to Eicke to arrange leave for Rahn to work undisturbed on his writing.

1939	Jan.-Feb.	Rahn returns to Muggenbrun, confiding to a witness that he could bring himself neither to read nor write. He cannot say where he had been but that he had seen things with which he could not come to terms (per Adolf Frisé).
	Feb. 28	Rahn submits St. Odile Grail report to Himmler. Himmler's records show receipt of "Gral" at the same time (no further information on what "Gral" was).
	Feb. 28	Submits letter of resignation to Karl Wolff. On the letter Himmler scrawls "yes" and his signature.
	Early Mar.	Visits Kurt Eggers apartment in Dortmund; publisher Von Haller present.
	Mar. 8	Meets publisher Otto Vogelsgang in Freiburg hotel.
	Mar. 12	After visit with old friends, the Lauermanns, in Schliersee, Rahn sets off for Kufstein in Austria.
	Mar. 13	Rahn disappears on Wilder Kaiser near Kufstein.
	Mar. 17	Rahn's resignation from the SS is granted retroactive from 22nd February and with immediate effect.
	May 18	*Volkischer Beobachter* publishes Rahn's obituary.
	July 17	Rahn's father writes to Otto's writers' association, saying that his son had died in a snowstorm at Ruffheim on 13 March.

Abbreviated Bibliography

Otto Rahn

Graddon, Nigel, *Otto Rahn & the Quest for the Holy Grail: The Amazing Life of the Real Indiana Jones*, Adventures Unlimited Press, 2008.

Rahn, Otto, *Crusade Against the Grail: The Struggle between the Cathars, the Templars and the Church of Rome,* Translated and annotated by Christopher Jones, Inner Traditions International, 2006.

Rahn, Otto, *Lucifer's Court, A Heretic's Journey in Search of the Light Bringers,* translated by Christopher Jones, Inner Traditions 2004.

Nazi Germany in the 1930's

Goodrick-Clarke, Nicholas, *The Occult Roots of Nazism: Secret Aryan Cults and their Influence on Nazi Ideology*, New York University Press, 1985.

Levenda, Peter, *Unholy Alliance: A History of Nazi Involvement with the Occult,* Continuum, 2002.

Von Lang, Jochen, *Top Nazi: SS General Karl Wolff, the Man between Hitler and Himmler,* Enigma Books, 2005.

Yenne, Bill, *Hitler's Master of the Dark Arts: Himmler's Black Knights and the Occult Origins of the SS*, Zenith Press, 2010.

The Cathar Revival Period 1299-1325

Costen, Michael, *The Cathars and the Albigensian Crusade*, Manchester University Press 1997.

Guirdham, Arthur, *The Cathars and Reincarnation,* The C. W. Daniel Company Ltd., 1990.

Ladurie, Le Roy, *Montaillou: The Promised Land of Error*, Translated by Barbara Bray, George Braziller Inc., 1978.

O'Shea, Stephen, *The Perfect Heresy: The Life and Death of the Cathars,* Profile Books, 2000.

O'Shea, *The Friar of Carcassonne: Revolt Against the Inquisition in the Last Days of the Cathars,* Walker Books, 2011.

Weis, René, *The Yellow Cross: The Story of the Last Cathars' Rebellion Against the Inquisition 1290-1329,* Vintage Books, 2002.

Gnosticism and Catharism

Churton, Tobias, *The Gnostics,* Barnes and Noble Books, 1997.

Oldenbourg, Zoe, *Massacre at Montsegur: A History of the Albigensian Crusade,* Minerva Press, 1968.

Smoley, Richard, *Forbidden Faith: The Gnostic Legacy from the Gospels to the Da Vinci Code,* HarperSanFrancisco, 2000.

Strayer, Joseph R., *The Albigensian Crusades,* Ann Arbor Paperbacks, 1992.

The Grail, The Knights Templar

Douzet, André, *The Wanderings of the Grail,* Adventures Unlimited Press, 2008.

Goodrich, Norma Lorre, *The Holy Grail,* Harper Perennial, 1993.

Partner, Peter, *The Knights Templar and their Myth,* Destiny Books, 1990.

Ralls, Karen, *The Templars and the Grail: The Knights of the Quest,* Quest Books, 2003.

Stein, Walter Johannes, *The Ninth Century and the Holy Grail,* Temple Lodge Publishing, 1988.

Von Eschenbach, Wolfram, *Parzival,* Translated by A. T. Hatto, Penguin Books, 1980.

Miscellaneous

Yates, Frances A., *The Art of Memory,* Routledge, 1999.

Acknowledgments

In writing this visionary and historical novel, I drew upon the thoughts and works of too many of my fellow human beings, past and present, to name here. To them all and to the Spirit of Inspiration that guides writers through the triumphs and trials of the creative process, I express my profound appreciation.

A special thanks to my fellow core team members of the Visionary Fiction Alliance, Jodine Turner, Margaret Duarte, and Eleni Papanou. Your dedication to making the Visionary Fiction genre a vital instrument for enhancing human growth in consciousness has helped keep me honest and focused as a writer for the past several years. I am honored to be your partner and invite all visionary authors, established and aspiring, to join us at visionaryfictionalliance.com.

Kudos to Richard Stanley, who, with his films, writing, and the Terra Umbra website (shadowtheatre13.com), serves as the consummate custodian of Otto Rahn's legacy from his home base in Montsegur, France. And to Anneke Koremans (Jean D'Aout), author and Languedocian tour guide, who shared her deep knowledge about the Cathar homeland during the days we spent in conversations while traversing the great American Southwest in 2013.

My thanks to the staff of the Goetheanum in Dornach, Switzerland, and especially to James Preston, who provided me with a private tour of the premises and its art treasures. There I was privileged to witness the continuing influence of the magnificent mind and soul of Rudolph Steiner, founder of the Anthroposophy movement and the Waldorf schools.

Much appreciation to subject matter experts, who took time to answer my many questions, especially Nigel Graddon (*Otto Rahn and the Quest for the Holy Grail*), and Frank Joseph (*Opening the Ark of the Covenant*). And from among the many visionary fiction authors who inspired me, a nod to that pioneer of the genre, Monty Joynes (*The Booker Series*).

The spiritual traditions behind *Channel of the Grail* have many sources. For the abundance of wisdom I received from all of them, I am thankful. I single out the Unity movement, with its practice of universal acceptance without exception, as having a profound impact on my life and work. Credit for a balanced approach to the study of the paranormal must be given to two outstanding spiritual/scientific research bodies, the International Organization of Noetic Sciences (IONS) and International Association for Near Death Studies (IANDS).

I acknowledge those throughout France, Germany, Austria, and Switzerland who generously gave hospitality and information to an inquisitive American who peppered them with questions in bad French and poorer German. And my admiration to the people of Languedoc and Provence who have beautifully restored so many of the Cathar monuments for our edification. The laurel tree of your valiant ancestors is again in bloom across southern France.

And a bow to the courage and honesty of modern Germany, my country of ancestry, for enshrining sites of national shame like Dachau and Buchenwald as a reminder to the nation and the world that the Nazi phenomenon did happen and must never be allowed to happen again.

Finally, and most importantly, a huge embrace of thanks to each of those who directly participated in the production of *Channel of the Grail*. Editors, proofers, beta readers, and consultants: Lauri Bonn, Kay Matthews, Robin Peel, Margaret Duarte and Jodine Turner. Cover designer and layout editor Jeff Danelek, himself an author of the arcane (ourcuriousworld.com). And a knowing wink to my friend Melissa Linn; it was in our many conversations that several key scenes in the novel popped into manifestation.